the last minute first lady

tinia montford

To Uncle Herman — Life is a duller without your random knowledge of Star Trek, Godzilla, and ninja stars. You are apart of my best memories and through them, you live eternally.

Playlist

Princesses Don't Cry – CARYS
Gimme Gimme – NNAMDÏ
Baby Powder – Jenevieve
Can't Help Falling in Love – GnuS Cello
Moment – Victoria Monét
Not Your Barbie Girl – Ava Max
Hurt You – The Weeknd, Gesaffelstein
Sweat – ZAYN
Nite and Day– Al B. Sure!
Through the Fire – Chaka Khan

Interested in listening to Jolie & Cassian's entire playlist?
Visit: https://rb.gy/txup0g.

Would you like to see deleted scenes, character interviews
and exclusive character art? Sign up for my newsletter at:
https://rb.gy/bbemfx

You can connect with me on:
My Website: https://tiniamontford.com/
Facebook I Instagram I Pinterest I TikTok:
@tiniawritesbooks

There is always something left to love. And if you ain't learned that, you ain't learned nothing.

— Lorraine Hansberry

one

. . .

160 days till Election Day

"We're sad to announce that after twenty years of leading our investigative unit, our beloved Walter Cabot will retire from the ten o'clock investigation segment. We will be searching for his replacement in the coming months."

Jolie's gaze shot up from her doodle. Walter had finally done it. It only took seven years of waiting the old man out. He was heading into the sun of retirement, and now fresh blood would reinvigorate the on-air investigation segment. She was the perfect fit for it. This was her moment.

She visualized it in her mind. *Thank you for choosing me. I'll be happy to fill the role.*

There was movement in the front of the room. Jolie's eyes narrowed, her lip curling as a young man stood before the room in an obnoxious Versace suit on a Monday. He ran his hand through his overly styled hair, and it took everything in Jolie not to scoff loudly.

Travis Osborne.

He faced the rest of his coworkers before making eye contact with Jolie. His gaze narrowed. "You don't have to look far, Dev. The replacement's right here."

1

Dev, her boss, looked unimpressed but gave a strained smile. "Thank you, Travis. Have a seat."

Travis was a waste of space and natural resources, not a reporter. He had hit on Jolie his first day in the office and did not take rejection well. In retaliation, he made her life in the office hell. Taking her stories or asking to be put on them because Jolie was "short of manpower," only to get the writing credits she worked hard for with no effort on his part. The only reason he still had a job was because his father was golf buddies with the owner of the channel.

"Nepotism at its finest," Helena, her best friend, muttered under her breath.

Dev's gaze landed on Jolie, and his smile went away.

"Let's not get ahead of ourselves, *Travis*," Jolie said out loud. "We have a few qualified people in this room, you know."

Travis waved her off. "*Obviously* I'm a part of that group. I mean, I broke the speeding camera story last month."

"That was my story, if I recall." Well, until the unfortunate incident.

"And why didn't you stay on it?"

Everyone inhaled sharply. Several spared glances at Jolie before averting their gazes to the floor or the ceiling. Her story on Congressman Jason Mills had been a disaster for Channel 12.

But Jolie would never let Travis see her sweat. She shrugged. Inside? She was beyond fucking pissed.

"I figured I'll toss you a bone."

There was a giggle from the right of Travis, and he pinned his gaze on an intern. "At least I'm not fixing paper jams—"

"That *you* cause because you can't operate a basic machine."

Travis's face went red like a tomato. "I'll have you know—"

"All right, let's move on." Dev pushed his wire-frame

glasses up the bridge of his nose as he turned one of the pages from the stack in his hand. "Primaries are over, and the Democratic nomination for governor has been announced. It's Cassian Anders…"

Jolie tuned out again till Helena nudged her.

"I bet if you were nice to Dev, he would let you back out on the beat," she whispered, tossing her braids over her shoulders.

Jolie glared at the back of Travis's head. "Dev's not one of us anymore."

The staff meetings at Channel 12 News these days were bullshit. Censoring and polite politics ran rampant in fear of cancel culture. Dev was always toeing the line to keep Channel 12 safe for their audience's palate, which went against Jolie's principles as a journalist in keeping it real.

"You keep this up, and Dev is gonna fire you for real this time," Helena warned. "You know how the Mills story went down."

Jolie rolled her eyes. "He knows I'd sue this place so damn fast—"

She had factual evidence that exposed Congressman Mills's son doing cocaine at a fundraiser for children's cancer, verified by the source himself, *the drug dealer.* Who gladly went on record in retribution for the two-thousand-dollar debt Congressman Mills's son refused to pay. That same son proceeded on a drug-and-alcohol-filled joyride, ending with him crashing his car into a family's home.

It was only right the fine citizens of Illinois, who were funding Congressman Mills and his son's lavish lifestyle, knew cocaine was being snorted off their hard-earned money.

Her mistake? The witness at the crash had been high and overemphasized details that didn't happen. They told the arresting officers, who then told the congressman's office, and now she was here.

Helena raised a brow. "I don't like that look on your face. What are you planning?"

"Are you in?"

"I can't keep borrowing bail money from my mama." Helena crossed her dark brown legs, shooting Jolie an annoyed look. But Helena was her ride-or-die. "Nor am I getting put back on suspension for you by going undercover again. Especially if we have to pretend to be a couple again."

"That was *one* time, and the lady said we were cute together."

Helena's shoulders shook as she tried to stop herself from laughing out loud. "Pretending to be partners to snoop on that sperm bank because you thought it was a money-wash front for a gang was a one-time deal."

"All the evidence pointed to Sunny Field Sperm Bank. That's a generic-ass name, and you know it."

"Ladies, is this something for the entire meeting to discuss?"

Dev's eyes were pinned on Jolie. Pursing her lips, she leaned back in her seat and caught Travis sneering at her.

"No, Dev," Jolie and Helena grumbled.

"I didn't think so."

Travis was still staring at her, so she cocked her head at him. *Can I help your ass with something?* Too bad violence in the workplace was frowned upon.

She waited a few moments as Dev lectured about how phone usage during work time was stealing from the company and then turned back to whisper to Helena. "Dev knows I'm the best damn reporter in this place. He can't give it to Travis. The minute they let his ass on the air, we'll all be in the unemployment line."

"You're already on Dev's bad side. You want to piss him off by continuing to talk right now?"

Jolie shrugged. "If I cared about pissing people off, I wouldn't be where I am today."

"Fixing paper jams and reporting on the senior citizen rendition of *Fiddler on the Roof*. Excellent use of that degree from Columbia."

"Bitch." Jolie sucked her teeth, and Helena grinned. "Fine. Turn your back on me. Listen to Dev while I plan my method of attack on not letting Travis Osborne wiggle his ass into my promotion."

Helena raised a brow. "This isn't war, Jolie."

"You, out of all people, should know it is. We're the only two unambiguous Black women in this office."

Before them, there had been one other Black woman. After Jolie was hired, she'd packed up and left for a station on the west coast. It was hard being a minority in a room of people who didn't look like you. Dev, being Indian-American, tried make the environment inclusive, but he had to play the politics game with donors and executives. If Travis tattled, then Dev's livelihood was on the line. Travis got away with all his microaggressions, malicious smiles, and snide remarks because of that.

"I guess I have to help, don't I?" Helena mumbled.

"That's what you signed up for when you became my friend."

Jolie needed this promotion with every fiber of her being. She was tired of being on the weekend news here and there. She wanted to be breaking the big stories in front of the camera during the week at primetime, and the small taste she'd had of it occasionally filling in for Walter wasn't enough.

"That's it, folks, get back to work." Dev clapped his hands, and everyone stood.

Jolie made a beeline straight for her boss.

This promotion would give her a six-figure salary with generous benefits. Many doors would open for her, like possibly moving on to a national news broadcast. That was her goal. To have the country knowing her name and face someday. Jolie knew she had the credentials for Walter's position. How many people and organizations had she busted since being here? Countless. Her dedication to this job? Unmatched. For the last seven years, she'd given her all to this station. She had to be recognized. Her motto was "If you aren't first, you're last."

Jolie trailed behind Dev. "Do you have a minute, Dev?" He glanced over his shoulder at her.

"I told you, either printer duty or reporting on the senior citizen center."

Behind them, Travis laughed, but stopped when Jolie shot him a deadly glare.

"Dev—"

"I said it once and I'll say it again, Jolie: the execs are still pissed, and they don't want any drama going on with any more public figures."

"The witness was high on *marijuana*. It's not shrooms or crack. He said the guy was driving a hundred miles an hour, and his car was reported seventy-three. Seventy-three in a residential! They conveniently forget that detail. They can't keep running that tired-ass defamation claim that didn't even go anywhere." Jolie edged Travis out of the way and behind them to press her point. "Are we the news if we cave into every complaint because we published a story someone didn't like? We are journalists foremost. We report the truth."

Dev shook his head. Crow's feet surrounded his dark eyes and made him look older than he was. The only bright thing on him was the gold band of his wedding ring. The stress was getting to him too.

"I didn't have this much gray hair until I met you, you know. My daughters don't cause me as much trouble as you do."

Jolie smiled. "I take it as a compliment."

"You got me against the ropes, Jolie. Don't do this to me," Dev groaned.

She couldn't let this go. After seven years of playing Dr. Jekyll and Mr. Hyde at Channel 12—forcing herself to appear nonthreatening and compliant to her non-Black coworkers so they didn't label her with the stereotype of an angry Black woman. Then flipping to be intimidating and cutthroat to assholes like Travis who undermined her skills and credentials. She surpassed these challenges, cranking out stories that ranked Channel 12 as one of the top news stations in the city. Her hard work had to reap her some benefits.

"Dev, I think—" Travis began.

Jolie made a dismissive sound. "The adults are talking, Travis."

Travis's jaw clenched.

"Dev, take me off the senior citizen watch and let me prove I'm the best candidate to take over for Walter. I've been here the longest." *Not Travis*, is what she wanted to say as she tossed a pinched expression at him.

"You are a liability risk. Why would we want you leading the most watched segment we have?" Travis asked.

Jolie's head whipped to him. "We? Since when do you speak for the station?"

"I—"

"Or do you think because your daddy is friendly with the owner, you can make that decision?"

Dev exhaled, "Jolie."

"My father has nothing to do with this." Travis's voice was strained.

"Is that right? How did you get that source for your last story on former mayor Rosenblum?" Jolie asked slyly, crossing her arms as they stood in the middle of the hallway.

"I got Vasco from city hall as a witness."

Jolie immediately knew Travis was lying. Jolie had both Congressman Mills and the Mayor Rosenblum story. Deciding she couldn't write two articles; Dev gave her hot and piping story to *Travis's* bumbling ass.

7

The former mayor of Chicago resigned after photos of him leaving a methadone clinic surfaced. His replacement was Mayor Charles, a promising leader with more than forty years of political experience.

"You talked to them?"

"We have a meeting scheduled." Travis sniffed.

Jolie's eyes narrowed. "When? Place? How long? What time?"

Travis began to stammer, and Jolie shook her head and turned to face Dev.

"I can't deal with you two right now. I need someone on the Anders announcement." Dev began heading down the hallway again.

The click of Jolie's heels filled the hallway as they headed to the newsroom. "Look, I'll apologize to the congressman if need be. But you know I'd be the best for Walter's role." Jolie had to rise higher than her past. Too often lately, she felt as if the ghosts and demons of her past were tugging on her ankles to drag her down.

Dev glanced at her, then Travis, as they walked into the newsroom. The buzz of phones, typing, and conversation crowded the air. Every time she walked into the whirr of activity, it felt like home.

Dev motioned to Travis to leave. "Give us a moment."

Travis begrudgingly walked away, but not before giving her another deadly once-over.

Dev motioned with his head for her to follow. Navigating through the cubicles, he dropped papers off on a desk.

"Please, Dev—"

He stopped and turned, and Jolie almost collided with him. She clasped her hands together and gave him her best puppy dog look.

"Don't kiss ass. It's unbecoming."

"I swear you'll get no more trouble from me. Let me back

onto the beat, and I'll show I can take over for Walter. That's all I'm asking."

She knew she could be the best on-air correspondent this station had ever seen. She could change the city she loved.

"I can't, Jolie."

Mindful they were standing in the middle of the newsroom with eyes on them, she tilted her head to lead him away from prying ears.

"Jolie—"

"I've been here for seven years. *Seven years,* Dev."

The seven years she'd sacrificed here at the station had to be for something.

"Remember when I worked undercover at the DMV and broke the story that employees were selling social security numbers?"

Dev scratched his beard and grunted.

"I discovered the ambulance service was billing people from the same accident random astronomical charges to the same hospital. They wiped those bills after my story."

Dev sighed, "I know this."

"I exposed the board-of-review worker for taking bribes. The state senator is resigning after I broke his wife's story about domestic violence. The private booting scam. The chief justice and the racketeering charges."

"Your point?"

Jolie frowned, crossing her arms. "Only I could have broken those stories. I've made this channel a contender against other stations. Donors, executives, and hell, even *you,* have benefited from my work. Don't deny it."

"You are a damn good reporter, Jolie, but you piss too many people off. I'm trying to keep you in this game."

Jolie held her breath, watching emotions war in Dev's eyes. The moment his shoulders slumped; she went in for the kill.

"Keeping me in the game is having me do bullshit reports

about senior bingo night?" she asked. "I committed myself to this station because I want to help people by shedding light on injustice. Everyone deserves an equal and fair chance for a happy life, and the scammers and frauds need to be called out. Please, Dev. I swear I won't cause another scandal."

People had vandalized her car. People tried to bribe her. People threatened her with lawsuits. People tried to get her fired. Through it all, the more those doing wrong tried to stop her, the more determined she was to write that story.

Dev stared at her for a hard second. Shaking his head, he exhaled loudly. "Fine. This is your last chance, you hear me?" Jolie grinned. "One more fuckup, Jolie, and that's it. You'll be back to community news, or worse, out of here."

"You won't regret this—"

"I better not. Take a mic and camera, and go report on Cassian Anders. Get us something good the other channels won't have."

Not Cassian Anders.

Jolie didn't buy the *I have a deeply ingrained sense of justice and fairness and blah, blah, blah* spiel he'd been doing around the city and state. She'd worked the politics and crime beat for years now. In her experience, politicians were shady and immoral. No one could change her opinion on that.

Cassian Anders was just another sham lawyer and a corrupt politician in the making that this city didn't need.

"I was thinking something better—"

Dev raised a finger. "No. Be nice to Anders. Prove to me I can trust you to act on your best behavior. Don't make me regret this." He walked off, barking orders to a group of nervous interns, who scrambled in a dozen directions.

First hurdle down. At least she was off copier duties. If she had to cover Cassian Anders, so be it.

two

. . .

**CASSIAN ANDERS TARGETED IN NEW ATTACK AD
LAUNCHED BY RADCLIFFE**

"Don't go off-script this time. I mean it, Cassian."

Sitting in a chair as the makeup artist touched up his face backstage, Cassian glanced up from the article that had been forwarded to his phone. Paul Samuels, his campaign manager, grimaced at him.

"He shouldn't be too bad this time." Margarita, an older, beautiful Afro-Latina with a lush twist-out Afro, waltzed in after Paul. She was his political consultant, and a damn good one. She smiled at Cassian, taking the spot next to Paul as the older man mumbled to himself.

"Do you want to end up on Channel 12 again by that same gossip reporter? You saw what they did to Congressman Mills." Paul shook his head.

"Mills got his ass handed to him," Margarita chirped happily. "He was a sloppy bastard. Good riddance."

"Look at this." Cassian offered Paul his phone. He took it, and his frown deepened into an abyss.

Margarita met his gaze in the mirror. "What's a little

11

scandal and drama now and then? Makes the people interested in what's going on. That's what we need. Attention."

"Cassian doesn't need any scandals or drama now. We have enough of that with these damn attacks on his bachelor status." Paul handed the phone to Margarita, who reached into her suit jacket for her glasses. "I told you not to go on any dates. They spotted you with three different women in two weeks. That's not demonstrating steady leadership while we're trying to assert you as a viable candidate for office. We've already got the odds stacked against us."

"One of those dates was my ex-fiancée, and all three of those meetings were pure business." His ex-fiancée had asked for legal advice for her startup. The other women were potential clients for his firm. Nothing more.

Running for office came with downsides. The limelight. People were exceptionally nosy about his personal life. A relatively young, rich Black man and no wife and kids? Blasphemous to the public.

From the press outlets to other candidates, to his campaign staff and supporters, to his own damn mother, everyone had been rumbling about his love life, or lack thereof. It pissed him off. He'd rather focus on his campaign. But apparently if he wasn't married or didn't have kids, he couldn't possibly know what it took to run a state.

"How bad is it, Paul?" Cassian asked. Tightness formed in his chest at the thought of the growing crowd outside.

For the last thirteen years of Cassian's life, he'd fought tooth and nail in the courtroom for his clients, who were usually victims of greedy conglomerates, circumstance, and tragedy. He got justice for them. Yet, the governor's race was an entirely new beast, one that bucked and threw him flat on his back each time he thought he'd mastered it.

This is the moment you've been fighting for. He'd sacrificed too much and for too long to let his goal slip through his fingers. Not when things were finally coming together. His mind wandered to the email he'd gotten that morning. After more than two years investigating, he finally knew who had caused his family's accident years earlier. Who had changed their lives forever.

Margarita handed the phone back to Paul, and he read the article out loud.

"'The race for Illinois governor is getting hot as Democratic candidate Cassian Anders was the target of Radcliffe's latest ad. The ad goes after Anders's record as a criminal defense attorney when he represented alleged domestic abusers and suspects accused of gang affiliation.'"

Cassian's jaw tightened. *This shit again.* "I proved those allegations were false."

"'Another ad from the group also targets Anders's family, or lack thereof, which has been a weak point for Anders's campaign. The rumors surrounding his ex-fiancée, a revolving door of women, his affluent lifestyle, and lack of relatability to middle-class families threaten the ten-percent popularity required for a candidate to stay on the Illinois ballot. After a recent survey, Mr. Anders's popularity is projected to fall to nine percent, jeopardizing his nomination. Governor Radcliffe says, "How can we expect Mr. Anders to lead a state of families when he doesn't have one himself?"'"

Cassian glanced at the man who had become another father figure. *It's the same shit every time. They need new material.*

Paul was the epitome of class, with a look that favored Giancarlo Esposito, his tight and silky salt-and-pepper curls glistening in the light.

"I don't think we should see this as a negative. Radcliffe sees you as a threat and he's trying to get ahead of it," Margarita offered.

"I've seen this before. Don't get cocky because you swept the primaries and snagged the party's nomination. That doesn't get you into office. We need to nip this gossip about your love life in the bud." Paul handed the phone back to Cassian and paced the small room.

Cassian was glad Radcliffe viewed him as a threat. All the campaigning, sleepless nights, and outreach events were paying off. It was time to get Radcliffe's ass out of office. He'd run the state with an iron fist for the last eight years, and poor and working families were suffering.

Margarita drummed her fingers on the arm of the couch. "Governor Radcliffe was a blue-collar worker for years. He won the lottery and bought his way into politics. It should be a walk in the park for Cassian to convince voters to elect him, regardless of his marital status. It doesn't determine his leadership style."

"Did you forget the only reason Illinois is Democratic is because of Chicago? The rest of the state is red. Conservative. *Traditional.* We can't cater to one city, we have to cater to all. They don't want to see a young, Black, and rich bachelor gallivanting with a different woman each night in office. It screams irresponsible, disrespectful, and gluttonous." Paul frowned at Margarita.

"Hmm." Cassian rubbed his temples. It was the same conversation rehashed for the millionth time. He dismissed the makeup artist.

He couldn't let his love life be the reason he didn't become governor. Surely they could move past this one...*fault.* It was outdated nonsense.

"I'll call James." Paul mentioned his PR rep as he reached for his own phone. "Have him release a statement denying all allegations."

"I say he should address the ad in his speech tonight. That has been our message since the beginning of this campaign. Honesty and transparency. Cassian's supporters trust him." Margarita stood as well.

"I say we leave that up to James. Don't bring it up, stick to the script, and don't bring up Congressman Mills or the *attorney general*." Paul pointed a finger at Cassian and narrowed his eyes.

A coldness settled over Cassian, and he had to call on all his former therapy techniques of counting back from five to prevent his fist from meeting the plaster. This was the bastard that he wanted to take down.

"Congressman Mills should have been out a long time ago anyway," Cassian forced the reply through his teeth. Flexing his fist, he exhaled shakily. He never liked the man from the several brief interactions they'd had. "Radcliffe is scared. Competition is looking a bit weak, and we're in a great position."

Once he was in office, he planned to clean up every department and seat in government if he could—beginning with the attorney general.

"Where's Rock?" Cassian asked, trying to change the conversation. Rock, his running mate, disappeared as soon as business talks started. Or when his wife, fresh off a new baby, made googly eyes at him.

"Evelyn needed him," Margarita replied.

Paul snapped his fingers in Cassian's face, jarring him. "Remember: stick to the script. Don't mention the ad. Ignore Congressman Mills. Stay away from the attorney general. Do you hear me?"

An assistant popped into the room. "It's time."

Get focused.

"You're the first person with a fighting chance to oppose Governor Radcliffe in eight years." Paul pressed his fingers into his chest, pinning Cassian with a grave stare. "We have more than enough obstacles. Stick. To. The. Script. No vengeance missions right now."

Vengeance mission.

It wasn't vengeance he was after. It was justice. His family's bodies would forever bear the trauma of the attorney general's decision.

"The young people nowadays love to do what… What do they call it?" Margarita snapped her fingers at Cassian as if that would help her remember. "Air out the receipts? Let's air them then. I've done it in the past, and we've won the election with flying colors."

Paul lifted his handkerchief to dab at the sweat on his brow. "Cassian isn't some sixteen-year-old rambling online with petty drama. He's a highly respected lawyer and political candidate. We stay high, let Radcliffe go low."

Justice for his family wasn't the only reason for wanting to be governor. It was also showing all the youth at his outreach center that someday they, too, could become governor or succeed in whatever arena they chose. That's what his father had instilled in him and what he was teaching to the kids.

"Paulie, you're gonna give yourself an ulcer. This will be like snatching candy from a baby. I've won cases that seem grimmer than this." Cassian tugged on the lapels of his jacket. *Rely on your instinct. It's never led you wrong.* He dismissed them as the assistant opened the door for him to exit.

No one could argue he wasn't one of the best paid and most accomplished lawyers in Chicago. He'd struggled with imposter syndrome through college and law school, even now during his campaign, but he forged forward despite the days when he wanted to say *Fuck everything and everyone* and walk away.

It was faith that helped him persist.

Margarita nodded. "That is the positive attitude we need to take onto the stage instead of your pessimism, Paul. Maybe you're too old for this job."

"My pessimism"—Paul puffed out his chest—"is what's going to get us to victory. I know the unexpected can happen."

Cassian exhaled deeply. When he had set out to hire the best of the best to advise him, he didn't know they would resort to squabbling like toddlers every moment.

Margarita sized Paul up with a smirk. "In all my years as a politician and serving as a junior senator, I know what passion can do. Our country is in a state of change. People don't want to stick to the past and what's been done before. It's time for a new dawn."

"Exactly. Thank you, Margarita. Paul, you are right too. Let's move on." *You both can have a pissing contest later.*

Cassian had spared no money on his campaign, recruiting Paul and Margarita to help him secure the spot. The two had a combined forty years of political experience and expertise. They planned meticulously, and yes, he had deviated from the script a few times, but the end was near. Risks had to be taken.

"You know what we've practiced, Cassian. Nothing negative. We go high," Paul insisted.

"Don't worry, Paul." He glanced at himself in the mirror by the door. He wore an expensive black suit paired with a white shirt and a red tie. His full beard was neatly trimmed and his curls freshly cut. "I'm always ready."

They were in the heart of Chicago at the McCormick Place, the largest convention center in North America. Earlier, he had glanced out the window to see traffic backed up on Lake Shore Drive, leading into the South Loop. Traffic control was swamped with directing cars in and out of the parking lots. Horns honked, music played, and the air was filled with excited screams for *him.* Most wore shirts with his campaign slogan, *We Are the Change.*

Security led him through the building. Those who couldn't snag free seats waited to see him in the halls. He nodded to people screaming his name, taking time to shake hands and take selfies.

Backstage, the sound techs placed a mic on him, and Paul grabbed Cassian by the arm, halting his entrance to the stage. "Are you sure you're ready for this? Once you formally accept, you can't go back. I've seen campaigns bring men to their knees."

I don't have a choice.

Cassian gave Paul a lopsided grin. "Don't get cold feet now."

Paul had asked him the same blunt question multiple times since they'd met. Cassian had flown to DC and ask Paul to manage him. They had become close over the year and a half of preparing for the campaign. Paul knew things about Cassian not even his parents knew. He should know no slick words of concern or doubt would make him bow out.

Paul squeezed his shoulder. "I understand finding out about the attorney general may have thrown you off—"

"I'm fine."

That's a lie. I'm fuming.

"You are better than a lot of men. The people of this state deserve someone for them, *and only for them.*" Paul poked a finger in his chest. "Don't turn into another Radcliffe."

With those parting words, Paul left. Taking a few deep breaths, Cassian tried to shake off emotions Paul stirred up. The crowd cheered as he stepped onto the stage.

Supporters pressed against the metal blockade separating him from them. News stations were at the back of the room with cameras and lights ready for an interview the moment he left the stage.

Waving, he plastered a practiced smile on his face as he crossed the stage to the podium to address the crowd. There was always a tiny feeling of nervousness addressing the crowd, akin to what he felt in court to give opening remarks. As he stood looking out toward the people, he thought about the shattered dreams of his father.

"Let me take this opportunity to reintroduce myself." Cassian paused, gazing at the sea of faces. "My name is Cassian Anders. I accept the Democratic nomination for governor of Illinois."

three

. . .

"You wanna know why I am running for governor?" he began. "I've sat, watched, defended in the courtroom the very people this state is supposed to protect. I've been in the trenches with you all." He pointed to the crowd. "I've seen the disadvantages in working-class neighborhoods compared to the elite on the Gold Coast and Millionaire's Row. I've seen families struggling to make ends meet, and youth struggle to stay out of street violence."

Cassian paused for a second, his eyes connecting with Paul's.

"I myself...I've been a victim of DUI violence. I've watched that same perpetrator get off because of connections. Someone needs to tell him his time is up. The skeletons are coming out of his closet." The crowd booed, and Cassian nodded.

"Everything we care about is under siege by Governor William Radcliffe." The crowd scoffed. "Our very identities do not fit in the governor's plan, nor will they ever. I grew up on the South Side of Chicago. Englewood. Chicago's murder capital. I've experienced poverty and crime, and I know the beauty there. I see amazing potential if we were to invest in the people there, not ignore them like Governor Radcliffe has."

A calm, collected feeling rolled over Cassian's body, obliterating the nervousness he'd felt. The crowd watched him with anticipation. It thrilled him. Fueled him.

"I will be a genuinely progressive governor for everyone. More opportunities for people to get ahead, not just get by. Youth enrichment programs. Healthcare for children and elderly. Inspiring spaces for local artists. We've got to tax millionaires and billionaires, not burden middle-class families with the cost of running this state."

The crowd roared.

"Illinois is losing jobs and opportunities. Creative minds. The fiber of our communities. If we continue to let Governor Radcliffe lead, there won't be a state for us to call home."

Cassian looked down in the crowd. He shouldn't have noticed, but he did.

In the center of the room, he spotted a woman. A beautiful woman. As they locked eyes, he recognized her. *Jolie Coldwell.* He couldn't forget the fierce reporter.

He observed her closely, his practiced speech faltering. She wore a pure white double-breasted blazer dress. From his position on stage, he could see it stopped midthigh, showing off the sexy, thick brown thighs. The dress wrapped around her curvy silhouette with decorative button details down the front that led up to her tasteful cleavage.

Jolie lifted her chin, meeting his gaze straight on, a small smirk on her lips. That's when he realized he had stopped talking. Clearing his throat, he returned her steady gaze, and something intense flared through him.

"I'm not here to only make history. I'm here because I love the people of this state. I want to remind everyone *We Are the Change.*"

He glanced at Margarita and Paul. They both had looks of satisfaction on their faces. Ignoring the tingling feeling of awareness of Jolie as the crowd erupted into applause, Cassian gave his thanks and made his way off the stage and into the growing line of supporters who wanted to shake his hand.

This was the best part. Meeting the people. Putting names to faces, especially those who had been supporting him since he submitted his bid a year ago.

Rock, his best friend, running mate, and the future lieutenant governor, finally appeared. He placed a hand on Cassian's shoulders as he leaned forward to whisper to him. "You ready? Here come the sharks."

The camera crews and reporters set up all their equipment in a line, waiting for an interview with him.

"Part of the job, right?" Cassian muttered.

"That's why I'm glad to be your running mate. They don't care about me."

"They care."

Rock pursed his lips, his bald head gleaming under the light. "I saw the article and the ad. The online comments are a mix between thirsty Gen Z and Millennials wanting to be your first lady and racist conservatives with conspiracy theories. Be prepared is all I'm saying."

Cassian sucked his teeth to stop himself from smiling. He'd read the thirst comments. "Is it too late to replace you?"

"Nobody else will deal with your type-A ass."

Cassian rolled his eyes at his friend, dabbing him up as he went to the first reporter.

"David Smith with Channel 2 News. After Governor Radcliffe's and Mayor Charles's disappointing handling of the uptick in crime, what are your plans to rectify that situation?"

Cassian made his face appear as if he was thinking about the question, but his answers had been memorized.

"My first steps would be what Governor Radcliffe and

Mayor Charles ignored. Make gun violence a state health crisis."

He watched as the camera pinned on his face, and the reporters' pens flew across the page to catch his words.

"The state has the funds to put resources in the hardest-hit neighborhoods in Chicago. Like my community of Englewood. Those funds, instead, have gone to highly affluent neighborhoods. I would've taken those funds and gave them to organizations focusing on violence prevention, at-risk youth intervention, and trauma recovery."

His eyes went to the right and caught Jolie a few feet down from him. Those mahogany eyes twinkled at him.

"This epidemic of gun violence is heartbreaking. If we equip these organizations with the tools they need, we will see a change."

Cassian's mind was split between smiling at the camera and reciting his practiced answers to each reporter and the anticipation of reaching Jolie. His pulse was at a gallop by the time he made it to her.

"Miss Coldwell, good to see you." He discreetly rubbed his sweaty palms on his pants leg.

Their first interaction nearly a year ago hadn't been nearly as cordial. She ripped into him and the other six Democratic candidates, and each one fell under her meddling investigations until he was the lone survivor.

"Mr. Anders, congratulations." She radiated a vitality that drew him like a magnet.

"That means a lot from you."

Jolie gave a tight smile before she glanced at him through her lashes. "You're a well-respected lawyer with influence who has fought banking corruption with a bunch of holy accolades. What's your response to commentators' concerns about your revolving door of women? Do you care people view you as the Black George Clooney? Who are these women and should we be expecting more soon?"

Cassian's face fell. *There are those claws.* Was this woman hired by Radcliffe? He wouldn't be surprised if she was.

"I thought Channel 12 News was about bringing the truth and current topics to the citizens of Illinois. When did it become a gossip station? Losing too much to Channel 8?"

Jolie scowled and silence stretched between them.

"I suggest you do more research with proper questions for the issues at hand." He dismissed her, not giving her a chance with a follow-up question. Her mouth parted, about to retort, but he moved on to the next reporter. He could feel her eyes lingering on him.

"Missy Johnson, TCW. You're the youngest contender in recent Illinois history to run for governor, and this state has always been hard workers and family—"

"Of course." Cassian was still shaking Jolie off as he listened.

"Recent poll results show that Illinoisans want their leadership to reflect their lives. Not to make it obvious, but you're not wearing a wedding ring. What do you say to family-minded voters who doubt your ability to connect with them?"

Cassian kept a smile on his face as his right hand covered his ring finger before he clenched it into a fist. In the public's eyes, a bachelor equaled a womanizer. He couldn't lose everything he'd worked for these last few years because of their unfounded doubt.

"Unless you're hiding something from us?" Missy asked leadingly. "There's no secret missus anywhere? Or do your female supporters have a chance with you?"

As he massaged his empty ring finger with his hand, his brain raced for a solution. He turned and caught Paul's eye. The man shook his head and mouthed, *Stick to the script!*

"I wanted to keep this under wraps, but..." *Just say "No comment."* "I'm proud to say I am recently engaged—"

The crowd murmured in excitement. Someone let out a

wail behind him, asking *Why?* Paul and Margarita stared at him in disbelief.

"Who is the lucky woman?" Missy grinned like a raptor with its prey.

"I won't be releasing that statement until after our wedding."

Missy pressed harder, and it looked as if she wanted to grab him. "Which is when exactly?"

"No more questions, thank you!" Paul jumped in.

Cassian stepped away with Margarita, Paul, and Rock following as he waved to the crowd a final time. The guards led them on a path to the hallway and back to his dressing room. In less than five seconds after entering the dressing room before Paul was on his ass.

"What the hell was that?"

Margarita and Rock shared equal looks of concern and confusion as Cassian fell onto the couch, the adrenaline from the crowd subsiding.

"I had to do it."

Paul pinched the bridge of his nose. "You told every major news outlet you were engaged! Who is this phantom fiancée? Is there even one? Or do you plan to order her online?"

"Don't worry, we can figure this out." Margarita nervously took out a cigarette and lit it.

Rock chuckled and leaned against the wall. "We're fucked."

Margarita inhaled deeply on the cigarette and she held a hand out to calm Paul down. "We can use this. If it's going to help him win, why not continue with the lie?"

Paul turned to Cassian. "What did I tell you about lies and the public? It will always come back to bite you in the ass."

His mouth went dry, and he forced himself to swallow, but it didn't alleviate the tsunami of regret washing over him. Cassian forced a smile.

"How hard could it be to find a wife?"

four

. . .

"You're going to the bar in that?" Helena's voice dripped with distaste as she jiggled her car keys in her hand.

Jolie looked away from her computer. "I have too much work to do—"

"Stalking Cassian Anders? Girl, let it go. You were in the wrong." Helena leaned forward, glancing at Jolie's monitor.

"You're on his side?"

Jolie devoted most of her day to looking for any dirt on Cassian Anders. *Asshole.* How could he walk away from her like that? If she dug deep enough into most people, she knew she'd hit an oil pipe of hidden unsavory behavior, but with Cassian…

It was hard not to see why he wasn't the perfect candidate. *He's too damn perfect.*

He graduated top of his class from Morehouse College. Finished his law degree in two years instead of three at Harvard University. Worked at the best law firms in the country before opening his own firm, which was growing to be the greatest full-service law firm in the Midwest. There was nothing bad she could get on the guy. And she hated that. Most of all, she hated her body's reaction to him.

The epitome of tall, dark, and handsome. That's what the women in the audience had been squealing about the moment he hit the stage.

The instant his eyes had met hers, her heart stuttered in her chest. He handled the crowd with ease, charisma, and a professionalism that further affirmed him as the perfect choice for voters. He gazed at her intently, and she had to subtly cross her legs at the low, husky timbre of his voice.

Damn, when was the last time I had a good fuck?

Her dedication to her career often put romance on the back burner. Right now, all she could think about was his big hands warm on her exposed thigh, those low, domineering eyes, and his body towering over her. That didn't happen often for her as a tall woman. He made her feel dainty and…protected.

When she met his eyes, she felt exposed. Raw. She never enjoyed that feeling. She was the one who did the exposing.

And yet, for the past couple of days she couldn't get the image of him commanding the crowd and looking sexy as hell out of her mind. She hadn't fantasized about a guy since she was sixteen and in love with Larenz Tate.

Cassian Anders was a temptation. Too bad the man was engaged. Damn Missy Johnson. She should have had that news first! Congrats to the mysterious woman who got to wake up to him every morning. Those lips…

"Hello? Earth to Jolie. You need a minute?" Helena waved her hand in Jolie's face.

"I was doing…research."

"You were staring at a picture of him."

There had to be *something* wrong with Cassian Anders, and eventually she'd find out.

"You're not flaking on me again. I'm setting you up with Clark tonight. We can get free drinks, and if you're nice, maybe you'll get some action. What's it been? A year?" Helena pulled out her chair from the cubicle across from Jolie's and plopped down in it.

Jolie's phone buzzed. "Ugh." Her mother had been calling all day and leaving ranting voice mails. She'd had the same number since she was sixteen, so it was easy for Liza to pop up whenever she wanted to give Jolie hell.

Respect. Guilt. Anger. Jolie experienced a complicated flood of emotions anytime Liza Coldwell made her presence known.

Helena looked at her in question.

"My mother."

"Have you talked to her lately?"

"Why would I do that?"

She didn't want to talk about her mother. There was nothing ever good to say.

"When was the last time you saw her?" Helena asked after a few seconds.

"Four months or six? I try not to go to the house if I can help it." A dark feeling came over Jolie as she thought about her childhood home.

"She's gotten better, right? Less Bible-thumping—"

"She still has white Jesus on the wall next to JFK and wonders if I'm fertile."

Helena cackled, slapping her thigh. "Not white Jesus on the wall."

"You don't know her like I know her. If she isn't hounding me, she's babying Aaron's ass." Jolie's mouth turned downward in distaste at the mention of her half brother.

"You need a drink. Come on, let's go."

Jolie sighed and shut down her monitors, and the women exited the newsroom, clicking toward the elevator for the garage. The elevator arrived, and they stepped on. "Is Aaron still working at the water treatment plant?"

"He got fired. Apparently, he's gonna go back to college for the third time."

The women emerged on the garage floor. It was only a matter of time before Aaron came around sniffing for money and pity—like he always did.

Jolie rubbed her temples. "I'm staying home, Lena. I'm gonna watch a movie, drink my wine—"

"Boo! Boring. Come out! Nate got Ginger Sparrow from *The Wake-Up Call* to put us on the list for Magnifica." Helena squeezed Jolie's shoulders and grinned as she unlocked the doors of her gray Mitsubishi Outlander.

Jolie rolled her eyes and opened Helena's door with more force than necessary. "I need to find a good story to give Dev."

"Please come? I'm serious, I don't want to go by myself, and if you don't come, I'm gonna cry—" Helena closed the driver's-side door, starting the car up.

"Lena. No. Please not the puppy dog eyes."

"Pleeease…"

"Fine." Jolie fixed her face into a semblance of normality and smiled at Helena. "You want to meet up with Nate so he can break you off." Helena looked guilty. "You ain't slick."

"Unlike you, I *like* romantic attention from the opposite sex. I'm not intentionally mean to them for no reason." Rolling her eyes, Helena put the car into drive.

Cassian's face appeared in Jolie's mind. She exhaled slowly, a tinge of regret creeping in.

"Like the great Maxine Shaw once said, 'Men are the speed bumps on the road to happiness.'" Jolie relaxed in the seat as they pulled out of the garage and into downtown traffic.

"You don't mean that."

"I do."

Helena gave Jolie a pitying look. "Braxton was an asshole and was intimidated because of how hard you work and the money you made, so he tried to gaslight you. No one told him to start a chain of vegan steakhouses."

Yes, her ex-boyfriend Braxton turned out to be a bum. He'd lasted for a good time, not a long time. She wouldn't be like her mom and ignore the red flags out of desperation for companionship. She got the hell out of there promptly.

"After him, it was Dre, the washed-up musician—"

"He wasn't bad. He could fuck at least and hold a tune."

"Another bum. Then it was Diego. Noah. Should I go on? Besides Braxton, these relationships all lasted max four months."

Jolie tugged at her earlobe. "What's the point?"

Most men nowadays didn't want more than a warm body to dump a nut in. She didn't need a man to exist. Helena slowed to a stop at a red light. "You know I love you, right?"

She rolled her eyes. Another come-to-Jesus chat.

"Lena—"

"Listen to me." Helena exhaled. "You've always been intense, and it was inspiring. Now, you're manic. A workaholic. I'm worried about you."

"There's nothing to be worried about."

"You're picking these relationships that go nowhere because of your mom."

Jesus, this again. They were apples and oranges. Her mother had the faulty picker. She was the one who dragged Jolie from relationship to relationship with her, even becoming homeless once after the guy they were living with put them out. Jolie could never imagine letting a man have that much control over her.

"You want control. Over everything in a relationship. If you don't have it, you freak."

"When did you become Dr. Phil?"

"I'm serious. It's like you pick these terrible relationships with one foot out the door instead of being vulnerable with a man and having him love you back."

"You and I have different views of love and relationships." Jolie bit her bottom lip, clenching her fist against the armrest. "I'm fine with my love life, or lack thereof."

Helena gave her a sad smile. "Take a chance with someone. I know it has to get lonely."

Jolie shrugged, turning her head out the window. Helena squeezed her shoulder softly before the low hum of the radio filled the car.

Her mother's life was a warning to Jolie. A prophecy of what could happen if she became unfocused. If she lost control and became a victim to vulnerability. She would be damned if that would be her fate.

"Meet me in a half an hour, okay? And smile when you get there, please." Helena dropped her off at her apartment in Bronzeville.

In the months since her breakup with Braxton, she had rarely let herself relax. There had been moments over the years when she was tempted to finally let her hair down, get a drink, and enjoy a one-night stand. Then her sensibilities kicked in. Memories of the past. Her mother. Her need to never be dependent on anyone. She was safer alone.

This promotion would expedite that goal. She'd be in control of her life. Never would she be like her mother.

JOLIE WAS MORE than a little late by the time she walked into the luxury lounge in Chicago's Gold Coast neighborhood.

Deciding to give in to Lena's urging, Jolie brought out a dress she'd ordered eons ago but never found the right occasion to wear—a green strappy minidress that molded to the soft curves of her body, stopping midthigh, with a slit that showed the right amount of skin.

Eyes were on her as she sauntered into the room with her head high and shoulders back in her five-inch pumps.

Magnifica was nearly impossible to get in without a connection. Jolie tried thousands of times, to no avail. Known for the politicians, high-society socialites, and local celebrities that often visited out of the eyes of the nosy public—and journalists like her. Nate in the Morning was a lot of things, but he came through in a clutch. Maybe she wouldn't give Lena hell about dating him.

Jolie's eyes raced over the beautiful people lounging about. Dressed to the nines in Gucci, Dior, Hermès, and Chanel, they moved and rocked with the live band on stage. Red lights shone low, adding a raw tension in the air.

The stage was on the far-right wall, and tables and booths were situated around it. In the center of the room was the bar. Jolie found an open stool and flagged down a bartender.

Jolie sent a text to Helena.

Where are you?

"What can I get you?"

Jolie set her phone down, observing the bartender standing in front of her. He was cute. Intricate dragon tattoos on both arms. He winked at her, and she raised an eyebrow.

"A dirty martini, please."

The bartender's eyes went down to Jolie's cleavage before he disappeared to make her drink. *Shit, Lena's right. I need to get laid.* If only Jolie were twenty-one again, maybe she would give the bartender the time of day. But she was thirty, and if she *wanted* a partner, it had to be a man who was steady in his career. Reliable. Caring. And it would help if they looked like Cassian Anders…

Dammit! The man is taken. Engaged. A goody-two-shoes. She shook her head. Where was Helena?

She forced herself to relax as she took a long sip. The familiar throat-burning sensation of the gin lit a fire down to her belly. She closed her eyes, feeling her muscles relax

31

already. There was a commotion from the entryway, and several people clapped. The hair rose on her arms as she noticed who had walked in.

Cassian Anders.

If she thought he was handsome before, he was downright sexy now.

A suppressed anger pulsated off him. He couldn't hide it from her. She had too much practice observing and studying body language. His black curls shone under the dim light, his muscles shifting under his suit like a panther as he crossed the room in long strides, nodding as a grin crossed his features. *God bless his fiancée.*

His thick brow slanted downward as he commanded attention in the room. He stopped and talked to everyone, plastering a smile on his face as he continued to move with a purpose toward the bar. Toward her.

He was definitely a politician in the making. Giving each person his sole attention, making them feel special. Under the lull of the jazz music playing, she could hear his deep voice rumble.

Forcing her gaze forward, she told herself she didn't like how his deep, husky voice sounded alluring. Braxton had never made her pulse race or ignite an achiness in her core just with his very presence. *Shut it down, Jolie. Not him. Anyone but him.* It didn't help that his announcement from a few days ago was playing silently on a TV in the room.

She wasn't sure why she ducked her head. Jolie never ran from a fight or cowered from anyone, but she felt severely outnumbered in a room full of his supporters.

"EJ, my man, get me a double Scotch. Neat."

Forcing herself to relax, from the corner of her eyes, she watched him pass a sleek black card to the bartender. She caught a whiff of his musky cologne and inhaled subtly.

"Miss Coldwell, nice to see you again," he said in a silky voice.

Ding, ding, ding. Fight's on.

Slanting her eyes to his, she pinned him with a vicious stare.

"Mr. Anders..." She set her drink down on the napkin. Her belly shouldn't be doing flip-flops like a fish on the shore. Squaring her shoulders back, she turned toward him.

Only a few inches separated them. The noise of the bar faded to a hum. Amusement flickered in his eyes before it died out, consumed with a look of polite irritation.

"Here you go, double Scotch neat," EJ said.

Jolie barely heard him. Her gaze remained fixated on Cassian. His curly hair, strong jawline, and full lips. *I really need to get laid if I'm lusting after him...*

"What are you doing here?" His voice was deceptively calm, but sharpness lurked in his tone.

Her heart fluttered as his eyes took their perusal down her body. Her foot accidentally grazed his when she uncrossed and crossed her legs.

"This is a public place, isn't it?" She sipped her drink slowly with a forced calmness.

"I didn't know Dan was letting reporters in here. Looking for more gossip about me?" He said the words nicely, but his distaste was obvious.

"Don't get too full of yourself. You're not that interesting."

Let's ignore the fact I've been researching you all day.

"I guess I should be thankful I'm not some poor bastard you destroyed. I saw the congressman story."

The corner of her mouth turned up.

"Good work. Mills had it coming."

They both took sips of their drinks. The clink of ice in a highball drink filled the silence between them, until he began again. "That article was a while ago. Now you're too busy reporting on seniors' plays."

Jolie drew back. "How do you know that?"

Cassian chuckled smoothly, and she hated how yummy it sounded.

"You're not the only one with internet access and a brain, you know. That's all you need to be a journalist, right?"

Jolie narrowed her eyes. "You know what I find funny, Cassian?"

"Cassian? We're on a first-name basis now?" He leaned against the bar, his cologne wafting toward her.

"You're not special."

His body stiffened.

"I've seen your type. You're a dime a dozen. Politicians get people to believe the lies and promises, but in reality, they're ruthless crooks and psychopaths."

A smile broke across his face. "I'm a psychopath?"

"You're another crook trying to get into office. You'll fail like the rest, and I will be the one that will be there with a camera and recorder."

Cassian's nostrils flared, his grip on the glass tightening. She grinned.

"You have a mouth on you. Don't let it write a check you can't cash."

Jolie waved her hands mockingly in the air. "Ooh, I'm cracking that façade, huh? That leads me to a question. Do you ever let your supporters see this real side of you, or is it just for me, because there are no cameras?"

He rubbed his jaw slowly, his eyes piercing.

"Miss Coldwell, you fail to realize you're not dealing with an amateur." Cassian pressed closer, and Jolie retreated, almost falling off the stool. "I see you for who you are. You like to scare people with big words and nastier threats." Cassian finished his Scotch. "I live for the threats, *doll*. Save your pretty words till you're ready to play with the big dogs."

They stared at one another till Jolie reached for her drink, finishing it in one gulp.

Cassian smirked. "I'm guessing that's the reason you're

here tonight? Spying for your gossip column? Traffic to your website is slow, and you need a payday?"

"Don't speak to me as if I'm a simpleton." She motioned to EJ for another drink, her mouth pulled into a sour line. "I'm an investigative reporter, not a gossip columnist."

Cassian grinned. "Don't back down now, Ms. Coldwell. We're getting started."

"As a political candidate, you should watch what you say, Mr. Anders. You never know what will find its way to the internet."

"Are you threatening me, Miss Coldwell?"

Heat bloomed in her chest as he angrily ran a hand through his curls. She recalled the thousands of women online admiring his looks. No doubt his little fans would be having coronaries left and right if they were her right now.

"You sure are something, Miss Coldwell," Cassian murmured as he licked his lips. Downing his Scotch, he slammed the glass on the counter.

"I know."

"Too bad about Walter Cabot. He was an honorable reporter, wasn't he? Shame he couldn't teach you a thing or two about that."

Shock jolted through her, and she spun to him. How did he know about Walter?

Cassian leaned forward, his voice dropping low, and she felt the vibrations of the tenor of his words on her skin. "Have a good night, Miss Coldwell, and don't worry. The drinks are on me."

EJ returned his black card, and Cassian slid away from her with a wink. Immediately he was embraced by others, and she felt her skin heat, not in arousal but anger.

five

. . .

J olie gripped the martini glass so hard she thought it
might crack as a flushed Helena sat down next to her
with a grin.

"Hey, girl! Why you looking like that?"

Her braids were escaping the knot on the top of her head
and her lipstick was smeared.

"Have you been fucking?" Jolie said bluntly, unable to
pull class as she glanced back toward Cassian. *Shame he
couldn't teach you a thing or two about that.* How fucking
dare he.

Helena had the gall to look sheepish. Nate in the Morning
came up behind her. His caramel skin was flushed red, his
cornrow braids untidy. He threw an arm around Lena's
shoulder and grinned at her. "Jolie-girl! Great to see you
again."

Jolie tapped her nails on the counter, stewing as she
turned to witness Cassian shaking someone else's hand
before glancing at his phone. A hard-pressed expression
passed across his face before he walked off toward the
hallway to the bathrooms.

"Is that Cassian Anders?" Helena whispered, and Jolie

rolled her eyes.

Nate squinted. "Eh, I saw homeboy on the news the other day. I'm voting for him."

Jolie's expression soured. "Do you know anything about him?"

"I know he's Black."

Helena giggled, leaning into Nate.

"That's making an informed decision." Jolie deadpanned.

Helena flagged down EJ, and gave Jolie a cheeky grin as EJ slid Jolie his number.

"Been busy?"

"I have not." *If you don't include bantering with a man who could keep up intellectually and who I should not find attractive.*

Helena wiggled her eyebrows. "He looks like he has stamina—"

Nate in the Morning choked on his beer, spitting it on the counter, and the women jumped. "Damn, babe, you can't say stuff like that."

"Cover your ears." Helena reached for a napkin to help him wipe himself up as she grinned at Jolie. "Remember what we talked about earlier?" she asked Jolie.

"I'm only interested in one thing, and it doesn't have a penis attached to it."

"You're no fun. But I guess that means you won't be pissed that Clark is gonna be late."

That prickly feeling she had about Cassian's earlier comment about Walter didn't sit right in her belly. She glanced toward the hallway he disappeared down, and downing the rest of her martini, she stood.

"Where are you going?" Helena called after her as Jolie made her way to where he disappeared. If he thought he was going to get the last word, it was a cold day in motherfucking hell.

Was she going to burst into the men's bathroom and curse him out? Yes, she was.

It helped that EJ made a strong martini. Stopping at the bathroom entrance, she heard Cassian's hushed voice.

"I know you're pissed, Paul. This is about the campaign. That takes precedence over anything. You of all people should understand that... Don't you know anyone who can do this favor for me?"

She pressed herself against the wall. Jolie couldn't hear the voice on the other end, but by Cassian's sigh, it was bad. Instinct had her reaching into her clutch for her phone. Clicking the record app, she inched closer to the entrance of the bathroom.

Her lips twitched, and warmth spread throughout her body. *It's the end for Cassian Anders. Pity. He fell so fast.*

"How hard is it to find a woman that will marry me? As long as she looks good and has some kind of intelligence, anyone will do."

A mail-order wife? Problems with the ladies? No surprise.

"I trust you out of anyone. Do it for me, okay? I know this wasn't the plan, but we can get through this."

Jolie's heart thundered. The golden boy had skeletons in his closet, and she was going to air them out.

"Find a wife. I'll draw up a contract. It will be airtight."

She didn't pay attention to Cassian's footsteps as he rounded the entrance of the bathroom and plowed into her.

Jolie stumbled and the phone clattered to the ground as he caught her from falling.

"I'm sorry, I didn't see you—"

He stiffened, recognizing her, dropping her like hot coals. She caught herself on the wall. Cassian glanced at the phone on the floor, then at her. Jolie dove for the device and took off.

"Hey!"

Cassian closed the distance between them and pulled her back into the alcove. She narrowed her eyes dangerously at him and yanked back; he refused to let her go.

"Were you *recording* me?"

"Get your hands off me before you find yourself with the biggest fucking lawsuit of your life!"

His brown eyes raged, and his full lips pulled into a snarl. She should resist him. Her body swayed toward his involuntarily.

"Give me the phone."

"It's my private property."

Cassian was silent. Then a slow smirk played across his features. "Everyone has rights to privacy and security and under the Fourth Amendment and the Federal Wiretap Act. Did you know Illinois is a two-party consent state? That means I have to give you my consent to record me. I didn't. Which is a gross infringement of my rights, which can cause a lawsuit of my own." He grinned.

"You wouldn't."

Cassian didn't loosen his grip on her arm; if anything it tightened. "I will sue you *and* Channel 12."

Shit! Dev would fire her if she got the station sued again.

"You're bluffing."

"I'm a lawyer, Miss Coldwell. I'm well versed on how to win a case like this."

How the hell am I going to get out of this one? Swallowing, she prayed for someone to come down the dark hallway.

"Tell me who told you about Walter retiring. That's not public yet." Her hand still gripped the phone.

"I won't repeat myself again. Give me the phone."

"Sorry, buddy, it's mine."

She pulled back from him again, he jerked her forward, and she shrieked as he forced her back into the wall. His body flush with hers. She tried to ignore the wave of arousal rising within her.

"I'll hate to ruin the reputation you've built, and I say that with much sarcasm."

Her eyes glittered. "You can try."

"I bet it wouldn't take much to have you on every black-list in this city."

Up close, he was lovely and dangerous. His eyes flickered from her lips to her eyes, and she could feel him shift against her, pushing her farther into the dark alcove, away from potential witnesses.

"What would your supporters think of you manhandling an innocent woman in the hall?"

The corner of Cassian's mouth twitched. "Innocent? Interesting way to spin things."

Wrenching herself from him finally, she rushed to the opposite wall, trying to gain the strength back in her knees as she faced him.

"I won't sue you if you give me that recording."

She stayed firm as her body trembled. "Why do you need a wife? Down bad in the female department, Cassian? Is it because of the polls?"

"I'm not going to tell you again, give me the recording."

She lifted her chin, ignoring the dark command of his voice. *Who knew a threat could be so sexy?* It sent a thrill down her spine but she narrowed her eyes at him. "You wouldn't risk your campaign."

"I'll do anything for this campaign. Even end you if necessary." The threat of his words wasn't lost on her.

"Tell me the truth about the wife."

"This is history in the making, Miss Coldwell. Do you want to destroy it for an exposé I'll just bury?"

"Answer me," Jolie demanded.

Cassian crossed the hall toward her, she inhaled sharply, stumbling back. He reached into his pocket and handed her a business card.

"You have forty-eight hours to turn over the recording, or I'm filing my lawsuit. You decide."

He spun on his heel, stalking down the hallway. Glancing at the phone in her purse, she cursed. *Dev is not gonna like this.*

six

. . .

"I told your ass not to drink all those martinis. Now look at you." Helena snapped her fingers in front of Jolie's face.

"Huh?" Jolie muttered stupidly as Helena stood in the entrance of Jolie's cubicle.

"Nate and I barely got you into your apartment last night."

Cassian Anders was fucking with her head. She had less than forty-eight hours to decide if Dev and the execs would have her head on a stake.

"Believe me, being drunk was better than listening to Clark talk about pork shoulders. Remind me to lay hands on you when I have the time."

Helena stuck her tongue out at her. "Do you know how much groveling I'm going to have to do to get back on Clark's good side? He's my meat butcher. You don't play with those relationships."

Clark had nothing on the sexy, mean, and vindictive bastard that was Cassian Anders. What she saw of him didn't match his public persona. She swore she still felt his grip on her arm long after he turned her loose.

"If you didn't like Clark, let me hook you up with someone else." Helena leaned on the wall of Jolie's cubicle.

"I have work to do."

She wasn't lying. Mulling over Cassian's threat had her avidly researching Illinois wiretapping laws. He was right. The law was there in black and white. *I'm fucked.*

"Why are you stubborn?"

"I'm a Scorpio."

"*Jolie*, where's my page one?" Dev's voice cut through the air, and Helena squealed, heading to her cubicle.

"Dev, I'm gonna need more time." How would she spin her blunder with Cassian? *Both* in public and private.

Dev now stood in the aisle between their cubicles. "I don't have time."

"The audio file for the transcript is corrupted, and IT is fixing it. We want exact quotes, right?"

Jolie clicked on an email with the subject line, *Please help me.*

"Fine, what about the story proposal you want to submit for consideration for Walter's position?" Dev crossed his arms, frowning.

Jolie spared Dev a sheepish glance. "Working on that too."

"I'm giving you a chance for the on-air role, Jolie. I need a page one proposal. Travis submitted his."

At the mention of his name, Travis came crawling out from beneath the rock he lived under. Pinning Jolie with a sly look, he snorted. "Hit the bottle a little hard last night?"

"Why are you speaking to me?" Jolie glared at Travis. "Shouldn't you actually do the tasks of a reporter, or are you waiting for me to do all the work again?"

"You mean cause another scandal?"

Jolie's eyes flashed, and Travis smirked.

"Can't wait till you leave, baby girl. I got plans on how I want to decorate this cubicle." He wiggled his brows at her before sauntering down the aisle with a whistle after Dev gave him a disappointed glare.

"If you want this, I need something from you soon," Dev stressed.

Jolie's mind flew to the roughness of Cassian's hand. His body, vibrating with anger against hers. *You don't like that man that way, Jolie!*

"Fine, Dev. I'll give you something by the end of the day." She turned her attention back to her email.

Dear Miss Coldwell,

My name is Lupe Lopez. I live in an apartment on the Lower West Side of Chicago. My landlord has raised my rent now over 68% in the last month—double my income. That price would make me and other residents in this building homeless.

My family has been here for over twenty years, and this is home. We need help, please, you need to investigate this.

Dev rubbed his temples. "Jolie, I wan—"

"I've got a proposal for you."

"What?"

Jolie normally didn't pick the first story that popped into her slush pile. People constantly submitted stories for the investigative team to report on, mainly domestic disputes or attempts at revenge or retribution. This one had her reporter instincts tingling.

"A story? That's what you want from me, right?"

Jolie scrolled to see the woman had attached a bunch of screenshots, pdf reports, and other documents from her landlord. "I have a story on rent gouging in Pilsen."

Dev frowned. "Pilsen? That area has been under redevelopment for years now. Rent is expected to go up."

"It's called gentrification, Dev. The rent is cheap to you, not to poor families and people on pensions."

This was like some stories Walter Cabot had done in the past. He'd always been a fierce advocate for affordable housing.

"Go see if it's worth it. I still need this written up by the end of day." Dev gave her a firm look before departing.

"You have that devious look." Helena peeked out of her cubicle.

Jolie gave a calculated smile.

This story had promise. It could easily join her long line of hard-hitting stories. She could help these people get fair housing. She would get views and ratings from it. The execs would love her again.

"Don't cause trouble." Helena watched as Jolie stood and slid her brown trench coat over her suit.

"I never cause trouble intentionally."

"Why don't I believe that?"

Jolie rushed out of the office and to the parking lot. It took her twenty minutes to travel from the Loop to Pilsen, historically a working-class residential neighborhood and gateway for many immigrants coming to the city of Chicago. First settled by the Irish immigrants, then Germans, and the Czechs, now it was a predominantly Mexican-American community.

Jolie surveyed the area.

The block bustled at midday. The sweet, doughy scent from the panaderías drifted to her nose and tempted her. There were several apartments on the street that had tarps and other construction equipment, with the sign Urban Properties in the window. There was a park across the street where several older people practiced tai chi. On the corner was a local grocery store with several guys standing in front chatting excitedly and smoking cigarettes. Jolie adjusted her dark sunglasses and checked the address again.

Apartment with a red door. This is it…

Lupe's apartment was next to a taquería. Freshly cooked tortillas and spicy marinated meat made her mouth water. Pressing the buzzer, she took a step back, observing several for-sale signs with "Sold" plastered on them on some of the other businesses' windows.

"Come on in!" A voice crackled through the intercom, and a buzz signaled the door unlocking as Jolie stepped inside. The apartment building was narrow, like a shoebox apartment in New York City. She ignored her claustrophobia as she climbed up the constricted stairwell to the third floor. Stopping in front of apartment 3B, she knocked and heard the click-clack of flip-flops heading toward the front door.

The door swung open, and an older woman gasped.

"It's really you!"

Jolie removed her sunglasses as she took in the older woman in front of her.

Lupe appeared to be in her mid to late sixties. Dark eyes with smeared mascara on her lashes, blue shimmery eyeshadow on her lids, a light blush, and red lipstick on her thin lips, and her hair pulled back in a messy salt-and-pepper chignon. She wore a floral, ankle-length dress with a fringe and a dirty apron tied across her front.

"You look the same from the television."

"Thank you, Mrs. Lopez. I appreciate you for allowing me over on short notice." Jolie asked, and the woman nodded before ushering her in.

"Please, please come in. I'm feeding my son right now."

Feeding her son? Nodding, she stepped inside the apartment. Immediately, it felt as if she was in her old childhood home. A small living room, barely any room to turn, but cozy. A worn green couch, with photos upon photos of children and other relatives plastered on the wall above it. There was a small bookshelf spilling over with books and DVDs, with a sleeping tabby in the window.

The delicious smell of meat and beans filled the air as Jolie followed the woman down the hallway and into a small bedroom. Jolie stopped midstep.

In a medical bed was a young man, no older than thirty.

Dressed in pajamas, he was propped up in bed, eyes open but fixed somewhere in the distance, his right arm curled tightly to his chest. Tubes connected him to various machines that beeped and hummed.

Lupe walked around, twisted the knob of an oxygen machine, and adjusted the tubes before taking a seat next to him.

Jolie slowly took the other seat at the foot of his bed. "I got your email, and it interested me."

"I'm so excited! I watch you on the weekends! It was amazing that you found out the ambulance was scamming people! Greedy. Just greedy." Mrs. Lopez frowned.

Jolie laughed. "Thank you, Mrs. Lopez—"

"Or those nasty DMV employees? That's why I hate going to the DMV. I'll never go again. I love your makeup, did the station do it?"

"Mrs. Lopez, your email—"

"Yes! I had my grandson help me make an email account. I knew you were made for my story." Mrs. Lopez picked up a bowl and fed her son some soup. "I had no other choice but to go to you since they've been ignoring me."

Jolie set her briefcase down, pulling out a notebook and pen. "Who's been ignoring you?"

"Urban Properties. They own this building now. The last owner sold it to them, and at first, everything was fine. Over this last year, the rent would increase in small increments of thirty or forty dollars to justify the city's increase in property tax." Mrs. Lopez spared a glance at Jolie. "A week ago, I get notice that the rent was increasing from twelve hundred dollars to twenty-five hundred dollars."

Jolie's eyes widened, and Lupe nodded sadly.

"I'm already spending most of my social security check on rent and utilities. I can't afford to pay more. I had to get a job as a cook at the local elementary school. I'm taxed heavily on that income."

"Have you tried communicating with the building manager?"

Lupe shrugged. "I've tried, and no one responds to me. Eventually I got a letter. It said they're abiding by the renter and landlord laws of Chicago."

Jolie felt anger boil in her belly.

"It's not just me. Maria downstairs, her studio went from five hundred dollars to a thousand. Frank's place went from two thousand dollars to thirty-five hundred. There doesn't seem to be any rhyme or reason."

Immediately, Jolie knew she was going to help her. This woman was obviously dealing with a lot, and she wanted to ease the burden off her as best she could.

"I don't have anyone else to help me. I can't afford to save and find another apartment. Especially with my son. He needs a caregiver almost twenty-four hours a day." Mrs. Lopez gently wiped his bottom lip with her napkin.

"If you don't mind me asking, what happened to your son?"

A sad look fell across her face as she smiled at Jolie. "My son's name is Miguel. He used to be a full-time transportation provider until his stroke—"

Mrs. Lopez sniffed, and Jolie's heart twisted. She reached into her bag to pass the woman a tissue.

"Thank you, sweetie. He recovered, then he had another. It was while he was driving. Luckily, he didn't crash into anyone else, but the damage to him was significant, and there was some bleeding in his brain."

Inhaling sharply, Jolie could only imagine the trauma this man and his family had been through.

"His fiancée at the time disappeared, and it was only me left. I've been caring for him for the last five years. With the rent increase, I have to pay for someone to watch over him while I'm gone."

"It's just one cost right after the other." Jolie's lips twisted.

Mrs. Lopez nodded. "I want to stay here in my home. If we can't, we'll be homeless."

Sitting in this space with Mrs. Lopez and her son, it felt like she was back in that small, cramped apartment she grew up in. Despite what Cassian or others thought about her, she cared about people. Mrs. Lopez represented the people she fought for. Everyone deserved basic rights as human beings.

Regarding the room, Jolie's eyes widened, and she jumped out of her seat, startling Mrs. Lopez. "Excuse me, Mrs. Lopez, what is this?"

There was a picture hanging on the wall of Miguel smiling with another man. Not any man. Cassian Anders. They both wore shirts with his outreach center logo on it. She couldn't tear her eyes away from Cassian. *I can't escape this asshole.*

"Oh, that's Miguel with his old boss, Mr. Cassian. Have you heard of him? He's running for governor!" The pit in Jolie's stomach twisted as the older woman continued to chat happily about Cassian.

"Miguel worked for him until his accident. Such a lovely young man. Did you know he paid for Miguel's hospital bills? Even gave us a stipend for a year to help."

"Lovely..." Jolie muttered. Cassian was drop-dead gorgeous with those intense eyes. A complete contrast to the man before her last night, who looked like he wanted to snatch her head completely off.

"A nice young man. Sends flowers on Miguel's accident anniversary."

Cassian Anders was ruthless *and* caring? A little voice said, *maybe he's not like the others.* She dismissed it. One nice thing didn't make him a saint.

"Excuse me, do you mind if I make a call, Mrs. Lopez?"

"Of course. Please...do you think you can help us?"

Jolie gave a firm nod. "I know I can."

Relief flashed across Mrs. Lopez's features. Jolie's phone

buzzed rapidly. After excusing herself in the hallway, she found there were three text messages from Helena.

OMG

Have you seen what Channel 8 ran today?

Bitch, you've been hiding secrets?!

Tell me it's not true.

Jolie clicked the attached photo. Gasping, she nearly dropped the phone. It was a photo of her and Cassian from the night before. It was slightly blurry, but his face was clear. Her back faced the camera as he pressed her against the wall. In big bold letters, it said **TROUBLE IN PARADISE OR SEX AND LIES?**

Channel 8 was accusing Cassian of having a secret affair.

They hadn't identified her yet, but it wouldn't be long. Cursing under her breath, she rummaged through her purse, looking for the business card Cassian had given her. She dialed his number and sent up a prayer as it rang. Her mind roared with possibilities of how to get out of this unscathed.

"Anders and Lincoln Law Firm, how can I help you?"

"Get me Cassian Anders. Now. It's important... My name? Jolie Coldwell."

seven

· · ·

"It's a fucking scandal!" Paul barged into his office.

Cassian couldn't remember the last time he'd slept a full eight hours. He'd left early in the morning to travel to the University of Illinois at Urbana-Champaign for a rally, and came back up to Chicago in time for his afternoon meetings with clients.

Caught between meetings, he foolishly thought he could take a quick catnap on his couch. Instead, he jolted up, eyes wide.

"What's the matter now?" He swung his long legs off the couch and to the floor, rubbing his eyes with the palm of his hand.

Paul shoved his phone in his face. Cassian blinked as he read **TROUBLE IN PARADISE OR SEX AND LIES?**

"What the hell is this?"

"*Four* women now, Cassian. The public has seen you with four women! We're trying to dispel philanderer rumors goddammit!"

"Calm down."

"I can't calm down. We got the Democratic nomination, and you're caught fucking a stripper in the hallway?"

"She's not a stripper." Cassian exhaled deeply, rubbing his jaw as he examined the photo.

He'd been so preoccupied with getting the phone from Jolie, he wasn't paying attention to his surroundings. Ever since the hallway, all he could think about was those mahogany eyes, that curvy body, and that sharp, *sharp* tongue.

"Oh, so a prostitute? That's nice."

Cassian sent Paul a look. "You're being dramatic."

"How many times have we gone over this? Politics and sex do not mix. You've fucked us being seen with *another woman* in public!"

Cassian stared at the photo a little longer. He was fucking terrified she might leak the recording. That would destroy his campaign. Was his threat enough to stop her? For the first time in a long time, he was unsure. She was unpredictable. Unpredictable opponents were deadly.

Yet, his brain ignored the threat, recalling the feel of her body against his. How her sweet rose perfume wafted into his nostrils.

"James and the others are in a damn scramble. You're giving Radcliffe ammunition!"

"It's not what it looks like." Cassian stood.

"It's clear to me."

"She's a reporter."

Paul's eyes were cold and flinty, a vein protruding from his temple. "A reporter! Oh, that makes me feel a lot better. You were caught making out with a reporter in a hallway where you were supposed to be schmoozing donors for our campaign. But don't worry, she's a reporter with connections that could cause every fucking thing we've worked for to come crashing down!"

Cassian stalked toward his chair, glancing at the family picture that sat on his desk. It was from last year, of him, his parents, and his sister at the lake. Their own private cabin on

Lake Michigan they escaped to every summer. Another luxury Cassian bought for his family. How he would have loved to be there right now.

"Considering the mess you got us into with Missy Johnson, telling her you have a fiancée, you're now an engaged man hooking up in a hallway! This shit is *bad*, Cassian. Have you talked to Margarita or Rock? I bet the press is lined up outside their offices." Paul continued to rattle on, and Cassian sighed.

Outside of being his running mate, Rock was the police chief for the Chicago Police Department. There had been a shooting and carjacking downtown the night before, and he was already fielding the media on that.

"They'll call when they get the chance."

"I don't like how you're so calm about this. You have ruined your chance—"

"She knows about the fake fiancée. She recorded me, and I was trying to get it back. Someone must have followed her and snapped the photo." Cassian rolled his shoulders, as if that would make all the tension he held there disappear like a wish.

For months, the heavy burden of responsibility, image, and anxiety had been growing more and more taxing. In a second of anger, he let his guard down, and this happened. He sabotaged himself. All because he was attracted to a beautiful—but annoying—woman.

"Tell me you're joking." The older man closed his eyes briefly, crumpling into the chair across from Cassian like he was depleted of energy. "A fake fiancée scandal, *and* you accosted this woman? I thought I was pissed that you went off-script. By the way, what did I tell you about *sticking to the fucking script*? Forcing us to deceive the public and find someone that won't run their mouths is nearly impossible, and you tell a fucking reporter! It's their job to spill secrets!"

Spit flew from Paul's mouth, and Cassian sat back in his desk chair, sighing.

"Calm down before you give yourself a heart attack. She won't say anything."

"How can you be sure?"

"I told her I'll sue if she releases the audio."

Paul shook his head slowly. "You can't be sure of that. She could leak it and disappear. Then what? We're ass out, anyway! You gave Radcliffe the election on a platter."

Cassian was thorough. He'd done his research on Jolie Coldwell, and he had friends at Channel 12. He knew she was standing on one leg at the station. She loved her job too much to put it at risk, no matter how juicy it would have been exposing him to the public.

"What's done is done. Have James release a statement denying the allegations." The older man groaned loudly, and Cassian ignored him.

Cassian weighed the pros and cons of lying to the public about a fake fiancée. His campaign was based on integrity, but there was no way out of the rumors. Each day Radcliffe, his supporters, and the media was relentlessly fixated on his love life, instead of his campaign. At first it was minuscule but now…

Winning the primaries magnified the gossip, and politely declining to comment did nothing. His opposition attacked persistently for his "We go high" campaign, and not burying this story for good only added fuel to his Radcliffe's claims that he was weak.

His ex and clients did not deserve having their lives poked and prodded because they were seen with him. *A philanderer bachelor.* As a lawyer, he knew evidence was king. He needed to *show* the public he could not only lead a state but a family as well. They couldn't keep the speculation going when it was evident he *had* a family.

This would be the only lie he told during his campaign. He swallowed the knot at the thought of the lie; it went against his values but it would be the *only* lie he told. He would continue to go high, ignore Radcliffe's attacks, and prove he was fit to lead the state. If he won, the ends would justify the means.

There was a knock at the door. He looked to see his receptionist, Leticia, peeking inside, and he waved her forward.

"Sir, a woman is trying to barged in, demanding to see you. She insists she spoke to someone earlier and has an appointment—"

Cassian rubbed his temples. "Get rid of her."

"Yes, sir. I will call security and tell them to remove Miss Coldwell and place her as persona non grata."

"Coldwell? Jolie Coldwell?"

Speak of the damn devil. His heart jumped, and he scolded himself for that reaction. He wasn't expecting her to respond so soon. He was sure she would be stubborn as hell and end up going to court. He felt slightly disappointed he couldn't go toe-to-toe with her.

"That's her."

"What do you mean her? *Her?*" Paul pointed to office door Jolie was behind.

Cassian nodded, then told Leticia, "Escort Miss Coldwell in."

Leticia nodded and backed out of the room. Cassian smoothed down the front of his suit.

"We can talk about this at a later time."

Paul got comfortable in his seat. "Isn't this convenient? I'm not going anywhere. We need to get this story under control now that you said you had a fiancée. We got the black-mailer. I say things are working out for us."

The door jolted open, causing the men to turn. Anticipation and desire made his heart race at the sight of Jolie blazing into his office like hell was nipping at her heels.

"Mr. Anders, I don't think I've ever had the pleasure of stepping inside your dungeon before."

"Someone sure knows how to make an entrance," Paul said sarcastically.

Jolie's eyes landed on Paul, who scrutinized her. His heart hammered with each passing second, she held Cassian's gaze.

"Dungeon? Dramatic, Miss Coldwell."

Jolie glided toward him, the light shining into the room illuminating her like a goddess. The modest pantsuit she wore made her more seductive than it should, clinging to those curves.

"I learn from the best. Blame my mother."

Her hair was pulled back into a sleek ponytail, but several tendrils had escaped, falling into her eyes and giving her a mussed, sexy look. It didn't fool him. He noted the way she clenched and released her hands rhythmically. *I see you.*

He liked everything about her, that sharp mouth and nasty attitude. He liked it too damn much. Inviting herself to sit in the open chair next to Paul, she crossed those lovely legs.

"Have a seat," Paul said coolly.

She turned to Cassian. "Your handler?"

"Handler?" Paul's voice rose a few octaves.

Cassian ignored him, his gaze never wavering from her.

"I'm his campaign manager, young lady."

"Don't take her bait, Paul," Cassian murmured, searching for a crack in her façade.

Jolie smirked, and Paul harrumphed. Oh, her mouth was a game changer. Those eyes focused back on Cassian, emotions flickering so fast he couldn't identify them all.

"If not a dungeon, is your office your lair? Is Paul your minion?" That shit-eating smirk bloomed into a grin that made him laugh loudly. He needed to get a handle on things.

She has the key to destroy everything you've worked for. Don't laugh with her.

"We need to add comedian to your résumé."

"Don't forget the best damn reporter there is, but I could be bragging."

"Have you seen Channel 8's report?" Paul asked her, cutting to the chase.

"I have, and I am not pleased."

Paul snorted. "What a shocker."

Jolie shot Paul a dark look.

"I don't think you came here to tell jokes, did you?" Cassian leaned back in the chair as he studied her face.

As a lawyer, he had gotten good at reading body language, and he watched as she gripped the arms of the chair. She shifted in her seat, biting her lip briefly before releasing. *Anxiousness. Worry. Anticipation?*

"You're right. I believe we have unfinished business to discuss, considering we're the talk of the town right now. Now tell me why."

"Why what?"

Jolie sucked her teeth. "Don't insult my intelligence."

Cassian's gaze dropped to her legs, her foot swaying back and forth slowly. With a desk separating them, he couldn't escape that damn rose perfume that reemerged.

"Why do you need a wife?"

Paul cursed under his breath, but Jolie kept her gaze fixed on Cassian. She thought he was just like other shady politicians going to these lengths to win the election. He didn't want her to see him as she did the others.

Cassian was thirty-eight. Over the last thirteen years since graduating from law school, he'd been calculating his every move. Establishing himself as a skilled lawyer. Winning an alderman then a councilman position. Growing a network of resourceful connections. The governor position *had* to be next for him. It was the only way to make proficient and effective change that would endure and help the people that utilized his outreach center. He couldn't let it go to waste because people were distracted by wild speculation into his bedroom.

"You shouldn't tell her anything," Paul interrupted. "You better hope we don't sue the hell out of you, lady."

"My popularity is focused on my love life instead of my campaign message right now. No matter what we do, it comes back to me being a bachelor. For people, that's synonymous with being unable to commit. Presenting as a married man could strengthen my credibility as candidate and help me dispel the rumors so people will actually focus on my message."

"Am I not speaking?" Paul asked.

"You aren't even going to wait to get into office to lie, huh?" Jolie's voice rose in volume her expression a mixture of smug confirmation and anger. "You're coming out the gate swinging."

"I don't take this decision lightly. My campaign—*I* base everything on integrity. If there was another way, I would take it, but the election's closing in. I need to act fast and get people focused on why I'm the best candidate rather than speculating that every woman they see me with is just another fling."

"Is that all?"

His father had instilled in him a sense of honor from a young age. For years, he followed his father's teachings, but the harsh reality was that the game he was playing wasn't always played fairly. Sometimes you had to play dirty.

"A drunk driver hit my parents head-on on their way home from their anniversary dinner years ago."

"You don't need to tell her this, Cassian," Paul insisted.

Cassian didn't know if he could trust the woman in front of him yet. But he also remembered something else his father always told him. *Sometimes it pays to tell the truth rather than to lie.*

Her shoulders deflated. "I'm sorry."

"My father was...*has* permanent scarring on his hands, arms, and face. His optical nerve was damaged when his head struck the steering wheel. Among many other physical injuries, it's difficult for him to walk without assistance. My mother's leg was crushed."

"Cassian, I—" Jolie's face was full of sympathy, and he shook his head. He didn't need sympathy from anyone.

"They lived, but it was several years of physical therapy and counseling to get where they are now. I've recently found out through private investigation the perpetrator of the hit-and-run was Attorney General Timothy Kinsella. There have been no charges against him for years. I want to change that."

Jolie's eyes flashed. "They didn't charge him for that? That should be automatic prison time."

He couldn't help feeling joy at the protective edge in her voice.

"That's the reason I went into law, why I've stayed in this career for years. There's only so much I can do as a lawyer. I need to be in legislation, making it so those who harm others are punished. I'm not doing this just to be another crooked scammer. I want to change things in Illinois for everyone's benefit."

Memories of the soft sound of Al Green on the radio. The light chatter of his family's conversation in the car. The cool breeze from the open window rolling over his skin. Then the crushing impact and shattering glass as bright headlights bore down on them faster than his father could avoid.

"Cassian, you're making a mistake." Paul tried to reason with him once more.

"Hmm." Jolie's brows drew together. "You're doing this for your parents?"

He nodded. "Not just my parents, for all victims of drunk-driving incidents. For my clients I've fought tooth and nail for."

Jolie clasped her hands together, leaning back in the seat. She paused a beat before nodding. "How about I marry you?"

"You've got to be kidding me!" Paul's eyes bulged.

"What?" Cassian's pulse thudded, echoing in his ears. "Excuse me?"

"I'll marry you. I'll be your fake wife."

Cassian observing her critically. *I don't believe it.* "You will marry me?"

"This is a joke," Paul said.

She sat up straighter. "You don't seem like a bad guy, Cassian. If you're in this to help people, that's something I can get behind."

What the fuck. It couldn't be this easy.

"What do you want out of it?" he asked, all traces of humor fleeing from him. He was a lawyer to his core; nothing came without strings.

"Can you tell me what you know about Lupe and Miguel Lopez?"

A jolt at the sound of his former employee's name caused him to look at her closely.

"Miguel Lopez? How do you know Miguel?"

Folding her arms, she mirrored his neutral expression. "Lupe Lopez sent me an email to investigate what I believe is rent gouging. This story is important to me. I'm going for a promotion at my job."

"Don't trust her, Cassian." Paul frowned at Jolie. "She could be lying."

Jolie cut her eyes toward Paul, looking him up and down slowly. "I still have the recording from last night. We haven't formally agreed yet, and I don't mind uploading it to YouTube."

"We'd bury you if you tried." Paul's voice was dark.

Cassian had to stay composed. "I don't see how Miguel has anything to do with you being my fake wife."

"I just need you to tell me all that you know. It helps me

write the Lopezes better, and get readers on their side." His body reacted to hers as she moved in her seat, the buttons of her shirt straining against her breasts. "We're already in the paper. It would make sense I'm your secret fiancée instead of some random woman."

"If the truth of this arrangement got out, it will be a scandal. How do I know you're not using me for information? Another story to secure your promotion?" Cassian finished.

Jolie rolled her eyes, rocking her crossed legs back and forth slowly. "If I give you my word, I mean it. If I marry you, I will hand over the file."

"You were going to have to do that, anyway."

Jolie gave him a spicy look.

"I don't *have* to do anything, Mr. Anders. Remember that." Jolie sat forward in her seat. "Since my covering of your announcement didn't go well, we can make up for it by your campaign giving exclusive interviews with Channel 12. We will also get first dibs on any images from your campaign. With an all-access backstage pass to your campaign headquarters on election day. I want Channel 12 to get even a whisper from you, first."

Cassian's face scrunched up. "You want everything I know about Miguel Lopez and exclusive access into my campaign?"

It unnerved him, not having the advantage in the conversation. What all did she know, and truly what was her plan?

Jolie shrugged, her leg still swaying back and forth. She propped her elbow on the arm of the chair, placing her chin in her hand as she observed him with a half smile. "Getting exclusives with you will make me look good to executives. You need to look stable. It's mutually beneficial."

The quiet finality of her statement rocked the room, and he sucked his teeth.

"Unless you have a harem of women clamoring to be your fake wife? I'm guessing you don't."

"I don't like this. I don't trust this. She's just some stranger off the street." Paul's caramel skin was red. "I think she's lying."

"Ironic you think I'm lying, considering *he* was the one who started the lie." She nodded to Cassian.

"We saw what she did to Congressman Mills. Do you know the irreversible damage she could cause if she was in our camp?" Paul shook his head.

"I don't think it's an awful choice, Paul. Being engaged to Jolie, a successful I-Team reporter, is beneficial. She has a platform, and her followers who don't support me yet might after this." Cassian rubbed his jaw and eyed Jolie.

"She's a reporter. Text messages, emails, private conversations—she could sneak her way into all of them. Then it's out there, and there's no covering up after that. How do we know she isn't wearing a wire right now?"

Jolie frowned, eying Paul like he was a bug that flew too close to her. "It's never that serious. People always tell on themselves sooner rather than later, and that's when I appear. I'm not interested in seducing Cassian for his secrets. I'm trying to help a family stay in their home and get my promotion. That's it."

"You have a bleeding heart?" Paul's voice dripped with disbelief.

Jolie ignored Paul's comment, keeping her eyes on his. His intuition told him to believe her. If they followed his set plan, they might just get away with this.

"Only you, Margarita, my political consultant, Rock, Paul, and I would know about the fake marriage. We keep it to ourselves. None of us will let it slip."

"This is a mistake, Cassian, and you'll regret it." Paul stood, the chair's feet scraping against the wooden floor. He looked at him with disappointment before storming from the office, slamming the door shut.

"A bit of a diva, isn't he?" Jolie murmured.

Cassian laughed. "Maybe. But he's damn good at his job."

"He doesn't give off the best first impression."

He was silent for a moment. "Are his suspicions correct? Are you using me for a story?"

I've lost my fucking mind.

"For now? No."

He would still have to investigate her more. He was too close to his goal to let it slip through his fingers. He folded his hands on the desk. "I already drew up a contract. All you have to do is sign it and an NDA. Take a few days to decide if this is what you really want to do." He opened the drawer, placed it on the desk, and slid it over to her, and she blinked.

"You work quick, huh? Before I sign anything, I have conditions."

"Conditions?"

He wasn't fond of conditions being placed on him.

"How do I know I'm not signing my life away or that you'll keep me as a sex slave or force me to have a baby?"

Cassian glanced down at the desk at the mention of a sex slave, hiding a smile. He could imagine her tied up in his bed in some sexy lingerie and a dark wanton look in her eye as she eyed him with anticipation.

"We'll be married for a year, if I'm elected. No child or sex enslavement required. After this is all over, we quietly get an annulment. Unless you have plans to get pregnant and trap me?"

Jolie blanched and he laughed.

"Never! I'll let you know now that I was arrested at sixteen for shoplifting. I changed my name blah, blah, blah. It'll come up in the background check you do on me, and no, I don't want to explain it." Jolie placed her hands on his desk as if to ground herself and nodded. "What about living arrangements?"

Charged at sixteen with shoplifting?

"For image's sake, it's better if we stay together after we

marry. I have several bedrooms for you to choose from at my home. By then we should know enough about the other to be comfortable."

Cassian considered every possible angle to this plan. It was June; elections were in November. They had five months to get to know each other and convince his supporters and the public.

"Are you expecting me to sleep with you?" Jolie asked bluntly. His body went hot as his eyes raked over her body against his will.

Consummating the marriage would complicate an already thorny situation.

"My professional life and my personal life never cross. This is business. If you don't have any outside affairs during the campaign, or keep them extremely discreet, we should be okay. Unless you have a current relationship right now?"

Jolie's face flushed. "I should ask you that too."

He felt a bit of hope and excitement bleed back into his veins. "It's important we convince the world our marriage is real. They must see us together in public as much as possible. We will be under constant scrutiny in public to be a model potential governor and first lady. The less we say to our friends and family, the better."

"Can I ask you another question?"

Cassian smiled. "Would I be able to stop you?"

The tough wall she erected crumbled a bit as she gave him a genuine smile.

"Are you sure you want to voluntarily tie yourself to a woman you don't love?"

Love… That deceptive emotion that always made things into a big mess. All love did was distract and cause unnecessary complications, things he didn't need in his life when he was so close to his goals.

"I'm not looking for love, Miss Coldwell." Cassian stood staring down at her, and she swallowed, her eyes briefly dropping to his crotch. "I am focused on something bigger than love. I want... I will become governor. By any means. Can you handle being a politician's wife?"

"Of course."

"We do our jobs and go our separate ways." Cassian exhaled deeply, the gravity of the moment weighing him down. "I would forever be indebted to you, Miss Coldwell."

"I just need you to do what I ask. Then you can thank me later."

Ouch.

"I can do that."

He had to remind himself not to let her get under his skin, especially with the election coming up. He had to think with his brain, not with his dick.

Jolie Coldwell was dangerous. Heat unfurled low in his stomach as she stood slowly, meeting him in front of the desk. He had quite a few inches on her as she reached her hand out, and time slowed.

"Let's get married."

This fake marriage would be a test of his willpower. *His integrity as a man.* No matter how he spun it, lying was bad, but his will to win this election was greater than his guilt. He had to play the game to win.

"Nice seeing you again, *hubby*."

Turning on her heel, Jolie sped out of his room, leaving him in silence.

I'm getting married.

eight

. . .

I t should have been easy to find information about Urban Properties.

Jolie combed her fingers through her hair as she leaned back in her chair, glaring at the computer monitor. *Give me something.*

Five hours. Five wasted hours she'd been scouring the internet looking for a crumb of information to get started looking into this company. It was after hours, and most of the office was empty. The light in Dev's office still shone brightly, and she bit her lip, debating how to convey the news of her impending nuptials to Cassian to him.

Hey, guess what? Save the date! Dev would probably think she was lying out of her ass. The truth sounded like fiction.

The website Mrs. Lopez gave her was conveniently broken. The social media pages for the company had generic stock images on it and hadn't been updated in years. Just as Mrs. Lopez had said, a call to the office number led her through a warren of robots and uninterested customer service reps.

Typing in *Urban Properties* in the search bar produced thousands of results: Urban Living Real Estate. Urban Proper-

ties Chicago. Urban Casas. All variations of real estate broker-
ages or services for various cities from Chicago to New York
to New Orleans.

The only solid information she sourced from local magazines in the area was Urban Properties was a real estate and
property management firm in Chicago. Since 2010, they'd
bought several abandoned and foreclosed properties and
rehabbed them into desirable homes.

There *had* to be paper or internet trails.

Jolie spread out all the papers Mrs. Lopez had given her.
She was missing something.

"Are my eyes deceiving me, or are you doing work?
Which councilman, mayor, or city clerk are you planning to
falsely attack and make my ass look good in comparison?"

Immediately, her temples throbbed.

"What do you want, Travis? I'm busy."

"Busy?" Travis's smile rivaled the Joker's as he placed his
hands into the pockets of his slacks. Crossing one leg over, he
leaned on the entrance of her cubicle. "Oh yes. That sad story
with the old lady that you think is going to get you Walter's
spot. C'mon, Jolie, you're smart. That won't be enough to
convince the execs."

Jolie narrowed her gaze on him. "You run your mouth
more than you work. Excuse me while I actually work."

"You're a smart, talented, *beautiful* woman, Jolie." Her skin
crawled at the way Travis complimented her, his eyes rolling
over her body and lingering on her breasts before he met her
eyes. "It pains me to see you act stupid."

"Stupid? I'm about this close—" Jolie held her index and
thumb inches from each other.

"Close to what? You step on a crack and you're out of this
office, and you know it. We *all* know it."

"Are you Dev? Why are you speaking for him?" Jolie
gripped the desk to prevent herself from jumping up and
beating his ass like he owed her money.

Travis stepped farther into her cubicle.

"I'm speaking for the future of this station, Jolie. I'm being nice here by telling you to give up now."

"Never."

He sneered and set the picture back down. She stood, forcing him out of her cubicle. She didn't want his grimy ass in her space. "You're so predictable."

"Goodbye, Travis. It's obvious you think I'm a threat and are trying to intimidate me, but it's never worked. I'll be here long after you give up and go back to being a pampered princess with your daddy's money." The tightness in Jolie's chest forced her breath through her nose.

"You ever get tired of being a diversity hire?"

Jolie's mouth dropped. "Excuse me?"

His eyes blazed as he took a step toward her, sizing her up.

"A pretty face that's brown. HR loves people like you. Hood, *ghetto*. Some flavor! It's good to keep the keyboard warriors from complaining about representation."

Coldness ran through her body, and shock froze her. Travis was *never* this bold before. He lost his mind, but Jolie was going to help him find it.

"This diversity hire has more skills, qualifications, education, and talent"—Jolie stepped in his face, forcing him back, and a brief look of shock etched on his face—"in her goddamn pinky finger than you have in your entire body. I didn't buy my Ivy League degree; I earned my shit. *If* you come at me out the side of your neck again, I'll forget we're in this office and show you the streets."

"Getting *gangsta* now?"

"Excuse me!" Dev's voice cut through the air as he walked down the aisle toward them.

Jolie and Travis stood there, chests heaving. Neither was willing to break eye contact, and blood rushed in her ears.

"Dev—" Travis smirked, but Dev glared.

"Cut the shit. Go home, Travis. That's a write-up."

"Dev—"

Dev moved in closer to them, forcing Travis away from Jolie. He positioned himself in front of her, crossing his arms as he stared down at the piece-of-shit excuse of a human being. Jolie shakily exhaled, willing her heart to slow as she closed her eyes briefly.

"I said go home. I heard everything. We'll discuss your behavior later."

Travis tried to glance at Jolie, but Dev blocked his view. Seconds passed before Travis huffed and spun on his heel. He made a scene, slamming cabinets and pushing his chair around, before he grabbed his bag and disappeared down the hall to the elevators.

"Are you okay?" Dev turned to Jolie.

Stay strong. Don't show fear. Be tough. You've heard worse insults in your life.

"I'm fine."

"Jolie—"

She turned back to sit in her seat. She gathered the papers, and placed them into a pile, tapping them on the desk. "I said I'm good, Dev."

Travis was a minuscule ant compared to the kinds of people she'd dealt with in college or at other local stations she'd worked at. This would only strengthen her.

"I won't let you be disrespected."

Too late for that.

"Fire him."

Dev sighed, lowering his gaze. "You know I can't do that. That's a lawsuit waiting to happen."

"Then don't lie and say you care about me."

Jolie focused on the monitor in front of her, but the words blurred. *You're strong. Prove him wrong. Prove everyone wrong.*

Dev turned to leave. Her hand trembled on the mouse,

and she exhaled a breath as she dropped her shoulders forward.

"Dev?"

"Yeah?"

"I need to talk to you about something…something important."

Might as well drop the bomb now.

"Go ahead."

"Not here. Your office." There was only an intern all the way across the room with headphones on and a janitor emptying trash, but she had to be careful.

Closing his door behind her, Dev sat at his desk and pointed to the empty seat.

"Sit."

"I'm marrying Cassian Anders." The words rushed from her mouth as she sat.

Dev snorted, laughing as he leaned back in his seat.

"You're kidding."

Jolie crossed her arms, her lips thinned.

"You're kidding," Dev said again, displaying a wide grin. He slapped his hand on his thigh as he shook his head. He waited for her join before his grin slowly dissipated. "Tell me you're joking."

She raised a brow.

"You're not joking. What? When? Jolie, I—I don't know what to say… How?" Dev ran his hand through his hair.

"It's kind of a long story—"

"Make it fucking short. I had you on the Cassian story! Do you know the conflict of interest you are putting us in?"

Jolie exhaled slowly and nodded.

"I didn't say anything because I wasn't sure where the relationship was going to go." The lie slipped easily from her mouth. She forced herself to hold his eye. "Things have obviously escalated. I'm marrying him, and I wanted you to know before we release the news to the public."

Dev narrowed his eyes, the humor gone from his face. "You're the woman. This secret woman in the picture?"

Her gaze fell, and her boss leaned back in his seat, letting out a string of curses.

"Jolie, you're a smart woman. You know what this can do to your career?"

She frowned. "It shouldn't do anything. I made my career before him." *I'll manage it after—No man will interfere with my career.*

"You're going to be under scrutiny. More than before. The execs aren't going to like this. You're forbidden to write anything about Anders and the election—"

"I expected that much. I arranged for him to give us exclusives. Interview, images, and election day, so say thank you for that. All I care about is investigating the Lopez case. Let me keep my shot for Walter's spot."

Dev watched her for several seconds. "Are you serious, Jolie? You're really marrying Anders?"

"Yes."

Shaking his head, he shrugged. "If you thought I was on your ass before, it's going to be worse now. You're going to be the subject of articles now, not writing them."

Had she prepared herself for that? For people digging into her life? A past she'd covered and buried. Her family would come out of the woodwork. *Did I think this through enough?*

Dev pointed at her. "No fuckups... I expect an invitation to the wedding."

nine

. . .

"Here we go..." Cassian shut off and stepped out of his silver Genesis G80, before walking up the steps of his parents' home with pastries in hand.

He should have been on the road heading to Peoria for another rally, but he never missed his family's weekly Sunday dinner together. The media continued to be brutal, and Margarita suggested upping the ante: *engagement photos.*

He favored posting a selfie, but Margarita insisted they commit to the act fully.

You want people to believe this? No one is getting engagement photos with a hookup. Don't get lazy. Do the work. Forty minutes later, she sent him a confirmation email for a photographer.

If this helped push him in favor to win, he'll do it. That would strike one thing off his never-ending list of tasks to complete. He could now focus on what to do about Attorney General Timothy Kinsella. After years of lament, the answer was here. The system had failed them, but he wouldn't let it happen again.

Using his key, he stepped inside the house. "Mama?"

Once he'd started making good money, he bought his parents a home. They'd chosen Wilmette, a beautiful and wealthy suburb in the North Shore of Chicago. He had it custom-built for them and hired gardeners to come every week to make sure the lawn was impeccable and gutters cleaned. He would have hired a maid service so his mother would never have to lift a finger, but she refused. As a Black woman, she didn't trust nobody to keep her house as clean as she could.

The home smelled amazing. The aroma of baked barbecue chicken, collard greens, corn bread, sweet potatoes, and baked mac and cheese made him drool.

"Mama, it smells good up in here. Luna's not helping you, is she?" He stepped into the kitchen to see his two favorite girls. His mother, Tisha, was standing at the stove with her apron around her waist. She turned around and her eyes lit up.

"My baby!"

"Mama, he's a grown-ass man." Luna, his sister, looked up from where she was buttering the rolls. Rolling his eyes, he balanced the pastries in one hand and flicked her on the forehead. She howled, pushing her cat-eyed glasses up the bridge of her nose, and swatted at him.

"Asshole!"

"You're ugly."

"Watch y'all mouth and don't start that arguing," Tisha snapped, and Cassian sucked in his breath as his mother's limp was noticeable as she crossed the kitchen toward him.

"Mama, why aren't you using your cane?" He met her halfway. Did she need to go back to the physical therapist?

"Are those my favorite macarons?" Tisha took the box from her favorite French bakery near his office.

"You heard me, Mama."

She hugged him and excitedly opened the box. They were carbon copies of one another. The same dark eyes and skin, identical moles on their chins. At sixty-two, she did not look a day over fifty, with warm laugh lines on the corner of her mouth, and her dark hair tinged slightly with gray was pulled into a French twist.

She pinched his cheek. "You treat me too good."

Cassian caught his sister's eye, and she nodded her head toward the entryway of the kitchen. His mother's cane leaned against the wall.

"You're my mama, of course I'm gonna treat you good."

"You don't treat me good," Luna spoke up. At twenty-seven, and earning her master's in clinical mental health, she held baby fat on her round face that made her look like she was eighteen, further heightened by the halo of her natural 4C hair.

"Since you wanna get on me, how 'bout I get on your tail?" Tisha narrowed her eyes at Cassian.

"Oooh, tell him, Mama," Luna instigated.

Washing his hands, he counted back from five, bracing his shoulders. "What you mean?"

"What you mean?" Tisha mocked in a deep voice as Luna giggled. "Are you bringing the girl you're having an affair with to Sunday dinner?"

Cassian went to the stove, lifted the lids off the pots, and snatched a piece of meat out of the collard greens. "Don't believe what you read."

"Hard to not believe it when the picture of you is everywhere," Luna muttered.

"It's a shame I had to be told at Bible study and not from my son." Tisha reached for a plate out of the cabinet for the pastries, a sad expression on her face.

"Mama—"

"That's yo' side piece?" Luna asked.

"Shut the hell up and get out of here." Cassian frowned at Luna.

Luna flipped him off. "Who you talking to, and first of all—"

"Luna, give us a minute," Tisha cut off the argument.

After placing the rolls in the oven, Luna slinked out of the kitchen slowly before flipping him off again.

"You hurt me, Cassian," his mother professed.

He had calculated the emotional burden his campaign would have on his family. By default, they would be scrutinized, but to a tolerable level. His family were good people. His fake-fiancée plan threw a wrench into everything. He hadn't thought enough on how the hell to prepare his mother emotionally for a fake wife she might get attached to.

"You know I didn't mean to."

Tisha's brows dipped. "Don't matter if you did or not— you did. For years since Kendra left you, I wanted to see my baby happy."

"Mama—"

"I was excited when I seen you both in the paper. Are you sure you're not gettin' back together? She was a good girl. You know I want you to have a wife and kids and be happy."

"Kendra and I are over. She just needed legal advice." Cassian approached the island at the center of the kitchen, pulling the stool out to sit.

Tisha frowned, crossing her arms she leaned against the counter. "You're burning from both ends, baby. You're still handling cases, running the outreach center, *and* campaigning. You shouldn't even be here right now. But now that you are, relax."

"I can handle things, Mama, don't worry."

Should I tell her about Kinsella? He weighed the options. She was already distraught over the fiancée situation. What would she do if he told her that it wasn't a hit-and-run by a random person, but a damn leader of the state?

"You can't keep this momentum goin'. You're gonna burn out," Tisha scolded, and Cassian stood.

Tisha crossed the space toward him, and he clenched his fists. It tore him fucking apart watching the way she limped.

She didn't deserve this. His father didn't. He couldn't stop now, not when the pieces were beginning to align.

"I can't stop, Mama. I'm too close. But I promise once this election's over, I'll take a vacation. I promise."

I'm marrying a woman to accomplish that goal was on the tip of his tongue.

Tisha shook her head slowly, and he hugged her, kissing her forehead.

"I guess I got nothing else to say."

Cassian stared at Tisha for several breaths. He wished he could tell her what she wanted to hear, but he couldn't.

"Where's Dad?"

Tisha pointed down the hall. "In his den."

Cassian watched his mother a second longer before disappearing into the hallway lined with family pictures. As he made his way toward his father's den, he heard a loud bang, then a thud before a grunt and a curse followed.

"Dad?" His breath rushed in and out as he ran down the hallway. "Dad!"

Bursting open the door, he found his father's walker tipped over, a spilled beer bottle on the ground, and his father leaning against his desk with an armful of napkins.

"I'm fine, dammit, I'm fine."

"What are you doin', old man?" Cassian's heart rate slowed.

The oak and smoky scent of cigars hung heavily in the air. Edward Anders's awards and accomplishments covered the walls of his den. On the wall, in a glass case placed high above the desk, was a leather jacket that said *Vietnam Vet*.

"You and ya mama in there arguin'?"

Cassian righted the walker, placing it in front of him before he helped him up slowly. Taking the napkins, he kneeled to clean up the spill. "We weren't arguing. She wants me to relax midcampaign."

"Listen to her versus givin' her trouble."

"Go sit down."

Edward obeyed, heading to the couch in front of an old box television. It played a black-and-white cowboy movie.

"I hate that beating-around-the-bush mess. Tell me what's up."

Cassian wiped the spilled beer. "What did your doctor say when you saw him the other day?"

"Nothin'. It's hell gettin' old."

If women online went gaga over him, they would swoon over his father. He was aging gracefully, with gray forming at his temples and threading through the dark strands of his full beard. A jagged scar, from his chin up to his right temple, was rough and ragged but didn't distract from Edward's force.

Eighty percent of Cassian's features may have been his mother, but his essence was his father.

"I doubt the doctor said that."

"You keep sending me to these fancy-ass doctors that have lemon water and coo-coo-smellin' shit in the waiting room. I don't need all that, son."

"You deserve everything." Cassian frowned, standing and tossing the soiled napkins into the trash. He took a seat next to Edward.

"You're too damn serious. Keep it up and you'll look like the crypt keeper."

"I'm tryin' to care for you." The exhaustion of the day settled in Cassian's limbs, sinking him into the cushions.

"Care about yourself. You a grown man now."

Cassian mentally checked each item off the list as he inspected his father. *No shaking in his hands, eyes aren't bloodshot, doesn't look gray.*

"Tell me what you here for. You ain't never been able to lie good. I don't know how in the hell you a lawyer."

"All lawyers aren't liars." *Hypocrite.*

"Or is it more serious? Don't tell me someone put a hit out

on you already?" Edward crossed his arms, his eyes briefly flickering to the muted TV and back.

Cassian's heart beat swiftly. *Can I lie to my father?* No one could ever strike fear in his heart like Edward could. The man always reverted Cassian back to being a little boy in his presence.

"I'm getting married."

"Wh-what?" Edward's voice rose, and he struggled to turn to face him, disbelief plastered on his face. "To the woman in the photo?"

"It's a long story."

"Get to telling it, dammit." His father reached for his remote to shut off the TV. He let out a strained sound as he tried to lift himself from the couch and Cassian grabbed it for him.

"I try to keep my...short-term affairs under the radar." He'd planned everything he would say in the car. The words now eluded him under the steady glare of his father. "This relationship...we've known each other for some time and things became serious—"

Edward lifted an eyebrow. "What you said on the TV was right?"

"Yeah."

"Hurt to find that out through a reporter and not my damn son... This was spur of the moment, or did you always know you wanted to marry this woman?"

"I know enough about her. We'll live comfortably."

Edward's voice was sharp. "I ain't ask you that."

Cassian inhaled sharply as he forced himself to keep his father's eye.

"A man knows when he's found a wife. Did you know when you saw her?"

He thought about the vicious tongue-lashing she gave him in the hallway of Magnifica. Jolie barreling through his office door, her strong, steadfast gaze on him. Not once had she wavered. The essence of her aroused him far greater than it should have.

"Yes. She's the one." He made a mental note to follow up on that email he'd been avoiding after dinner in the car ride down to Peoria.

Edward sucked his teeth. "I remember when weddings were formal, traditional. Get to know the family first."

"Jolie and I aren't traditional."

"Jolie, is it?"

Cassian said, "I want you, Mama, and Luna to be at our wedding."

Edward had an indecipherable look on his face.

"Tell me about this soon-to-be wife of yours."

"She's a reporter for Channel 12. You remember that big news that came out about Congressman Mills? Jolie wrote that."

"Well, she's got gumption, then. Bet she pissed in some people's cornflakes." Edward's voice held a note of awe. "Few people got the balls."

Honesty. Shit, I'm a fucking fraud in the making.

Cassian nodded. "That's my woman." The words felt foreign on his tongue, and he kept his face neutral. "You'll like her. Mama too."

"When's the wedding?"

"Our engagement party is next month, then I need some time to wrap up commitments at the office. I'll say the end of September into October?"

"Four months ain't a long time to plan a wedding. On top of you running for office. It's too much, Cassian."

"I can handle it."

Edward's brows furrowed. "You can handle it, but can Jolie?"

He knew she could handle the pressure and weight of appearing in public.

"She's strong."

This would be a purely platonic, beneficial relationship. He was getting what he wanted, and so was she. Then they would go their separate ways. Easy.

He changed the subject. "You're not going to like this, but I did some more digging into your and Mama's accident. I found out that the man who did it was the attorney general, Kinsella," Cassian told him.

Edward pressed his lips tight before letting out a heavy sigh.

"I told you to let it go."

"I know that—"

"Yet you're tellin' me you know who did it. What you expect me to do? Turn fuckin' cartwheels?"

Cassian clenched his jaw. *He knows it's haunted me for years. He knows it fucking hurts me to see them this way, and he wants me to let it go?*

Edward shook his head, pushing himself up and slowly, and Cassian immediately stood to help, but Edward shooed him away. "Ya mama was right. You're like a dog with a bone. Nearly twenty years, son. Let it go. What's done was God's will."

"I'm tired of you and Mama saying it's God's will. For you to be marred?"

"I've made my peace. Let. It. Go. But no, do what you want." Edward's words were like a dose of cold water. "Back to what I care about: did you know Jolie was your wife, or are you using her as a means to an end?"

He's dismissing this? The biggest news of my life, and he doesn't care who ruined his life all those years ago?

"That's bullshit, and you know it," Cassian snapped. Edward observed silently. "You of all people should know that they should try the attorney general for what he did to us, and who knows how many others."

"You have a savior complex, Cassian. You couldn't protect us then so now you do that with all your cases. With that outreach center of yours. The women you date. If you're being honest with yaself, runnin' for governor might fall into that bucket too. You're atoning for a sin you did not commit."

"How can you say that?" Cassian shot up, pacing away from his father. "You shouldn't be walking with a fucking walker, and Mama shouldn't be limping. You should be angry. Why can't you ever be angry?" He was practically yelling.

"It's not your fault we were in that accident."

Control yourself… Control. Don't lose control.

"You want me to sit here and act like everything is good?"

Edward's features turned down. In a soft but firm voice, he said, "You can't tell me how to feel, son."

Cassian sighed, reining himself in. He placed a look of neutrality on his face. "Don't try to psychoanalyze me. What life do you have, Dad? To be almost bound to this house?"

The silence between them vibrated with tension and anger. Edward shook his head slowly. "Make your peace, son."

"Not until I get justice."

In whatever way possible.

A sad look passed across his father's face, and Cassian exhaled shakily, trying to gather his composure as he flexed his fists.

"Whatever you say, son, whatever you say."

"Dad—"

"Don't bring your parents' issues into your marriage."

Cassian stood up and let out a harsh breath. He was tired of hearing how God was going to handle things. "Dad…"

"You're going to have to learn, son, and don't worry, it's going to come to you sooner rather than later. Let's go eat."

His father moved slowly with his walker out of the room, leaving Cassian alone to feel like shit.

ten

· · ·

"I think Nate could be the one." Helena giggled behind Jolie as they trudged up the stairs to her apartment. After signing the contract, she felt as if she'd sold her soul to the devil. There was a brief email from Cassian saying:

> I'll be in touch.

Since then, radio silence.

"Bitch, are you listening? Don't drop the food!"

The plastic bag holding their Chinese takeout almost slipped from her grasp. Shaking off the dazed thoughts of Cassian, she trudged forward up the stairs to the second landing. "Nate? Are you sure?"

It had been a long day. Researching Urban Properties had led her down a rabbit hole of several shell companies. Like Matryoshka dolls, one was owned by the other, and the other. It would be a while till she got to the bottom of it. *If I can.*

Helena made a noise in the back of her throat. "You don't like Nate?"

Jolie's keys jingled, and she pulled them out of her purse. "He wasn't mad I barfed in his car. That's a keeper."

The same night I went home and masturbated to the thought of Cassian Anders fucking me in the hallway.

"Could you imagine me married?"

I'm getting married. To a guy I barely know beyond a headline.

Jolie's resolve was hanging by a thread by the time she finally left his office.

Compared to the politicians she reported on, he wasn't bad. His work with the outreach center, Mrs. Lopez, and countless cases he worked prove it. But she wasn't convinced, yet.

He could make her look good to the executives and to Dev. She had to beat Travis for the promotion, and all-exclusive access to the hottest candidate in the last fifteen years? They would offer the promotion to her on a silver platter.

She only had to suffer through sexy fantasies of him for possibly the next year.

"You'll be an awesome bride, Lena," Jolie forced the words out as they made it to the third landing, Cassian's face running through her mind.

"Really?"

It had to be the way the suit held his body, or those curls, or those damn eyes...

"Total white picket fence material."

Ignore him. Ignore his body. Ignore the butterflies you get around him.

"Unlike you."

Jolie jerked back and glared. "Excuse me?"

"I'm open to things. Jolie, you should have tried Clark."

Here they went with this conversation again.

"Can you see me married to a butcher? Don't play with me." Jolie frowned as they made it to the fourth landing.

"It's an honest living. He would treat you right, and maybe massage your feet."

Jolie had worked too hard to get where she was now. She couldn't afford to get distracted by any man. Marriage and love weren't things she fantasized about, and Cassian was purely business. Her stability in her career meant more than a man giving her butterflies.

"Why can't you let someone in and love you? See the real you? Instead of this bitchy exterior?"

A memory appeared in Jolie's mind. Her mother crying in the dark living room, repeatedly dialing her new man of the month over and over again, begging him to give money so they could eat that day. Never would Jolie let a man use her and leave her with scraps of her dignity. That's why she was in control in this…situation with Cassian. She only needed his image, nothing more. *Ever.*

"I'm fine being by myself and the bitch of the office in order to get what I need."

They made it to the fifth floor, and Jolie fished for her house key on the key ring.

"Are you really? Or are you telling yourself that because you're scared?"

"We can live without love. We can't live without food, money, and air. I'd rather focus my attention on making my money and creating a legacy." Jolie put her key into the lock and turned as Helena snatched her back around.

"Jolie—"

"I'm marrying Cassian Anders."

She couldn't not let Helena know she was getting married. Even if it was a sham. Her bestie wasn't a snitch. Despite pissing her the hell off right now, they were sisters and she would need her in the coming months.

Helena let out a scream, making Jolie jump. "What the fuck?"

Why don't we put the cherry on top?

"Next month is our engagement party."

Helena's mouth opened and closed.

"What?"

"It's fake. I got dirt on him."

Helena's brows rose to her hairline. "Bitch, are you joking?"

"Get inside, I'll tell you everything—" Jolie turned and unlocked her apartment door, stepping inside the apartment, only to find all the lights on...but she had definitely turned them off this morning.

Helena muttered, "You're marrying Cassian Anders? Stop lying—"

"Wait, shh... Listen."

Jolie and Lena stopped talking, straining to hear anything. Then she heard her cabinet close and a bag rattle.

Helena pressed closer to Jolie. "You think someone broke in?"

Jolie's heart was beating as she handed Helena the Chinese food, rummaging through her purse for her mace. Whoever was in there was about to get the shit maced outta them and their ass kicked.

"Let's call the police."

"We're capable women. We got this. And by the time the police get here, they'll be halfway across Chicago with my shit." Jolie stepped into the foyer of her apartment.

"What if they have a weapon?"

"No weapons formed against us will prosper," Jolie muttered.

She held the mace in one hand and had the other hand balled into a fist. She heard a bang, then a crunch. This mothafucka was eating her food? More than ready to kick some ass, Jolie barreled right into her open-concept living room, yelling, "If you don't get the hell out of my apartment!"

Jolie only saw the mass of the man and started spraying. Helena screamed and rushed forward with her eyes closed and Chinese food in hand, bumping into the counter.

"Jolie, shit! What the fuck!" a familiar masculine voice exclaimed.

He cursed, bending over and gagging. Jolie coughed too from the spicy kickback of the mace.

"Aaron? What are you doing here?"

Her younger half brother was supposed to be halfway across the country. Not in this city. Not in her apartment. Not in her life.

He looked no worse for wear than when she'd last seen him nearly a year ago. His caramel-brown skin was now tinged red from the mace and he sniffed rapidly. A red beanie covered his low waves, and gold chains hung around his neck. A hoop piercing in his right nostril glittered under her kitchen lights, and he wiped his face on his bomber jacket.

She used to pinch that nose when he was a baby. That had been the last time they'd ever been close. At twenty-five, Aaron had stopped being her little brother a long time ago.

"I can't come see my big sister?"

"You called me 'a dumb, coldhearted bitch' the last time we talked. I don't see why you're here." Jolie blinked rapidly as he came into focus and the burning subsided.

"You were being a bitch then, like you are now."

Jolie wouldn't tolerate being disrespected in her own place, not where she paid the bills.

"Get out, Aaron, and don't come back." Jolie sniffed, the spicy scent of mace fading. He'd always hated her, and she'd long ago stopped wishing for different.

"Don't be like that—"

"You called me a bitch."

"'Cause you always act like it's a chore to talk to me or somethin'."

Jolie went to the sink to wash the residue of mace off her hands. All she wanted to do was take off her heels, eat, and sleep.

"You're a grown man, but you act like a child."

Aaron's eyes were tinged red and he rubbed his nose and sniffed. "Anyway, I'm here."

Jolie sucked her teeth, unpacking the Chinese food.

"I had a music gig in New Orleans."

"Helena, can you grab some plates?" She motioned to her friend. Helena looked between them. She thinned her lips and shook her head slowly as she went for the cabinet.

"Hey, Helena, how you doing?" Aaron said in a sing-songy voice, looking a mess with red eyes and smeared snot on his face.

"I have a boyfriend," Helena shot back immediately.

Jolie focused on counting the soy sauce packets. *One, two, three—dammit, I should've gotten extra. Think of something, anything but Aaron in front of me.*

"Hello? Wake the fuck up. Are you going to ask me about my gig?" Aaron snapped his fingers at Jolie.

"Get out."

"Ask me."

Jolie balled her fists, and spoke through her teeth. "Don't make me call the police."

"Really? That's fucking cold. Wait till I tell Mama you're the one that put me in jail. What do you think she gonna do?"

Aaron tilted his head with a smirk. He knew he had her there. Liza Coldwell would have an absolute fucking melt-down to know her "baby" was in jail. Jolie already teetered on the edge of no-contact with her mother, but a stupid, tiny, tiny part of Jolie still wanted to connect with her. It was a foolish.

"What happened to the gig, Aaron?"

"We went our separate ways because of artistic differences."

"Artistic differences?" Helena handed Jolie the plates with a look that said *I didn't forget what you said earlier.*

"He wanted me to wear a tie and shit. The fuck I look like wearin' some goofy-ass tie?"

"You'll look like someone employed," Helena chirped, opening the bag of egg rolls and biting into one.

"Shit just ain't me."

Pinching the bridge of her nose, Jolie focused on scooping fried rice onto a plate. "Why not wear the tie?"

"And go against my beliefs? Are you crazy, girl?" Aaron reached for an egg roll, and Jolie slapped his hand.

"You have morals and beliefs? Funny..." Helena finished her egg roll. She found Jolie's half-empty bottle of red wine in the fridge and poured them both a glass.

Jolie took the mug of wine and downed half.

"That's why I'm here. I need a lil' bit of money till I can get my unemployment check—"

Jolie scowled. "That's why you're here. How did you get into my apartment, anyway?"

"Picked the lock. Don't look surprised and shit. Some buddies taught me. You should get them changed." Aaron shrugged, leaning against the counter.

"I will immediately in the morning." Jolie narrowed her eyes at him. "Buddies? Criminal buddies?"

"*Real people.* People that get money the only way they know how. None of this fake wannabe *Leave It to Beaver* rich-folk shit y'all got going on in here. We ain't grow up with this stuff, and you don't need it." Aaron made a sweeping gesture around her apartment. It was neat and modern, all the latest tech with a big flat screen TV on the wall.

"Don't start that—" Jolie scowled.

"You got a lil' bit of money, and now you act like you can't see Mama?"

The real reason he was here. He wanted money from her, and since she wasn't going to give it willingly, he was going to guilt her.

"It's not about that, and you know it."

"Why she say she ain't seen you in months?"

"Why aren't you over there with her?" Jolie threw her hands up.

"I can't come see my sister?"

At far too young of an age, she was forced to accept the

reality of their positions in the family. Aaron was the baby. He could do no wrong. Jolie was the oldest. She had to bear the burden of raising him, making up for *his mistakes.*

"I'm not giving you money."

Aaron smacked his lips. "You act like you ain't got it. Just enough to last the week, that's all I'm askin' for—"

"Didn't you just judge me for having money?"

Jolie's phone buzzed in her pocket. It was a text from an unknown number:

This is Cassian. Meet me at my office in the morning, nine o'clock sharp. Dress nice.

"You bougie and shit, and I see you got it." Aaron followed her, and she kicked off her heels before turning to him.

"Don't be a dick." A headache pulsed from her temples. She wanted him out. Out of her apartment. Out of her life.

"Excuse me, Miss *Investigative Reporter*. I would love to look pretty on TV and write some shit and make bank from it."

"I don't know about making bank," Helena muttered.

Jolie sent her a look.

Aaron glared at her. "You don't do shit or contribute to society like us workin' people. You type words, I'm out in the trenches."

"*You* have no job. Remember?" Helena pointed out, opening the container of egg foo young.

Jolie slammed her hands on the counter. "Do you always have to be an asshole?"

Why Aaron could never grow up and constantly bummed off others, she didn't know. As she looked into his eyes, a pang of what could've been hit her. A loving relationship with her brother. Like the ones on TV she used to wish for. It never happened.

"Look, can you give me the money? I'll go." He held out his hand, making the "gimme" motion.

"You must be on big drugs if you think I'm giving it to you after you insulted me and demeaned my career."

"*My career, my career, my career.* That's all you ever fuckin' talk about. Get a life. Get some dick or somethin', I'm sick of it." Aaron placed his hands on his hips. "You say the same shit every time. Can we ever have a new conversation?"

"Grow the hell up, and maybe we can." Jolie's fingers tightened on the counter.

"You aren't better than any of us, no matter how much you push us away. These rich people don't know you like me."

If the tightness in her chest didn't make a deep breath impossible, Jolie would have screamed in frustration. "Get out. Go to your parents' place."

"We have the same parents. You don't have to say it like that."

"Daryl is not my father."

Jolie stood in front of him, their chests rising and plummeting. Neither dropped their gaze.

"I wish you wasn't my sister. I see why your father got shot. It wasn't an accident. You just weren't good enough for him. He died to get away from you."

A sense of vertigo hit her. The sound of Helena's chair scraping across the floor as she yelled at Aaron to get out was muffled. Jolie's face went slack, her gaze flat on her brother's face. Coldness swept through her as he spoke to her.

"Get out, Aaron! Get the hell out and don't come back." Helena tugged him toward the door.

Realizing he fucked up, Aaron tried to backtrack and laugh. "Come on, I was playin'. Don't look at me like that."

Jolie exhaled slowly, her eyes fixed on the wall as Helena forced Aaron out into the hall and shut the door with a slam. She heard Helena's steps, then felt her hands on her shoulders.

"Come on, don't listen to him. He's a dick."

"I'm fine. It doesn't matter."

Weak. Foolish. Alone. Jolie managed a calming breath, then another. The throbbing in her head receded into numbness.

She despised who Aaron had become. She didn't only blame him; she blamed her mother, the root of his evil. She needed to get away from her family, and maybe it was rash of her to marry Cassian. He could never meet her family. She would never let Cassian see this weakness within her.

I've been alone for years now. It'll always be that way.

"This fake marriage to Cassian Anders. Tell me about that."

"I'm going to bed."

Jolie ignored Helena's calls. With each step she took to her bedroom, a tear fell, and any love for her family dissipated with it.

eleven

. . .

Jolie stepped onto the forty-fifth floor that housed Anders and Lincoln Law Firm. Closing her compact mirror, she sat her shoulders back after confirming that her eyes were not at all puffy from the night before.

I'm sorry. I didn't mean it.

Aaron sent her several texts during the night until she finally blocked him.

The sound of phones ringing, papers shuffling, and the odd cough here and there made it feel like her own office. She passed by some partners' offices with open doors, her heels clicking confidently against the floor, drawing glances and whispers from the employees.

"Miss Coldwell, it's a pleasure to see you again. Congratulations on your engagement." Cassian's receptionist gave her a big smile.

Engagement... Jolie inhaled and gave her a curt nod. "Thank you."

"Mr. Anders is waiting. Please step inside."

After a talk with Helena that morning explaining her

marriage deal, she avoided any more conversation about Aaron. Instead, she took the day off to prepare for this next round with Cassian.

"It's good to be back in the dungeon—" Jolie paused as she noticed the full room. "Oh."

Cassian was not alone.

There was Paul, and two people she recognized as part of Cassian's team. She cleared her throat.

"Rock, Margarita, I would like you to meet Jolie Coldwell. My fiancée."

She shouldn't like the way her name rolled off his tongue.

Inadvertently, Cassian and Jolie had complemented the other. He wore a navy blue suit and red tie, while her suit was a replica of Gabrielle Union's in her iconic introduction scene in *Two Can Play That Game*. Bloodred, molded to every curve, and exposing more of her thighs than what was strictly professional. The suit jacket was cinched tight enough to elevate her breasts.

Cassian's gaze drifted down the length of her body before returning to her face as she crossed the room. *Walk straight, be calm.* By habit, she ran her hand through the end of her high ponytail.

"Fiancée?" Rock had golden-brown skin and a trimmed goatee, and his bald head gleamed in the light. He raised a brow, eying her appreciatively. "Are you sure?"

"Thin ice, man." Cassian's voice held a threatening tone as he stared down at his running mate.

There was obviously a joke she was missing. Cassian moved around the desk. *Confident. Sleek.* His arm slid around her waist before she could stop him, the sarcastic comeback jammed in her throat.

"The woman of the hour. I've been dying to meet you," a woman with nut-brown skin, wearing a black Givenchy jacket that made her look like the ultimate badass, said. "I'm Margarita José—"

"I know. You were the first Afro-Latina woman to represent Oregon in Congress."

"I have a fan?"

"I make it my business to know successful women breaking the glass ceiling."

Margarita's eyes lit up as she turned to Cassian. He watched Jolie intently, and a lurch of excitement coursed through her as he squeezed her side. That electric touch tightened her nipples and forced her to press her thighs tightly together.

Margarita laughed loudly. "You got a keeper here, buddy. Too bad it's fake."

And like that, the balloon popped. She wasn't here because she was a love-blind fiancée of his. She wasn't his *friend*. Taking a step away from Cassian, she grabbed the open seat next to Margarita.

"I told you that there was nothing to worry about." Cassian sat behind his desk.

"I don't have to comment how I feel about this," Paul said scathingly.

Jolie rolled her eyes, focusing her gaze on a picture of an older couple and a young woman on Cassian's desk faced outward. *His family?* Family she would have to meet. *Soon.* Her nerves rumbled. Damn, how did she forget his family in all this? Her confrontation with Aaron replayed itself. *He can never meet my family.*

"You've made that clear," Margarita muttered drily, and Paul shot her a look.

"It could work." Rock suggested.

"This is wrong, on many, many levels." Paul looked Jolie up and down. "This is not the way into office."

"Paul—" Cassian rubbed his temples.

"I beg to differ. We are playing the game. Albeit a different way. Don't you want to see history made, Paulie?" Margarita asked.

"Don't call me Paulie. I'd like to bring up the ethical ramification of grabbing a random woman off the street and Cassian calling her his wife."

"Excuse me, he didn't pluck me off the street like I was a stray. I *offered* to be his wife," Jolie said.

"After you illegally recorded him or before?"

"You're the campaign manager. Next time, advise your client about speaking on personal matters in public spaces." Jolie pinned Paul with a dirty look.

"You're a stranger. You don't belong here."

It wasn't an accident; you weren't good enough for him.

Jolie's breath caught, and Cassian slammed his hand on the desk, jarring everyone.

"Enough. Paul, if we all are going to work together to help get me into office, we need to agree. Is that clear?" Cassian looked between Paul and Jolie.

"I'm on board," Jolie said with mock sweetness. Paul's mouth pinched as Margarita snickered.

"Can I expect this kind of pliancy during our marriage?"

He captured her eyes with his as a smile crossed his face. How would it feel to kiss him? They would have to eventually. Instincts screamed to her that under those suits of his? Dynamism.

"Don't get used to it. I would hate to get your hopes up." *Don't forget why you're here.*

"I'm glad we got that settled. Introductions weren't the only reason we called this meeting today," Margarita said. "We have all the players in the game now, so let's take advantage and strike now rather than later. Beginning with engagement photos."

"Engagement photos? You said we'd just have an engagement party." Jolie turned to Cassian.

He shrugged. "We have to sell this, don't we?"

"What we need to do is stay on this high with Cassian's

nomination acceptance. That would drown out Radcliffe's smear campaign," Margarita said.

"I think it's an effective strategy." Cassian's eyes never left Jolie.

"I've found some society magazines we can release the photos to. A few stations will do a spotlight."

Jolie sat up. "Stations?"

"Channel 9 and WBNC are the most willing." Margarita smiled.

"Per the terms of our contract, Channel 12 has first dibs on any developing from Cassian." Jolie squinted at Cassian. *No way he's two-timing me on our deal already.*

Margarita gave Cassian a look of surprise. "Contract?"

"Jolie and I have our own private contract."

"What's all in that contract?" Rock winked at Jolie.

"It's nothing you all need to worry about. I agreed to give Channel 12 exclusive rights to any interviews, photos, and statements during my campaign."

Margarita frowned. "Wouldn't that be a conflict of interest, Jolie?"

Her confrontation with Travis replayed itself. *This is for your promotion.* "It's handled."

"For now, let's release the engagement photos in the society mags and on WBNC. Do you want to go on *The Wake-Up Call* with Ginger Sparrow? A large population of women watch the daytime show, and it would do well in boosting a loyal support group for Cassian."

Jolie raised a brow. "Manipulate voters by getting them to fawn over him?"

A smirk played on Cassian's face. Of course he would find that amusing. Cassian possessed a raw sex appeal that was dangerous. For both her and his potential fans.

"Every bit counts," Margarita agreed.

With a soft knock, Cassian's receptionist interrupted and

said, "Mr. Anders, I have Gillian Miller from Picture Perfect here to see you."

Jolie's eyes widened. "We're taking the photos now?"

"I told you to dress nicely for a reason." Cassian tugged the lapels of his jacket.

Jolie scowled. She would have prepared differently if that information hadn't been withheld from her.

"I have to stay and see this." Rock chuckled.

Margarita stood. "We'll be right out. Let's go, team."

Everyone filed out of the office.

In the hall, a woman and several people held black bags and huge pieces of equipment. They ushered Jolie into a conference room. Paul watched for a moment before he threw his hands up and stormed away.

"Why do you look nervous?"

Jolie jumped. She'd been staring out the window and down to the busy street and Lake Michigan below as the crew set up, and hadn't heard him come up behind her. "I'm not nervous."

"Liar."

Jolie raised a brow, eying him from head to toe. "Excuse me?"

She had been glossing over the true responsibilities she would have as his wife, but the meeting had thrown them into stark relief. *Me, a reporter and politician's wife?* How did Michelle Obama balance being a senator's wife and lawyer and then being first lady of a nation running several social initiatives, being a mother, and writing memoirs? Michelle didn't have a terrible family to worry about. Michelle didn't have to constantly fight to prove herself. Michelle wasn't in a marriage of convenience.

"I'm sure if you bring as much energy as you did the night in Magnifica, we'll both be fine." Cassian reached into his pocket. The clatter of setting up the room ceased as she watched him pull out a small black box. "We need this to make it real."

She held her breath as he opened the box. Never in her life had she seen something beautiful. It was a huge emerald-cut diamond ring with a diamond-studded band. This probably cost as much as her student loan debt.

It's only for a year. If he wins. You'll stay the same.

Who was she kidding? She would never be the same after this. Was she truly prepared for the ramifications of this agreement? How her life would change? *Is Channel 12 worth this?*

"It's a bit late for romance."

"You deserve romance regardless. This would make a good photo, right?"

How do I remain myself?

Jolie stood frozen, her heart beating a dent in her chest. She slowly extended her hand toward him.

No longer would the public see her as Jolie Coldwell. She would soon be *Cassian Anders's wife.* Or *ex-wife,* eventually. That's what she'd be reduced to. *This promotion will be worth it.*

She watched him slide the ring on, and her stomach plummeted to her heels the moment the weight of the diamond settled.

"Didn't get this from a gumball machine, did you?" She needed something light to cut the intensity of this moment. "You could have handed me the ring."

Cassian's gaze was laser-focused. "When I play, Miss Coldwell, I play to win. Now we are going to take pictures and we're going to sell to people that we're deeply in love, so I need you to stop looking sad."

"I'm not sad."

How far is the press going to dig into my background and ruin the reputation I spent years crafting?

"Don't lie to me."

He stood tall, backing her up into the glass window behind her. Her eyes nervously glanced at the surrounding workers; Cassian leaned forward to whisper in her ear. "We need to look like we're in this for the long haul. Let your guard down."

Jolie fought to keep her breathing neutral as he released her and headed over to the photographer. She exhaled shakily. That would never happen. Life… *Liza* had taught her that.

This is all pretend. He couldn't see her. Not the real her.

In no time, the photography crew had cameras, tripods, and reflective umbrellas set up. Eventually, she and Cassian were directed to the center of the room.

"Let's start with a kiss, shall we?"

Whoa.

Cassian advanced, slowly unbuttoning his suit jacket. She licked her bottom lip.

"Only if you're comfortable," he murmured.

"For the photos."

"For the photos."

Jolie swallowed as he wrapped his arms around her stiff body.

"Relax," he affirmed, his hand cupping the back of her neck. He gently dragged his fingers in tiny little circles, and her body jerked closer. His fingers played with the end of her ponytail. "Can I try something?"

Jolie nodded.

Cassian's gaze traced over her face, and her belly exploded with butterflies. Never had she had a man stare at her the way he did now. Like she was truly beautiful.

Her cheeks flushed, nerves tossing and turning like waves. *Your goals, Jolie. Promotion. Urban Properties. National news.*

His hand around her waist squeezed tight, drawing her from her thoughts.

It was unnerving how he made her relax. After so many years of being independent, all it took was a man gently massaging her neck and holding her delicately for her to consider giving up control. She felt a tug, and her hair came tumbling down around her shoulders.

"Hey!"

"That's better. Good girl."

She nearly melted at his words before freezing, realizing what he said.

He chuckled. "You like being praised?"

"Excuse me, let's get this going. We're paying by the hour here," Margarita cajoled.

Needing to regain control, Jolie planted a hand on Cassian's chest, and lifting to her toes, she pressed her lips firmly to his.

"Okay, perfect!"

She vaguely heard the shutter of the camera.

His lips melded into hers, forcing her to stay with his pace. The kiss deepened, and her blood heated into molten lava. Cassian's other hand cradled her jaw, slowly tracing the contours of her face. Her heart galloped and her lashes fluttered. She tried not to moan out loud as erotic images of him fucking her on the conference table popped into her brain.

Not appropriate in a room full of strangers watching!

His tongue teased the entrance of her mouth and she parted her lips.

His tongue dipped inside, licking her teeth, and she gasped as he tunneled farther in. In her mind, those big, long-fingered hands swept over her bare skin, cupping her heavy breasts, pinching her beaded nipples...

What would Cassian look like with his body over her? Sheltering her. Protecting her. Straining against her as he sent them both over the peak of ecstasy.

Gillian cleared her throat. "Should we get some of the two of you... not kissing?"

"Or should we step out?" Rock asked slyly.

Jolie retreated gradually from Cassian, the adrenaline draining from her and making her limbs feel like lead.

"What's the next pose?" Cassian's voice was rough.

"Let's get cozy, I want you to look like you're hugging—"

She circled her arms around his neck, tilting her head to look up at him. He rested his hands on her hips. The butterflies in her stomach morphed into a tsunami of fretfulness as her eyes drifted to his lips.

"You looked upset earlier. Why?" Cassian questioned.

Jolie's smile faltered as Gillian snapped another photo. "What?"

"When you walked into my office, you looked upset. Did something happen?"

Jolie's smile swelled to obviously fake proportions as Gillian stepped closer with the camera.

"I'm cool."

"You're not telling the truth," Cassian grumbled. "It's all over your face."

Gillian ordered them back to front, and he intertwined their fingers together to rest on her belly.

Jolie did not want to rehash her argument with Aaron again. "Why do you care?"

"I can care, can't I?"

"You don't have to pretend to care. Let's do what we need to do and go about our day." *It's better to leave the past in the past.*

"If we're going to be together—"

"This is fake, Cassian," she whispered, mindful of other people in the room. "We're not really fiancés, we're not friends, we're barely acquaintances. I don't plan to spill the dirty secrets of my life to you. Drop it."

Cassian was silent, and Gillian snapped a photo, nodding as she inspected it.

"Yes, perfect."

"Is that it?" Jolie swallowed thickly, pulling herself from

Cassian, and avoiding the guilt she would feel when she looked in his eyes.

"This should be enough—" Margarita said.

"Tomorrow, we're having a sort of fundraising party at Loft Lucia. Be ready at nine o'clock sharp." Cassian's face was neutral. Nothing gave away his emotions, despite the robotic way in which he spoke.

"Fine, I'll send you my address."

"I'll send you some dresses too! Mayor Charles is an important potential ally. Let's get on her good side, right?" Margarita chirped.

Cassian pushed past Jolie, heading out of the room. Rock sent Jolie an apologetic look and followed him. Despite the tendrils of regret trying to clamp on to her, she made the right choice to reject Cassian's olive branch. Nothing good would come from him knowing about her personal life. Nothing at all.

twelve

. . .

"You like her, you *really, really* like her," Rock sang into the phone. Cassian rolled his eyes as he sat in the back of the rented limo in front of Jolie's house. A glance at the clock let him know she had two minutes before she should appear.

"You're regressing to being a child now?"

"I'm commenting on what I witnessed."

"You saw everything going according to plan." *This is all for the campaign.*

Rock scoffed. "You can't lie to me man."

Cassian sometimes wanted new friends. He and Rock been close friends since freshman year in college. They'd both been studying law, from the city, and with dreams to make a change.

"Ass," Cassian mumbled.

"Jolie's fucking beautiful and can tough it out with Paul's mean ass? You got yourself a winner."

"Is this why you called?"

Yearning churned in Cassian's gut as he thought about Jolie's soft body pressed against his. Her heavenly rose perfume wafted from his clothes long after she turned him loose. It made his heart beat faster to remember the brief shot of desire he'd seen reciprocated in her eyes.

Stay focused on the plan, asshole. He needed to win. There would be no intimacy involved.

"You jackin' off over there or something?"

You're losing your mind over a woman.

Cassian rubbed his temples. "You have five seconds to tell me what you called for, or I'm hanging up."

"I'm all for the dedication to the cause, but did you think this through, Case? I thought you were joking, but shit... You're *actually* marrying a woman. One I think will eat you the fuck alive if given the chance."

Cassian tapped his fingers on the armrest. *She has one more minute.*

"I don't joke."

"Fucking understatement of the century. Isn't it just easier to pay Jolie off? Is the campaign really worth this?"

Cassian glanced at the blacked-out privacy divider separating him from the driver.

"Absolutely. We'll get to know one another. I've arranged for some media to catch us at my outreach center. We can talk there."

There was the sound of a door bursting open on Rock's side of the call. Then the pitter-patter of feet. *"Daddy!"*

Rock groaned. "Diana, what did I tell you about running in the house?"

"Is that Uncle Case?"

Cassian smiled at the five-year-old's high-pitched voice coming through the phone.

"It's me, sweet pea."

Diana giggled, and she heard Rock grunt and the shuffling of the phone.

"Are you coming to my birthday party?"

The little girl wouldn't let it be forgotten that her sixth birthday was coming up fast. She'd demanded a backyard BBQ complete with ponies, jumping castles, and clowns.

"I told you yesterday I was coming."

"Are you sure?"

Cassian loved spending time with his goddaughter. The little girl had both Cassian and Rock wrapped around her finger. "Don't I always keep my word?"

Diana screeched excitedly. "Yes."

The phone was muffled, and he heard Rock's voice clearer. "Go help your mama with dinner. I'll be there after I finish discussing business."

Diana whined and Rock sighed loudly. Cassian heard the door close as he laughed.

"You spoil her."

"Don't act like you don't."

"Did you prepare Jolie for tonight?"

Cassian dragged a hand down his face, sucking his teeth. "She's a journalist. She's been to a ton of public events."

"Not the ones with snotty-as-hell, uber-rich people."

"We need to fund this campaign."

The clock struck nine, and he glanced at the door of her apartment building.

"I don't think she'll like ass-kissing as much as you do. Definitely not as much as she enjoyed kissing you the other day."

"Rock..."

"In all of your majestic planning, when is the consummation of the marriage scheduled for?"

Cassian's breathing slowed, and he tried to ignore the electricity that struck his spine at the thought of that. He would enjoy tasting her, touching her, pleasing her till they collapsed, both from passion and exhaustion. But he wouldn't, because he needed to stay focused on his campaign.

"This marriage will be purely platonic."

"Platonic?" Rock snorted. "When was the last time you got laid?"

"That's none of your business."

Rock cackled, and Cassian looked toward Jolie's apartment. He would ask the driver to honk.

"That long, huh?"

Fantasies of her legs spread wide and thrown over his shoulders as he sank into her over and over, her nails scratching up his back... All from merely being in her presence. He was going to need to hit the gym more often to get rid of all the tension.

Rock switched to a more solemn topic. "What about Kinsella? What are you going to do?"

"There's thousands of things I could do about him, but picking one is nearly impossible."

It should have been something he "made peace" with, but his gut screamed *bullshit*. It wasn't until a year ago that he told his parents he'd be investigating what the police failed to discover. In the haze of the accident, Cassian only recalled a dented red Chevrolet Camaro peeling away, and the first three letters of the license plate, *SLR*. That should have been enough for the police. It wasn't. Their case became cold and forgotten.

"You're planning something, but don't let it ruin what we've built. The goal is the election, not Kinsella."

The door of Jolie's apartment building opened, and his breath caught at the sight of her. Her dark hair was pulled into a sexy chignon with several tendrils falling in her face, making her appear dainty and sweet. He knew it was a trap.

"I gotta go."

"You're my brother. I'm not gonna stop worrying about you."

"I know, man, I know."

He stepped out of the car, balancing the phone between

his shoulder and ear and motioning to the driver to return to the car.

"Give Gerald time with the Kinsella issue. I put him on your case for a reason, and he's a damn good PI."

"Thanks, man."

Cassian ended the call. He forced the knot in his throat down as he stared at Jolie.

Jolie wore a red one-shoulder satin gown that formed to her curves like water. The fabric glittered under the streetlight as she held up the hem.

"Shit," he muttered.

He was lying to Rock. Having to be in a marriage where he tempted to touch her or kiss those full lips would be absolute torture. He willed himself to be stronger than his dick. As her leg extended, he noticed the dress had a split that stopped midthigh. *Damn.* He focused on her strappy gold heels.

"You're mighty impatient tonight, Mr. Anders," she said once in front of him.

"I said nine o'clock."

"Most people say a lot of things but don't follow through."

Cassian noticed a faint speckle of glitter on her skin, making it look delectable.

"You'll find I'm better at keeping my word than most." He smiled at her. "You look beautiful."

"Not bad yourself, partner." Her cheeks flushed, and she looked away. The corners of his eyes crinkled as his lips tugged to the side in a grin.

"Should I get used to these compliments from you?"

"You're welcome, and no," she shot back.

He walked her over to the limo, and held the door open as she slid inside, trying to ignore the shiver that went down his body as her body brushed against him.

In no time, they were on the expressway heading toward

the Loop. Out of the corner of his eyes, he noticed her tracing the diamond on the engagement ring with a finger.

"Are you okay?"

Jolie didn't look up, her gaze pinned on the ring. "You like to ask that a lot... But yes. This is outrageous, though, you know."

"The ring?"

"This plan." She folded her arms and glared. "Do you really think people are going to believe this? You and me?"

His heart pounded. No way she was getting cold feet now. "They shouldn't have a reason not to."

Jolie eyes fell to the ring then him. "What's the agenda for the night?"

He was grateful for the conversation change. "It's a relatively small gathering. Some influential acquaintances, politicians, and businessmen—"

"Your typical upper crust."

Cassian frowned. "Mostly people who I've worked with closely in the past and now support my campaign."

"We're trying to wring money out of lazy rich folks? I gotcha."

"Not like that."

"Be for real, Cassian. You're runnin' through their pockets. Got to have this circus funded some type of way."

"Don't generalize. You don't want to offend or alienate anyone." *Maybe Paul is right. She's too rash.*

Jolie raised an eyebrow. "I don't alienate people."

Cassian gave her a look of disbelief.

"Fine. I won't say anything to their faces."

He stared at her a few seconds longer before saying, "Thank you. Mostly tonight is just wining and dining and easing you into your new role." Her brows dipped briefly at the mention of a role. "The topic of tonight is us. People are going to ask."

"Why not? I'm the new prize pony. I doubt they want my résumé," Jolie said sarcastically.

"Let's get the story down."

They drew closer to downtown, the Willis Tower a beacon in the night sky.

"We met at a party," Jolie began.

"What party?"

Jolie gave him a look. "Does it matter?"

"Your story is too vague. If we're as specific as possible, that will leave little room for people to ask questions."

Her voice grew quiet. "How about…we met at the opening for your outreach center."

Cassian blinked, brows furrowing. "You were there?"

"Front row. My hair was shorter then."

The day returned to his mind. It had been a flurry of screaming kids, media, and families from the local area. He was answering questions from the media, but he remembered a beautiful woman raising her hand to ask, *Why do you think you'll last when others have quit on this community time and time again?*

Back then she didn't shy away from the tough questions, and neither did she now.

A smile crept across his face. "I remember you…"

Jolie's eyes rolled toward the ceiling but she smirked faintly. "Don't. I'm just saying I was there, and it would make sense why we know each other."

He smiled at her, and she huffed.

"How about we find out some things about one another that we couldn't find online?"

That would help and wouldn't give away how little he knew about his fake fiancée.

"Okay, like what?" Cassian stretched his legs. Their driver pulled them off the Dan Ryan Expressway and onto the 511.

"What's your middle name?" Jolie asked.

Cassian pursed his lips. "Do you really need to know that?"

"How am I going to put on a winning performance if I don't even know your legal name?"

"Arthur. Yours?"

Jolie snorted before covering her mouth.

He gave her a sharp look. "What's wrong with my middle name?"

"Nothing." Jolie shook her head and bit her lip. "Nothing at all."

"Obviously it's something."

Another glance at him, and she exploded into laughter. "I was thinking more biblical. Bartholomew. Emmanuel. *Hezekiah*."

He chuckled. "Sorry to disappoint. Would it help if I told you my mother almost decided on Isaac?"

"It would, very much."

Cassian huffed playfully. "Tell me yours."

"It's—" Jolie started to speak, instead clearing her throat. "Jolie. My middle name is Jolie. My first name is too embarrassing to say."

"Tell me."

"No."

Cassian sat up. "Your first name cannot be that bad. Unless it's Quasimodo. Or Karen."

Jolie shot him a look. "Karen?"

"No one likes a Karen."

She took a deep breath, facing forward, and she crossed her arms over her chest. "Sparkle."

"Excuse me?"

"My first name is Sparkle. Like the film from the seventies?"

It wasn't...horrible. It fit her personality perfectly.

"Why did you change it?"

She still refused to meet his gaze, facing the black partition. "My fifth-grade teacher called it ghetto."

Cassian sucked in a breath, and he watched her close her eyes briefly, shoulders sagging.

"She said I wouldn't get a job that wasn't flipping burgers. As I got older, I wanted to prove her wrong. I did my own test when applying for jobs. Jolie got more callbacks than Sparkle. After I got to college, the reactions to my name were the same as that teacher. Who would take me, a Black woman from Chicago, seriously with a name like Sparkle?"

A pain hit him in the chest. He remembered those early days in law school and his first firm. The crushing and paralyzing feeling of imposter syndrome, and the constant pressure to prove himself and go above and beyond the bare minimum of his privileged peers.

"I understand you, completely."

Jolie turned to him, apprehension in her gaze. "It sucks to conform, but it's sometimes necessary if you want to get ahead."

Like what we're doing now.

The sound of a faint pop song filled the surrounding space, cutting the tension between them.

"You never answered my question." Cassian's voice was soft.

"Which one?"

"Why did you look sad in my office?"

"Why do you care?" Her body language was elementary.

Rigid body posture. Squinting eyes. A lowering brow.

"I'm not the enemy, Jolie."

"I never said you were."

"Despite how we came to be, we can leave this arrangement as friends, you know."

Everything about her appealed to him, especially her intellect. She would be the downfall of both himself and his plan.

Yet he couldn't get that hurt expression on her face out of his mind. He wanted to beat the shit out of whoever put that look there. She deserved to have a grin on her face. Laughing. Talking shit to him, and him loving it.

"Would it help if I told you I have a fear of frogs?"

Jolie's head snapped toward him. She let out a bark of laughter. "What?"

"They are completely bizarre the way their limbs bend. Slimy. It's repulsive, and the worst part about fishing with my dad."

A weak smile appeared on her face, and she swallowed visibly. "You fish with your dad?"

"Since I was ten. The first time, I got the hook caught in my left ass cheek and vowed never to go back. That was over twenty years ago, and he still makes me go out there."

Jolie nodded slowly, a frown engulfing her smile. "Must be nice."

Gone was the sexy seductress. Her mask had dropped, and he was seeing the *real her*. Damn it, he wanted to protect her…from whatever was hurting.

"What about your—"

"Murdered."

Silence. He grimaced, glancing at the window, then back at her. "I'm sorry."

Her mouth tilted, and she wrapped her arms around herself. "Can't miss what you never had."

Defensive. Defensive. Defensive. She's not gonna make this easy.

"My brother." She glanced at him.

He blinked. "Your brother?"

The car was silent as they pulled in front of a luxury high-rise.

"The reason I was upset at your office. It was my brother."

Jolie offered no other explanation, and he didn't push

111

further, grateful that she had given him a tiny bit of insight into her. The driver opened the door.

Smiling his thanks at the man, Cassian extended his hand toward her, helping her out. He placed his hand on her waist. Jolie stiffened, then relaxed. His hand smoothed up her spine, and she leaned into him, his body singing at the small progress.

CASSIAN LED Jolie through the throng, stopping repeatedly to greet people he recognized or who recognized him.

The guests were in their element, drinking and laughing, taking all the opulence for granted. As promised, Jolie smiled and nodded at the precise moments, and like expected, people inquired about their relationship. It felt weird to make goo-goo eyes at her, but after a while, it felt completely natural.

"Paul." Cassian clapped the older man on the shoulder when he found him and Margarita at the bar. "Which number drink is this?"

"How's the new reincarnation of the Kennedys doing this evening?" Paul's voice dripped with sarcasm. Jolie narrowed her eyes at him.

"I think they're doing well." Margarita laughed.

Cassian was used to the social politics game, but since his nomination, he felt scrutinized. Like a goldfish in a fishbowl.

He sent Paul a sharp glance, squeezing Jolie's side till she relaxed into him. "We've heard enough of your opinion at the office, Paul. Not here."

"When should we?" Paul demanded, and shook his head.

"You need to keep digging into *her* background. The skeletons will emerge."

"I'm sure we won't find much," Cassian said, sending Paul a look that said, *We'll talk about this when she's not standing in front of us.*

"I'm right here, you know. And I was honest about my past," Jolie hissed at Paul.

The bartender set a cocktail in front of Paul, whose eyes didn't leave Jolie. Cassian glared at the man for his tactlessness.

"You better hope and pray to God I don't find anything."

Jolie sliced her hand through the air. "You really want to talk about this in public? Who's going to cause a scandal now?"

"You are a problem."

"Paul," Cassian growled.

Jolie scowled at Paul. "The feeling's mutual."

Margarita patted Paul on the shoulder. "This is a fundraiser for Cassian. Let's show a united front, not a civil war."

They turned to notice more than a few curious gazes on them. They all relaxed, feigning smiles till the attention waned.

"Keep it together till the morning. Can you do that?" Margarita demanded, looking between Jolie and Paul.

Paul's mouth parted to speak as applause erupted.

Cassian's gaze shifted to the foyer, where Mayor Ida Charles was holding court. The mayor was an older biracial woman with sandy-blond natural hair and hazel eyes. She appeared calm, but he knew enough about the mayor to know what she was doing. She was calculating everyone in this room as a potential vote for herself.

"Shit," Paul muttered, finishing his drink.

Mayor Charles, her husband, and her entourage made it

through the crowd. Cassian, Paul, Margarita, and Jolie stood up straight as she approached them.

Cassian spoke first. "Mayor Charles. Phil."

Mayor Charles's husband grunted. A tall, lanky man who resembled Lurch from *The Addams Family*, he never said more three words at a time.

"Congratulations are in order, I hear." The mayor looked between Jolie and him. Her eyes fell to Jolie's left hand as she wrapped her arm through his.

"Thank you. It means a lot to hear that from you," Jolie said, surprising Cassian.

"Hmm." Mayor Charles pinned her gaze on Jolie.

He wasn't sure if Jolie had meant to sound mocking.

"Yes, thank you, Mayor Charles." Cassian cleared his throat, nudging Jolie subtly in warning.

"I didn't know a young lady had your eye. You seem so focused on work." Mayor Charles pressed her lips into a thin line, her intense gaze unblinking.

"You of all people know the requirement of discretion with relationships in the public eye."

"I know all too well." Mayor Charles nodded. "I thought we were close, Cassian. You were once a top supporter of mine."

He exhaled deeply; he knew what this was about.

"Can I have a word with you alone, Cassian?"

Cassian nodded, untangling himself from Jolie. She briefly gripped his hand, and he gave her a slight smile.

"Give me a moment, baby?"

They didn't have time to analyze the affectionate nickname as he followed Mayor Charles across the room, toward the open balcony. With a look from the mayor, those guests on the balcony observing the skyline scattered.

He leaned against the railing to look back into the room and saw Jolie pick up a glass of champagne.

"I called your office several times but couldn't get through."

"When you demolished the Well Housing Projects to open a luxury gym and boutiques, you and I had to part ways. I don't regret my decision. Tonight is just formalities," Cassian said through clenched teeth.

Mayor Charles tilted her head to the side. "C'mon, Cassian. You're a lawyer. You know risk and sacrifice. It was a good deal for this city."

"It was a good deal for you to line your pockets. That's not the message you told the voters. That you told me when I was helping to fund your campaign."

Mayor Charles scoffed. "It was a small sacrifice for a larger gain. The city had three large tech firms move from Menlo Park in California to the Magnificent Mile. The revenue and jobs we will see will be unparalleled."

Cassian's hands tightened into fists. When Mayor Charles came onto the political scene, he thought there'd been hope. After the last mayoral scandal, Mayor Charles was city council president running for office with Cassian and his law firm as one of her biggest backers.

She'd promised to uphold justice. Fund local housing projects and antiviolence groups. Increase tourism in the city. Like many before her, she'd declined in favor during her time in office. Her approval rating was at an all-time low at twenty-seven percent, and activists were calling for a new bill that allowed for the recall or impeachment of a Chicago mayor.

"Money over the people?" Cassian's jaw clenched.

"Investment for future generations. Where do you think those kids you're mentoring are going to work someday? You want them at a fast-food joint?" Mayor Charles turned toward the open door.

He spotted Jolie laughing with several people

surrounding her, her smile drawing in men. He forced himself not to go over and tell those men they needed to back the hell off.

"You want them to get up out of the hood like you did? Have a better life? We need companies that will supply the salary so they can attain that life."

"Not like this."

Mayor Charles nodded. "Yes, like this. You accepted my twenty-five-thousand-dollar donation to your center last year. You've funded my campaign. We're interconnected, don't forget that."

He'd seen that donation as a gift from a friend. He'd been able to supply five of his boys with college scholarships.

"I've changed, Cassian, and the city is changing. Things don't last forever, and if you keep that mentality, you'll never be successful as governor."

Cassian's nostrils flared. "I'm going to do everything in my power to make your time in office hell until we can replace you."

"Shame, Cassian. I came here to personally tell you I won't be donating to your campaign. I'll be supporting Martin Gomez instead."

"What?"

"You may have the Democratic nomination, and Radcliffe has the Republican, but Gomez will be independent. I'm going to pour all my resources into getting him into office instead of you."

He cracked his knuckles. "You're paying that man to run?"

Mayor Charles shrugged, a smirk playing on her face. "I'm securing the financial future this city needs."

With those words, the mayor stalked from the balcony. Her husband and entourage immediately fell in by her side. Not only was he fighting Radcliffe, he had to fight Mayor Charles too? *Fuck!*

If Charles's recent approval rating meant anything, she knew her time was limited. That made her dangerous and unpredictable. Standing in the doorway, his muscles rigid, he caught Jolie's eye. Now more than ever, he needed her. This plan had to work. There was no plan B.

thirteen

. . .

Cassian just arrived back from Rockford, a city almost two hours from Chicago, after making appearances at the local university when he got the call he'd been waiting for. Ducking out of his board meeting, he jerked his tie loose as he sat at his desk. He was reviewing the documents that Paul had forwarded to him and laughed.

First Lady Training… He doubted Jolie would agree to Paul's training. He bit his tongue and decided to see how this played out. After Jolie's brief interaction with Mayor Charles, Paul did not trust Cassian's urging that Jolie would have the sense to act with decorum and professionalism in public.

Every first lady should strive to be like Eleanor Roosevelt. Eleanor is the model prototype of a first lady, and all should rise to her level of excellence.

Cassian whistled. This would not go well, and he was excited to see the shitstorm Jolie would rain down on Paul. His thoughts darkened at the thought of Mayor Charles, but his body came alive at the way Jolie placed her hands on his shoulders afterward and whispered in his ear, *I can do a leak on the mayor that will hurt if you want.*

It made him laugh, and eased the heaviness of his spirit.

"Mr. Anders, Mr. Flowers is here to see you," Leticia said through the intercom.

Closing the email, he shut off his monitor and smoothed out the lapels of his jacket. "Send him in."

"Good morning, Mr. Anders." The older man was punctual and perfectly discreet. He gave a solemn nod and extended his hand to Cassian.

"Gerald." Cassian stood, clasping his hand. "Tell me some good news."

With the campaign ramping up, he'd turned over his investigation into Kinsella to Gerald. Rock has recommended him highly—a retired cop, now a PI—and Cassian hoped the man was worth every penny he was spending.

"I think you'll like what I've found." Gerald sat back in his seat, setting his briefcase down onto the ground and finding a brown envelope that he handed over to Cassian. "She's clean. Minus the conviction you notified me of. Just minor traffic tickets."

Cassian was staring down at an off-guard photo of Jolie. There was a bright smile on her face as she laughed with another woman with braids. A coffee cup in one hand, eyes closed, and head tossed back. He hadn't had the pleasure of seeing this side of her yet.

Cassian flipped through the basic run-of-the-mill information. "Nothing else?"

Keep digging. You'll find something on her, I know it. Paul's voice rang in his mind.

Flipping through the file revealed standard information. She was born in Memphis. Got her undergrad degree from the University of Illinois at Urbana-Champaign. Worked at a few newsrooms before Channel 12.

"No men, as far as I can see."

Cassian let out a breath and the tension fell from his shoulders. She was telling the truth.

"Perfect."

Cassian hadn't prepared himself in case she had lied about having a relationship with someone else.

"There was an issue with her birth certificate. There's no father listed."

"What?"

"Seems like a purposeful omission. Did she mention that?"

"She only said he was murdered." Cassian's gut twisted.

"If you give me a name, I can find his death certificate."

Asking Jolie the name of her dead father, when he could barely get her to open up about her brother? "I'll run this by Paul first."

Gerald grunted before handing Cassian another file. "This is what you really want."

There was the bastard himself.

Attorney General Timothy Kinsella.

A pounding began in Cassian's ears. The man aged like a banana. A once-lean and toned figure now a potbelly. Blond hair now white. Aged lines creased around his mouth, crow's feet around his green eyes. There were no term limits in Illinois for attorney general, and he'd occupied office for the last twenty years consecutively. The public respected him, clueless as to what he'd done to Cassian's family.

There was no fucking way Cassian was taking any advice from that man if he won the governor position.

Kinsella had more than overstayed his welcome. He'd never been held accountable for his crimes, and here he was just...*living.*

In the past year and a half of relaunching an investigation into the crime, it turns out there had been ten Chevrolet Camaros in the state with the license plate beginning with *SLR.* They were registered to owners located in the southern part of the state bordering Missouri. Two of the cars had been registered to the attorney general. It was an obvious cover-up;

Cassian just didn't know how far it went. He'd need indisputable evidence.

"I got a record of a receipt from an auto body repair shop a few days after your accident."

"A receipt? That's all you got?"

Gerald frowned. "I'm finding all the information I can."

Cassian didn't want to hear that shit. He wanted results. He dropped the files on the desk, tapping them with one finger. "I'm paying your exorbitant price—"

"Don't doubt my skills, Mr. Anders. The people you're trying to go against are just as game."

"He's sleeping at night with the fact he crashed into my family." *And destroyed our lives.* "I need more."

"I can track down the witnesses that pulled your family out of the car."

He remembered it had been an older couple in their early fifties. By now, they would be eighty and it would be a miracle if they remembered anything. *Fuck!*

"Give me some time. Focus on your campaign."

"I need this information. Soon. Not later." Cassian flipped through the document.

"There's only so much power I have, Mr. Anders. Relax—"

There was a knock on the door before it opened and in stepped his founding partner.

"Why in the hell are you still here?" Meg Lincoln, the Lincoln in Anders and Lincoln, stepped inside the office.

Her locs were pulled high into a bun, her dark skin flushed with sweat and irritation. Her long-legged stride made her glide across the room hastily as she sent Cassian a murderous glare. "You dip out on our important meetin', but you're still sittin' here and not on your way to the outreach center. Who's this?"

Gerald cleared his throat, and Cassian sat up, closing the envelope of the file, and sliding it into his desk drawer.

"This is Gerald Flowers, a colleague of Rock's."

"Ma'am." Gerald offered Meg his hand, and she shook it, the suspicion still visible on her features.

"Mr. Flowers. I'm sorry you have to be witness to me tearin' Cassian a new asshole, but that's what you're 'bout to see."

Cassian's brows lifted. "What did I do now?"

"What haven't you done?"

Meg slammed a magazine down. His and Jolie's faces were plastered on the front. They'd used the photo of her arms around his neck, her eyes closed as he stared down at her admiringly.

"I'm in New York for a month, and I come back to you engaged?"

The phantom scent of Jolie's rose perfume wafted to his nose.

"What can I say? When you know, you know."

Meg rolled her eyes. "I will kill you."

Cassian barked out laughter as Gerald stood up and nodded toward Cassian. "You have my number, Mr. Anders."

"Thank you. I'll be in touch."

Giving a curt nod to Meg, the older man abruptly exited the room.

"What the fuck is really goin' on? You're gettin' married?"

He and Meg had been friends since law school, right along with Rock, and Meg had always treated him like he was her fourth sibling. She had two younger sisters, and her brother, Marsh, had just passed the bar and would be coming to work with them soon.

"Language."

"Fuck off, Cassian. This is big news, and I shouldn't be blindsided by with your picture on a magazine."

He lifted a brow. "What are you doing reading society magazines?"

"What are you doing *in* them?"

Cassian exhaled loudly. "When have you ever been interested in my love life?"

"Since when have you had one? I don't think you've taken a day off in over ten years."

Meg was right but he kept his poker face. "I get out and… mingle. I'll manage the wedding and the campaign. Paul, Margarita, and Rock have my back."

"I didn't know you were datin' at all."

"Who are *you* dating right now?"

Meg rolled her eyes. "Don't switch the subject."

Cassian grinned at Meg. "We can talk about your dating life or my campaign."

"I saw the video of you at the McCormick Place online. You did good. I also saw Radcliffe accusin' you of sleepin' with prostitutes. You've been makin' waves."

"As I should."

Meg flipped him off. "I came to remind you the equity partners are gettin' antsy. You were fallin' asleep in the meetin' you were late to. Clients are complainin' it's taking weeks to hear back from you. Or you're runnin' out of here for your center. You can't keep this up, Case. You have too many balls in the air."

"Things got busy these last few weeks. I'll get back on it soon."

Meg looked at him like he was smoking crack. "What the hell do you mean? You can't work here and run the damn state."

Cassian tipped his head back and briefly closed his eyes. "I built this firm. You're not kicking me out, Meg."

"*We* built this firm. No one is disputin' that. It's grown, and you're heading for bigger things—"

He would be governor and work at the firm and the outreach center. Those were all products of his hard work and dedication. "I'm not leaving."

Meg sighed. "You're tryin' to do too much. Be reasonable, Cassian."

"I got this. I haven't disappointed you in the last ten years."

Meg was quiet for a few moments. "You're one of my closest friends, and I just don't want to see you crash and burn. That's where you're headin'."

"I'm handling everything." Cassian shook his head, standing up.

"What about your fiancée? When are you goin' to be a husband to her?"

If only you knew.

"Jolie has her own career. She's not waiting for her man to come home." *Her man?* Cassian ducked his head, a smirk playing on his face. What if Jolie had heard that?

"No one wants to be alone in a relationship. I need to meet this fiancée. Make sure that she's right for you."

"I'm a grown-ass man, Meg, not one of your siblings."

Meg rolled her eyes. "That means nothin'. Did you forget I went through that En Vogue obsession with you? Terry Ellis?"

Cassian frowned and flipped her off. "Of course you remember that."

"It was the toughest five years of my life watchin' you salivate over that woman. I'm bringin' it up every chance I get—"

Cassian snorted, reaching for his briefcase. He quickly put the file from Gerald in with some random papers. He needed to change out of this suit and get to the outreach center.

"I'm serious. You need to learn how to delegate tasks."

"You mean well, Meg, but I'm fine and nothing's changing around here."

"Things can't stay the same. Stop bein' a control freak. You're movin' on, and we're adjustin'."

"YOU'RE LATE."

Jolie stepped inside of Cassian's outreach center on the far South Side of Chicago. She hadn't made it two steps when Paul appeared out of nowhere and accused her of being late.

"Traffic during rush hour."

Paul scowled. "I find you entirely too reckless. I don't condone this dreadful lie, and I do not trust you. You're hiding something, I feel it."

"Do you ever take a break from being an ass?"

"Do you have decorum?"

Jolie's lips thinned. She had a phone call with Mrs. Lopez earlier. They both had tried the headquarters number, to no avail. It was pissing her off, but that was the fuel she needed. Going through the shell companies ate up a lot of her time, but she finally had a lead. She went through almost twenty pages of Urban Properties–owned properties in the city, and she found an address located in a strip mall. It was progress, but slower than she liked. She didn't have time for Paul's bullshit today.

"I need you to get with the program, Ms. Coldwell. Leave. Give us the recording. For the sake of everyone involved in this charade. We'll figure out something with your so-called engagement."

Jolie sneered at him. "I need you to get off my damn back and let me breathe."

It was a stare down as the front door of the center opened.

Her breath caught as Cassian approached. She'd thought he looked drop-dead fucking gorgeous in his cocktail attire for the fundraising gala. But now? They were going to have to mop her off the ground.

It was her first time seeing him dressed down. Jeans, T-shirt, thin chain and combat boots. Perfect attire for mingling with teenagers. He captured and commanded her attention as his dark eyes swept over Paul to linger on her. She noticed the deep bags under his eyes and dark circles. The sleepy glaze appeared in his gaze before he blinked and it disappeared.

She recognized that look. A bone-gritting exhaustion, but there was no reprieve when so much was expected of you.

She shouldn't care. She was getting exposure and noto-riety from his name. So what if the man ran himself ragged? This marriage would serve as a means to an end for both of them. Pesky feelings need not enter.

You're not that cold, Jolie.

"Paul, Ms. Coldwell." Cassian stood in front of them, and Paul simmered down. *Ass.*

"We're engaged. You don't have to be formal, you know," Jolie told him.

A mischievous look came into his eyes, and that melted her further. His gaze cascaded down her face and over her suit. The mischievousness fled his eyes, replaced with a look she wasn't ready to confront yet. She felt her body respond to his gaze, and pulled the lapels of her jacket closer, focusing on kids drawing on the wall nearby. *Control yourself, Jolie!*

"It's a habit," Cassian noted.

"Break it."

"Like we need more unwanted attention," Paul muttered.

"Causing trouble today, Paul?" Cassian asked.

Jolie snorted loudly, and Paul's eyes were hard.

"Out of this little ragtag party, I'm the last one causing trouble. You remember what I said, Ms. Coldwell."

Her gaze slid back to Cassian, and his head was tilted, observing her and Paul.

"What did you say?" Cassian's voice was crisp.

Paul sniffed, and Jolie cleared her throat. "The usual. Reminding me I'm not wanted."

Cassian's eyes were sharp on Paul, but the older man shrugged and didn't deny it.

"We'll talk later, Paul." Cassian turned to her. "Thank you for coming today. I thought it would be good for you to see what I do here. We're having our weekly guy chat."

"Guy chat?"

"Yeah." He chuckled. "Uh…it's informal. We talk about school, their lives, or whatever wrestler they're obsessed with now. A lot of them are seniors in high school this year, so we're starting the college and trade school talk."

She didn't think he took such an active part in the outreach center. Of course, years ago when she attended the opening of the center, she'd doubted he was going to be doing anything beyond cutting checks.

An effusion of warmth expanded in her chest. "You hang out with the kids?"

"I consider them friends, and I hope it's reciprocated."

He would be an amazing father. Images of him holding a chunky brown baby with a riot of curls and dark eyes hit her. Her biological clock never ticked. Why was she hearing it now?

The sound of heels clacked speedily down the hallway. "Casey? Casey, you finally showed up? Boy, I should tear ya butt up, you so late!" An older Black woman approached. She looked immaculate in an all-white pantsuit that Jolie wondered was the best fit for an outreach center full of kids, cream-colored high heels, and her dark brown hair pressed silky into a bob cut with bangs.

"Hi, Miss Arnell—"

"Don't hi me. You're not too old for me to take you over my knee."

A gentle look passed across Cassian's face as Miss Arnell opened her arms toward him, pulling him into a bear hug and swaying him excitedly from side to side.

"You know you always supposed to see me before you go in." She placed a hand on his cheek, patting it.

"I always make time for you, Miss Arnell."

"As you should. Got me runnin' this place, and these kids about to turn my hair gray." Patting Cassian once more, she released him and turned to Jolie. "Who might this lovely young woman be?"

"I'm Jolie Coldwell, Cassian's fiancée." Jolie offered her hand before Cassian could speak.

Miss Arnell gave her an appreciative look before turning to Cassian.

"I'm glad to see some young woman has finally snatched his heart. I was afraid he was gonna end up a monk. With a height like his, it'd be a shame to lose those genetics in the world."

Cassian grimaced. Jolie instantly loved Miss Arnell. The woman approached her with a hug, which she readily accepted.

"Don't worry, I'm trying to teach him to relax." *Why am I lying?* The older woman's eyes widened.

"Miss Arnell—" Cassian groaned.

"The kids are waiting for you in the classroom."

Jolie followed Miss Arnell and Cassian as they chatted with a sullen Paul trailing behind. On the walls of the hallway were corkboards with announcements and class schedules for subjects like math, science, personal finances, and navigating government health insurance.

Entering the classroom, they were met with the laughter of teenage boys. The desks were arranged in a circle, with some kids sitting on top of them. Others sat in their seats with cell phones out. Miss Arnell gave a sharp whistle, and the kids' faces lit up at Cassian before storming toward him.

"Mr. Cassian!"

They all surrounded him, and he gave a few of them daps. Cassian made it to the center of the room, ordering everyone to their seats. Staying in the back with Miss Arnell and Paul, Jolie watched as the kids sat and waited for Cassian to speak.

"Let's start with our normal check-ins. What's something good that's happened to you since we last met?" Cassian looked around the group.

The kids were quiet, each looking at the other to see who would be brave enough to go first.

"I'll start with something good." Cassian spoke with experienced authority that demanded attention. "I got engaged."

The kids whooped and hollered. Cassian hushed them before turning to her.

"She's here. Meet Jolie."

Fifteen pairs of eyes all turned to the back of the room toward her. She gave a small wave. Several of the youngsters grinned mischievously, and one let out a wolf whistle. "Damn, man, she fine!"

"Maceo," Cassian reprimanded.

"My bad, Mr. C. She's a baddie… How'd you get her?"

Everyone laughed, even Jolie. She made eye contact with Cassian. He returned a smile.

"Mr. C, you got game?" Maceo smirked, leaning back in his seat, and dapped with the boy next to him. "No offense, she doesn't look easy, and you a square." *The kid was right.*

"This isn't an appropriate discussion. Let's move on." Miss Arnell sent Maceo a withering look.

The kids simmered down, and one by one they all reported out the good things that occurred. It ranged from getting paid from their summer jobs, beating a new level on a video game, to getting a text back from a girl.

Cassian was at ease with the boys, and Jolie had to fight to quench the unchecked desire burning within her as he crossed his arms, making his muscles bulge.

"Last time we talked about volunteer opportunities here at the center that you can take advantage of to put on your college application. Did everyone sign up for one?"

"Man, I ain't doin' that shit." A wiry young man in a bright red hoodie waved him off.

Cassian and Miss Arnell tensed, and the teens' eyes widened.

"Why, Malcolm?" Cassian asked.

Malcolm shrugged and crossed his arms. "I'm not going to college."

"You don't have to go to a four-year college. There's community college and trade schools too."

"What I look like wastin' years of my life when I could be makin' money now?"

That launched a few murmurs of agreement, and Cassian frowned.

"You're seventeen. What money are you makin'?"

Malcolm grinned. "My rap career 'bout to set off. I already been in the studio, and I got a thousand followers on IG."

"Your rap career?" Cassian gave Malcolm a doubtful look. "Are you sure?"

"Yeah, I'm sure."

"Gamblin' on making a thrivin' and promisin' rap career is like winnin' the lottery. Many enter, few win," Cassian said.

Jolie respected the way Cassian switched his language, mimicking the pattern of the boys to capture attention. *Perfect politician.*

"You ain't seen the views I got."

Cassian nodded. "I am sure you have them. How many of those views are convertin' into real-life fans? How many of the fans would pay to attend a show you put on? Have you investigated the costs of venues for a performance? What about representation? Merchandising? Licensing?"

"You tryin' to take the fun out of it." Malcolm waved a hand dismissively.

"I'm tryin' to get you to think, Malcolm. If music is what you want, then pursue it, but understand it's a business fore-most. There are celebrities with a college education or equivalent. They don't mindlessly perform. They know their worth, how to charge, and add tax."

The boys laughed, teasing Malcolm, and he flipped them off. Cassian called their attention back.

"You have a brain, and I want you to use it. I also want you to have a backup plan in case things don't work out—"

Malcolm stood up abruptly. "You like my fam, man. Tryin' to kill my dreams and shit."

"I'm sayin' dream, but be smart."

"I need money now. My mama got bills to pay. It's either rappin' or the other way."

The kids fell silent. A tense, solemn recognition of the unspoken truth filled the room. Jolie felt for Malcolm. She knew the hunger to get out of poverty. How suffocating it could be not only to one's mental health, but to one's dreams as well.

"There's nothin' for you in the streets but jail or death." Cassian faced off with Malcolm, and Jolie held her breath.

"It's money."

Cassian's forehead crinkled. "Money isn't everything. If you're tryin' to convince me that the streets are the only way, you must be stupid."

The boys inhaled sharply.

"The only thing you're going to do is end up on a T-shirt and become a forgotten statistic of gun violence in this city, leavin' your mother and friends to mourn you because you made the idiotic decision to play a game that's fixed. The streets will always win. Now and forever."

Cassian didn't wait for Malcolm's reply as his gaze fell on the other boys.

"There's the emergency grant for personal expenses and education. I'll be damned if I catch any of you hangin' on a street corner."

The stern look Cassian gave the boys made them all sit up straighter.

"I'm here. Miss Arnell and others are here to help you succeed. There's no excuse not to get any help. Do you hear me?"

The boys all chorused in agreement, even a deflated Malcolm.

"All right, let's move on."

Malcolm grumbled under his breath but remained quiet. Jolie tried to pay attention to Cassian encouraging the boys to sign up for the bottle drive, but her eyes focused on his lips. She tried not to think about the way they felt against hers. They were as soft as they looked, and his tongue...

Stop thinking hoe thoughts!

It was interesting watching him be himself. No camera. No voters to convince.

"It's great to meet you," Miss Arnell whispered to her. "I was worried that with his work at this center, at his firm, and now the campaign, he would collapse walking."

She turned to Miss Arnell. "What?"

"He's a workaholic. Always has been, even when he was younger, and he's stubborn as hell. He won't listen to nothin' nobody says."

Jolie looked between Miss Arnell and Cassian. This sweet older woman and Cassian were a hodgepodge. "If you don't mind me asking, how do you know Cassian?"

"I was Cassian's high school English teacher. He's always been a bright, bright boy, and it's an honor to see him successful now."

"Really?"

Miss Arnell nodded. "Always kept in touch with me. I love him like I gave birth to him. I retired a few years ago, and he called me up and asked me to help him oversee the kids' education here at the center."

Jolie's brows rose, and Miss Arnell continued, "Yes, girl. Now I'm ready to retire after thirty years—I don't wanna work for nobody no more, but he made a convincin' case. How could I tell him no?"

Jolie glanced at Cassian. His gaze zeroed in on hers and held it.

"Offered me more than what I had been makin' all my career along with benefits. But that wasn't what convinced me. It was his dedication. Birthday parties, holidays, and sports events. He shows up. He tries to get to the boys before the streets do."

Jolie's heart cracked. *Why is he making this hard for me? Why does he have to be a good guy?*

Miss Arnell nodded. "I'm sure you know how easy it is for kids out here to get into bad things. Cassian avoided it, but if it wasn't college, he was going to go to the military to get away from the streets."

Military? What would he look like in a combat gear? Probably sexy.

"He doesn't seem like the military type."

"You know his father, Edward, served in Vietnam. That boy loves his daddy. It was a shame what happened to Edward and Tisha."

Jolie stiffened, and she thought about meeting his parents very, very soon. "The accident?"

Miss Arnell frowned. "I nearly bawled seeing Cassian come into school on crutches. Face bruised and scarred. The cheerful boy I saw was gone, and he was going to go off the rails. Then one day everything changed."

"Changed how?"

"He got back on track. Extremely focused. Pulled his grades up, got a full ride to Morehouse, and he was back in my classroom years later, offering me a job. It's funny how the world turns, isn't it?"

Why couldn't he be an asshole like every other lawyer and politician? Why is he forcing me to see him differently? She had assumed a bunch of negative things about Cassian. How wrong had she been?

"What else does this place do?" Jolie asked.

"After-school and summer academic program. We also offer transitional housing, job training, and some older adult services like transportation—"

"Did you know Miguel Lopez?"

Miss Arnell's eyes widened. "You know Miguel?"

"I'm helping his mother."

"What a shame. He was a nice young man. Cassian took it hard. He was supposed to drive the van that day, but he had to help a client in court."

Jolie thought about the shocked and guilty expression on Cassian's face the day she brought it up.

"He couldn't foresee his stroke, but does Cassian listen? No. He starts a medical emergency fund in Miguel's honor for employees here."

Her entire perception of Cassian was changing, cracking, and peeling away to reveal a man who was selfless and compassionate. Someone who truly wanted to make a change for his community.

"Wow… He started this all on his own?"

Miss Arnell nodded.

Jolie's eyes focused back on him. Is that why he was going to these lengths to become governor? He had this much passion and interest in his community?

Cassian wrapped up the conversation, but many of the kids lingered by his side to ask him questions or share tidbits of personal news. He caught her eyes once more, his dark eyes scouring her frame before his right eyebrow lifted a fraction and he smiled at her, its brilliance rivaling the sun up above. She returned the smile, a little hesitant at first, then relaxed, as she felt a wall within her crack.

fourteen

. . .

J olie leaned against her car in the parking lot outside
the outreach center and watched Cassian and Paul talk
furiously. Why was it Rock, Cassian, and Margarita
could trust her, but Paul couldn't?

Crossing her arms, she rocked her right heeled foot back
and forth. She knew she was charming. Most people loved
her. She wasn't gonna grovel for Paul's acceptance. She'd
vowed to never grovel for anyone's approval ever again. She
was here to stay for a while. Whether he liked it or not.

Cassian's face twisted and Paul's brows dipped. Jolie's
attention was piqued when Cassian hand Paul an envelope.
What is that? Paul nodded and crossed the parking lot quickly
to a shiny gray Cadillac XT5 and peeled out.

Cassian drew closer. "What did you think?"

He knew how good he'd done. She'd play along.

"Standing ovation."

He grinned brightly at her, and she avoided the temptation to smile back.

"What was in the envelope you gave Paul? Seemed
serious."

Cassian's expression coolly shifted from irritation to masked calmness.

"It's a dossier on Martin Gomez." His gaze flickered to the right and back to her. "I don't know much about him, but if he's working for Mayor Charles, I want to know every possible thing."

Jolie gave him a dubious expression. "You couldn't have emailed it?"

"Paul's old school. He's paranoid of being hacked. He'll find the weak spots on Gomez."

Cassian mimicked her stance, leaning on the opposite car.

She changed the subject. "You did well with Malcolm today." Lawyer. Politician. Mentor. *Who else was he?*

He frowned. "I see myself in them, especially Malcolm."

"You wanted to be a rapper?"

A ghost of a smile played at his lips before he shook his head. "No. But I was angry. I'd just turned eighteen when the hit-and-run happened."

Sadness and discomfort filled her body, and she stood up straight. "Miss Arnell said you had it rough after the accident."

Cassian shrugged. "We're lucky Luna was at cheer practice. She's the only one in our family without a scar."

"How do you know she doesn't have a scar? Her family was in a horrific accident, and she'd witnessed the aftermath. Have you ever asked her how she felt?"

Emotional scars are just as painful as physical ones.

A sheepish look passed across his face.

"I take that as a no."

His dark eyes were unreadable as he stepped toward her. "Watching my parents broken and bloodied... My dad had so many tubes in him, he looked dead. I thought they were waiting for us to pull the plug on him."

His hands flexed, a darkened expression clouding his face. Instinctively, Jolie placed her hand on his upper arm.

"I never thought about my parents dying before. It just wasn't something that occurred to me. My parents were so lively. My dad was a soldier. Fear hit me in a way it never had before."

"You were a kid, Cassian. We all think our parents are invincible, but they're human just like us." She started to pull her hand away, but he caught her wrist. She froze as he slowly rubbed his thumb back and forth on her inner wrist, sending sparks through her.

"It's my fault they were in the accident. I didn't want to go to the ma-and-pop restaurant near our house. That's where we always went for dinner when my parents got a little extra cash. I insisted we go somewhere nice. Get dressed up. They humored me, and look what happened."

Her heart began to beat faster. Didn't she insist on no hair-braiding and heart confessions? She should tell him she was sorry for what he'd been through, be polite, and leave, but why couldn't she pull her arm away? Why couldn't she turn and drive off?

"I should have been the one hooked up to machines, fighting for my life."

"Don't say that."

Cassian's eyes were sad. "I started hanging out with the local guys smoking and drinking to forget. My broken leg paled in comparison to my parents. Nothing got rid of the soul-wrenching guilt I deserved. I did it to them."

Jolie closed her eyes and she felt him move closer. *Guilt.* It was a funny thing, being shackled to a ghost of the past with no reprieve. Hadn't she felt that about her mother? Aaron? Wishing she could have done something to change who Aaron had become? Guilt that'd she should have been a better daughter and maybe her mother would love her.

"Is that why you helped Mrs. Lopez with Miguel? It was like history repeating itself?"

"I had a last-minute court hearing. But if I had said no,

Miguel wouldn't have been behind the wheel. He could have been saved in time."

She pulled her hand from his grip and, surprising herself, placed it over his heart, feeling the steady beat.

"You can't take responsibility for every bad thing that happens to the people in your life. That's not healthy."

"That's easier said than done."

"*Do it* with no excuses."

The corner of his mouth tipped up. "Can't give me one, can you?"

"I don't endorse pity parties. I learned a long time ago it doesn't solve anything."

Her body became rigid with memories of her days after she left her mother's house.

It was Cassian's turn to study her. "Your father?"

Jolie wished that was the only reason for the way she'd turned out. Liza Coldwell's grip on Jolie some days felt like the woman was within her skin.

"People assume losing a parent young makes it easier. It's worse. If I was older, I would have memories of him. A recollection of the man he was. I have nothing. He's an enigma in my mind."

The words tumbled out too willingly. The outreach center made her too comfortable with him.

"Your mom didn't tell you any stories about him?"

"She didn't even have a picture of him up. Hell, I don't even know his last name. I wasn't getting a story out of her. When I was sixteen, she had this lockbox under her bed. I broke into it. I found a picture of him. Lamar was his name. If I hadn't, I wouldn't even know what he looked like."

"What about his family?"

Jolie grimaced, pulling away from him, and her back hit her car. "Do you know how many Lamar's exist? If they reached out, I never knew. My mother never told me a word about his side, and I used to want to find them, but I just... didn't."

"Why?"

"Why be hurt again? What if they were"—*what if they rejected me like my mother?*—"people I didn't want to associate with? That would sully his memory. So that's that."

She pinned her gaze on a spot over his shoulder.

"Jolie—"

"I'm done with this conversation now, Cassian."

The lines had to be drawn between them. They had a contract. A means to an end, for both. She wasn't ready to talk about her family with anyone.

"Will your mother come to the engagement party?"

Jolie cut her eyes toward him. "No, she will not. Nor will my brother. I want them as far away from your campaign and me as possible. And no, I don't want to talk about my relationship with them."

The air between them grew tight, hot.

"Who are you, Jolie?" he murmured, his eyes searching hers.

"*Who are you*, Cassian? The lawyer, the politician, or the bleeding heart?"

"Multiple things can be true at once."

The heat flushed across her skin at the silkiness of his words, and flowed between her legs, and she inhaled deeply. The man hadn't even touched her. *Yet.*

"Speaking of the engagement party, but we should talk about the physical boundaries of our relationship." Cassian purred.

"You ask this after kissing me?"

His gaze dipped toward her lips, and back to her eyes. "What are you comfortable with? People are going to expect us to act loving."

"How much acting are you suggesting?"

"Hand-holding. My arm around your waist."

"That's fine." Jolie's voice wavered slightly.

"We'll have to kiss again."

Her heart thudded against her chest as she forced her face to remain impassive. "We've done that."

"On the lips, but here too." Raising her arm to his mouth, he kissed her palm and then the inside of her wrist.

"Really?" she breathed.

Jolie was a rational woman. Never had she let her body override her common sense. Yet here she stood. Flushed. As if she might burst if he didn't touch her again.

"And here," he murmured, pressing forward, trapping her against the side of her car, his mouth close to her ear. He drew back, his lips brushing her cheek.

"I think the cameras would like that," she swallowed the knot in her throat.

Putting his fingers under her chin, he lifted her face. Jolie needed to focus. She was just another link in the chain of his plans. Nothing serious would come from this, and she would be the one left with scars if she allowed him too close.

He cupped her face, caressing her cheek with his thumb. "That's only in public."

"Are you suggesting we...do something in private?"

"That would make our contract difficult. Wouldn't it?"

The air thickened, pushing the parameters of suffocation. He tucked her hair behind her ear. Her heart thundered in her ears as his fingers grazed the side of her face.

He pulled away, leaving her plastered on her car.

"I...I think you're right. Public only. Private off-limits."

Cassian gaze honed on her.

"That's the first time you've agreed with me. I better memorialize this."

Jolie started to speak, but his cell phone rang.

"Give me a moment." Cassian took a step away from her.

Pressing her hands to her belly, she breathed low and

even. *You will not jump into bed with Cassian Anders. It will be a disaster. Do you want to be like Liza?*

The purpose of this deal was to help her career. Not bring a man into her life who distracted her from her goals and possibly ruin her. And Cassian could do that. If she viewed him as a distraction, she could ignore the butterflies in her belly or her mind tempting her to indulge. *Just once.*

"I have to go. Margarita wants me to talk at one of the city colleges on the west side."

Jolie sighed. Cassian yawned loudly as he texted.

"You need to rest."

He flashed her a tired grin. "You're sounding like a concerned wife already."

Jolie raised a brow.

"I'm fine. You focus on chasing your story, and I'll do what I do best."

"Which is?"

He smirked. "Win."

"YOU HAVEN'T STOPPED STARING at her," Paul said flatly.

Guests mingled on the rooftop patio of the Viceroy Chicago as the setting sun illuminated everyone in an orange glow. The clink of champagne glasses, sirens from the traffic below, and laughter filled the air as everyone toasted the couple of the hour.

The wedding planner he'd hired was a miracle worker. In under a month and a half since they announced their engagement, they'd been in nonstop correspondence with Cassian and Jolie, who surprisingly helped, voicing her opinions on the decorations of the party. And now he was witnessing the results.

They had transformed the place into a romantic summer soiree, perfect for welcoming July. Soft flickering candles illuminated the rooftop, and red roses were everywhere, from the tabletops to scattered petals on the floor. The major highlight for the guests was the ten-foot-tall rose flower wall with Jolie's and Cassian's names in glowing, neon light centered in the middle.

"She's my fiancée. I'm expected to stare." Cassian gripped his champagne flute. *Liar*, his mind screamed at him.

Jolie was clad in a white crepe ruffle shoulder dress that molded to her sexy body. Her hair hung in big, silky-looking beach curls well past her shoulders. He was amazed by the way she navigated the room. She smiled and acted like the perfect wife-to-be, tossing flirty glances his way. It took everything in him to keep composed.

"I'm sure Margarita is more than proud." The disgust in Paul's voice was apparent.

Cassian followed his line of sight to Margarita, chatting animatedly with her wife and a director of a nonprofit Cassian worked a case for a few years back.

"Be good tonight," Cassian requested.

Paul's gaze flicked upward. "No father on the birth certificate? Another red flag."

"She can't control that."

"Don't be naïve because you're attracted to her. The woman's bad news."

Jolie hadn't flinched earlier when he'd stroked her arm or he held her close. She returned his flirting with winks and giggles, pressing her lips to his when the crowd demanded another kiss.

"I don't believe she is." She had granted him a moment to truly see her the other day. After years crafting his skills in reading bullshit, he hadn't got that vibe from her. It was real.

"We can't let her ruin what we've built."

Who was the real Jolie Coldwell? He'd seen the hurt in her eyes. He knew what it was like to bury pain so deep it took root in your soul.

"Dig if you want, but my gut tells me she's being honest."

Paul crossed his arms. "She's distracted you. You need to focus on continuing to build your supporters—"

"If we want her to help us sell this marriage and get those supporters, you can't continue to attack her. She's a part of our team now. Relax. Come to Diana's party next week and judge her there."

How could he break her walls? Someone made her this defensive, and he desperately wanted to know who hurt her. He should step away from the budding feelings craving to take root, but couldn't.

"I guess we should be glad she is behaving herself tonight," Paul said, studying Jolie as she spoke with Rock and his wife, Evelyn. "You know what I find weird? She brought her best friend and her boss. Where is her family?"

Defensiveness emerged in his chest for her. "She's not in contact with them."

"No father on the certificate, and not in contact with her family?"

Cassian frowned. "Paul—"

"Skeletons. That woman has many, and it's going to destroy us."

Cassian cleared his throat, taking another sip of champagne.

"Speaking of in-laws, have you mentioned the arrangement to your parents?"

Cassian averted his gaze.

"Why would I do that?"

He already felt like shit, knowing his mother had been talking about the engagement party for weeks and meeting her new "daughter."

"At least you're smart about that. Who is going to be your best man? Surely you don't want to ask me?" There was a lilt of humor in Paul's voice, and Cassian rolled his eyes.

"Rock would kill me. You can be the ring bearer."

Paul chuckled. It'd been a while since he'd laughed with his mentor. He clamped a hand on the Paul's shoulder and shook him.

"You need to laugh more, man."

Jolie turned, catching his eye. She nodded toward the couple and her friend, Helena, before making her way toward him. Standing straighter, he tried to ignore those red, glossy, pouty lips of hers.

"Gentlemen, aren't we supposed to be having a party? Why are you standing by the wall? I know why Paul is." Jolie slid an arm around Cassian's waist, narrowing her gaze on the older man.

"Why am I standing by the wall?" Paul asked, confused.

She tilted her head back to rest against Cassian's shoulder. Amusement flickered in her gaze. "You can't dance."

Cassian laughed as Paul's face went beet-red. He pushed his body closer to hers, pressing a kiss to the top of her head, her rose perfume filling his nose.

"I can dance. I just choose not to."

Jolie goaded Paul. "You don't strike me as the type with rhythm."

"I beg your pardon!"

Paul was about to have an aneurysm, and Cassian squeezed her waist. "Don't antagonize him. The party is going smoothly."

Jolie smirked as Paul glared. "I'm just getting started."

"Is that my baby?"

Cassian's head jerked at his mother's booming voice.

Tisha Anders had on her Sunday best. Low heels, a modest teal dress, and matching cardigan. She had on what some would call her "church Mother's Day hat" complete with flowers and a veil that fell into her face with matching gloves.

"My baby?" Jolie repeated.

Cassian shot her an annoyed look as Jolie grinned.

"This place is fabulous, honey! Is that my new daughter-in-law? Oh my gosh, you are beautiful!" Tisha gushed.

Cassian grimaced as Tisha called Jolie her daughter. He caught Jolie's amusement morph into strain.

"Mama."

Leaning on her cane, Tisha crossed the space toward the couple. His sister followed behind her in a shimmery pink summer dress, holding on to the arm of his father as he moved slowly with his walker. He glanced at Jolie, thinking there would be some type of judgment in her eyes. Instead, they held a disconsolate, faraway look.

Tisha reached out for a hug, her cane wobbling dangerously, and he gently dislodged himself from Jolie to hug his mother.

"Be careful, Mama. Was traffic easy? You let Luna drive, right? How was the spa?" Cassian had sent all his favorite girls for an exclusive all-expenses-paid day at the spa. He glanced at Jolie again, and she plastered on a practiced smile.

"Lovely, lovely. I got to go back. The young man, River, did such a good job. He touched places your daddy ain't touch in years."

Cassian blanched, and Jolie's eyes widened.

"Get over here, daughter-in-law! We're family." His mother pushed him to the side, blazing ahead with open arms for Jolie. Cassian held on to his mother's other side to keep her balance.

"Mama, be careful."

"Look at you! Your skin is gorgeous, and you're smart too. Cassian told us all about you and your work." Tisha brought Jolie into a tight hug.

Jolie stiffened, shooting a glance at Cassian. Slowly she raised her arms, hugging his mother back. "Thank you…"

"Mama, let her go." Cassian gently pulled Tisha back.

"Mrs. Anders," Paul said, giving the older woman a respectful nod.

"Always wonderful to see you, Paul." Tisha beamed.

Cassian gently peeled his mother from her, replacing himself at her side, and she clung to him. "Jolie, please excuse my mother, Tisha Anders. My sister, Luna, and my father, Edward."

"I love the dress, girl!" Luna hugged her before returning to her father's side. "Daddy, meet Jolie."

A chill cut down Cassian's back as he met his father's gaze. Edward gave him a curt nod, which he returned.

"Nice to meet you." Edward offered a handshake instead of hugging her.

Jolie swallowed. "Same to you, Mr. Anders."

"Edward, why do you have to be formal?" Tisha frowned.

"I'm not trying to get all up in the girl's space like you."

"I was not all up in her space. I was welcoming her into our family. First impressions are everything. You remember when I met your mama? Couldn't stand her, rest in peace." Tisha did a motion of the cross.

Cassian sighed.

"Please, not this story again." Luna knitted her brows.

Jolie's eyes flickered between the four of them. She stepped back, but he pulled her closer, forcing her to stay in the circle.

"You both are giving Jolie a terrible impression of us." Cassian frowned.

Luna snorted. "I doubt that, if she agreed to marry you. Have you seen you?"

"Shut up."

"You shut up."

Tisha snapped her fingers. "Not today. We're in public, and we're celebrating."

Edward watched him and Jolie closely. He noticed his father's grip on his walker shook slightly, and he instantly began looking around for a chair.

"Luna, get Dad a chair." Luna nodded and headed toward the tables by the dance floor.

"Are your parents here, Jolie?" Tisha said.

She stiffened in his arms.

Cassian cleared his throat. "They couldn't be here tonight."

"Really? That's too bad."

Luna appeared with a chair, and helped Edward ease himself down slowly. Tisha placed a hand on Edward's back, stroking. Luckily for them, his mother's mind was a hamster wheel.

"Let's talk about the bachelorette party." Tisha grinned.

Luna squealed. "I know some nice strippers with big di—"

"There won't be a bachelorette party. Or strippers." Cassian glared at his mother and sister. The thought of some man grinding on Jolie with his dick in her face made him want to murder someone.

"Boo, you're no fun." Luna pouted.

"Come on, son, let the girl live a little. I had a stripper at my bachelorette party. His name was Diesel, and he had this trick—"

"Tisha, don't make me get out of this seat." Edward sent his wife a look.

Cassian's cheeks flushed. "Why don't y'all find a table, and I'll have the server bring you some hors d'oeuvres? We can talk there. Paul—"

Not needing any encouraging, Paul offered his arm to his mother, and began leading them to an open table.

"Wait, can I get a kiss? I want to post this to Facebook."

Tisha scrambled for her phone out of her purse, and Luna did the same.

Thickness settled in his throat. Jolie turned to him, giving a slight nod as his family huddled around.

Cassian cupped the back of Jolie's neck, bringing his head close to hers. Their eyes locked, and he drew her closer. Her hands wandered over his chest, around his neck, into the hair at the base of his neck. His hand settled on her lower back as he leaned down, pressing his lips to hers. He was a damn addict for her kisses. When he felt her tongue brush his lips, he obliged her. The excited squeals of his sister and mother faded to the background, as desire overrode his logical brain.

"Ain't this a mothafuckin' party?!"

The atmosphere went silent as Cassian pulled away to find a young Black man stepping onto the rooftop with a Colt 45 beer can in his hand and a joint behind his ear. The guards rushed in behind him, grabbing him by the arms, the head of their security detail trailing in after with his hand pressed to his ear.

"Excuse us." The guard nodded at the shocked party.

The man wore low-slung jeans and a wife beater stained with sweat under an open button-up Hawaiian shirt. The guards stumbled over one of the flower vases after he staggered, his beer sloshing over the sides.

"Jolie! Got damn, you mothafuckas are strong!" The young man pulled against the two guards.

Jolie trembled violently against Cassian as the man continued, seemingly uncaring about the attention he was getting. He fought the guards as they tried to pull him out. "Hey! Get your bitch hands off me! I'll knock you the fuck out. Where you at, Jolie? Jay?"

Several of the guest stirred and whispered, and Jolie took a step from him. He heard the sharp intake of breath from his mother, and his father grumbled something unintelligible.

The man squinted, looking around the crowd before his eyes fell on Jolie and Cassian. He grinned and pointed.

"Found ya mean ass! That's my sister! I'm allowed to be here. Tell them, Jay." He dropped his weight, sending him and the guards to the floor before they caught themselves.

"Shit, I'm sorry, Cassian," Jolie muttered, not looking at him or his family.

Cassian grabbed her arm, turning her to face him. "You know that guy?"

"That's my brother. Aaron."

fifteen

. . .

B rother? Cassian glanced at Paul. His expression said *I told you so*, but he ushered Cassian's parents away from the drama unfolding. Jolie's expression shifted from shock and embarrassment to annoyance as he signaled for the DJ to play music once more.

Jolie marched toward her brother. Cassian grabbed her hand, forcing her to stay by his side. She stared at their entwined hands before fixing her gaze on her brother.

Cassian nodded to the guards to drag him back into the hallway and pinned his head of security with a glare.

"I'm sorry, sir. He attacked a guard and ran past him into the elevator. We were on it as soon as possible."

"This is completely unacceptable." Looking the young man up and down slowly, Cassian noticed the barest of resemblance between him and his sister.

"Aaron, what the hell do you think you're doing here?" Jolie stepped forward, glaring at her brother.

Cassian motioned for the guards to let him go.

"What's this? You got a party and shit goin' on." He flung out his arms, splashing some of his beer onto the floor. "You ain't tell Mama or me you were gettin' married. You that cold-hearted of a bitch not to invite family."

"Watch your mouth," Cassian snapped. The young man stumbled back from the intensity of Cassian's stare before looking him up and down with a smirk.

"This the corny-ass dude you're marryin'? Shit, you can do better. I didn't know you were getting' married till I was scrollin' on Instagram and saw you two. Fucked up, sis."

Jolie pushed Cassian behind her. "I don't want to know how you found this party. Get out of here, Aaron."

He waved away her demand. "I came to wish you blessin's and all that happy shit."

"I think it's time for you to go." Cassian grabbed Aaron by the arm, and the young man knocked his hand off.

"I don't know you like that, bruh."

Before Aaron could protest, Jolie pushed her brother farther into the hallway near the bathroom as he stumbled along, complaining and cursing the entire time.

"I don't want to talk to you, Aaron."

"I apologized. Damn, you want a mothafucka on his knees beggin' you for forgiveness, and I'm ain't gon' keep doin' it —" Aaron groaned loudly, leaning back against the wall as he gulped down beer, some spilling from the corners of his mouth.

"Leave. You weren't invited."

Regardless of what Cassian felt about Jolie, he couldn't have a violent, drunk brother causing unnecessary problems. This whole engagement and marriage was for his *campaign*.

"You think homeboy would still want to be with you if he knew the truth?" Aaron turned to him with a calculating eye. "God knows if you'll still want to fuck her."

Cassian's frown deepened as Aaron laughed. Now, Cassian had a growing list of reasons to beat this dude's ass, the first being how he treated his sister, *his fiancée*, but for his general disrespect of his family and guests in attendance. "You need to go."

"Tell him, Jolie."

Shit, we cannot have this. What if reporters outside saw him?

"Go," Jolie seethed.

"I ain't goin' nowhere. You in this fancy place with these rich people, lookin' down your nose at Mama and me like we didn't live in the same neighborhood. All the money and changin' your name can't erase your past."

Cassian's heart thudded as he recalled her revelation of her name. He pressed a hand to her back, offering comfort.

Jolie crossed her arms. "I told him about the charge, but I did not change my name for that reason. And it's never been about money, Aaron."

The guards stood, antsy, at the end of the hall, waiting for Cassian's signal.

"You left… *You left me* at seventeen and never came back. You abandoned your brother, your family, and now you gonna live all high and mighty like this—"

"Mama kicked me out!" Jolie's voice broke, laying a splayed-out hand against her chest. Cassian took a step closer to her.

"That's a damn lie. You left and never said goodbye. You're still pushin' me away!" Aaron slammed the can to the ground, making Jolie jump back.

The beer sloshed over her heels, and Cassian advanced forward, ready to haul his ass out of there.

Jolie blocked him, pressing her body against his front as if she was holding him back, but avoided looking at him, her face twisted. He wanted to pick her up and move her to the side to handle him, but this was her brother. He bowed to her demand, but was ready if Aaron got too fucking crazy.

"Aaron, are you not listening to me?"

The sounds of the engagement party back in full swing drifted down the hall.

"You need to get yo' life together and stop lyin' all yo' damn life." Aaron kicked the can down the hall. "Your lovely fiancée here got caught shoplifting from the store."

Cassian hated that Jolie's head fell slightly. Her hands clenched into fists. Despite her earlier warning, Cassian placed a hand on her back.

"I know that."

"The whole story? I doubt she told you what happened after."

Jolie shook her head. "Since you want to air out my business, tell him why I was stealing."

Aaron faltered for a second as Jolie's sharp gaze never left his face. "Tell him, Aaron."

"'Cause you wanted to steal!"

"It was because Mama decided she wasn't going to buy me any pads. Fucking pads for her sixteen-year-old. Do you want to know why? She loves you, but she's never loved me."

Cassian inhaled sharply. To go to your parent, who's supposed to love, protect, and provide, only for them to reject you? That was a disgusting mindset for her mother to have.

Aaron shook his head, wagging a finger at her. "Mama didn't say that."

"You and her hate the idea despite what she did, I'm thriving. I always will, and I hope that eats your damn hearts up." Jolie's muscles jumped under her skin, visible sweat appearing on her forehead.

"You shoulda listened to her. Maybe she would love you more." Aaron's voice was weak as he stumbled back into the wall, sliding down slightly.

Jolie pushed a finger in Aaron's chest. "She should have been a parent! Why should a child have to convince their parent to love them?" A lone tear fell from Jolie's eye. She wiped it fast. "Don't you dare show up on my day—*on my fiancé's day*—claiming I should be ashamed of my past. Or of not inviting someone who's never loved me."

"Mama would love you if—"

"Nothing will make her love me."

Aaron glared at the opposing wall rather than Jolie. Cassian placed his hands on her shoulders to bring her back.

"It's always been about her, and what she feels. Or what you feel, Aaron. No one gave a *damn* about my feelings or my needs in that house. Even now, this scene is about *you*," Jolie shouted.

Cassian pulled Aaron into his arms. "You need to leave." He motioned toward the guards, and they came rushing down the hall.

Aaron glared at him, some sobriety in his drunken eyes. The two guards yoked him up.

"You left after that." Aaron's voice was ice. "You left me and didn't speak to me for years. You ignore me now. What type of sister are you?"

"And what type of brother are you?"

"One that wishes he wasn't related to you."

Cassian had enough. At a tilt of his head, the guards hauled Aaron down the hall. The head of security pressed for the elevator, and it appeared immediately.

Jolie stood there staring at the space Aaron had occupied, her hands going to her knees as she inhaled and exhaled deeply.

"It's okay," Cassian tried to comfort her, and she pushed him away.

"Please...don't. I'm fine. *I'm fine.*" Jolie muttered the words repeatedly, the tears spilling from her eyes. "Why can't I get away from them? I'm strong. I'm strong—"

A cry broke through, and Cassian ignored her dismissal, pulling her into his chest. She clung to him.

"Let it out, baby, I'm here. You have me."

Jolie shook her head, her voice muffled. "I don't want you to see me like this. Let me go."

She fought against him, and he cupped the back of her head, cooing softly to her till she settled down from fighting.

"Cry."

An emotional knot formed in his chest as she hit his chest with a weak fist. Then he felt a sob rack her body, and she buried her face in his chest.

"You're not alone anymore, Jolie. I'm here whenever you want to talk. We're family now."

His campaign came to mind again, but he put that to the side for now. They'd spin things if anything popped up in the media.

The laughs and steady beat of the music settled like a wet blanket over them. Her body trembled until her cries quieted down. He heard soft sniffles then silence, the beer tacky under their feet.

There was no fucking way he would leave her now. She had him. His parents, Luna, Rock, Margarita, and even Paul's mean ass. This arrangement was temporary, but he couldn't abandon her like her family had. He was her family. That was a vow.

sixteen

. . .

"You're being dramatic. Just talk to Cassian. He's not going to judge you," Helena said as Jolie stepped out of her car, balancing her phone on one shoulder.

"I would rather die."

It was only noon, but the place looked closed. *This should be the address.* The strip mall address was strange for a company reporting over five hundred thousand in income last year. To the right of the office was a liquor store with old men loitering outside, bottles and cigarettes in hand. On the other side was a beauty supply with half of the letters illuminated on the sign above, and farther down, a fish and chicken restaurant. Potholes and trash littered the lot, making the place feel even more desolate and unkept.

"He saw you cry. So what? You've avoided him for a week now."

Aaron's ass was lucky that the only thing that appeared in the press was a report of a mild "scuffle" with a drunk bystander. That's all Aaron would be in her life now. A bystander.

"He probably wouldn't see me till we were walking down the aisle if Rock hadn't invited me to his daughter's birthday party." Right before her life imploded, she'd had a great conversation with Rock and Evelyn. "He saw me cry, Lena. I hate that shit so much."

A lump formed in her throat, and she blinked rapidly to stop the tears from coming. *Don't you cry again.*

There was the slam from a cabinet through the phone. "You're human, and you cry. You're gonna be married to this man. Will it hurt you to trust him? Has he run away yet?"

He hadn't. In fact, he'd reached out to her every day. Sent her a bouquet of two dozen red roses to her office with a simple message: *I'm here.*

"He hasn't…"

Her instincts screamed she should keep her distance. He saw her behind her well-placed walls, and she didn't know how to reclaim her power again.

"You are marrying this man to help him get into office—" Helena's voice lowered. "He's trusting you with this secret. He's told you about his family. Give him the chance. Don't reject him just so he can't reject you."

I don't know how to let him. Not when I've been forced to show him something I haven't revealed to the men I've dated in the past.

Jolie clutched the phone tighter. "Shut up."

"I'm right. Have you given that man some yet? That could sweeten the deal. I mean, he deserves it for staying with you all night with your mean ass."

She'd spent the last fourteen years being strong. How could she break and let Aaron get to her. What did Cassian think of her now? That she was some broken charity case with mommy issues? Would he want to fix her like he was fixing the boys at his center?

Walking up to the abandoned-looking storefront, she tugged on the door handle. Locked. Peeking through the dirty glass of the front door, she saw some chairs and a desk for a waiting area but no other obvious sign of life.

"It's not the time to talk about sex."

Jolie needed all her blood in her head. He'd taken her home after the engagement party. Helped her out of her dress. He helped her remove her makeup. Waited patiently while she showered before he lay in bed with her till eventually she fell asleep.

She'd never fallen asleep with a man before.

They were moving too fast. He didn't have to comfort her in private. That wasn't a part of the deal. He was encroaching on her space she heavily guarded.

It was unnerving, waking in the morning to his cologne clinging to her sheets. Or finding he'd made her breakfast and kept it warm in the oven for her.

He was making it really fucking hard to keep her walls up.

"Come on! It's obvious between you. You know you want to. You were eye-fucking him like crazy at the party."

"I was admiring him in his suit."

Helena snickered. "You wanted to sit on his face, didn't you?"

It was much easier to kiss him and compartmentalize it as her required duty. The emotional involvement was deeper than she'd expected, especially after his family had welcomed her like she was one of their own. He had the family she used to dream of.

How could she fit into this idyllic family when she'd never experienced that?

Your promotion. Mrs. Lopez. Beating Travis.

She needed this deal, and as much as it killed her to think of Tisha being disappointed once they divorced, she couldn't walk away now. She had to put on her big girl panties and toughen up. She only prayed Cassian forgot about that night.

Most importantly, how could she keep her emotions detached when things were tumbling fast?

Helena was right. The sexual tension was there. Sex was easy. It was giving your body to the other, then you wiped your hands and walked away. Sharing emotions? That created a bond. From the heat in his eyes and his assessing gaze that crawled over her body every time they were in the room, she doubted she'd have any complaints if she slept with him. But she couldn't allow him closer than that.

Having someone know your weaknesses was like giving them a loaded gun to put to your temple. Relying on a man? That was the worst. Cassian knew and saw too much already.

"Ha! You're fantasizing now."

"Get the hell off my line—"

"You look like you need some help, young lady." An older Black man with wiry gray hair approached her, a cigar on his bottom lip. He inspected her from head to toe. "Don't look like you live around here."

"I gotta go, Lena." Jolie dug into her pocket for her business card, handing it to the man. "I'm looking for Urban Properties. This is supposed to be the place."

The man laughed loudly. "You another sucka that got scammed?"

"Scammed?"

"Yeah, doggy. You're the fifth person up here today."

She reached into her pocket for her recorder and notepad. "Do you mind if I ask you a few questions?"

"Shit, I got a few seconds. Call me Blue."

"All right, Blue, my name is Jolie Col—"

"Why that sound familiar?" Blue scratched at his beard as he squinted at the card.

"I'm a reporter with Channel 12."

"Hot damn! I know you!" Blue wagged his finger at her as if he solved the mystery. "You be on the news on the weekends. I seen you all cuddled up with that young cat runnin' for governor!"

Jolie tucked a strand of hair behind her ear. "Let's focus on this place."

"He's a nice-looking young man, ain't he?"

Jolie smiled at the man. Blue reminded her why she loved hitting the beat. She got to be around real, hardworking people. The opposite of what Aaron accused her of.

"Yes, he is. Blue, Urban Properties?"

"Talk like he's gonna make some sort of change."

"Cassian will do what he promised." Jolie cleared her throat. "Start with telling me about this scam?"

"Maybe a few months ago, a bunch of rich-lookin' white folks came through, passing out flyers for a few apartments. Stuff like that. Real cheap too." Blue scratched his belly. "I ain't believe the shit the moment I saw it. They offered discounts if you were on public aid."

Jolie's bullshit meter was going off like crazy.

"I know when I'm bein' fucked." Blue patted his pockets and pulled out a pack of cigarettes and a lighter. "Tried to tell them people, but they had a line out the front door the day they opened to fill those apartments."

A pensive look passed across Blue's face as he lit the cigarette and inhaled deeply, blowing out a cloud of smoke.

"Bought most of the buildings on 63rd and 64th Street too. They put up some playgrounds, gardens, and shit, then *poof.*" Blue flicked his cigarette's ashes. "My buddy Albert got him a spot right there." Blue pointed at an apartment complex across the street. It was above a barbershop with a faded blue awning. "The inside of that place? You might as well be living outside."

"That bad?"

"Damn right. They just painted over the walls to make it pretty. Carpet is old and stained. Water's cold. Bed bugs runnin' rampant."

Jolie's anger rose.

"He called the landlord, a greasy, shady-lookin' guy.

Finally, he sent somebody, but the guy ain't know what the hell he was doin'! Then he turns around and raises the rent. Some could manage, but others couldn't. Albert ain't have a choice 'cause he got priors."

"What'd he do?"

"Armed burglary in '78. The man's been clean since, but don't nobody wanna rent to a felon."

"But Urban Properties would. What's the landlord's name?" Jolie pressed her lips together.

Blue nodded. The picture was still blurry, but clear. Urban Properties was preying on the poor and working class, and those with records. To do what? Drive them out of the area?

"Leo...Leroy or Leonard. I know his last name is Gambino. He left when rent got raised. One complex down the block is nearly empty now, but the rent was three times it was before."

She quickly jotted down the name, excited about the break.

"You see, they put up an organic grocery store right there." Blue pointed a little way down the block. "A bunch of different franchises popped up. Restaurants and bars. It's more police drivin' 'round here too. I give it six months before they buy this whole mall, tear it down, and build a spa or gym."

Jolie turned to look at the outdoor shopping mall. Blue was right. It was like the last bit of the old West, a relic of the past trying to remain in the present.

"Mayor Charles promised all kinds of shit to revitalize this neighborhood. She ain't done shit."

Her introduction with the mayor of the city was brief, but her instincts screamed the woman wasn't who she portrayed herself to be. *I'm on your ass, Mayor Charles. Urban Properties too.*

"She don't care 'cause she got the rich people votin' her into office."

161

"That's not right," Jolie said. Now she was pissed. If there was one thing she hated, it was a bully, and she wasn't gonna let Mrs. Lopez, the tenants, or Albert be another victim forgotten.

"What can we do about it, other than survive?"

Jolie wished she had the money to take back this neighborhood. Make it a safe and vibrant place for working-class individuals, families, and children.

"I'm gonna do something about it."

Blue raised a brow and laughed. "What you gonna to do?"

"Do you think your friend Albert would speak with me?"

Blue looked at her with curiosity and a bit of respect.

"Pass my information to any other tenants that have been affected by Urban Properties. Tell them I want to get their stories."

"Albert is home. You wanna talk to him now?"

Jolie nodded. "Lead the way."

JOLIE WATCHED Cassian lift Diana to twirl her around in a helicopter motion. A line of kids laughed and screamed, waiting for their turn.

"Again!" Diana screamed as he set her down.

"Who's next?" Cassian sounded winded as a little blond boy held up his hands toward him.

Diana's birthday party was in full swing. Jolie sat at an empty picnic table closest to the fence and out of the mix of the party. She hated that her body reacted before her mind. She thought Cassian was sexy and at ease at the center, but seeing him right now in a sweat-plastered T-shirt soaked to his body, showing off wide shoulders and a solid chest? The familiar coil of desire filled her belly. *I hate when Helena is right.*

His dark eyes found hers. They warmed immediately, and she offered a tentative smile.

Why are you more scared of him than he is of you? You have an audio recording of him that could destroy him. I plan on giving it to him on the wedding... Just in case anything happens and we don't make it to a wedding.

Cassian broke from the horde of children. His party hat was tilted to the side. Breathing heavily, he cocked his head, getting closer, and smiled. "A butterfly?"

Evelyn insisted the moment she entered the backyard party to get her face painted. He cupped her chin gently, tilting her head side to side as he took in the neon pink, yellow, and green wings painted on her face.

"Evelyn is persistent, and I was feeling wired off punch."

"I love it." Cassian's voice was gruff.

Jolie dropped her gaze. Focusing on the ground, she kicked at a stray piece of confetti trapped in the grass.

Stop being scared.

"Can I get the same thing?"

"What about your beard?"

He stood. "I'm sure she'll make it work."

Ten minutes later, he had a matching butterfly on his face as he sat next to her.

"You're ridiculous."

"You gonna stop avoiding me now?"

Here we go.

Jolie fixed her gaze on the table, tracing an indentation in the wood.

"I wasn't avoiding—" She stopped at the way his brow rose. "I was. It's... Cassian. I'm embarrassed."

"There's nothing wrong with being vulnerable."

"I don't like it. I can take care of myself. I've always done it."

Her heart raced as Cassian observed her for several seconds. "Stop that."

"What?"

An itchiness built under her skin. She picked at the skin around the bed of her nail, pulling at it. Cassian reached over, grabbing the hand she was fidgeting with, and heat erupted as he intertwined his fingers with hers.

"Just talk. I'm not here to judge." Cassian met her eyes, the intensity in his making her breath catch.

Jolie dropped her gaze, a light sheen in her eyes as his thumb rubbed back and forth slowly.

"Whatever you think that has you feeling like I look down on you, stop it. I don't... I—I know what it feels like to not be in control of a situation. You know how I told you about the attorney general and my parents' accident? I keep finding more and more about it, and it just... I can't believe how much he's gotten away with."

"What do you want to do to him?"

Cassian's eyes were cold. "I want to ruin the man like he did us."

"Cassian..." Jolie inhaled sharply.

"That's what my mind tells me but...I can't forget and I can't forgive. I don't want to risk my campaign but I can't let this go. Criminal charges need to be pressed, and he needs to be stripped immediately of his title. He's lucky he's still walking this fucking earth."

Cassian exhaled deeply, running his hand through his hair.

"I would never tell you to do that but... Have you talked to your parents about it?"

He stared at their feet. "My father knows. My mother and sister don't."

"Why?"

His lips thinned.

"My dad wants to let it go. I can't. It hasn't been too long since I started looking into it for myself, pulling favors from people, and right as I get nominated, I find out it's him."

Jolie leaned forward, sliding her hand across his. It was too late to take back her act of tenderness, and he gripped his hand.

"The guilt's still controlling you."

"You can't expect that if I win governor, I'm going to be able to work closely with Kinsella? That won't fucking happen." Cassian's words were cold, and Jolie swallowed.

"If your family's moved on—"

"I need this, Jolie. I have to fix it, and there's no other way than by removing him. By becoming governor and getting that power. His cover-up runs too deep."

"Is that why you wanted to become governor all along? Vengeance?"

Unease filled her chest as he removed his hand from hers. *Is he just like the politicians' I've exposed? Shady?*

His gaze fixed forward. "Never. It's always been about helping and protecting people. There's only so much I can do as a lawyer and a rich guy. How much more can I keep pouring into the center, into my clients, if the laws are fixed to screw them? I have to start there, and now throwing in Kinsella... The system's protecting him, so I have to change the system."

"You should hate me. I could ruin your entire campaign and stop you from helping people yet you want to...reveal these things to me? Get to know me?" Jolie murmured.

"We're a team now. We have to trust each other."

She took a deep breath and made a decision. *Don't do it. Protect yourself.* "I got arrested and charged for shoplifting," she began. Jolie closed her eyes briefly, reimaging the shame and terror she felt when the clerk caught her walking out of the store. "It's not something I'm proud of. My mother and I, once I hit puberty, we could not get along."

Her brows drew down into a frown.

"She was never the warm and fuzzy mom before then. At thirteen, she told me I had to pay my own phone bill. I got a job babysitting to afford it. As I got older, I had to put money in for groceries, the light bill, and gas. She blamed me for whatever went wrong, especially if it was about Aaron."

How long she wept for that sixteen-year-old girl who'd been abandoned by her mother and her family, she couldn't say. Cassian stiffened against her.

"If Aaron needed anything, especially something of mine, she expected me to give it to him. I was forced to be a second parent to him. Every little thing fell on me. Any money I got, she took. I could never get ahead. I learned not to ask my mother for anything. I always had to give her something in return." Jolie sighed, leaning back as she rubbed her palms up and down her thighs. Cassian placed a hand on her right hand.

"My life didn't matter to my mother. She called it learning to be tough. She didn't want me being a woman depending on a man, while she turned around and did the same thing over and over again. Fucking hypocrite." Jolie swallowed, finally meeting Cassian's eyes. "I had a boyfriend. I kept it a secret because she didn't want me to date."

Her heart rattled in her chest as she forced herself to recount the story.

"I was having sex with my boyfriend, but we always used protection. My mom's friend caught me getting out the back of his car one night and told her. She yelled at me all night, calling me horrible names, but she didn't throw me out the house yet."

Her breath snagged in her lungs. She glanced at him. Compassion. Tenderness. Sorrow. No pity.

"You didn't deserve that."

"I had really terrible, irregular periods when I was younger. I got awful cramps one day, and bled so heavily it went through the pad. I told her I needed to go to the emergency room. She wouldn't take me." Jolie laughed dryly.

She stuttered at the next part. It was too much to bare herself, and everything screamed at her to get the hell up and walk away. Cassian sensed it, holding her hand tighter. She briefly closed her eyes.

"I had paid my mom for my phone bill, and she asked for extra for lights too. I didn't have any money. I needed thicker pads, and I didn't know of any other way—"

"Baby, no," he objected fiercely, his brows drawing down in a dark frown as he leaned closer. She opened her eyes, and his face was close to hers. "You were a child. You should have never been put into that predicament."

"She came up to the precinct and made a fucking scene, Cassian. Talked down to me while everyone watched. We got in the car, and she said to me, 'What would your daddy think, huh? He's dead and rolling over in his grave at the disappointment you are.' I snapped. I'd asked her for years to tell me about my father. Or give me a last name to find his family, and she turns it on me? We were screaming. She told me to get out of her life. I got out of the car and never came back."

Why did I tell him? Why, why, why. I'm fucking stupid.

"You've been on your own since?"

"It wasn't hard. I'd been alone for a while." Jolie's voice dropped.

"Will you look at me?" Several heartbeats passed before she could return her gaze to him. He circled a hand around her nape, a thumb stroking the side of her neck while the other hand continued to cup her face. "I admire your strength."

He didn't judge you.

"You proved your mother wrong. You go hard for those in need. You don't take shit, and you're one of the most honest and trustworthy people I've come to know. You have a thriving career." He paused, his eyes roaming her face. She leaned in closer to him, her walls shaking and trembling. "I'm sorry you lost your father. I'm sorry your mother didn't protect you. I'm sorry that you've had to grow this tough shell in order not to feel like that scared sixteen-year-old girl again."

She leaned forward, pressing her lips to his.

He smelled so damn good. Her hands came up to wrap around his neck. She bit back a moan as his hands encircled her waist.

Jolie put everything she couldn't say into the kiss. Gratitude. Relief.

Heat and desire drove away sorrow and hurt. He pulled her closer, lifting her legs over his thighs, and she felt her heart in her throat with his crotch pressed into hers.

"This is a child's birthday party!" Evelyn shouted across the lawn, causing everyone to look over. Jolie ducked her head in embarrassment as Cassian's body vibrated with laughter.

"Sorry, Lyn," Cassian yelled back. Jolie couldn't look up. She was about to bust it open at a child's birthday party. *Help me.*

"You free tonight?" she whispered in his ear, leaning back. His butterfly was a smeared mess of paint on his face.

"Yeah." He shifted, removing her legs from over his thighs. His hands rested on her upper thighs, rubbing slow circles to soothe her.

"Want to come over?"

Cassian paused for a beat. "Are you sure?"

"Yes."

The party flew by in a flash of confetti and ice cream. Once the birthday girl made everyone sing to her twice, Jolie and Cassian said goodbye, him following behind her in his car. Fantasies of Cassian marking her body with pleasure made her press harder on the pedal. She turned onto her street and was met with flashing red lights and fire trucks, ambulances, and police cars. Her neighbors stood in front of the building.

She jumped from her car, and sprinted across the street, looking all around.

"What happened? Is someone hurt?"

Her neighbor who lived below her said, "The building flooded."

seventeen

. . .

The crowd erupted into shouts of protest as their landlord said, "The main water line broke on the top floor. We're going to have to shut down the building."

The residents exclaimed at once, their words a buzz of noise.

"We pay all this money in rent, and this happens?"

"Who's going to replace my stuff?"

"I will sue the hell out of you."

The landlord shushed the crowd. "Due to water getting into the electrical system, the building must be evacuated. I'm sorry."

People booed. The landlord tried to answer the barrage of questions, and Jolie rubbed her temples as Cassian's voice rose above the noise.

"Being evacuated from their homes is an inconvenience. How long will the building be uninhabitable, and what accommodations will be in place for residents?"

That quieted the crowd. "It's still not clear how long it will take to get everyone back in. We'll have an engineering crew come in the morning."

An older man with a cane raised it above his head and shouted, "Cut the bullshit! How long?"

"We'll book accommodations in local hotels as long as there is availability, and we will keep you updated every step of the way. For now, we'll go floor by floor to allow you to collect what things you can."

The landlord and the firefighters had to step to the side to avoid being run over by the crowd stampeding to get inside. The walls and ceilings down to the carpeted hallways were all sodden, squishing underneath Jolie's feet as she headed to her unit.

Her apartment wasn't extremely flooded, but the hardwood floor was damaged. She packed quickly, and what couldn't fit into her Mini Cooper was placed in Cassian's car.

She didn't trust the landlord not to put them up in a Motel 6, so she sat in her car and searched for local hotels on her phone as Cassian closed his trunk.

"Everything's secured." Cassian bent to peer in her driver's-side window.

"I'm going to go to a hotel—"

"Are you crazy?"

"This is my problem, and I have money, Cassian."

He exhaled deeply. "Didn't we already have this discussion?"

Jolie huffed and stared forward into the dark street. "I don't want to intrude on your space."

"You're not staying at a hotel."

"We planned for me to move in *after* the wedding."

He gave her an intense look, and she felt herself get run over with *feelings.* Icky, sticky, gooey feelings, all without him lifting a finger.

Give up control. Just this once. "Fine. Only for tonight."

"Was that hard?" He leaned forward, giving her a peck on the lips before jogging to his car.

Forty minutes later, she was parked in front of Cassian's

gorgeous townhome in Lincoln Park. There was no reason for her to be nervous, but as she helped Cassian carry her things inside, she realized that it would only be the two of them. In close proximity.

"That's the last one." Cassian maneuvered through her pile of bags by the front door.

"Your place is beautiful, Cassian."

His gaze held her hostage, heavy-lidded and intense. "It's our place now."

"I'll only be here for a while."

"You don't need to feel like a guest here. It'll be as much your home as mine."

Her mouth dry, she murmured an agreement as heat crawled up her spine. The darkening of his eyes sent a thrill through her as he headed down the hallway. "Let me give you a tour."

The place was a mix of uber-modern and rustic décor with a limestone façade and rounded dormer windows. The kitchen belonged in a Michelin-star restaurant. Strolling behind him, she was more distracted by admiring his wide back flexing than the extra home office she could use.

The only awkwardness, if there was any, was the sleeping arrangements.

"The guest rooms are crowded with my campaign things right now. I'll clean that out in the morning, but you can have my bed tonight. I'll sleep on the couch."

"The couch's too small for you. We can share the bed. I don't snore." *What the hell are you saying?* Jolie clasped her hands together and shrugged. "If you want."

Cassian stared at her for several blinks before he nodded slowly.

"Yeah… That's fine."

They still had the stupid face paint on their faces.

"All right then, bed? You want to shower first, or should

I?" Jolie's voice was shrill as she brushed past him, savoring the feel of his body against hers.

Awareness settled between them, and she could feel the heat of his eyes on her ass as she climbed the stairs.

Jolie took the quickest shower ever as Cassian waited outside the bedroom while she used his en suite. She had a razor, and though most of the mood had been ruined by the flood, it wouldn't hurt *not to*.

She quickly finished in the bathroom, then hopped into his bed in a silk slip she feared was trying too hard. She placed her hands on either side of her and smoothed out the sheets, and ran a hand over her ponytail.

"I'm ready," she called.

The door opened. She felt a lurch of excitement within her as Cassian entered barefoot. The corner of his mouth turned up at her bundled in the sheets.

"Comfortable?"

"Just like home."

Her fingers flexed on the sheets as she watched him pull at the belt buckle of his jeans. Holding her breath, he unfasten his belt, sliding it slowly from his waist. Her mouth went dry as he lifted the bottom of his shirt and removed it in a flourish.

"I'll be a minute."

Undeniable desire raced through her veins. Her eyes traveled over the smooth, hard lines of his abdomen that looked chiseled by Michelangelo himself. Her reply was stuck in her throat as she watched the door softly close.

Jolie was playing with fire, but that didn't stop the curiosity that had been awakened. She'd had sex before—some good, some bad, but nothing that rocked her world. From the way he kissed her, passionate and demanding, Cassian would humble her between the sheets and leave her weak and invigorated.

What would it feel like for those muscles to comfort and

cradle her? She'd need to retain pieces of herself for when the inevitable split happened so she wouldn't be broken by it.

The lull of the shower, mixed with the long day, made her lids droop. She faintly heard the door to the bathroom open. The covers lifted, the bed dipped, and she felt the warm heat emanating from Cassian's body next to her.

Immediately her eyes opened. He exhaled deeply, eyes on the wall ahead.

"My mom wants to take you wedding dress shopping."

She cleared her throat, his nearness kindling a fire. "She doesn't have to."

"I told her that, but she demanded time alone with you. Luna will be there too."

Going dress shopping with his mom wasn't part of the plan. I'm supposed to keep my distance from them.

"I'll just tell her you're not interested."

She frowned. "I'll look like the bad guy."

Cassian turned to face her. "If you're not comfortable with it—"

"No, I'll go. I like your mom and sister. I can bring Helena too."

Jolie should be strong. Tell him no and keep herself far away from his family. But the selfish part of her wanted to experience what being immersed in a family that loves each other feels like, even for a short time.

Cassian smiled. "She'll like that."

They both returned to their backs, staring at the ceiling. Jolie's body felt a powder keg of anticipation, lust, and excitement.

"Good night." His voice was a dark, husky whisper.

"Night."

No emotions involved. If you give in, only give your body. Keep your emotions unattached.

Pushing herself up to her elbows, she circled one arm around Cassian's neck, pulling him over her.

She laughed loudly as he smirked slightly before she gasped. Her legs parted, and the unmistakable bulge straining against the front of his boxers pushed against the satin thong she wore. She wiggled, rubbing her pussy against his stiff dick, and he released a soft groan. His mouth took hers in a long, deep kiss. She moaned as his tongue touched hers and explored her taste. She savored the delicious way his lips moved on hers.

"Cassian..." Jolie exhaled breathlessly as his lips trailed down her throat.

Her eyes fluttered closed at the delicious friction of her slip brushing against his chest, causing her nipples to ache.

"Shh." He caressed her breast, kneading, teasing, as his thumb circled her nipple and she choked on a scream. He'd barely touched her, and she felt like a live wire. Curling her legs around his waist, she pulled him closer. The thick ridge of his erection rubbed against her sex, mimicking fucking but not giving her any satisfaction. She wanted it fast and hard. Rough and gritty. She wanted all of him.

"So fucking sexy..." He placed kisses down her chest before he tugged at her slip, taking one nipple into his mouth.

Jolie inhaled sharply. Rocking her hips against him, she dragged his erection down her cleft, stirring the heat in her loins. All he had to do was remove the little thong and send them both into paradise.

Releasing her breast, he sat back, watching her every move with rapt attention as his hand traveled down her side and over the flare of her waist.

"Hurry up. I need you to touch me," she demanded. Her stomach flip-flopped as his natural masculine scent, mixed with the freshness of his soap, filled her nose. She couldn't wait any longer. If he didn't move faster, she would snap.

Cassian laughed. "Relax."

Relax? He's fucking joking. His finger brushed the inside of her thigh, gliding over the crotch of her thong.

"Cassian—" she gasped, releasing him briefly as his fingers pressed snug against her pussy. *Yes!*

Jolie spread her thighs wider. Her head fell back as his fingertips teased along her inner lips. He was playing, dipping a finger in then quickly retreating. She raised her hips to follow his fingers, but he forced her hips to the bed with his opposite hand. She trembled as he pushed one finger in deep.

Jolie's sigh turned into a cry as he added another finger. She tossed her head back as he leaned over her, his lips sucking at the base of her throat.

His thumb found her clit, and she jolted—just as the phone rang.

Cassian broke away, breathing heavily. "Shit. One second."

Jolie's eyes popped open. It was nearly midnight. Who was calling him?

"What? No." *We just got started!* A vibrator and her fingers wouldn't do. She needed him. Over her. Under her. His dick deep inside her, forcing her over the peak of pleasure all night long. Desperate for more, she caught him by the arm, forcing his back to hit the bed.

"Jolie—"

"Ignore it."

The phone continued to ring as her hand dipped into his boxers. Cassian cursed as she wrapped her fist around him.

He was hard, warm, and vibrant. Pulling his boxers down, he pushed himself into her hand as she squeezed him lightly. She licked her lips, kneeling between his legs, as the phone's ringing faded into silence. She let the fat mushroomed tip drift along her lips before she enveloped the smooth head with her mouth.

"Fuck, you're doing so good," he murmured.

A sense of power filled her. She wanted to push him the

same way he'd pushed her. Her mouth touched his, her voice a mere whisper, she asked, "Please."

Gripping the base of his erection, she swirled her tongue around. A shiver racked his body as she brought her lips to encircle his length. She couldn't help but moan as she hollowed her cheeks, bobbing her head slowly. She kept her pace slow, toying with him as payback from before.

His brows twisted with frustration as filthy moans tumbled off his tongue. She stroked him more, sucking harder and faster than before.

"Jolie—"

A grin creeped at the corners of her mouth at the sight of Cassian's face.

She needed the taste of him on her tongue, and her lips sealed around the head of his dick once more as his hand cupped the back of her head.

The phone went off again.

"Goddammit!" Cassian drew her off and away from him, and snatching his phone up he snapped, *"What?"*

Jolie's back bounced on the bed as her chest heaved. She licked her lips slowly, savoring the taste of him.

"Fine. Just shit, fine. I'll be there in the morning. I'll have Paul reschedule the Edwardsville talk… Yeah. It's fine, Meg. Bye." Cassian pulled up his boxers, his dick straining against the front.

She exhaled slowly. "Is everything okay?"

Cassian lay next to her, pulling her onto his chest. She could feel their rapid heartbeats fall into sync.

"An associate missed an intellectual property deadline for an important client, which is the worst thing he could have done. The client might lose rights to their trademark. I have to smooth things over in the morning."

Cassian sighed deeply, and she felt the stress stiffen his body.

"Cassian—"

"Sleep. You need it."

Jolie sucked her teeth, annoyed they were interrupted, but after a few moments, exhaustion smacked into her. Yawning loudly, she pressed her face into his chest. She felt the soft rustling of the sheets over her body before she drifted off into a deep sleep.

eighteen

. . .

"Oh, this is so exciting!" Tisha exclaimed as they walked into a bridal boutique in downtown Chicago.

"Welcome to Lovely Bride. My name is Stephanie. How can I help you today?"

Lovely Bride was an inclusive shop featuring modern and classic bridal gowns across a vast range of sizes. Stepping inside was like visiting a French bistro. White couches and pink roses filled the entrance, classical music played over the speaker, and a small diffuser bubbled softly in the background.

"This is my future daughter-in-law, Jolie. Ah! Off that phone! You've been on it all day."

Leonard Gambino was one slippery son of a bitch, but Jolie finally had an address. There was a property on the west side of the city, with an Ella Gambino listed as the owner... *Bingo.*

"Jolie?" Tisha asked.

"I'm sorry, what?" Jolie locked her phone, placing it inside her purse.

She was already feeling overwhelmed. Revealing her past

to Cassian. Being intimate with him. There had been no more contact from her family, but she was waiting for the other shoe to drop.

"I would love to see her in a traditional gown. Is that okay?" Tisha batted her eyes toward Jolie.

"Aw, I would enjoy that!" Luna gushed.

Jolie winced. Tisha and Luna were too damn sweet. So observant and catering to her when her place in their lives, *their family*, was a sham. But she was a greedy bastard because she ate up all their love and attention.

"Some crystals too," Helena added.

Jolie shot Helena a look. *Stop encouraging them.* Helena kept her mouth shut about the fake marriage, but she was urging Tisha and Luna on, making them take pictures and posting them to social media. It was fucking torture.

Jolie could not tell Cassian's mother she was not marrying her son out of her undying love. It was a contract. They didn't need to make her feel like family but she wasn't expecting to enjoy his mother and sister so much. The love they shared for each other, Cassian—it was admirable. Something she'd never experienced nor witnessed before.

"We want a long veil. Is that right?" Tisha added.

Luna took a picture of the place. "I'm thinking she will look sexy in that piece right there." She pointed to a dress on a mannequin in the window.

It was breathtaking. Intricate details and floral lace appliques lined the silhouette dress. It's beaded sleeves and illusion back with cascading crystals was the main selling point. Not to mention the train was a dazzling mixture of lace and satin.

"Definitely that one." Jolie knew her taste didn't line up with Tisha's and her gut told her this dress on the mannequin was hers, but she would appease Cassian's mom a bit.

It was the least she could do.

"I'll take the bride with me." Stephanie motioned for Jolie

to follow her as Tisha, Helena, and Luna sat in the waiting area.

Stephanie returned with a dress Tisha suggested. Slipping into it, Jolie knew it was an immediate no. The bodice was sequined and that was fine. It just got weirder the more you looked down. A peplum ruffle skirt with sequins flowing down to a cathedral train. She didn't know you could have a train with a peplum skirt. But that didn't make her want to gag. It was the feathered shoulders.

Jolie gathered the skirt as Stephanie held her train. The moment she rounded the corner, Tisha looked as if her eyes would pop out of her head. Helena's and Luna's lips turned downward.

"Oh my God. Oh. My. God." Tisha held a hand over her mouth.

Stephanie wasn't impressed, but Jolie admired her professionalism. "Mom likes it?"

"You are beautiful! Oh my God, look at the sparkles and those feathers—"

"Mama, that dress is ugly," Luna declared.

Jolie was glad Luna said it. Tisha looked offended as her gaze flickered from Luna to Jolie.

"That dress is gorgeous. It's—"

Luna shook her head. "She looks like Big Bird, Ma."

"It's not bad, but it's not good," Helena offered tentatively.

Tisha frowned. "What do you think, Jolie? You love it, right?"

She twisted and turned in the mirror, contemplating words that wouldn't hurt Tisha's feelings. "It has some elements I like—"

"Not the feathers," Luna muttered.

Tisha hit Luna on the arm as Jolie licked her lips to stop from smiling. "The feathers... They do—they take it up a level."

"It's not wowing you?" Helena suggested.

Jolie shook her head.

"Do you think your mother would like it?" Tisha asked.

That was an ice-cold bucket of water.

Tisha didn't mean to be insensitive with her question; she just didn't know the turbulent history between Jolie and her mother. Helena gave Jolie a sympathetic look.

"She wouldn't like this. She wouldn't like anything I chose." Jolie kept her face impassive. *Be calm, don't think about her.*

"That's a shame. A mother should support her daughter," Tisha said.

Luna cleared her throat loudly, nudging Tisha in the side with her elbow. Realization passed over Tisha's features, her mouth parted.

"That's my mother." Jolie shrugged.

"How about we move on to the next one, then?" Stephanie offered with a tight smile.

Tisha wanted to be redeemed so she sent Stephanie back with more gowns for Jolie to try. It was *fun*... Jolie would never admit that out loud. For a moment, she let herself get lost in the fantasy of being an excited bride.

She exhaled slowly, leaning back on the chair as Stephanie removed the reject gowns, looking for more. Her phone rang, and she fished it out of her purse to see an unknown number.

"Hello?"

"My ungrateful daughter."

Coldness ran down Jolie's spine, and the phone almost slipped from her grasp. "Mom?"

"Where have you been at? Jesus only knows. Good to know you ain't dead in a ditch."

"Mama, why are you calling me?"

The last time they talked it ended with both women demanding the other to forget they were alive.

"I can't call you?"

"You don't ever call."

Hang up the phone. She doesn't deserve to speak to you. Hang up.

"I seen you on the news with that young man, Anders or whatnot, talkin' about you gettin' married? My daughter gettin' married and she not tellin' me?"

"Why would I tell you?"

"Don't get smart—"

Jolie exhaled heavily. "I'm not getting smart."

Liza muttered under her breath about how disrespectful Jolie always was. How the devil had to be in her. What had she done in a past life to get a daughter who hated her?

"I'm busy, I gotta go—"

I'm not sixteen anymore. I'm a grown woman. She doesn't have control anymore.

"I'm talkin' to you, Sparkle. Don't act like your ass is grown that you can cut me off." A foreign feeling rolled over Jolie as her mother ranted. "Aaron called after your fight. You kicked him to the street? You're evil, Sparkle, a pure evil spirit. You aligned yourself with the dev—"

"Aaron is a grown man, not a child, and I'm not obligated to do anything for him. And don't call me Sparkle."

"That's what your daddy wanted your name to be! God rest yo' daddy soul, *he* named you. Aaron is your brother, and he's right. You always thought you were too good for what I could give you. Family is family, and you goddamn help family. But you conveniently forget that. There ya go, disappointin' ya daddy again."

"Don't bring up my father. Each time I see Aaron, he's drunk or drinking. I don't want that in my life."

Liza inhaled sharply. Jolie knew what was coming. Balling her fist on her knee, she tapped her foot rapidly, willing herself to calm down.

"I'm the one that fucked your father, that's why you're here. I can say whatever I want!"

Jolie shook her head. "You keep bringing up a man that you won't tell me anything about."

"I demand you let your brother and me come to your wedding."

Heat flooded her body, and her heart pounded in her ears. "Do you hear yourself? Let you and Aaron come to my wedding? For what? You hate me—"

"You're just so damn selfish! Aaron's your blood. I'm your blood."

Jolie went rigid. "Mama, if I'm that way, it must be the way you raised me. Look in the mirror."

"Moments like these make me regret giving birth to you, Sparkle. I pray to God every day Aaron doesn't end up like you. That's why you are not allowed home."

"What did I do in a previous life to end up with a mother like you?"

"Bitch, is this how you talk to your mother? You will respect me above all—" Liza screeched.

"From this point on, I'm done with you and Aaron."

"I'm in you, Sparkle. I gave you life. My blood runs through you, and I hope it prevails over all of your evil—"

Jolie hung up the phone.

Calm down, calm down. Don't let her ruin your day.

She refused to cry, even as the tears threatened to fall. Every conversation she had with her mother, she reverted to a scared sixteen-year-old. How many years had she prayed for her mother to like her? To give her the love she gave Aaron? What was wrong with her that her mother couldn't love her?

A knock on the door made Jolie look up as Luna poked her head in the dressing room. "I wanted to catch you before you tried another dress to plead that you put us out of misery. Wear the dress from the mannequin. Stop my mom."

Pulling her robe closer, Jolie sniffed and nodded.

Luna's smile fell. "Are you okay?"

"Peachy."

An understanding expression passed across Luna's face as she closed the door, holding the gown Jolie had been eying earlier.

"I can see that you aren't, but I'm not gonna be nosy and ask why—"

"Thank you."

"Unless you wanted to talk about it with me? You're about to marry my brother, which is a sacrifice of its own, but we're not talking 'bout that," Luna joked.

She shouldn't take her pissed-off emotions out on Luna. "I don't want to think about it." Jolie rubbed her temples, forcing a fake laugh. "Let's take a dress and go."

"Just take a dress? Are you crazy?" Luna eyed her like she'd committed a sin. "This is your day. It's all about you and finding the dress of your dreams."

This isn't real. Even if I wanted it to be.

"I'm not in the mood anymore—"

"Don't let anyone or anything have that much power to ruin your day," Luna told her seriously.

Jolie tilted her head. "Is that the therapist in you coming out?"

"Maybe, or maybe I don't want my mama sending you out in a circus dress."

Jolie laughed. "Fine. That is the dress. I know it."

Luna smiled and she looked so much like her older brother.

"You can talk to me if you need anything. You're family, Jolie."

Tears appeared in Jolie's eyes. They were making this harder for her. "Don't get me emotional. I hate it."

"I'm sorry! I'm sorry, but my big brother's getting married and now I have a sister after praying all my life —and now I'm about to cry." Luna fanned her eyes. "Let me help you into the dress so we can see it before you buy."

Luna helped Jolie into her dress, allowing Stephanie to add the matching veil.

"Is this it?" Stephanie fixed the veil leading down her back.

The lace overlay on the bodice and the beading at the neckline caught the light when she moved. It hugged every curve from breast to hip and down to the floor. She looked like a goddess come to earth.

"Let's show my mom," Luna urged.

Jolie followed Luna out to the waiting area, with Stephanie trailing behind. Helena's eyes widened, and Tisha's jaw dropped. Jolie smiled brightly, still emotionally raw as she stepped onto the dais.

"What do you think?" Crystal sleeves hugged Jolie's arms to her wrists and twinkled, catching the light of store.

"Well?" she asked as everyone stared.

"You look…" Helena's words trailed off. Tears spilled from Helena's face, and Tisha leaned over to rub her best friend's back.

"Incredible," Tisha finished. Her eyes were bright with tears.

"This is it," Jolie said. "That's the one."

Helena clapped her hands. "Now we drink!"

Jolie needed double shots of the strongest liquor legally allowed. Maybe that would stop her mother's words from echoing in her mind.

nineteen

· · ·

Cassian—

I've found civil cases against Kinsella buried deep. I had to call on some important people to get this. One is six months after your family's accident.

Gerald.

The front door slammed shut as Cassian scanned the files Gerald had emailed over. He bowed his head, balling his fists as he forced himself to read the details of the case. *Six months after.* At that time, his father had been induced into a coma for swelling on his brain. His mother had undergone another surgery to place a rod in her leg. And Kinsella was still out fucking up people's lives. Curtis Lyon. Nettie Walker. Davy Sweet. All victims.

How the fuck hadn't Kinsella been discovered? Who was hiding this information?

Cassian leaned back, pressing a fist against his mouth as he puffed out his cheeks.

"Oh my God, please. I can't handle you looking like that." The lights in the living room turned on.

His head shot to the doorway, and Jolie leaned against the wall of his living room.

"What's wrong?"

He needed to contact those people and see if they would testify that Kinsella had in fact crashed into them under the influence… If they hadn't been paid off.

Anger and guilt stirred like a storm inside of him. Jolie didn't need to see him like this.

"You know what you're doing." She shook her head, her hair a dark shadow falling on her face.

He swallowed, forcing himself to keep her gaze. He was hit with immediate curiosity and desire for her. He had already resigned himself to the fact that he would always feel that way in her presence.

"I don't."

"It's—*you!* You're wearing a robe and reading glasses. You look like a DILF." Her eyes danced playfully as she dropped the heels she carried to the floor.

He looked at himself. His gray cotton robe was splayed open, and his hair was a mess from running his fingers through it. He was wearing worn-out basketball shorts he'd had since college and a tank top. Nothing amazing.

"DILF?"

Jolie flipped him off and stomped toward him. "Is this another manipulative campaign tactic? Look hot to get votes?"

"Are you drunk, Jolie?" Cassian shut his laptop, mentally filing away his next steps. He slid the laptop away from her, and she collapsed on the couch next to him. Her cheeks were flushed, and she giggled lightly. *Jolie fucking giggled.* What the hell happened to her with his mother and sister?

"I'm okay," she mumbled, peering up at him.

"Jolie," Cassian frowned, "are you drunk?"

Her nearness was overwhelming. The sweet, fruity scent of her hair. The way her body pressed into his side. She shifted, laying her head on his shoulder, and positioned her legs across his lap. "No. Your mom was worse than me. Luna had to carry her inside."

He held his breath, not wanting to break the moment and send her running back behind the wall she'd built. Tentatively, he placed his hands on her knees, squeezing lightly.

"You did shots with my mother?"

"It got kinda awkward at the bridal store when she brought up my mother." Jolie's head was tilted down, and he sat up to see her face but she pressed her weight onto his chest and forced him back.

"I'm sorry if she offended you."

Jolie lifted her head, observing him with big brown eyes that made his pulse quicken and his body tighten with awareness. *Shit, it's been a month of living together.* Cassian shook his head, forcing himself to keep the blood in his head and not his hardening dick.

"She didn't know."

He couldn't stop himself from running his hand through her hair. It felt so silky-smooth. His fingers grazed her scalp in a gentle massage, and she let out a purr that made his gut clench.

"Other than that, how was dress shopping?"

"Your mom picked out some ugly-ass dresses. No offense." Jolie chuckled, and he cupped her chin and she grimaced.

"Why are you making this hard for me?"

Cassian lifted a brow. "How?"

"Emotions weren't supposed to be involved in our deal. You're not supposed to make me open myself up to you and confess things I don't tell anyone. Or make me love your family."

"I didn't do it on purpose," he murmured.

"But you did, and now I'm—" Jolie sighed, closing her eyes before running a hand through her hair. "I'm stuck because I'm not supposed to let you into my life like this. It's not a part of the contract."

A flash of sadness flickered across her features, and his forehead creased at the sight.

"Is it that bad to let me in?"

"Vulnerability is not my thing. Especially with men. Nothing good comes from it."

Cassian forced himself straight, and staring into her eyes, he saw shadows of fear.

"Why let me in then?"

Jolie's eyes held the same sad, dark look. The urge to bring her into his arms, to force her to release all the pain and sadness she felt, was so close to the surface. She had mentioned their contract. They didn't want to muddle the boundaries, but sense faded from him as Jolie climbed on top of him, her knees planted on each side and her hands on his chest. He bit back a groan and gripped her ass to steady her.

"Jolie—"

"I've been thinking about my job lately... I don't know if it's the right place for me anymore." A grim look passed over her face.

"You love your job."

"But am I heading for a dead end there?"

His brows furrowed. She shifted, grinding on his dick, and he forced his gaze to stay on her face. "You have a master's degree. The doors should be opening, not closing."

"I can't fight nepotism, Cassian. There's a lot I can fight, but with Travis... The man wouldn't know his head from his ass if it wasn't attached, but I have to prove myself against *him*? I've written countless stories that have brought respect and attention to the channel."

Anger blazed through Cassian for her. He knew the game; he'd been an unwilling player in it since he stepped out of law school.

"I'll save you the long story but I got an outrageous email congratulating him on his one-year anniversary and everything he's accomplished. They've never done that for me. I've given them years of my hard work, and I'm not a shoo-in for the promotion? They put me on television on the weekends during the dead hour. Yet when it comes time to cash in the money from advertisers, I'm their best friend because they know my stories will bring traffic." Jolie's eyes were cold.

His dark eyes were full of concern.

"It's unfortunately the games we have to play, Jolie. We can bust our asses getting every degree in the world, but sometimes all they want to see is a Black man or Black woman who should just be grateful for being let in the door."

Jolie squeezed her eyes shut, and he grabbed her wrist, rubbing gently.

"Baby, the game won't ever stop unless you fight back. Ask yourself, is it worth it to make a change at Channel 12, or do you need to leave to get what you want?"

She stared at him thoughtfully. Looking like this, Jolie was temptation personified. And then she leaned down to kiss him once, twice on the lips. Her lips trailed down his neck, sucking at the point where his neck and shoulder met.

Immediately he acquiesced. He was so damn easy for her. Their sorrow and anger merged into a kindling of simmering desire threatening to destroy the last boundary between them. Her hands ran over his chest, down to the edge of his shorts, and he caught her hands.

"Jolie, baby…"

"I want you. I need this. Please?" She gently removed his glasses before he crushed her to him.

He chuckled low, heated as he let his nose brush along hers, then tilted her head back so he could kiss her slow and deep. A low moan tore through him as he urged her lips open, their tongue melding.

He should have protected their deal, but the lust inside him was an untamable beast. Jolie was a damn firecracker; he couldn't stop her from incinerating him from the inside out.

Jolie lifted her shirt above her head, revealing a lacy black bra and hardened brown nipples pointing through the flimsy fabric. Sliding his palms across her belly, his fingers featherlight as they traced up her rib cage, he brushed his hands under the swells of her breasts then tweaked her nipples.

After a month of near brushes, heavy looks, and jerking off till his dick was damn near raw, it thrilled his body to give in and let this woman use him. He squeezed her ass, then released it to slap it through her jeans. They both felt his hardness pressing through his shorts, and she ground against him slowly, teasing him.

Panting slightly, she unclasped her bra, and his mouth watered at the sight of her full breasts.

"Jesus... Fuck, baby," Cassian groaned weakly, swallowing thickly as his mouth encapsulated her fat nipple. His pink tongue ran circles over the hard nub, tasting the sweetness of her skin.

"Cassian!" She tugged at the hem of his shorts again.

"Touch me," he murmured.

Cassian lifted his hips into her. His hardness brushing against her core, a smile broke across her face as she kissed him.

He let her slide his shorts down, and Jolie tossed their pants onto the floor, her underwear trailing afterward.

"How do you want it, baby? Underneath me? On your stomach and back arched? From the side? What?"

She whimpered; eyes half-closed as she licked her lips. "I really want to see you beg."

He hissed as she stroked his dick to his achy tip. Her eyes on his face, memorizing every twitch as his body melted into the sofa. He pulled her close, hungry for her taste, the speed of her hand pumping him growing faster and faster.

"Wait, baby, let me taste you—"

Jolie's eyelids fluttered. "I'm ready now."

Breathing harder, he locked his jaw as she lifted her hips, teasing his dick with her pink folds.

"I need a condom, baby."

"I—I can't wait. I'm on birth control, and my last test results were all clean. What about you?"

"Clean. No STIs."

Jolie sank onto him as he slowly rocked up into her.

"Fuck, baby," he rasped. There was no way he could fight her. He was at her mercy.

Both were panting as her pussy clenched and released around his dick. A gasp escaped her as she rose and dropped.

"Damn, Cassian…" she breathed as she bounced up and down on his dick, her ass slapping against his thighs. He kissed her tenderly once more, open-mouthed and seeking.

"Feels fucking good, baby."

He wasn't sure when it happened. It was that day he saw her in the crowd at his acceptance speech. Or the way she tore into him in the hallway of Magnifica. It could have been the way he watched her eyes light up as she explained the story she was working on. This woman had burst into his life and disrupted all his best laid plans. He had no idea how he'd ever recover from her.

He'd never considered the possibility of developing feelings for his fake fiancée. Especially when he would have to let her go in a year.

"You like how I fuck you, baby?" she crooned, slowing her pace, rocking against him harder.

Sweat broke out on their bodies. He couldn't contain his rumble of pleasure, his lips cascading downward toward her nipple. He'd never felt like this before. So, fucking horny, so in tune with her body, so consumed with pushing her to ecstasy.

Cassian moaned around her breast. "Baby—shit, Jolie. I need you, baby. Keep going, don't stop."

Her hips slammed back, and she shivered when his thumb teased her clit.

"It's so good, Cassian." Jolie yanked his head back, forcing his head back onto the sofa. Her hand slid to his throat, squeezing as his fingers dug into her ass cheek.

He nodded eagerly, entranced with the beautiful sight of her coming apart for him. "I'm glad you like it, baby."

He would have done anything she said at that moment. With each stroke, she demanded everything from him.

Her grip tightened on his throat, pausing their fucking. She rose slightly, reaching to grip his dick, rubbing her pussy over the tip of it before sinking down again. "You gonna let me come on this big dick?"

"Shit, what are you doing to me, Jolie?"

He wouldn't last much longer.

"Damn." Jolie ran her fingers through his curls. "I want you bad… Cassian, please…"

Her hand loosened on his throat, and he watched her eyes close. Their gasps and the soft squelches of their sex were a nasty symphony that edged them closer and closer to the brink.

"Cassian!"

"Shh. Keep going, you're almost there. Almost there, baby." Cassian returned his teasing to her nipples, sucking and releasing in time with his thrusts.

She let out a tiny slither of a moan before her body surrendered to him. Her eyes rolled back as she cried out.

"Fuck…fuck." He closed his eyes as stars exploded behind his lids.

"Cassian!"

He forced his eyes open as she said his name like a prayer. Biting his lower lip, he rutted up into her as she dug her nails into his shoulders, her head thrown back, mouth wide open.

She collapsed onto him, her breathing rushed before slowing to an even tempo. He crumpled back onto the sofa, rubbing mindlessly patterns on her bare skin.

He had to grab a frayed strand of control, but the truth couldn't be denied. He was falling in love with her.

twenty

• • •

"Jolie, you look amazing," Helena whispered behind her.

She stood in her wedding gown in the mirror of the dressing room at Café Brauer at Lincoln Park Zoo. Between Cassian jet-setting off to every corner of the state to rally voters, her investigation, and their relationship tipping and tumbling into inescapable levels of closeness, they'd finally made it to the wedding.

You can't back out now.

Her life as Mrs. Cassian Anders would begin in less than an hour. Jolie gripped her phone tighter as it buzzed with a message.

> Congrats. If it's worth anything.

Aaron. He'd gotten a new number.

Cassian had a scheduled appearance in Bloomington that morning, so they settled on an evening wedding. That was perfect because after a two-day stakeout, Jolie had hit a wall in her investigation. Leonard Gambino wasn't talking. That led her to going back to her elementary tactics. She followed him, and he'd led her right into city hall and the Chicago Development Commission meeting.

The CDC assisted with private redevelopment projects and selling properties. Only fifteen members from the public were allowed at a time. Jolie was on the list for the next meeting, but before the doors closed in her face, she saw Leonard shake the hand of Kathleen Wilson, the CDC commissioner. Kathleen Wilson was a very accomplished woman, and very hard to get a hold of. Jolie's emails to her had gone unanswered, so she began poking around the DPD and CDC boards to find someone to talk about Urban Properties.

"Do I?" Jolie murmured.

Helena nodded. "Don't tell me you want to back out?"

The executives at Channel 12 had loved the exclusives Cassian's team had been giving them. He gave her everything she needed to know about Miguel Lopez as well. Cassian was honoring his word. She was in the executives favor again, but each day cemented an irreversible link between her and Cassian.

She would be forever tied to him.

Jolie understood this now with much more clarity than she had that day in his office. Her reputation. Her mind. *Her heart.* All territories in which Cassian claimed. She willed herself not to think much into the words Cassian whispered in bed when they lay together, exhausted from passion. She was playing his game, making *his dreams* come true. He'd made it clear his campaign was his chief priority, and she couldn't forget that no matter what confusing emotion awakened in her heart.

"I'm not backing out."

Helena looked beautiful in her burgundy mermaid bridesmaid dress, her braids twisted in an elegant bun. "Why do you have that look on your face?"

Jolie tried to swallow the lump in her throat.

"Oh my fucking God, you like him! You like him!"

Jolie felt her phone ringing. The call buzzed twice, then stopped. "Shut up, Lena."

"This is great! Why do you look like the world has ended?"

"This is *fake*. This is all about getting Cassian into office, then we go our separate ways."

She would only give her body to Cassian. She could not give up her heart. Her promotion was her sole purpose. No matter what she felt about Channel 12 or Travis, she put years into that station. She was going to leave with the job title of her dreams. She would ignore her budding feelings. She would ignore tender touches and whispers. She would move forward with this marriage. She would divorce Cassian once the year was up. Her eye was on the prize.

Jolie's phone vibrated with a voice mail. There was soft knocking at the door before it cracked open, and they turned to find the wedding coordinator.

"We're ready for you."

Helena passed Jolie her bouquet.

"Wait, I need to listen to this voice message. It could be about my story."

"Jolie…"

"It'll be fast." Helena huffed as Jolie pressed to listen. There was a muffled sound, then the crunch of something rattling before a gravelly voice began.

"You keep diggin' your nose in business that don't belong to you, Miss Coldwell. Leave Leonard alone. Stop calling Urban Properties' offices. Leave Kathleen and the CDC alone. This matter ain't none of your concern. Don't have this escalate. You won't like it."

Jolie froze to the spot.

"Jolie? What's wrong?" Helena held her veil.

She gulped down a breath, forcing her pulse to slow. "Someone threatened me."

Helena's eyes bulged. "What? Who?"

"I don't know. Blocked number. I'll handle it when I get back to the office."

Jolie gave a strained smile. They thought they were intimidating her, but they were only igniting her. She was going to take Urban Properties down to its fucking knees.

"This is serious, Jolie. It's not just about you anymore. Cassian could get hurt too."

"They mentioned leads in my story. I'm not worried by an incensed anti-Cassian hater. I was pushing at city hall, and obviously someone's threatened."

"You need to tell Cassian and Rock."

"After the wedding." Trepidation knotted inside her. "Come on, Lena. It's time."

Helena placed the veil gently on her head, flipping it forward. She gazed in the mirror one last time. She looked like a true bride, even though she was a phony.

The wedding coordinator led them to the great hall, lanterns lighting the way. They made it to the double doors, and Helena turned. "I always got your back."

Jolie hugged her best friend tightly. They embraced, and Jolie exhaled shakily and drew strength from Helena till the coordinator cleared her throat.

The doors opened into the wedding hall, and Helena marched forward.

The instrumental version of "Can't Help Falling in Love" commenced as the coordinator motioned for Jolie to start down the aisle. All guests turned their eyes on her, and she kept her shoulders squared back, head high, until she met Cassian's eyes.

All her anxiety was gone. Evaporated. Instead an indefinable feeling of rightness filled her. He was breathtaking.

His curls glistened under the light, accentuating the hard angles of his face. The fitted tuxedo made his shoulders look impossibly broad, and he exuded power and certainty. For this moment, lie and all, he was hers. *I'm so screwed.*

That look of desire and something akin to love appeared on his face. His eyes didn't leave hers for a second as his gaze guided her down the aisle.

The guests sat, and Cassian took her hand once she reached the altar. Her heart stammered as he lifted her veil, his eyes warred with emotion.

"You're beautiful."

"I know," she breathed, and Cassian chuckled.

She handed her bouquet to Helena, and the minister began his sermon. Jolie tried to focus, but her gaze kept drifting to Cassian, only to find he was watching her.

"Do you, Cassian, come here freely and without reservation give yourself to Jolie in marriage?"

"I do."

Butterflies swirled in her belly. The moment the ring was on her finger, their countdown would begin.

She was careening toward an unknown that rocked her to the core.

"Jolie, do you take this man to be your husband? Do you come here freely and without reservation to give yourself to Cassian in marriage?"

A searing sensation burned through Jolie's veins. "I do."

"Cassian, the ring."

Jolie's hand shook slightly as Cassian slid the wedding band onto her finger, then she did the same for him.

"Let the wedding rings you exchanged today remind you always that you are surrounded by enduring love. May you cherish the home and family you will create together, and let it be filled with moments to celebrate and renew your love. Remember marriage is love, a lifelong source of devotion for one another."

There was a sniff from behind her, and Jolie peeked to see Helena wiping a few tears away. She glanced out into the audience. Cassian's family sat in the front row, their eyes glistening with tears. Dev sat behind Cassian's family, his eyes glossy.

"It is my honor and delight to declare you husband and wife. You may kiss the bride," the minister said.

Cassian drew her closer, his smile outright tantalizing as he sealed their vows with a kiss bursting with passion and a possessiveness that made her shiver. She returned the kiss with a hunger that belied her outward calm, and made her hungry for more.

"I am pleased to present, for the first time, Mr. and Mrs. Anders."

The guests erupted into applause. Intertwining their arms together, Jolie smiled like a pageant star. She tried not to think deeply about their vows and the sacredness of them, or how they'd both lied, knowing there wouldn't be blissful years to come.

SHE WAS OFFICIALLY Mrs. Cassian Anders.

"How are you feeling?"

They swayed side to side to the music wrapped up in each other's arms. She was hyperaware of the photographers and all the eyes on them. Like that night at the bar, her body sang as she pressed up against him. *Tell him about the voice message.*

"Great, good. Minus these heels, they're killing me." She couldn't ruin their wedding day with a random threat.

"I think you look hot." He purred, and she snorted.

"Flattery gets you nowhere with me."

"Just because we're married means we lose the romance?"

They were a union now. Not forever, just for now. Intimate teasing just made her resolve crack more.

Jolie looked at Cassian's parents on the dance floor. The

way they embraced her after the ceremony nearly brought her to tears. She never felt shittier.

"Your parents look happy," she said, her voice trembling.

"They are." There was a catch in his voice.

She watched him look at his parents with a pensive expression. As quickly as it came, it disappeared.

"I have to tel—"

A flash went off.

"Please tell the photographer to lose that flash," Jolie grumbled, white spots appearing in her eyes.

They turned to glare at the photographer.

"Margarita wants all the best photos to release to the public." Cassian kissed her cheek.

Jolie swallowed. Of course, his campaign came first.

"Cassian!" a voice called.

A couple made their way toward them. A young woman in a pink dress and matching braids dragged along a handsome guy with low waves in his hair and a full beard with a slight limp.

"Marshall, you made it." Cassian grinned and shook the young man's hand.

"Call me Marsh, man. And you're the boss. I had to come." Marsh responded in a Southern accent, and his eyes fell on Jolie. "Nice to meet you, Mrs. Anders."

"Yes, a pleasure to meet the new Mrs. Anders. It's sad I couldn't do it before the wedding, but *somebody* was too busy." Cassian's law partner, Meg, who Jolie had met earlier, appeared behind the couple in an elegant black gown.

Jolie's skin flushed darkly. Would she get used to that? "Thank you. Nice to meet you both."

"I've seen you on the weekends on Channel 12," Marsh continued. "Your piece on the congressman was dope. He totally deserve that shit too—" The girl next to him nudged him in the side with her elbow, and he hissed out a breath. "What?"

"I'm Cami Clinton, Marsh's fiancée, since he rudely forgot to introduce me."

Marsh pouted at Cami. "I'm sorry."

"When's the date?" Jolie asked, and the two looked at one another with stars in their eyes.

"Not soon enough. I'm tired of being dragged to bridal shops," Meg muttered.

Marsh kissed Cami's cheek. "As soon as she gets a break from her dance tour. Cami's with the Leblanc troupe. Our wedding might not be fancy like yours, though. We're thinking of eloping."

"You know Devin will be upset about that," Cami said. "And Deja and Winter would kill me if they couldn't be my maids of honor."

"Maids?" Jolie asked. "Isn't it usually one?"

Meg and Marsh glanced at one another before smirking.

"I don't want to ignite a war." Cami shook her head.

"Wait, Leblanc? I love them! I saw your group's performance in New York last year. It was amazing."

Cami's eyes glistened with excitement.

"Marsh is coming to work for me. He's going to do great work," Cassian said with pride, and Marsh waved him off.

"I've learned from you."

"You learned from me," Meg interjected.

Marsh rolled his eyes at his sister, and she nudged him playfully.

"We wanted to give you both this." Marsh handed them a card, and Jolie took it.

"You didn't have to do that, Marsh." Cassian clasped Marsh's shoulder. The younger man shook his head.

"Where's the honeymoon?" Cami asked.

Jolie realized that was one bit of information she'd forgotten in this entire plan.

"We're going to San Francisco. Napa Valley."

Jolie whirled on him, her brows raised, and he grinned sheepishly.

"It was a surprise, but Pacific Grove University wants me to speak to their law school. I thought we could spend a day in the city and spend the rest of the weekend in wine country," Cassian explained.

"Aww! We should go back and visit soon. Can we?" Cami turned to Marsh.

After reminiscing about their undergrad experience at Pacific Grove University, the young couple said their goodbyes.

"If he gets out of line and you need help, call me, Jolie. I know how to put him in his place," Meg emphasized. "Don't let him intimidate you."

Jolie laughed. "I'll need your number then. He's a wild one."

Cassian pinned Jolie with a shocked look.

"*I'm* the wild one?"

"How about we get lunch when you get back? I can tell you about his En Vogue phase."

Cassian groaned.

Someone cleared their throat. "Can I have a moment with the bride?"

It was Cassian's father. The dashing older man looked at her with a sort of fatherly pride she wasn't expecting.

"Or are you being stingy, boy?"

Cassian grinned before stepping away from Jolie and passing her to his father for a dance. The two settled into an easy rhythm.

"Welcome to the family," Edward said.

"That means a lot, Mr. Anders."

Edward snorted.

"You don't have to call me that. Edward is fine." He twirled her around as gently as he could with his cane, and she laughed. She wondered if her own father would have been like Edward. "Do you love my son?"

Her pulse beat erratically, and her mind fluttered in anxiety. *Love.* Could she love Cassian? *Did* she love him? She loved his dedication. To his job. The boys. He had an innate sense of when she was upset. Most of all, he made her feel secure. *Safe.* Something that eluded her most of her life.

Love? It's too early for that. How can I love him when this is fake?

"Yes." Jolie's heart clenched, and she forced herself to continue to move with the music.

"Don't let him lose himself in the campaign." Edward's voice dipped low. "I don't want him to abandon his integrity going after the attorney general."

Jolie's spine stiffened. Over the past weeks she'd seen Cassian be consumed more and more with Kinsella. Stepping out of the room the moment Gerald called. Dropping everything to meet him. Staying up into the early hours of the morning studying document after document.

"Don't let him lose focus just because he wants to avenge us. I can see him gettin' lost now." Edward stopped their dance. "Can you do that?"

Jolie swallowed. How could she do that when she was complicit in Cassian's need for justice?

"May I cut in?" Cassian appeared again.

"Of course. She's all yours." After kissing Jolie on the cheek, Edward made his way back to his seat with Luna's help.

"What happened?" They watched his dad sit and release a breath as if he'd been on his feet too long. Tisha rubbed his knee.

"I don't want to hurt your family, Cassian. I don't want to be the villain in the end." *And I don't know how to deal with the fact that I'm feeling things.*

"You won't be."

"You can't promise that," Jolie said.

His large hand took her face and held it gently. "Don't worry."

A contract didn't mean anything when it came to feelings. It also didn't spare the fallout of their actions against his family, the public, or most importantly, themselves.

twenty-one

. . .

"*Kiss, kiss, kiss!*"

Rushing through the aisle made by the tipsy and happy guests, Cassian held Jolie close to his side. They made it to the limo amid sparklers and rice, and he gave her another soaring kiss while trying to tame his body's reaction to *his wife*.

His kiss was slow and thoughtful as his tongue traced the soft fullness of her lips. Tiny whimpers escaped her mouth, and she grabbed the back of his head hungrily. How had she become his addiction so quickly? In a blur of smiling faces and well wishes, they bid their guests and his family a hasty goodbye and headed for The Peninsula Chicago.

The lights of the streetlights passed over them, and his gaze fell on her. She rested her head on his shoulder.

He stroked her hair. "In all this craziness I forgot about the speaking engagement in San Francisco. Do you think you can take the time off?"

"Yes."

"I'm glad," he whispered, and he couldn't help himself from placing a soft kiss on her lips.

He should be celebrating that they'd accomplished this

wedding without major scandal. Margarita would release the photos. He had several interviews lined up with local stations when they returned. His popularity rating was shooting up. His mind continued to drift toward Attorney General Kinsella. The more Gerald unearthed, the more Cassian found it increasingly hard to keep his composure and not scream the evidence to the world.

Kinsella deserves to be destroyed.

When the limo arrived at the hotel, Cassian stepped out first, reaching a hand to assist his wife. *Kinsella needs criminal charges. Every victim of his needs compensation, and I'll lead the fucking charge in court.*

He guided her through the lobby and to the elevators. Electric energy surged between them as he contemplated how she would respond if he confessed how he felt.

He needs to be fired. Pay back every cent this state paid him, and his name wiped from state history.

"Margarita had a bag packed for you for tonight." He began loosening his tie and undoing the top buttons of his shirt. Anticipation vibrated in his veins as he noticed her eyes riveted to the hollow at the base of his throat.

He deserves humiliation. Public shunning. He needs to fucking grovel to not just the victims but my parents.

"Thanks?"

"She'll release the wedding photos to the press by Monday."

Pushing herself away from him, she slid to the other side of the elevator.

I'm so fucking close. I'll release the documents to the police. It won't be slander if there's proof. He won't be able to deny it, or ignore what's he's done. It is time to face the consequences.

"What is the speaking engagement about?" Jolie ignored his statement, leaning against the elevator wall.

A buzzing sound began, and he reached into his pocket for his phone. "Typical encouragement spiel. Letting them know what they're signing themselves up for by practicing law." It was Gerald. *What now?*

Jolie spoke but he was too focused on his phone. *A disciplinary record.* If he had this, and he reported to the governor… *Fucking Radcliffe.* There's no way Radcliffe couldn't have known, yet he chose to do nothing.

"Cassian?" Jolie questioned.

His fist tightened around his phone to the point of pain. "I'm sorry, what?"

"Never mind," Jolie muttered. The elevator dinged as they arrived on their floor.

He groaned, running a hand over his face. This was their wedding night, and Jolie deserved his focus. Having his hands on her, calming him, grounding him, was what he needed. His eyes were on the way her hips swayed seductively, his guiding beacon into the hotel suite.

A bottle of champagne on ice with two glasses and chocolate-covered strawberries sat on the table. She spun on her heel, leaning down to pick up a strawberry. "What time is the flight tomorrow?"

"Ten."

Kinsella is getting what's coming to him.

Jolie bit into the strawberry, letting out a tiny moan at the taste. "What airline?"

Don't think about Kinsella.

"I want to make love to my wife now."

His heart pounded in his chest, his blood slowly lighting on fire. She ducked her head away from him.

"I guess the gentleman in you is gone?"

He swept her into his arms and drank in the strawberry's sweetness in her kiss. Carrying her to the bedroom, he set her gently down on the bed. Shoving off his suit jacket, he kneeled on the bed over her. Her arms circled his neck, and she parted her thighs to allow him in.

First, he kissed the tip of her nose, then her eyes, and finally, he kissed her soft mouth. "Baby… I need you, okay?"

His hand stroked down the side of her body, and he watched her shiver as she nodded.

Don't think about Kinsella.

The city lights were the only illumination in the room. He yanked down the fabric of her dress to expose her breast. His fingers pinched and pulled at her nipples, rolling the buds between them, making her moan into their kiss.

"I need you bad." Cassian kissed her neck slowly, making her squirm in response. "It's all I thought about today."

Should you be making love to her, or righting the wrong against your family's?

He pulled away for a moment. Shaking his head, he closed his eyes before unbuttoning his shirt. Jolie pushed herself up to her elbows, removing the pins that held her hair up, and her curls tumbled down.

"Cassian…"

His gaze slowly crawled over her. He caressed her thighs, teasing her, then he pulled the silky thong down her legs. Cassian placed his hand on her narrow waist and soaked in the incredible sight.

You need to win this election so your family will no longer be victims. You'll have the power to finally give them the justice they deserve.

"I want to taste you this time," he rasped.

"Yes."

"Spread your legs. Hold them up."

Drawing a quick breath, she lifted her legs, holding them close to her chest, her soaked pussy on display. Goosebumps broke out on her skin. His senses felt as if they were short-circuiting.

He lowered himself to his belly, positioning himself so that his tongue could lap slowly between her wet folds, his lips suctioning around her clit, pulling gently before releasing. His head dropped, and he positioned her legs over his shoulders, using his tongue to relish the taste of her arousal.

"Cassian," she whispered.

He rumbled low in his throat without stopping, his sole focus on distancing himself from dark thoughts about Kinsella.

Her eyes rolled back, and she bowed as she let out a breathless cry of his name.

"I love it when you're agreeable, baby."

The L-word made him feel too much. Even when used in banter, he was hungry for her, and he could not help the noises that left his lips as he pressed two fingers into her moist sex.

"God, Cassian."

"Lift that ass up, baby. Open up."

Her hands fisted in his hair, and he gripped the backs of her thighs. His eyes never left her face as he studied her facial expressions as he slurped at her cunt. When his tongue caught her clit, they both moaned, and Jolie rocked her hips upward again.

If I died here, I would be happy. This is where I should always be. In between her thighs. By her side. In her life. How would he go back to normal when their time was done?

"Spread your legs as wide as they can go… Good girl."

"Shit! Yes, yes, yes!" Her thighs shook, and he kept her on his tongue. He hummed on her clit, and his dick throbbed painfully. He was entranced with how her skin flushed. How she choked on her breath. The way her lashes fluttered.

"Mmm, baby, that pussy is pretty. Keep those legs open while I eat this pussy."

"Cassian!" she screamed.

Gasping, he gulped down every drop.

"Oh my God, Cassian. Please—"

He released her, and immediately Jolie was on him. Her mouth met his in a sloppy kiss, lips barely releasing before he unfastened the buckle of his belt and dropped it to the floor before pulling down his zipper and finally relieving his heavy dick with a breathy sigh out of his nose.

"You feel good, right? You came so much in my mouth."

She moaned pitifully, watching him with heavy eyelids as he lowered his pants and boxers, his dick springing up. She pushed herself into a sitting position, her fingers wrapping around his pulsating shaft. He hissed as Jolie jerked him slowly, then lowered her head to suck on the sensitive tip.

"Ah, fuck, baby. Fuck, fuck, fuck." He rested a hand on her head, his eyes shutting briefly as he thrust his hips upward. Tugging her from his dick, he urged her onto her back.

"You make a mess of me, baby."

The corner of her mouth lifted. "Do I?"

He sat back to grab a condom. Chuckling softly, he sheathed his dick before he took her mouth with a fiery possession.

"Minx," he muttered, and she laughed. She opened her mouth to reply. Instead, her nails trailed down his scalp, and she cursed wildly as he pressed slowly into her.

"Please, please…"

He situated himself inside her, feeling her pussy clench and unclench around him. Her mouth fell open, and she shuddered, retracting her hips from him.

"Stay there."

"Mmm. Fuck! You feel good, baby." Her eyes rolled as he bottomed out.

All thoughts were suddenly wiped from his brain. His hand grabbed her ass as she ground herself on him. Electric desire and nerves drove his body faster and faster, circling his hips continuously.

"Shit, shit, shit, baby," he choked out, her noises sending him over.

His only goal was pleasing her, fucking all the breath out of her till she couldn't utter a word.

You won't be the same when she's gone.

"Ung! F-fuck! Cassian, I'm gonna come. Right there, baby!"

He didn't want to be the same when they were done. He wanted to walk this city with her brand seared into his soul, long after she left him and moved on to better things. He fucked hard, going deeper, forcing her to feel the emotional rollercoaster she was putting him through as prickles of pleasure burned his scalp.

Looping one arm around his back, Jolie tilted her head back, allowing him to kiss and suck on her neck as he hit her spot from a new angle. Cassian lost his rhythm as he felt her body jerk.

"Shit, are you comin' again?" He pressed his face into the side of her neck and thrust deeply once, twice, then ground his hips hard into hers. "Oh—f-fuck yeah, you are. Gimme that, baby, shit."

"Ooohhh!"

He bit and nibbled on her ear before saying, "I could look at you like this all day." *I could look at you forever.* Cassian's fingers were on her clit, rubbing slowly.

"Baby, baby, look at me," Cassian instructed her, his hand guiding her head toward him by her jaw. At his words, her eyes fluttered open.

"I want you to look at me while I'm fucking you, okay? Can you do that?"

Her gasps escalated into wails as he took her hard, massaging her swollen clit. Cassian placed one hand around the front of her neck, and another on her waist, and crashed into her till they broke.

She screamed his name, spurring his own orgasm. Her legs fell away, and he lowered his weight onto her, attempting to catch his breath.

A declaration sat on his tongue, but he held it back. Neither of them were ready for that.

"You mean more to me every single day," he said instead.

Pushing himself to his elbows, he observed the emotions flickering over her face like a kinetoscope.

"You don't have to feel it back toward me—" Pain seared through him at the thought that she wouldn't reciprocate his feelings. "Just know, being with you feels right to me."

Jolie sucked in her cheeks, her eyes glistened, and she closed them briefly. He grunted an agreement before he lowered himself again, giving a tentative thrust, and she moaned. "Gimme one more."

"What?"

After discarding the used condom, he quickly put a new one on, and pressed back into her tight heat. "Beautiful."

Her eyes rolled back as her body convulsed, as his hips retreated and pressed deeper.

"Cassian!"

Her nails clawed at his back as he continued to drive into her until they both collapsed on the bed in exhaustion.

"CAN I ASK YOU A QUESTION?"

Being with you feels right to me.

She wanted to lie to herself that she didn't feel that way, but she couldn't. Their eyes locked, and her heart thudded once more. Their flight to San Francisco was smooth. A driver picked them up from the airport and dropped them off at the St. Regis San Francisco. Cassian treated them to dinner at a luxury seafood and steakhouse before he whisked her back to the hotel and made love to her till the early hours of the morning.

Their driver was taking them to the Pacific Grove campus. Cassian looked up from the notes he was typing on his phone. His mouth curved with tenderness.

"Ask away."

Scraping a hand through her hair, she cleared her throat. "What will you do if you don't win?"

What happens to us?

Seeing him sexy in his suit and back in his "on" mode for the public made her think of Edward's plea to her. It made Mrs. Lopez and Urban Properties fade temporarily. All she could think of was him. She wanted him around her always. She loved laying with him. Talking to him. *Loving him.* He was consuming her thoughts, muddling her brain. This wasn't her.

You're becoming your mother, Jolie, letting a man take precedence over everything.

Cassian was silent for so long that she thought he'd changed his mind about answering. Finally, he spoke. "I will win."

"Don't tell me you're that cocky."

You're not her. You're not her. You won't let a man distract you.

Cassian nodded assuredly. "I believe in myself. That's enough for me to have confidence I'll win."

The threatening voice message was on the tip of her tongue but now was not the time to tell him; it would distract him. He'd want to save her and pile another problem on the ones he already needed to solve. She could handle this threat alone. She'll fix it before she told him so he wouldn't feel more overwhelmed than he already was. It would prove she still had a handle on herself. Her career. Her life.

"Can I ask *you* a question?" Cassian's expression stilled and grew serious.

"I'm an open book." *Liar.*

"What will you do if you don't get the promotion?"

It would crush my entire fucking world. To work under Travis?

"I'll set my gaze on something better."

I would have to leave Channel 12. For good.

Why did she keep letting him in? It's too late. He was inside. In her psyche. *Encroaching on her heart.*

They arrived at campus. The moment he entered the lecture hall, he was swarmed with faculty, staff, and students. She trailed behind, before sitting in the front row. She smiled smoothly, betraying nothing of her warring emotions.

She admired the way he worked the stage, and she loved the sound of his voice as he dished out everything the students needed to know about entering law.

Love? That was silly. She admired the man. He could be a hell of a lot worse. But there was no love. This new, vulnerable Jolie wasn't her. She had to retreat into her old independent self. That Jolie was more comfortable than the one forming within her.

Her phone buzzed, and a look at her phone showed an unknown number.

Call me. It's important.

Aaron again. Jolie sucked her teeth, blocking the number and deleting the text message. There was nothing else they had left to say to one another.

"How do you find the motivation to keep going? Especially with tragic or abuse cases?" a young woman asked, and Cassian nodded.

"I think about who the victim may have needed at the time and didn't have, then I try to be that for them in the court. Throughout my time representing them, I know that I'm helping someone at their lowest, and giving them the support and strength that they need. If I lose a case, I at least know my clients are better than when we met."

Jolie's phone vibrated once more, and it was an email from Dev with the subject line: *Hurry.*

Cassian's voice faded into static as she read the message:

Travis submitted his proposal. He got an exclusive about a complaint about CPD. It won't look good on your husband's running mate, but execs like it. I'm trying to talk him out of it; we're getting exclusives from Cassian so we don't want to anger him. You need to send your story soon.

Travis was going to attack Rock. Just as they were rising in the polls. Anxiety steamrolled Jolie. Travis was threatening everything she built. The executives would be upset, and they'd pull all the exclusives she'd gotten from Cassian. She might be desked, permanently, this time. She couldn't let that happen.

Why am I still fighting for a spot at a company that continues to make me prove myself all the time?

Time. Hope. *Liza.* Jolie sacrificed too much for this channel to walk away. She needed a story to trump Travis, to direct the attention away from Cassian's campaign.

"Any more questions?" Cassian clapped his hands, jarring her from her thoughts.

After he finished his speech, he ushered her outside to a royal blue Corvette Stingray on the curb. Urging her into the car, he ignored her questions as he pulled away, leading them out of the city.

An hour into the drive, he reached into the armrest to fish out a blindfold. He handed it to her.

"I don't think I'm into BDSM," Jolie told him.

He rolled his eyes. "Put it on, and I'll take it off when we get to where we're going."

"Another surprise?"

"Another surprise."

Jolie tied the smooth silk around her face, and Cassian tested the knot before she settled back in the seat. Ten minutes later, the car came to a stop. Cassian's door opened and closed, and she heard the crunch of gravel under his feet before her door opened. He gently grabbed her hand, helping her out of the car.

"You're ready?"

"Burning with anticipation."

Cassian chuckled, slapping her behind softly. "Ass."

Jolie grinned as he pulled the knot of the tie, and she blinked several times, gathering herself. They stood in front of a rustic cottage. Ivy climbed up the front, giving it a charming feel, and there was a private front porch with two rocking chairs out front.

"Cassian, this is…" She couldn't find the words.

"Ours. For the weekend."

Jolie turned to him and kissed him soundly. She wound her arms around his neck, and he wrapped his arms around her waist, bringing her up to her tiptoes. Jolie broke the kiss to stare into his dark eyes. *I'm not going to let Travis ruin your campaign.*

"Are you going to carry me across the threshold?"

Cassian grinned, lifting her up in her arms. Jolie pushed away all thoughts of Travis, her promotion, the voice mail threat, and her family. Cassian carried her into the house and into the bed where they stayed in their own little world for the rest of the evening.

twenty-two

. . .

Jolie closed the front door of the cottage. Balancing her laptop and phone in one arm, she sat in the rocking chair on the porch. The honeyed scent of blossoming flowers and newly cut grass drifted by with the morning breeze. Opening her laptop, she started the video chat.

"Miss Jolie!" The slightly distorted voice of Mrs. Lopez came through the speakers.

"Mrs. Lopez, it's great to see you." Jolie kept her voice low, glancing at the front door where Cassian slept inside.

"You're glowing!"

Jolie flushed. "Thank you."

"Did it happen yet? Are you married?"

Jolie held up her left hand and Mrs. Lopez squealed and clapped her hands.

"That is wonderful!"

"I came on to talk about what I found, Mrs. Lopez—"

A panic flashed across Mrs. Lopez's face. "I just received a thirty-day notice to vacate!"

The laptop nearly slipped from her lap. "What?"

"Foreclosure of property."

"Foreclosure? After the rent increase, and now they're foreclosing on the property?" That didn't make any sense.

"I don't know what to do."

Jolie inhaled deeply. "You don't have to do anything. You're staying in your home." A violent energy ran through her veins, and she sucked her teeth. *It is on.*

"Miss Jolie—"

"I got a lead at city hall. I'll be there as soon as I get back. Take care of yourself and Miguel, okay?"

I have to help Mrs. Lopez. I can't let her and Miguel be out on the streets. Hell, I can't let Blue's friend Albert end up on the streets either.

Mrs. Lopez agreed, and Jolie ended the call. The countdown was officially on now—for Cassian's election, her story, and their marriage.

"YOU LOOK like the monster from the deep!"

Jolie poured mud over Cassian's head in the mud bath, cackling as it trailed down his body. Cassian was treating her to a trip to Calistoga, which was renowned for its hot springs and mud baths.

She watched the mud cling to his head, slowly dripping down. The corners of his mouth turned up as he wiped his face. He scooped mud into his palms.

"You better not—"

The mud connected with her face. Cassian's deep laugh filled the air as she kept her eyes squeezed shut.

"You got it in my hair!" she whined, flicking the excess off into the pool.

"You'll be fine."

Jolie flipped him off. "These tape-ins are expensive."

He gathered her into his arms, holding her snugly he eased them down into the pool. The faint sound of the water burbling from the fountain muffled the groan she released as Cassian kneaded the point where her clavicle met her neck.

"That feels good." Jolie's head fell forward.

All morning she'd been considering how to help Mrs. Lopez, and how to stop Travis's story from coming out.

"It's the last free time we'll get before the election, so we better enjoy this," Cassian pressed a kiss to her neck, mud and all.

Jolie's throat tightened. *How do I protect you, help Mrs. Lopez, and save myself?*

"Your campaign…"

Cassian placed his chin on her shoulder. "It's going to come down to the wire."

She withdrew from his arms and moved to the right. "Are you sure you're running for the right reasons?" Edward's words reverberated in her mind.

His eyes grew sharp. "What are you talking about?"

"Have you truly thought about the weight that's going to come down on your shoulders if you win? On your family?" *On me?*

A guilty look passed over his face. "They'll be able to handle it. You'll handle it."

"Your father told me he's worried about you concerning Kinsella. I am too." Jolie crossed her arms, eyes narrowed on him.

"He did what?"

"You don't think I noticed how distracted you've been? You're constantly on your phone. Calls, emails, texts at all hours of the day and night. Are you still truly focused on the right goal? It should be about the people, not about your revenge."

Cassian crossed his arms over his chest, a deep frown forming on his face.

"Why are you asking me this? You know the people have always been the focus."

"Cassian, you're a good man. Don't become like every other politician."

"Kinsella can't keep getting away with what he's doing, Jolie." He moved closer to her, and she retreated, her back hitting the wall. "My reasons for running haven't changed, but I can't ignore Kinsella. He needs to be dealt with. Immediately."

"Cassian…" Jolie shook her head, and he moved closer, trapping her against the wall of the mud pool. "What happens to us after? If you win? If you get Kinsella?" *How will I recover from losing you?*

"What do you want to happen?" His voice drifted to a low whisper and when she didn't answer his hands gripped her sides. "What do you want to happen, Jolie? What do you want?"

There was an edge of desperation in his voice. Jolie chewed on her bottom lip, dropping her gaze.

"You know what you want, don't you? Just say it." Something akin to hope crept into his expression.

"How do I know this"—she waved a hand between them —"won't go south? If I decide to… Want more?"

"Are you saying you want this to be real? No contract?"

Her breath caught in her throat, and she felt her heart pounding in fear, but also in…excitement?

"Yes."

Joy bubbled in his laugh and shone in his eyes as he scooped her into his arms. Wiping the mud from his mouth, she kissed him, lingering, savoring the moment.

"We'll be all right." Cassian gave her another dreamy kiss. "We will be fine. Nothing will change me or the campaign or us. Believe that."

Jolie wanted to believe what he was saying, but she'd worked the political beat too long not to see the writing on the wall. Cassian was heading somewhere she couldn't save him from.

twenty-three

. . .

J olie stood in Cassian's luxury kitchen, trying to figure out how to make breakfast with the few ingredients in his fridge. Jolie had gotten access to today's CDC meeting, and she was going down there to ambush Kathleen Wilson. Her story had to come out to help Mrs. Lopez before her eviction.

Jolie got out the skillet, eggs, and butter to make an omelet. Once the butter was melted, she beat the eggs and poured them into the skillet. Her phone vibrated with an incoming email. Nervous it was Dev, she quickly picked it up.

I need your attention, Miss Coldwell, or I will make your next twenty-four hours miserable. You have one day to end your search. Otherwise, your bosses are going to get some compromising photos of you and your husband. Final warning.

Attached to the email were intimate photos she'd taken on her phone. She hadn't posted those online.

They've hacked my phone.

Jolie forced herself to remain calm as her body vibrated with violent energy. *This is my career. I won't let anyone interfere with that, but I can't let Cassian's campaign get ruined either.* She folded the omelet, and she forced herself not to cry in anger. Jolie turned to plate the omelet and jumped.

Cassian was lounging against the wall near the fridge, wearing only low-slung pajama bottoms. Her heart rate sped up as she eyed the silky trail of hair that led into his pants. Her eyes followed up his broad chest, to his crossed arms, then to his sleepy eyes pinned on her.

She gave him a smile that didn't meet her eyes. She tugged her black silk robe tighter. "Breakfast is ready."

"Breakfast?"

He pushed away from the wall, crossing the kitchen toward her. He stood behind her, his arms circling her waist.

"It was supposed to be a surprise."

He was going to be pissed when she told him about the threats, now escalating to sextortion.

He kneaded her hips, then pressed a lingering kiss to her neck. "It's the thought, baby."

She couldn't meet his eyes as she turned off the stove, and gently dislodged herself from his embrace. She grabbed both plates, setting them on the kitchen island and poured them both orange juice. They ate in comfortable silence.

"What's your plans for the day?"

"Going over the details for the governor's debate. Martin Gomez still being in the race is throwing everyone for a loop." Cassian's brows drew tight.

"Don't worry, you'll do great." She reached over and placed a hand on his thigh, squeezing.

"Domestic life has made you nurturing. Breakfast *and* encouragement?" Cassian teased.

She rolled her eyes playfully, scooting her chair away from him. "You ruined it."

"Come on back over here. I was loving it." He leaned over, pulling her chair closer, and she laughed.

Tell him. Let him know what's happening.

"What's wrong?"

She twirled her fork in her hand. *Fuck it.* "I'm being threatened."

"What?" he roared.

She opened her mouth to reply but swallowed instead.

"The first thing we're going to do is go to Rock. Get a detail on you, my family—" Cassian's skin was flushed.

Jolie placed a hand on his arm, and exhaled.

"It's about my story. Someone doesn't like that I'm digging. They just sent me another threat."

Cassian stiffened. "Another?"

"They hacked my phone. They have pictures of us."

Cassian's stool skidded across the floor as he stood. He stared at her with a palpable rage, and she froze.

"Another threat? What photos?"

"Nothing nude, but the photos are intimate."

He finished his glass of orange juice; he sucked his teeth.

"Let me guess, they want to leak them."

Jolie nodded, and Cassian cursed, running his hand through his curls.

"Why didn't you tell me about the first threat? Jesus, Jolie… Paul's gonna fucking freak when he hears this."

"I can handle this."

He pinned her with a look of disbelief. "You'll handle this? Are you crazy?"

"Excuse me? You think I haven't been through this before?" Jolie reared back from him.

"This isn't just about you, Jolie. This person has pictures of us. I'm in the middle of a campaign—"

"It's about you then? I know how to handle this."

Cassian exhaled deeply. "I love your tenacity, baby, but this is not the time. You need to get off this story. Your safety is my first priority. We need to start doing damage control—"

Jolie stood. "I'm not folding on this story. This is my job. And Mrs. Lopez will get justice."

"You're not a vigilante. This could ruin my campaign."

She took a step back. "Your campaign? So, screw my whole career because everything is only about your campaign?"

"That's not what I meant—"

"That's what you're saying. Fuck my career, my hard work and passion, because all that matters is your campaign. I can't believe you."

She wanted to strangle him. She began storming out of the kitchen, but Cassian caught her wrists before she could, walking her back into the counter.

"Don't *touch* me, Cassian."

"Shh." Gently, Cassian kissed her. "You know that's not what I meant."

"Don't insult my intelligence. You meant it." She struggled to free herself.

"I just want you safe, baby. You didn't tell me about the first threat," Jolie couldn't meet his gaze. "This isn't about demeaning your career or you. Yes, my campaign is affected, but your life matters more to me, dammit. We both talking but not listening to the other. I'm sorry, I was being selfish but there are crazy people out here, and if something happened to you, I would lose my mind. I lo—"

Cassian stopped abruptly, and Jolie's frown deepened.

"You what?"

She stared at him, her breathing ragged, his burning gaze pinning her to her spot. His knuckles brushed her cheek softly.

"My life is so much better with you in it. I want you here, and I want you safe."

She felt shy. She was *never* shy. Jolie freed her arms and pushed him back slightly. "I don't want to hurt your campaign, but this is my career. You can't tell me to give it up."

"You're my wife. We're a family, and that comes first."

We're a family. And with that, he completely defused her temper. He lifted her off the floor and sat her on the counter. Undoing the sash of her robe, he exposed her bare body. His mouth encircled her nipple, and she whimpered, dropping her head back. Cassian chuckled.

"Don't distract me. It's not fair."

"I like when you're greedy like this, as if I'm not fucking you every day." He grabbed her chin roughly before locking his lips with Jolie.

She welcomed the distraction from her thoughts. He lowered himself to his knees, and then his hot mouth encased the flesh of her thighs, trailing wet kisses down to her pussy and brushing against her clit.

"Yes, Cassian…" she gasped, her hand curling in his hair.

She needed this. She needed him worshipping her body, taking away the stress and worry, making her give up control. She couldn't last long under the expert flick of his tongue and the heat of his mouth. She exploded, her climax rippling through her. Cassian stood, capturing her in another soaring kiss.

He began to work his dick into her with a steady roll of his hips. Her mouth parted as she let herself experience every vein, every throb, that perfect curve that hit just the right spot.

"Yes! Please," she gasped.

Cassian reared back to thrust just as the shrill ring of his phone sounded.

"No!" she gasped.

"Fuck," he grunted.

Cassian retreated from her warmth, and immediately she was met with cold. She grabbed for him, but he gave her a fleeting kiss before pulling up his pants.

"I'm sorry, baby, that's Gerald. It's important. I'll be back."

"Cassian!"

He didn't wait for her reply as he took off toward the stairs.

She had a day to decide. When the time came, which would she choose? Cause another scandal for Cassian's campaign, or shelve a career-changing story and sacrifice the promotion of her dreams?

twenty-four

· · ·

Cassian sat in the dressing room on the set of *The Wake-Up Call* with Ginger Sparrow. He watched Margarita and Paul debate the level of enthusiasm he should have when Ginger revealed the wedding photos.

"Excited, be excited."

"I say be calm. Respectful. He's a political candidate, not some half-brained celebrity. Give the marriage a spotlight, but pivot to the campaign." Paul frowned at Margarita.

The revelation that someone had intimate photos of Jolie and him made his stomach churn. They could release them at any time. His campaign would careen into the toilet. His love life would become the focus of attention *again*.

Margarita and Paul were working with Rock by reporting it to the law enforcement. Online alerts had been set up on their names. Cassian was working with one of his blackmail attorneys in preparation.

His phone buzzed. It was from Gerald again. That morning he'd been thrilled to be notified one of the victims from Kinsella's crashes was willing to talk. That changed *everything*.

See attached. Told you things would pop up.

It was the police records from the night. Details of the description of the crash had been erased, his witness statement altered in the police report. They hadn't included the partial license plate Cassian reported.

A grave expression passed over his face, a heaviness settling in his limbs as he struggled to control his thoughts. *Forged police reports.*

He wanted to beat the shit out of Kinsella and the police officers involved. His family had never stood a chance against the corruptness of the department that night, or years after.

Margarita continued speaking. "Bad news. My sources say Radcliffe's starting a whisper campaign about you."

Cassian closed his eyes. *The bullshit keeps piling.*

"That's not all." Paul hesitated for only a second before adding, "Gomez is gaining traction thanks to Mayor Charles. You three are heading to the governor's debate."

Cassian gave Paul a black look. "What should we do? Gomez is retribution from Mayor Charles. He won't win."

"He's still a legitimate candidate." Margarita sat on the couch, crossing her legs. "It's time to get serious. Mayor Charles and Gomez are a problem. It's time to take them out. Shed light on Gomez's inefficiencies and push him out of the race. Then we can focus on Radcliffe."

"Are you suggesting we do a negative ad run on him?" Paul asked.

"Fight fire with fire. It's time to put on the big boy underwear and—"

"No." Cassian frowned. "We don't go any lower than we already have."

The guilt of his family's involvement in his marriage made it hard enough to deal with. Now with Jolie's confession of wanting to dissolve their contract and have a real relationship... He wanted to prove to her that he was a man she could trust both as the leader of the state, and as *her partner.*

Yet, Jolie wouldn't get off her story and it could destroy them both.

"Fine. Do it your way, but we need him out. Capitalize on his connection to tech and Mayor Charles, then undercut him."

There was a knock on the door, and an assistant peeked in.

"We're ready for you, Mr. Anders."

The trio followed the assistant on set, where he spotted Ginger Sparrow talking with another woman with headphones on.

Cassian had gotten used to interviews over the course of the past year, and he knew what the basic interview questions would be. *Why are you running for governor? What would you do to make a difference? Why should the people vote for you?* Now it was time to throw in some razzle-dazzle with his marriage.

Ginger Sparrow was a well-known local TV host whom he had met at several functions around the city. Her dark bob swished excitely, turning in time to see Cassian approach.

"Mr. Anders, it's a pleasure to have you on the show this morning." Ginger extended her hand. Cassian shook her hand, and the producer's.

"Thank you."

He pushed thoughts of Radcliffe, Jolie, and Mayor Charles out of his mind. It would all get solved, he'd make sure of that.

"The photos Margarita shared were beautiful," Ginger continued.

"They were, weren't they?" Margarita grinned.

Paul snorted and Cassian smiled.

"We're ready to begin whenever you're ready."

Cassian nodded. "Lead the way."

The techs attached his microphone, and the cameras turned on him.

"Congrats on your recent nuptials. How are you enjoying married life?" *No warmup, straight to business.*

Cassian gave a polite smile. "It's been wonderful, Ginger."

"The wedding looked gorgeous. What are the next steps for you both?"

"Right now, we're enjoying the bliss of being newlyweds."

Ginger was luckily not a pushy interviewer on personal issues. "Governor Radcliffe made a comment in a recent interview that your views are too radical for Illinois. For example, in making gun violence a state health crisis, and moving funds from state prisons and infrastructures to public health. What do you say to that?"

Cassian rubbed his chin, pretending to be in thought. He'd been waiting for this question.

"Governor Radcliffe is scared. The messages I've sent out in my campaign and what I stand for highlight the differences between me and Governor Radcliffe. His ideologies do not belong in this state anymore."

From the side, he could see Margarita give him a thumbs-up.

Ginger crossed her legs. "What about Martin Gomez? He's still in the race."

Cassian's voice was mild, but bored. "Mr. Gomez is new to politics and his background is in tech. I don't see how that's a transferable skill to state policy. I would doubt his leadership."

Ginger was a great interviewer, and by the time they were done, he didn't feel drained of energy. Paul pressed the button for the elevator to exit the studio as Margarita argued with him about the necessity of creating GIFs out of his interview as the doors opened.

Cassian faced Governor William Radcliffe himself.

Radcliffe's piercing blue eyes focused on him, evaluating Cassian slowly from head to toe. "Cassian Anders, the man of the hour."

Cassian's skin pricked at the poorly disguised judgment in

the governor's phony voice. He looked to Radcliffe's right and nearly dropped to the floor.

Attorney General Timothy Kinsella.

There were many ways Cassian had imagined meeting Kinsella, but none of his revenge fantasies amounted to this moment. Cassian staggered back, and Margarita placed a hand on his back, steading him.

Radcliffe beamed. "Cassian, meet Attorney General Timothy Kinsella. A long-time friend and key supporter of mine."

Kinsella's eyes showed no recognition of Cassian.

"Nice to meet you."

Cassian blinked rapidly at the man.

"It's been a pleasure, but we should go." Paul cleared his throat.

"I hope I will see you at the gala on Friday night. A friendly meeting before the debate?" Governor Radcliffe asked.

Paul made a strangled sound.

"We haven't decided—" Margarita said.

"I'll be there." Cassian's eyes never left Kinsella. "There's no doubt about that."

Cassian's moment was here. It was time for Kinsella to pay what he owed.

twenty-five

· · ·

"Who threatened you?" Rock said through the phone.

Jolie looked around to see if anyone was being nosy. Helena stared at her with wide eyes from across the aisle in her cubicle. So, no one.

"I don't know who threatened me, but the person stole pictures from my phone."

"The call is coming from inside the house?" he joked.

Jolie sucked her teeth. "Can you find out who it is? This person might leak our photos."

Her job meant everything to her, and she wasn't going to be bullied into silence. Nor would she give up her story like Cassian demanded. She didn't want Cassian to be collateral damage, and she could only hope her story got out before their pictures.

"Did you tell him about the voice message?" Helena hissed across the aisle.

Covering the receiver, Jolie shoot Helena a look. "Why don't you scream it to everyone?"

A siren sounded in Rock's background. "Send me the

email, and I'll get some guys on it. I don't want to take any chances. I'll send a police car for you—"

"I don't need this to be a big scene." It was weird enough walking into work and having everyone whispering and staring at her ring finger.

"Jolie, a threat to you is a threat to us."

"I don't want a detail following me or whoever it is to think I'm scared."

"It can be unmarked."

Jolie's gaze flicked upward. "Find the asshole who threatened me and lock him up. That's what you can do for me."

"Is this what Cassian is having to deal with?" Rock sighed, and she heard his chair squeak.

Jolie took that as a compliment. Sitting in the CDC meeting that morning had been fruitful. Jolie overheard a developer she'd seen talking to Leonard Gambino mention his car had broken down near Leonard's office in the Fulton River District.

That area was strictly warehouses turned into lofts or start-up techies' offices.

She'd spent the entire morning going through all of the shell companies' "physical" locations, and what did she find? An office owned by McMullen Realty. The giveaway was the registered agent for Urban Properties and the other shell companies was the same for McMullen Realty.

Gotcha.

"Do this for me, Rock."

Helena tossed a pretzel at Jolie. It bounced off the side of her head, and she turned, frowning. Helena pointed in front of them. *"Travis!"*

Travis was walking briskly to Dev's office, his arms filled with a folder stuffed with papers. *Shit.*

"Gotta go. Thank you!"

Rock sputtered. "Jolie, no—"

Helena rolled her chair across the aisle and into Jolie's

cubicle. "You don't think Dev would give him Walter's spot? He wouldn't do that."

"Travis is being a piece of shit like usual. I just have to finish this story as soon as possible." Jolie opened the webpage with the registered agent's address. She felt a jolt of adrenaline hit her veins. She stood, forcing Helena to slide her chair back.

"Where are you going?"

"To make sure Travis doesn't get my promotion."

"Don't go alone. Let me come with y—"

Jolie slammed the laptop shut and hurried to the elevators with a shout back to Helena. "I'm fine, Lena. Cover for me."

If Travis thought he was going to get that promotion without a fight, he had another thing coming.

JOLIE KNOCKED SEVERAL TIMES, but there was no sign of life, even when she pressed her ear up to the door of the loft office of the registered agent, Chase Blake.

Using a paperclip and screwdriver, she began picking the lock until she heard a click. Yes!

She opened the door slowly, entering the dark office. Flicking on the light, she was greeted with boxes of files stacked along the wall. Exposed pipes and loops of loose wiring hung through holes in the ceiling. The smell of musty cushions and mildew drifted to her nose, and she covered her mouth.

She walked in slowly, pulling out her phone to record. "Chase Blake? Hello?" No one was there.

More boxes lined the walls as she entered the main lounge area. Two enormous tables sat in front of the industrial windows. There were stacks upon stacks of newspapers in one corner, and black garbage bags filled the open space on the floor. On top of the tables sat files and shredded papers.

Jolie noticed the name of condominium Albert, Blue's friend, lived in on a box. Another box had another property name. On the right wall there was a map of the city, with red pins placed at various points.

"You have got to be kidding me."

The pins indicated each of the developments Urban Properties owned. Albert's complex, near their storefront office, was there. Mrs. Lopez's apartment building. Jolie grabbed a box and dropped it on the table.

What the hell is going on here?

These were records of the purchase of properties for the previous year—homes, apartments, and condominiums owned by families and working-class people. They were buying people out to renovate these properties. *Something isn't right.*

She opened one of the black trash bags and pulled out strands of shredded paper. She began to lay the strips piece by piece and peered at the lettering on the page.

Residents' contact information. Rental income. Their social security and home addresses. Letters to a company called MGA. *What the hell is MGA?*

Jolie went from bag to bag to bag, lining up the shredded papers. It looked like she was a conspiracy theorist the way her eyes scanned them wildly. The shredded papers only told her so much and were taking too long to assemble, so she decided to return to the boxes of files. She picked another pile, discovering it was records of purchases. Yet, the names of the purchaser changed on each receipt.

Urban Properties. McMullen Realty. Hawk Real Estate. That confirmed that these shell companies were controlled by one entity. The properties were first sold cheaply to these companies and then to…MGA Corporation. There were development plans in the box, along with receipts totaling thousands of dollars.

"MGA, MGA..." Jolie muttered as she used her phone to do a quick Google search.

MGA Corporation was a large real estate investor from Menlo Park, California. Jolie placed her hand on her chin, looking at the documents in front of her.

Rent gouging. Selling properties. Delinquent and fore-closed properties. Renovating properties. Corporation name switches. A real estate investor from California. Thousands if not millions of dollars in rental income. Mrs. Lopez's thirty-days-to-vacate notice.

Jolie researched eviction procedures in Chicago. It could take nearly ninety days at most, possibly longer if the tenant fought back. It could be harder if the tenant had good standing with the landlord. There was virtually no way to kick them out, and evictions were often a long-drawn-out process. The only way to get people out of a property with relative ease was to sell the property to another.

"I solved it," she gasped, looking down at the documents.

It was money laundering but with property. They would buy a property, sell it to another and another until it was inte-grated back onto the market. Raise the rent, and hide behind the shell companies so the public couldn't decipher it was essentially the same entity. That didn't answer the question of who was behind this scheme.

Whoever it was, they had to be able to network with high-level entrepreneurs and politicians that the average person wouldn't have access to. Jolie needed to gather as much evidence as she could. She picked up another box, dumping the contents onto the table. To her surprise, a black book tumbled out and landed on the floor.

Kneeling, she was surprised to find it was a ledger. Line after line of names of prominent Chicago businessmen and city leaders. It all made sense, and the book almost fell from her hands.

"Mayor Charles owns Urban Properties, and Martin Gomez is the acting president of MGA Corporation. She's buying the apartments and selling them to him through her company and the city. They're a damn team."

twenty-six

. . .

"**Y**ou are never going to believe this!" Jolie exclaimed as she bounded into their home.

She'd broken several speeding laws coming from Channel 12's office. She'd gathered as much information as she could from the loft and immediately went to the office and started writing. It was past midnight but she completed her article, citing Mayor Charles's and Gomez's involvement, in record time. She was ready to place it on Dev's desk in the morning.

Jolie froze as she rounded into the kitchen. Cassian's back was toward her, his palm placed on the kitchen sink, shoulders hunched as his head hung. He gripped a wine bottle without turning to her.

"Cassian?"

"Welcome home, baby."

His voice was rough and scratchy. Not the clear and confident voice she'd heard on the phone this morning. Ignoring the dinner he'd laid out for her on island, she stalked toward him and forced him to turn.

"What happened?"

He squinted at her, rolling his shoulders back as he leaned against the sink.

"Pinero."

"The interview didn't go well?"

Jolie had been against Cassian going on the *Pinero Radio Show*. It was a known traditionalist station, and Jolie had run-ins with Mark Pinero in the past. He was a rude and abrasive man. With Cassian's liberal ideologies, she didn't think he could sway Mark. But Cassian and Paul had been insistent that appear *everywhere*, and not to exclude any avenue to secure voters.

"Isn't it obvious?"

She ignored the sarcasm in his voice.

"I told you not to go. Was it that bad you're drinking?" She pointed at the bottle. That was one of the many odd behavior changes in Cassian lately. Drinking. Irritable. Absentminded.

"You don't know the half of it."

Jolie placed her hand on her hip. "Tell me."

He unlocked his phone and offered it to her.

CASSIAN ANDERS SAYS GOMEZ SUPPORTERS ARE "LAUGHABLE"

"It took them less than an hour after we ended to post that. It's trending online, and I've lost over a thousand followers and counting," Cassian tugged at his hair.

"You and Paul had a plan, what happened?" Jolie's eyes skimmed the article.

"Pinero took it completely out of context. He asked about a comment I made in Rockford when a reporter there asked me about Gomez's bid and Mayor Charles's support. I said it's *laughable* to discredit anyone in the race yet. He spliced the audio, and now people are saying 'the Saint isn't so holy anymore.' Which is ridiculous."

Over the past few weeks, the attacks from Radcliffe and

Gomez had gotten harder, and the more Cassian chose to "go high" the more his opponents called him *Saint*.

"You know the closer you get to the governor's debate, the more they're going to attack," Jolie said softly.

Cassian grunted, taking a swig from the bottle. Jolie swallowed. This agitated and anxious Cassian wasn't what she was used to. All his time was divided between with Paul and Margarita or Gerald, staying up all hours of the night. Permanent bags had developed under his eyes, and if it wasn't the race, it was about—

"Gerald found several more insurance claims against Kinsella. He was out there drinking and driving like he was winning a damn carnival prize."

Jolie sighed deeply, biting her tongue. *Kinsella, Kinsella, Kinsella.* It's all she heard nowadays from him. Jolie empathized with his pain, but he was obsessed. She told him that, but he brushed her off as being dramatic.

"I need more. The more I can get on him, the less he'll be able to weasel his ass out of it."

"Cassian."

"The more I find out, the more it pisses me off! He can't get away with this. I need to expose him and put his ass in jail."

"Cassian."

"It's not right…" Cassian ranted.

Jolie stepped closer, placing her hand on his chest and a finger over his lips. "I know something you'll be excited about."

Cassian raised a brow as she removed her finger.

"Can I share?"

"Sorry, baby. Go ahead."

Jolie rocked back on her heels, a grin splitting her face. "I know who's behind Urban Properties."

"What?" A light came in Cassian's eyes, it temporarily

relieved her anxiousness. He nodded eagerly for her to continue.

It had been odd at first, to have someone as supportive and engaged in her work as Cassian had become. She liked that no matter what, he switched gears when it came time for her to share anything regarding her career.

"It's Mayor Charles and Gomez."

Cassian's face fell. "What?"

Jolie hurried to the bag she dropped on the floor by the stool to show Cassian the evidence on her phone.

"She's paying him, and vice versa! There are aldermen and council people involved. Cassian, this is the biggest story of my *life*. I'm taking Mayor Charles down, and this will get Gomez out of your way. It's a win-win."

Cassian's face remained grim as he flipped through the images on her phone.

"I've already written the article, and I'm submitting it to Dev in the morning."

He swallowed. "You can't."

"Why the hell not?" Jolie's head jerked back.

"Your article is going to be seen as an attack against Gomez. I'm trending already for an attack against Gomez. This will give the media even more fuel against me."

"I've been working on this story for months. You know this."

"It's not the right time. Can you hold it till this Pinero situation fades?"

She took a step back from him.

"Hold it? I can't hold it. This is breaking news. *News* that will discredit your opponent. Why would you want me to hide it?" Jolie swallowed as adrenaline rushed through her veins.

"I'm not saying you should hide it, but Jolie, this will backfire against me. You're my wife now. Anything you write politically about an opponent of mine will be criticized and seen in favor of me." Cassian sighed. "You're not Jolie Coldwell anymore. You're an Anders."

You're not Jolie Coldwell anymore.

Jolie understood Cassian's campaign value of going high. She'd come to be an avid supporter of his, when each day he proved himself to her as one of the good ones—something she'd rarely seen in politicians—but there was a greater good to think of.

Mrs. Lopez and Miguel's home was at risk. Albert was being exploited.

She couldn't back down and leave them in a lurch. This article would be a stepping stone in her career. The executives would hand her that *promotion on a silver platter.*

"I'm not missing out on a career-changing opportunity because you had bad press one day. This is crucial to me."

Cassian nodded slowly, setting down her phone. "We've been working toward this governor's debate. We raised my popularity, and we can't waste it with a double whammy of looking like we're grappling against bad press by redirecting it toward Martin Gomez's main supporter."

Jolie turned from Cassian. She had not forgotten the reason she lived in this house. She'd signed the contract to help Cassian, but that didn't mean sacrificing her career. She had forfeited blood and spirit at Channel 12. She wasn't letting this story go.

Michelle and Barack hadn't gotten into issues like this in the White House, had they?

She'd hoped her and Cassian's careers wouldn't come into conflict, but now they had. Those early doubting thoughts returned. Barack would have supported Michelle. Like Cassian should be doing for her. *Do you know what it means to be a politician's wife?*

How could they balance what they both wanted without jeopardizing the other?

"Think about it. This is good. I have evidence on both of

them. It won't be seen as defamatory. We both win from it."
Jolie watched the conflict war in his eyes, and he grabbed the
wine bottle, gulping it all down.

"The media won't care. They are already doubting me
more because of your job. I can't look bad when I'm trying to
get Kinsella. You'd do the same thing if you were in my
position."

They are already doubting me because of you.

Her cheeks flushed and she clenched her fists. Shouldn't
she be accusing him of that? Her credibility had been on the
line at Channel 12 since that ring went on her finger. Was that
stopping her? No.

"Kinsella? Cassian, you're obsessed! What about the
people you're trying to help by becoming governor? The boys
at the outreach center look up to you. Your clients. I'm not
pulling this proof out of my ass. This is real and verifiable,
and these are not good people. I need my promotion. You
need Gomez out of the race. It benefits us both."

Cassian's gaze fell to the ground.

"You're obsessed with Kinsella. Admit it. What's the
difference between your plans against him and me helping
Mrs. Lopez?" Jolie clenched her jaw.

"I'm not obsessed with Kinsella."

"That's a damn lie. It's all you talk about, Cassian. You're
running out of meetings, running out of this house—hell, we
were making love, and you took a call from Gerald!"

Cassian tipped his head back and groaned. "What if you
posted the story anonymously? Or put Helena's name on it?
It still goes out, and we avoid the conflict of interest."

Her chest hitched.

"Helena didn't do the work! *I did.* My name is the only
one going on this byline. That's not up for discussion."

"You're not compromising with me."

She gave a slow, disbelieving head shake.

"You're offering bullshit compromises that favor *you*. It's not a conflict of interest when I'm working for the greater good. What happened to truth and justice? Or does that not matter?" Jolie pinned him with a hurt stare. "We're saying to hell with my career?"

"With Pinero gathering people against me, your story, and when I expose Kinsella soon, it'll be too much negativity. Voters won't believe I'm going high. Take your emotions out of it Jolie, and look at it from the campaign's perspective. We're playing chess here, not checkers."

"I can't believe you right now." Her voice cracked. *When did I lose focus? This was what I wanted to avoid. Jolie Anders, the politician's wife and not reporter.*

He rubbed the back of his neck. "Mayor Charles is not going to take your article lying down. The woman is ruthless. You need a plan for going against her. I'm trying to protect you— *Don't look at me like that.* Baby, be reasonable." His phone began to ring, cutting the conversation. "I have to take this."

"It's almost one in the morning. Who could possibly be calling you?" She narrowed her eyes.

"Gerald. I told him time doesn't matter."

Jolie ground her teeth and shook her head. "Cassian, we need to talk about this."

He turned on his heel, heading out of the kitchen for his office. "Hello? Talk to me, Gerald."

"Cassian!"

"Give me a moment, baby," he shouted from the stairs.

"Cassian!" Jolie yelled again before falling against the counter. Rubbing her temples, she closed her eyes, willing the tears of frustration not to fall. *Am I a wife first, or am I a reporter?*

"CASSIAN!" Someone from the crowd shouted out his name as he stepped out of the SUV and turned to assist Jolie.

"Cassian Anders!"

"It's him! It's him!"

He thanked the supporters with a smile that didn't match his eyes. A glance at Jolie showed a tense smile, as a few supporters shouted her name as well.

It preoccupied his mind, knowing Kinsella was here. *After all this time.* His stomach was in knots, and his head felt light. Tonight wasn't just a gala dinner with the elite of the city. It was an unofficial showdown. Like boxers at a weigh-in, Radcliffe, Gomez, and he had all come to size up the competition one final time.

Supporters of Cassian, Gomez, and Radcliffe crowded the entryway into the Shedd Aquarium. News vans and press stood taking pictures and calling out his name. Ignoring the media, he turned his head and helped straighten the small train of Jolie's pink, off-the-shoulder Pamella Roland gown that made her look ethereal.

"Are you ready?" Cassian whispered as he placed his arm around her waist, forcing his features into staged happiness. Another camera flashed.

Her brows pinched together. "Ready to perform like always."

Cassian frowned at the way *perform* fell from her lips. Obviously things weren't going to be mended quickly between them. As much as he wanted to expose Mayor Charles, after his blunder on the *Pinero Radio Show*, he didn't need any more negative media attention. He also knew how calculating the mayor was. He loved Jolie's tenacity, but she wasn't a match for the reach Charles had over this city. He was trying to protect her, just until he could get himself in a position of power to finally boot Charles out.

"Mr. Anders, do you have a moment?" A young man stepped closer to them with a cameraman.

In a strained voice Cassian said, "Not right now."

The young man continued, "How do you feel about finally meeting Martin Gomez after your attack against him on the *Pinero Radio Show*?"

Jolie shot the reporter a black look, and Cassian exhaled deeply. He was not in the mood to field questions, or respond to unnecessary attempts at demonizing him further in the media.

"It's a race for governor. Things will be said. I have no further comment—"

"You've been tryna to appear almighty this whole campaign. Can't answer questions about your fall from grace, *Saint*?"

He gritted his teeth. This new nickname of "Saint" was growing old fast. He started to respond before Jolie cut him off.

"You only want Cassian's name for clickbait. Traffic must be slow to your tabloid, so either find another sucker or be a better reporter."

Cassian's fingers dug into her side as she scowled at the reporter. Giving the man a terse but apologetic smile, Cassian ushered her inside the building and out of the view of the cameras. In the empty hallway in front of the elevator, he turned on her. "What did we say last night?"

"I don't need you to remind me how to act in public."

"I know you're mad at me, but I need you to be on your best behavior tonight. We're too close, Jolie, for you to act how you used to act—" *Kinsella is here, and I can't focus on him if you're fighting me too.*

"How did I used to act, Cassian? Enlighten me." Jolie

cocked her head to the side, narrowing her eyes in that universal look that said, *I dare you to say the wrong thing.*

"Don't… You know what I meant."

"I really don't."

Cassian clenched his jaw. Kinsella was all that mattered tonight. He walked over to the elevators, slamming his hand over the button. He felt jittery, his breathing erratic as the seams of his control slowly unraveled.

"Any other time, baby, I'll cater to you and grovel, but I need you to put your stuff to the side and understand what tonight means—"

"Your vendetta against Kinsella."

He ran a hand over his face, fighting back the memories of the accident. He kept a tight lid on his anger and pain, but the more he discovered about Kinsella, the more his soul screamed for justice. He wanted to demand an answer to the question that plagued him: *How can you live with yourself, knowing the lives you've destroyed?*

"This is a partnership. A contract you signed to help me win."

Jolie's eyes widened. Cassian stepped toward her. She took a step back.

Ignoring her stubbornness, he moved her hair from her shoulder before grabbing the back of her neck gently. He felt her tense, her body trembling with irritation. Yet, even in their anger with one another, their bodies still swayed toward the other.

"I gave you options, Jolie. You're the one who refused them."

Jolie pushed him from her and he stumbled. The elevator arrived with a ding and she stalked inside.

"You don't give me options concerning shit about my job. If we're going according to our *contract*, you agreed to help me. How are you fulfilling *your* end of the deal if you're stopping me from my promotion?"

Cassian's skin crawled at the way they tossed around the word *contract.* The doors closed and they ascended, a charged silence dropping over them.

"I care about your job, but Jolie, you're being selfish. You know how much this campaign means to me. You would put my campaign at further risk? It's not just *you* anymore. We're a team. Or did you forget that? After I've continuously defended you against Paul—"

"Defended me against Paul?" Her voice became shrill. "After everything, you still don't trust me? I told you *everything* about me. I let you into my life, *into my past.* You should understand what this story means for me! You know how I've struggled at Channel 12 as a Black woman. Now you want me to hide a story that can elevate me and effectively hand the promotion over to Travis?"

Cassian's dark eyes locked with Jolie's, the distance increasing between them.

"I don't want you to hide anything. I just think you should come out with the information after—"

"You want me to choose you and this campaign over my job? Over my dream?" Jolie replied in a low voice.

"No, you're choosing your job over me and screwing over *my dream.*"

Her eyes glistened with unshed tears, and his heart ached.

"Jolie—"

The elevator arrived at their floor. She bolted out of the car, leaving behind only the remnants of her rose perfume.

A few seconds later, pain, anger, and regret came crashing down. He followed her out, but a few guests milled by the elevators. Immediately he plastered on a smile, nodding to them and shaking the hands of a few here and there. Paul, Margarita, Rock, and Evelyn were already sitting at a table. Jolie was in conversation with Margarita. The moment he sat next to her Jolie scooted her chair away from him, never turning from Margarita.

"Don't look too happy there," Rock whispered jokingly to Cassian from his right.

"I'm not in the mood."

Rock sucked his teeth. "Better get ready because yo' boy will be here."

He didn't like any of this. The distance with his wife. Mayor Charles's conniving ass. Kinsella walking and breathing. Cassian motioned for the server to fill his glass with wine.

"Are these seats empty?"

Standing at their table was Governor Radcliffe and his wife, and Attorney General Kinsella. Cassian's eyes locked with Kinsella. He was knocked with blazing rage and hatred. *This motherfucker.*

Rock cursed under his breath as Paul reached for his wine.

"Please, sit." Margarita tossed an awkward glance at Cassian.

Cassian's eyes never left Kinsella.

Kinsella lurched forward into a chair. His suit was disheveled, and his hair in disarray. He stumbled into the table, causing the silverware to clatter and everyone to reach for their glasses.

"He's fine," Radcliffe tossed out, waving his hand at Kinsella as if it was nothing.

Kinsella shifted his body back and forth, trying to find balance. His eyes were dazed, glittering under the light, and the man belched. Cassian recoiled, the heavy smell of beer wafting across the table.

"I believe this is my first time meeting your lovely wife," Governor Radcliffe said, lingering on Jolie longer than Cassian liked.

Don't get fucked up at this table. I talk and look nice now, but I wasn't always this way.

"Jolie Anders, Channel 12 investigative reporter." She

scooted closer to Cassian, still refusing to touch him, but he was grateful at her portrayal of a united front.

Governor Radcliffe narrowed his eyes at her. "You're the one that stirred up such trouble. Congressman Mills was a friend of mine."

Cassian lifted his glass, finishing the drink. "Considering what he did, should we doubt your morality?"

The table's eyes followed Cassian's to Attorney General Kinsella.

"Excuse me?" Kinsella's voice sounded like gravel. He snapped his fingers at a server, demanding wine. The table watched as the server filled Kinsella's glass halfway.

"All the way to the top," Kinsella demanded.

Cassian gritted his teeth, and he gripped the table.

The server filled the glass, and Kinsella snatched it, wine sloshing over the side. Margarita was closest to him and shifted out of the way. Kinsella swallowed half of it, sighing as he frowned at Cassian.

"Morality? You sound like a true politician, Mr. Anders," Dr. Mia Radcliffe, the governor's wife, chimed in. The older woman was a petite blonde with dark blue eyes, and was dressed in a lavender draped one-shoulder gown that swallowed her figure. Her beady eyes were pinned on Cassian, mouth drawn tight as she held a glass delicately between her thumb and forefinger. "Morality and values are always such tricky subjects."

"They're simple concepts. Children understand them," Jolie noted in a brisk tone.

Cassian placed a hand on her lower back.

Dr. Radcliffe bristled as Paul cleared his throat, commanding the attention of the table. "Thank you for joining us tonight, Governor."

"Are you enjoying your night, sir? Seems like it," Cassian questioned Kinsella.

The older man observed Cassian with those drunk eyes.

Kinsella picked up his wineglass, gulping down the remainder. He raised a hand to call the server back.

"I am. Considering how damn trivial these things are." Kinsella laughed, while the rest of table remained silent.

Governor Radcliffe smiled, revealing a row of ultra-white teeth. Cassian had never seen someone smile that wide and bright and disingenuously.

"These events are necessary. You get to meet some new blood, get a pulse on the ci—"

A thud followed by shattering glass cut through the air. The table turned to see a partygoer bump into a waiter carrying a tray of empty wine bottles and glasses. The guest looked clearly drunk, and it was only pushing eight thirty. He mumbled a slurred apology, reaching to help the waiter up but went tumbling to the floor.

"Is he okay?" Margarita sat up in her chair. Several other servers went to his aid, helping clean the mess.

"That man should be ashamed of himself," Paul muttered, glaring at the drunk man as his friends tried to pull him up.

"I hope he's not driving home," Kinsella joked. There was a roaring in Cassian's ears as his gaze snapped toward the older man.

"Drive drunk often?" Cassian snapped.

Rock, Paul, and Margarita sucked in breaths. Cassian kept his gaze on Kinsella. Jolie glanced between the two with a displeased expression.

"Me? No. Many people like to mix alcohol with entertainment. I know the time and place."

To say the elephant in the room had crashed down at their table would be an understatement. The man was judging people, *but he was drunk?* Cassian snorted loudly; Kinsella frowned.

Paul cut Cassian a strained look. "Yes, no one should drive drunk."

"It's totally irresponsible behavior. That's why I passed

that DUI bill last year to force drivers to compensate victims."
Governor Radcliffe's smile didn't budge an iota.

Fucking hypocrite with a drunk man you've covered for beside you!

"I should be compensated then?" Cassian's grip tightened on the glass. He wanted to curse this man out and explode all his pain and anger onto him, but he swallowed down what he wanted to say. His campaign. His damn campaign.

"Cassian," Paul hissed.

"You were a victim? I'm sorry to hear that," Kinsella muttered.

Cassian's back went ramrod straight. Jolie released a muffled sound that was a mix of disbelief and anger.

"I was," Cassian snapped.

Kinsella looked him up and down. "You look good. Was it recent?"

Cassian pushed his chair back as if he would stand, and Jolie's hand darted over into his lap, gripping his thigh.

"Twenty years ago, with my parents, who were badly injured. The man got away. People covered it up."

"Cassian…" Margarita said in a stressed tone.

Kinsella eyed Cassian. "We haven't met before, have we? It feels like we have."

He doesn't even remember… Cassian's face dropped. How could the man sit here, knowing that he destroyed lives?

"Well, Timothy won't be around much anymore. He's retiring. Liam, his son, is soon gonna take up the mantle. We expect he'll snag the title in the next election cycle." Governor Radcliffe grinned.

Jolie's brows rose. "Nepotism in action?"

The governor, his wife, and Kinsella froze. Paul's eyes were bugging in shock.

Jolie smiled at the attorney general, her hand still on Cassian's thigh. "That's a good story."

"Is that a threat?" Kinsella swiftly recovered, but the way he swayed undermined his power.

Cassian sat up. "Watch your tone with my wife."

"Let's calm down," Margarita told the table.

They ignored her.

"It's not a threat, just an observation. These elections aren't even here yet. Who's to say your son will win?" Jolie wasn't deterred at all by Kinsella. In fact, she looked amused. Despite the current problem between them, he knew she was fit to be a powerful first lady.

"A story is that picture we've seen of the two of you at Magnifica." Governor Radcliffe pointed a finger between Cassian and Jolie. "Don't tell me you think you'll win. With that scandalous cover of you two? Then your comments about Gomez?"

A shrill ring of a phone startled the table, and Jolie fumbled for it in her clutch. Grimacing, she hit ignore.

"That was a private moment taken out of context," Cassian said firmly.

Governor Radcliffe looked Cassian up and down. "You knew you were running for office. It should have never gotten out, period."

Cassian wanted to pick Radcliffe and Kinsella up and hurl them over the balcony into fucking Lake Michigan, raising a toast as the fuckers went under.

Jolie tilted her head at him. "Aren't you one to talk about scandal, considering your history as governor?"

"Excuse me, girlie, you don't know my past." Governor Radcliffe's eyes flared.

Jolie's own eyes flared. "I know enough to know you shouldn't be one casting judgment. Glass house and stones, right?"

"I would be careful, Mrs. Anders," Governor Radcliffe said.

Anxiety ran up Cassian's spine as Radcliffe pinned his

glare on him. "We all have skeletons. Would hate to see yours come out—"

"All of my favorite people are here."

Mayor Charles approached the table. She wore a royal purple tulle gown with an embroidered neckline that clashed with her green eyes. Cassian cursed under his breath when he saw Jolie clench the cloth on the table, and Paul made a sign of the cross.

Fuck.

SPEAK OF THE DAMN DEVIL.

Jolie was beyond pissed. She'd been hurt when she brought her evidence about the mayor to Cassian, and instead of leaping on it, he'd told her to *wait*, to save it for after his election?

This is fake. Did you expect him to care about you?

She'd thought they'd had something real when they decided to be more than the contract. Over the last couple of months, she'd let herself fall in love with him. It happened at some point before she could stop it. Even now, she wanted to strangle him and kiss him at the same time.

"I don't normally see two opposing sides sitting together for dinner." Mayor Charles smiled.

I didn't think this politician's wife scenario through enough, and now look me.

Both sides eyed the other warily, no one responding to the mayor's lame joke as she chuckled, unperturbed by the lack of response.

"Mayor Charles, I'm surprised you could come by. Don't you have techies and billionaires to swoon over?" Margarita tilted her head, a sarcastic smirk on her face.

The mayor squinted at Margarita for a moment, before wrinkling her nose in distaste.

"Margarita. It's always so...*interesting* to see you. Martin Gomez couldn't be here tonight, so I'm representing him."

Jolie's phone vibrated again. Aaron for the third time with a new number tonight. She hit ignore.

"Mayor, always a pleasure to see the woman who's running our fine city." Governor Radcliffe reached for her hand and gave it a kiss, and the woman ate it up.

"William, always the charmer."

This is all bullshit. I bet Radcliffe's names are somewhere in those shredded documents too.

Mayor Charles smiled politely, clasping her hands on her belly. "I wanted to let my presence be known. I'll be on my—"

"Mayor Charles, can I have a word?" Jolie stood as her phone rang once more.

Cassian gripped her side in warning. "Don't do it."

"I'm not sure what we would have to talk about."

"Lots, actually."

She felt Cassian's eyes on her but ignored them. *I can't bury this. Not even for you, Cassian.*

"That's interesting." Mayor Charles's eyes narrowed.

Jolie stood and rounded the table. Cassian couldn't stop her without causing a scene. "Let's get some more wine."

The mayor inspected Jolie closely, and then acquiesced.

Jolie led the mayor away from the table and from Cassian's prying eyes. They walked toward the Amazon Rising exhibit. The room was empty except for them.

Mayor Charles turned, her dress creating a small arc. "I assume what you have to say is important, Mrs. Anders, considering we aren't friends."

"I doubt we'll be friends after."

Her heart skipped for a moment, Cassian's pleas filling her mind. Was she being selfish? Could she let Travis get the promotion?

Maybe Cassian is right… No, fuck that, you have never backed down before, and you aren't gonna let her get away with her scheme.

"You know what Seneca says, right?"

Mayor Charles looked perplexed.

"Veritas numquam perit." Jolie crossed her arms. She could feel her phone buzzing with text messages in her clutch.

"That is?"

"Truth never perishes."

Mayor Charles raised a brow. "Right…"

How much do I love Cassian to let this ride? Or do I stand up for what I believe in, and let the chips fall where they may?

Jolie stepped closer to her. "I know what you've done."

Mayor Charles stared at her for a long moment before bursting out laughing.

"What I've done?"

"MGA Corporation? Urban Properties? Ring a bell?"

The smile left Mayor Charles's face.

"Should have covered your tracks better." Jolie smirked.

"I don't take threats lightly, Mrs. Anders. I understand you're not familiar with politics the way I am, so I hope you got some damn good evidence. Otherwise, Channel 12 will hear from my lawyers, and you'll be out of a job."

Jolie crossed her arms, taking a step toward the mayor. The women stood eye to eye.

"You are a disappointment to office and you should step down. Before I make you resign."

"I am the reason this city is in the economic green now. You think you'll expose me? Ha, sweetie, I've done research on you. You've burned too many bridges to think someone is going to come to bat for you." Mayor Charles pointed a finger in Jolie's face. "You release that information, it will be the end of your career."

"I'll gladly take my chances in order to see them throw your ass in the back of a police van," Jolie snapped.

Mayor Charles nodded. Taking a step back, she circled Jolie slowly. "Hmm. That's hypocritical, don't you think?"

"Excuse me?"

"You're too reckless. You should have stayed quiet and ignored sob stories from the tenants. You went poking your nose around city hall, *my domain*. You brought it on yourself. You don't take threats by voice mail or email seriously. I guess I underestimated you."

Jolie's eyes widened.

"Since you've come onto my radar, I've done some research about you too, *Jolie*. You have some secrets to hide, do you not?"

Her mind went to her contract with Cassian. Jolie exhaled deeply, keeping her face impassive. "I don't have anything to hide."

Mayor Charles stopped in front of Jolie. "I think you do, Mrs. Anders. I hope your husband is more forgiving than the public."

Turning on her heel, the mayor left her standing in the hall.

Jolie's body was a shaky mess, and she closed her eyes, gathering herself. Her phone rang, and irritated, she answered it. "What!"

Aaron's slurred voice, along with rock music, came through. "C-can you come g-ge-get me at the bar? There's a bunch of d-dudes that wanna fight me."

Another drunk man. Fucking amazing.

"Handle it yourself, Aaron. I'm busy."

"P-please—" Aaron smacked his lips.

"No." Jolie's heart raced, and she placed a hand on her chest to will her heart to slow.

"I'm s-sorry. F-for everything. I—I been thinking some things. P-please can you get me? I won't c-call you ever again."

"Aaron. We have nothing to talk about. Ever."

There was the sound of glass crashing, and a curse from his side. "I d-don't have anyone. Please, Jolie. I swear you'll n-never see me again."

Jolie knew she had to be strong. "I'm busy with Cassian."

"Fine. I—I'll drive h-home."

She couldn't let Aaron kill anyone on the road, especially knowing what Cassian and his family had been through.

"Where are you?"

twenty-seven

. . .

"**Y**ou didn't have to come. I can handle this," Jolie mumbled to Cassian as they entered a small, dingy bar in Greektown.

"I'm not letting you go to a bar late at night alone with drunk fools." Cassian's voice was tight as he glared at a group holding beer by the door.

"It's a gala dinner. You need to be there. They won't miss me."

Jolie had returned to the table and explained that she had a "family emergency" she had to deal with. Only Cassian knew about her relationship with her family. Immediately he stood, stating that he was going with her and insisting that Rock, Paul, and Margarita could cover for him. Even with the disagreement between them, he was willing to do it, and internally she was grateful for it.

Jolie entered the bar, Cassian trailing behind her. A small neon sign hanging in the smudged and darkened window, depicting a woman slinging her top on and off, flickered steadily.

"I don't want to be here longer than I have to. Let's find Aaron and go." Jolie glanced at Cassian.

He grunted, his eyes not meeting hers.

Gambling machines sat in one corner, pool tables in the center, with older men smoking cigars and standing with sticks in their hands. The news played on the TV, overpowering the soft murmur of chatter from the patrons in various booths and tables.

"Aaron," Jolie said.

She spotted Aaron at the bar, slumped over, arms surrounding a few glass bottles, and head nodding back and forth. Picking up the bottom of her dress, she stomped toward her brother.

"Hey!"

Aaron twitched, turning his head. His eyes were bloodshot as a stupid grin went across his face. "M-my favorite s-sister!"

Jolie exhaled loudly, ready to be out of this bar, this dress, these heels, and the chaos of her life right now. Cassian stood by her side silently, watching Aaron with keen eyes.

Jolie snapped her fingers. "Get up, let's go."

"Forget I called you. Imma stay h-here," he slurred. His elbow slipped off the table, and he nearly went tumbling to the ground.

"Aaron, you did not call me and drag me from a gala to stay here." Jolie ignored how everyone in the bar stopped eating and drinking to listen and watch. "Get your ass up."

"It was a mistake c-calling you. I'm staying here." Aaron glared back at her, his eyes dazed. He could barely keep eye contact with Jolie.

"If I have to drag your ass out of here, I will. Get. Up."

Grumbling, he slammed the bottle on the bar. "Fine!"

He slid off the stool and pulled himself up as straight as he could, then squinched up his face to yell as his eyes crossed.

"Aaron—" Jolie reached for him.

"Shit." Cassian snatched her out of the way and she almost twisted her ankle in her heels.

Aaron swayed, stumbling back into the bar stool. It squealed and scraped against the floor as Cassian reached forward, missing Aaron by seconds as he keeled over and fell into a heap at their feet.

"Damn." An older man with wiry hair and a beer bottle in hand peered at Aaron. "He's out cold."

"Thank you, sir," Jolie snapped at the man. She nudged her sprawled-out brother with her foot. "Aaron, get up."

He moaned loudly, and Jolie nudged him again with her shoe. Cassian strolled forward.

"Get up, Aaron. Hey, you guys over there—" Cassian motioned to some biker-looking men. "Help me get him up."

He, along with the two other men, got Aaron sitting up and on his feet. They plopped him into a chair from a table, as Cassian went out to bring the car to the front of the bar. Aaron's head hung pitifully as he whined.

"Hey, lady. Is that you?"

Jolie looked up at the TV screen to see a Channel 8 anchor plastering two pictures—one of Cassian and Jolie smiling as they left an event, and a mugshot of a gnarled old man she'd never seen before. "Secrets and Lies—Cassian Anders hiding criminal family members?"

The entire bar went silent. All eyes turned to her.

"Just in, an anonymous source has identified sixty-four-year-old Lamar Francis as the father of Jolie Anders, the wife of gubernatorial candidate Cassian Anders. Francis, an inmate in the Shelby County Department of Corrections, is serving twenty-five years to life for the slaying of an unarmed police officer, Dennis Simpson, in 1996."

Aaron snored loudly, and her knees buckled. Her photo and...*her father's* were placed next to each other. The resemblance was uncanny.

Her dead father.

What the hell…

Her mother had lied to her.

Her head felt light as her breathing gradually increased into a panic. The door of the bar opened, and Cassian stepped inside again. He called her name, but she couldn't tear her eyes from the screen.

"With elections nearly a month away, we will see how this affects Cassian Anders's camp," the news anchor said.

The news changed to the weather, and Jolie didn't want to turn to face Cassian. He moved closer as the anchor spoke, and she felt his eyes blazing on her.

"Why didn't you tell me?" Cassian shouted.

Her throat felt as if it was constricting. Placing a hand on the counter to steady herself, she said, "My father is dead. He's been dead for over twenty years."

"Who is this then? He randomly decided to stroll out the grave?" Cassian pointed at the TV.

"I—I didn't know—"

"What happened to letting me into your life? This is you being honest with me?" Cassian clenched his jaw, running his hand through his hair.

"My father is dead!"

Cassian glanced at the audience they had, and cleared his throat, "Let's get him in the car."

With the help of the men from before, they got Aaron up and shoved him into the back of Cassian's car. Once they were in the car and on the road, it was silent for several minutes.

"Paul was right. I didn't listen to him. What were you thinking, hiding this from me? When we're this close to the election?" Cassian's hand thumped against the steering wheel.

Jolie dropped her head for a second before she remembered who the fuck she was. He wasn't about to talk down to her, especially about this photo of a man she'd never seen in her life.

For years, she had studied her father's photograph, and the old and weathered man in an orange jumpsuit didn't remotely resemble him. Her mother told her most of her father's side was old and died off when she was a baby, but Liza had never given her names or locations.

"Paul was right?" she echoed.

Cassian gave her a look mixed with anger and regret.

"You really believe I would lie about this? You've been thinking I've been lying to get some story on you this entire time?" she asked through gritted teeth. *My whole world is falling apart, and you don't even care.*

"This is a fucking disaster! I don't need more of it. Jolie, you know how much this—" Cassian pointed between them. "My campaign, my image, my goals mean to me."

She snapped. "Why would I lie about my father being dead?"

Cassian's eyes flashed at her in disbelief. He was a stranger.

"Did you plan this? Has this been your plan all along? Pretend to want me, then ruin me?"

Nausea sent her stomach rolling, and she gripped the armrest, forcing herself to stare at him.

"How can you fix your mouth to say that? What about me right now? You have not once asked me how it feels to be outed on a news station with the knowledge my *dead* father is alive? And yeah, that matters more to me than if you can get into office to settle a score for something your parents don't even care about anymore!"

"I don't want to lose what I've built!" Cassian slammed the steering wheel again, and Jolie jumped.

"My mother told me my father was dead."

She was so stupid. She had taken Liza's word for it when she was younger, and over the course of her adulthood she never had any interest in looking further into her father or his family. Now she was paying greatly for it. She never believed her mother could be that fucking evil.

Aaron let out a loud snore, then coughed, gurgling down something in his throat. Jolie turned on him. "You better not throw up back there!"

Aaron settled down, and she felt the car jerk forward as Cassian pressed down on the pedal.

"From what we've seen from your family, you believed that? Nothing ever clicked in that big brain of yours to find out if it was true? You can judge and analyze everything and everyone else, but believe the mother you hate?" His eyes were sharp at her.

Jolie's ears rang and she clenched her fists.

"Don't overstep your boundaries, Cassian," Jolie said darkly. Burning with humiliation, disappointment, and anger, she shook her head. "I need to talk to my mother. Take us to her place."

Cassian's phone was connected to the car, and it rang, jarring them all. He hit the button, and immediately Paul's voice said, "I told you, Cassian. *I told you.* Look what she's done. She's ruined our chances. The media will never let this go!"

"Paul—" Cassian stressed.

A sharp pain flashed in her chest. Her fingernails dug into her palms as she rapidly inhaled and exhaled. *They've both turned on me. After everything, they think I planned this.*

Paul continued. "This was a mistake from the beginning. I should have found this information sooner. I should have—"

"Paul, you need to calm down." Margarita was on the line too.

Jolie's voice thundered. "First of all, watch yourself, Paul. You're getting this close to me cursing you out like you deserve. I do not appreciate being blamed for something I did not know. After all that I've done for you, and this campaign, you all are going to turn on me?"

"No, it's not that at all—" Margarita began.

"Tell the truth. We're already in a bad position because of you," Paul demanded.

Through it all, Cassian remained silent, and that stung most of all. With how late it was, and Cassian's driving speed, they got to the far West Side in no time, pulling off the expressway and heading to Jolie's childhood home.

"I will not apologize. I was honest from day one. Take it or not. I don't give a fuck anymore," Jolie declared.

She wanted to grab Cassian and shake him. For months she let herself play into the game, but she wasn't going to allow Paul to speak to her as if she was the scum of the earth.

"I'm not lying to you. If I wanted to set Cassian up, I would have been done it." Jolie looked directly at Cassian as he parked in front of her mother's house. The old duplex apartment stood like a relic from the past, and dark memories swirled.

Regret flashed across his face and his voice broke. "Shit, Jolie, I'm sorry I—"

"You are the biggest disappointment right now."

Cassian looked away from her, the orange light of the streetlight illuminating the inside of the car. One thing was for sure: she would not cry over a man.

She should have listened to herself. She should have turned down this deal. She should have exposed him and taken the flack. She shouldn't have shared her body or *her story* with him. Cassian wasn't different than anyone else. He disappointed her and betrayed her—just like her mother.

Anytime she let someone into her heart, it came back to bite her in the ass. *I'm so fucking stupid.*

"Jolie, I was just angry. I believe you."

"We're done here."

Taking her rings off her finger, she kept a straight face as she tossed it at him. He failed to catch it. Grief and despair tore at her heart.

"Goodbye, Cassian."

"Jolie, Cassian. Come on, we can work this out," Margarita panicked.

Jolie threw open the door and moved around to the back to get Aaron.

"Wait, Jolie—"

"What I do isn't any of your concern. Not anymore, to any of you. Aaron, get up! Now."

Her brother groaned, then began mumbling a string of slurred words she couldn't decipher. With one hand under his left armpit to keep him steady, she put one foot in front of the other. Away from Cassian and her broken heart.

"Jolie!"

"Keep walking," she commanded to Aaron, not once looking back as she led him into the house and slammed the door behind them.

twenty-eight

. . .

She felt as if she'd been snatched back into the past.

Her mother had always been particular about her home. A plastic runner led all the way toward the back of the kitchen and to the stairs leading up to the bedrooms. To the left was the dining area that hardly anyone used. To the right was the small living room. Cozy couches that Jolie remembered as a child, a small TV, and the smell of mothballs.

"Ugh, I think I'm gonna be sick," Aaron groaned.

"You shouldn't drink like you do."

She guided him to the couch, and he collapsed. The upstairs light came on, and she heard the shuffling of feet.

"Aaron? Baby, is that you?"

Jolie tried not to let the affectionate way her mother addressed Aaron hurt. Setting her shoulders back, she stayed firm as her mother came down the stairs in a fuzzy and worn pink robe.

"Hi, Mama."

Liza froze, her eyes wide, and her hair tied with a silk scarf with rollers underneath. She descended another step. "I must be dead to see you standing in front of me."

Oh, how she'd missed her mother… Not.

"I came to talk to you."

"I thought we said all we need to say on the phone." Liza narrowed her eyes.

Jolie sighed, willing her anger to calm. "Have you heard the news?"

"What happened to my baby? What did you do?"

Pushing past Jolie, Liza kneeled to sit on the couch, placed a hand on Aaron's forehead, and cooed at him. "Why is it when he's around you, he always comes back worse for wear?"

"Why did you lie?"

"Excuse me?"

"Why didn't you tell me my father was alive? If this man is *even* my father. Why have you been lying for all these years? What do you have to gain from hiding him from me?"

Liza stood up slowly, pulling her robe tighter to her body. "I know you been living a new life with a different name, money, and whatnot. I am your mother. You will respect me."

"Just answer the question. Why did you lie?"

"Your father is dead."

The sound of her heart thumping boomed in her ears. "He's alive and in prison in Memphis."

"You heard what I said."

"How are you still lying when they have the man's mugshot on the news?" Jolie shouted, and she wanted to shake the delusion out of her mother.

Liza recoiled. "Are you goin' to believe me or those people?"

"Those people."

Liza caught her breath, and it looked like she wanted to hit Jolie. It didn't matter if she did. After this moment, Jolie was disowning this entire family. She would be alone. Without them and without Cassian.

"You lied to me. You made some phony-ass obituary for

him for what? What could he have done that you took me from him? You knew my father was alive all these years, and you never said a word!"

"I was trying to protect you."

Holy shit. Jolie laughed drily, running her fingers in her hair, ignoring the mess she was making of the curls.

"*You* protect *me*? The woman who threw her daughter out at sixteen? Who has never loved, cared for, or protected me, and has been a constant source of toxicity I can't get rid of? How fucking dare you lie and say that!" Jolie advanced toward Liza, and the woman stumbled back, placing the coffee table between them.

Liza shook a finger at her. "That's why you're evil! You got *him* in you, and no matter what you do, he won't come out of you."

You're just like him, and you're going to hell just like him. The memory of those words her mother said when they were in the car heading from the police station all those years ago rang through her.

"That's why you kicked me out. He committed a crime, I committed one. It was too much for you to handle?"

Liza shook her head. "What I did in another life to be surrounded by just evil, unsanctified people, I don't know."

"Don't start that holier-than-thou shit right now. You never loved nor liked me. Why deprive me of a father who could have cared about me?"

Liza moved to the left as Jolie followed her around the table. "How dare you? All the years I've sacrificed for you and your brother. The dreams and goals I gave up. If I didn't like you, you wouldn't be here."

"You abandoned me!"

"I set my rules—"

A tear fell, and Jolie wiped it away quickly. She closed her eyes, trying to stop the world from spinning. She'd spent much of her life wondering what could have been if she'd had her father. How different her life could have been if he was there. In prison or not, he was her family. She wouldn't have spent so long alone.

Behind Liza, there was a picture of the four of them. Daryl, Aaron, Jolie, and her mother. *The image of a happy family. Fucking hypocrite.*

"I don't know what I did as a child to make you hate me, but you're wrong. You know you're wrong, and you're trying to justify it, but you can't. You have to live with this deception, and knowing you've ruined my life further. I hope your god punishes you, and I hope you never have a moment's rest." Jolie had nothing left in her to give.

Liza advanced on Jolie as if she was going to hit her, and at that moment there was stomping and clattering down the stairs as Daryl, her stepfather, appeared.

"Liza, what's all that screamin'—" Daryl's eyes widened when he saw Jolie. "Jolie?"

She ignored Daryl as he rushed and caught her mother, pulling her back. Aaron stirred. Sitting up with bleary eyes, he tried to make sense of the commotion.

"Tell me why!" Jolie screamed.

"You trapped me!"

The room went silent at Liza's confession. Jolie stiffened, Aaron struggled to sit up straighter, and angry tears flowed from her mother's eyes.

"I didn't want a baby at sixteen. You think I wanted the responsibility of a daughter? I was a child myself, but Lamar wanted you. He was the one who asked me not to abort you. I had dreams!" Liza tried to shake Daryl off. "I lost my body. My life. My brother put me out."

"So you do it to your child?"

Tears fell down Liza's face, but Jolie felt nothing. "I wanted to live like you're living now. Free. Fun. I didn't want to breastfeed you or stay up all night with a wailing child. I didn't want to stop livin' my life when it had just begun."

"You could have given me up to someone that would love me." Jolie gulped hard, hot tears slipping down her cheeks.

"Lamar wouldn't have that. He adored you. Worshipped you. What about me? I'm the one who did the work."

My mother is jealous of me...

Liza stepped from Daryl's hold, pointing a finger, and advancing on Jolie. "Then he decides he wants to rob a corner store. We were out of money, and you needed diapers."

Jolie shook her head, the tears falling steadily.

"He robbed a corner store for diapers, and the lord sent a cop inside at that moment. I could have gone to the WIC office, but he said we were better than that. He killed the cop and left me alone with you. That's my consequence of sleeping with the first guy that showed me any attention. I'm paying for it for a lifetime!"

Jolie felt a hand on her arm.

"A-are you okay?" Aaron had a sympathetic look on his face, and she shrugged him off.

Jolie pinned her mother with a vicious glare. "When I think my opinion of you can't get any lower, it does."

Jolie felt nothing for this woman. All her life, she'd made Jolie feel as if she'd done something wrong when it was her own issues that she had never resolved.

"How about I talk to him?"

Liza's eyes widened. "What?"

"He's my father. I should meet him." Jolie gathered the bottom of her gown, moving toward the hallway to leave this place for good. As she hurried past, she paused in front of the photograph of the four of them.

A picture-perfect family that never existed. Liza continued to yell at her, and she grabbed the frame and slammed it to the ground. Glass shattered, and Liza screamed.

Jolie swallowed, staring into the innocent eyes of her young self.

"Don't go down there talking to that man, Sparkle. It's for

your own good. Forget him like I did. It's for the best," Liza shouted.

"For you? Or for me?" Jolie turned and strode down the hall.

"Sparkle!"

Jolie snatched the door open. Rushing down the stairs, she wasn't sure where she was going as her mother screamed her name.

"Wait, Jolie, listen to Mama—" Aaron stumbled after her.

Jolie didn't turn, stomping down the street.

"That woman is not my mother. As far as I'm concerned, I'm an orphan."

Aaron's voice was slightly clearer, but still slurred. "Don't go there!"

"You can't do anything to stop me."

"Wait, wait, please. Can we talk about this, Jolie?" Aaron hollered.

Jolie didn't turn back. She heard Aaron's steps stop. It was dark, getting cold, and she had no ride, but she'd find a way home. She'd always found a way for herself.

twenty-nine

· · ·

"**Y**ou need to eat something." Helena set a plate and glass down.

Jolie had hardly slept. She wanted to go to Cassian, but betrayal played on a loop in her mind. That night, Jolie barely made it to Helena's apartment before more tears came. She rarely cried, but her mother...Cassian. The hot tears streamed down and never stopped. Her face and *her father's face* replayed on the news.

This was Mayor Charles's doing.

Helena's place was the only solace. Jolie sat up, peering at the plate. Bacon, eggs, and toast with orange juice. Jolie turned her nose up at it.

"At least drink the juice and nibble a bit on the bread. Want me to feed you?"

"Screw you."

Helena laughed as she wiped her face. Her expensive gown was on the armchair, and she was wearing Helena's triple-XL *Someone who loves me very much went to New Orleans and got me this shirt* tee— that Helena stole from a past hookup—and shorts. She reached for the piece of toast, taking a sizeable chunk out of it before swallowing some orange juice in two big gulps.

"You want to talk about what happened?"

"You mean how the mayor exposed me to the city or Cassian pulling a Judas move?" Jolie ate a piece of bacon. "No."

"You still need to talk to Cassian. Jolie, you were happy with him. I've ne—"

"He called me a liar and accused me of ruining his campaign. There's nothing left for us to say."

Jolie tossed the toast on the plate and sat back on the couch. Everything she worked for, it all came crumbling down. That morning, Dev had sent her an email titled *TROUBLE*.

Jolie, you promised no more scandal. Now YOUR face is all over the news. I'm pissed. The execs are pissed. They're demanding we remove every exclusive involving Cassian. If you wanted to blow this promotion, you've done it. When you return to the office, we need to discuss if Channel 12 is still a good fit for you.

The dark, gaping hole in her soul spread, swallowing what life was left in her.

"Believe me, I stand behind you one hundred percent. Cassian was wrong for wanting you to hide the story but... you shouldn't throw him away. You both can work this out."

"What?"

Helena sighed, sitting next to Jolie.

"Was he an asshole? Yes. Does he need to get on his knees and grovel till the end of time? Yes. He's been calling nonstop. He's realized he fucked up. You can't tell me you weren't happy with him."

Jolie wanted to lie but she couldn't. *I love him.*

"You were the best I ever seen you, Jolie. You were living! You weren't obsessively focused so much on your career or proving your mom wrong. You were you. With a man who loved you. You have to learn that you aren't alone anymore.

Partnership takes work, forgiveness, and sacrifice. Sometimes sacrifices have to be made if you love that person."

She tossed the last bit of toast at Helena.

Helena shrugged. "If you don't want to talk about Cassian, how about Aaron?"

"That's like talking to my mom." Jolie sucked her teeth.

"Jolie, you need family. Aaron is the only one left from your mom's side, and you need that connection. Despite what you believe."

The night played repeatedly in her brain like a horror movie reel. Jolie squeezed her eyes shut.

"Don't use this as an excuse to swear off everyone."

"I have you."

Helena rolled her eyes. "You need more than just me. Don't let Cassian go completely. Your mom fucked up. She led you to believe because you weren't enough for her, you're not for anyone. You were afraid she was right, so you hide in this shell so you won't feel that hurt. But by keeping people out, you don't let the ones who will love you in."

The little voice she tried to hide rang clear. *I can only count on myself.*

"I'm going to Memphis."

Helena sighed. "Do you want me to go with you?"

"I can do it myself."

It was luck her landlord let her know the other day that she could return to her apartment. Helena drove Jolie back to her home, and thankfully no press was there waiting for her. Once she changed into jeans and shirt, she began searching. She found him in the database and stared at the mugshot. She also discovered he was in a prison-hospice facility. *He'd only been seven hours away my whole life. Why didn't he ever contact me? And now he's dying?*

Jolie jotted down the information, grabbed a bag with a change of clothes, and walked to her car. Helena and Nate grabbed it from Cassian's house for her. She found Aaron standing next to it.

"If you've come to defend Liza, I don't want to hear it," Jolie snapped at him as she unlocked the car.

Aaron had bags under his eyes. "I'm not letting you go to Memphis alone."

"I'm surprised you remembered that with how piss-drunk you were."

Jolie got into her car, and Aaron slid into the passenger seat.

"Get out."

Aaron reached for his seat belt. "I'm going with you."

"This has nothing to do with you."

Jolie eyed him warily. She didn't know what he was planning. Did he want to report back to their mother? To laugh and point in her face? To see the "dead" father he insulted her with?

"You're my sister."

"Aaron, don't come here with the kumbaya mess right now. I wasn't your sister when you called me a bitch. Or when you insulted me with my father. Now you have a change of heart?"

"Look—" Aaron huffed out a breath, running a hand over his head. "After last night and what Mama said to you…it upset me. You don't have to talk to me again, but I want to make us right."

"You have a guilty conscious and want to make amends? Too late." Jolie started the car, typing the coordinates into her GPS.

"Unless you going to carry me out of this car, I'm not leaving." Aaron fastened his seat belt and scooched farther down in his seat. Jolie stared at him and sighed before pulling the car away from the curb.

"Fine."

SOMEONE WAS BANGING on Cassian's front door.

"I'm coming!"

It was four in the morning, and he'd just gotten back from Springfield a few hours ago, where he was inundated with questions about his *father-in-law*, Jolie, and the future of his campaign. It was a shit show, and he was drowning.

He'd fucked up royally. Jolie wouldn't take his calls, text, or emails.

She was done with him.

The only way he stayed sane was by working. If he wasn't at his firm, he was at the outreach center. At Rock and Evelyn's home. Or with Margarita and Paul. Or on the road. Anything to avoid replaying the last conversation with Jolie.

Her wedding ring sat on his bedside table, a burning reminder he'd strayed from the goal of his campaign. Last night, he finally passed out after downing the entire bottle of Jack Daniels. Regret. Anger. Denial. It all ran together in his brain, and every time he closed his eyes, he saw the hurt look in Jolie's eyes. The way she walked away, never looking back.

The banging started again.

"I said, I'm coming!"

Assuming it was Rock, Paul, or Margarita, he flung open the front door, grumbling under his breath. "Why are you at my front door?"

"Let's go fishing, son."

Cassian blinked. His father stood there, leaning on his cane and the railing. He wore an army-green chest wader with boots over a plaid shirt. His old Vietnam vet cap was securely on his head, and he had a grim expression on his face.

"Dad." His father liked to get up early to go to the and

fish. Today wasn't a day where he wanted to go sloshing out to some lake. He needed to avoid the sun. Society. The truth that he was a piece of shit.

"Throw on some clothes. Let's go."

Edward slowly made his way down the stairs. Cassian did not disobey his father. He changed and was sliding into the passenger seat of his father's 1980 red Chevy truck twenty minutes later. Otis Redding sang as they drove out of the city in silence.

Cassian was sixteen again the moment his father turned onto the dirt road.

A trip to the lake with his father used to always clear his mind. Gear and chairs in hand, their old fishing boat was waiting at the dock. He helped his father into boat, pushing them from the shore.

They floated quietly and cast their lines before Edward said, "Been a while since we been out here."

"It has." Cassian reached for the thermos Edward packed.

He passed the thermos to Edward, watching his father blow the steam away from the hot coffee.

"You wanna talk about it?"

Cassian grimaced. "I fucked up."

His campaign was in jeopardy. Governor Radcliffe and Gomez would win. But most importantly, he'd lost the woman he loved. Returning to the silence of living alone, he realized how dependent he was on her presence in his home.

Having her makeup and clothing across the bathroom counter. Her shoes in the middle of the floor. Making dinner together in the kitchen. Sitting on the couch in silence, her leg thrown over his. His fingers in her hair. Basking in the other's presence till they fell asleep. His campaign and his marriage were falling apart, and he didn't know what to do to salvage either of them.

"First off, how is your wife?"

"She's not speaking to me."

"Why is that? Ain't she the one with some harsh news about her daddy?"

Cassian swallowed as he observed the lake. Shame cast over him as he thought about how Jolie was handling all the scrutiny alone.

"You don't know why your wife isn't speaking to you, son?"

"I asked her when we first"—Cassian couldn't let it slip about the contract—"started *dating*, if she had anything in her past the press would find and use against her. She told me no. I believed her, even with Paul in my ear but... Shit. I didn't believe her when the news came out. The moment I accused her, I realized I fucked up. She was telling the truth."

"You are a damn shame."

"What?"

Edward shook his head sadly. "You been journeying down a road that's only gonna get you one thing—"

"We've discussed this."

"You can't control life." Edward frowned at Cassian, looking away toward the open water. "You been trying to save people for too long. I'm sorry you had to see me the way you did after the accident. I'm sorry you felt you had to become the man of the family. Bad things happen in life, and sometimes the people who do those things don't get punished right away, but God... He gets them. You've been dead set on Kinsella, and you let it ruin you—"

"I was this close!" Cassian snapped, holding his hand out to show the small space between his index finger and thumb. "It's not fair to you, Dad. You didn't see Kinsella sitting there, drunk and guzzling wine like everything was okay! You could have lived your dream, but now—"

"I've moved on. Made peace. Found success as an engineer with two wonderful children."

Cassian ran his hand through his hair. In desperation, he croaked out, "How?"

"It ain't complicated. *I. Moved. On.*"

Let go of the years I've been fighting for this moment? All that work. Gone.

"After seeing the man, then his son possibly taking up the role next? The fact *I* may have to work with the son of the man that damaged us? I can't. I cannot let it go."

Edward shrugged and tugged on his line. The sky continued to lighten to a grayish-pink. "You're holding Jolie to blame for this?"

"I only blame myself. And now I'm afraid. Of losing this campaign. Of losing my marriage."

Edward looked at Cassian with a disappointment he'd never seen, and he felt lower than ever.

"I don't know what's gonna make you realize you need to forgive." Edward leaned over, placing a hand on Cassian's shoulder. "Forgiveness benefits two people—the giver and receiver."

Cassian remembered the earnest look on her face, and guilt roared in his chest. He'd been shameful to his wife. More than that, he'd deserted her. He should have gotten out of the car and followed her. Pleaded with her.

"Do you love her?"

Cassian looked from his father toward the rising sun, a golden hue shining over them.

He nodded. "I do. I love her."

A slow smile spread across his face. A feeling of breathlessness seized him as heat radiated through his chest. *I love her.* He loved everything about her. Her smart-ass mouth. Her passion and dedication. The soft parts of her she hid from everyone but him. Without her, without hearing her voice, his life had become stale. Unlivable. He needed her more than he needed his next breath.

"You need to forgive. Kinsella. Me." Edward pointed at his chest. "As your parents, your mother and I didn't do enough to help you get rid of this guilt. You couldn't have known the man would drive on the road that night, son. If you want your wife back, you need to let go."

"What if she wants a divorce?"

Edward shrugged, "That's your punishment. You learn from it. You do better. I've seen how that girl looks at you. Her love for you isn't gone. You love her. That's all you need to know to make the best decision for you both."

The sky brightened and the sun burst from the lake's horizon, and Cassian felt something inside him release.

thirty

. . .

"You didn't have to come," Jolie muttered as they passed the Welcome to Tennessee sign.

Aaron glanced at her. "For the tenth time, you couldn't do this alone."

"I'm more than capable of handling this alone. I always have been."

She flexed her grip on the steering wheel, rolling her shoulders. Rows and rows of evergreen trees lined the edges of the highway as she retreated deeper into her thoughts.

Her father was currently at a licensed prison-hospice facility. She'd called the facility and identified herself as his daughter, and she was able to glean a small bit of information. Lamar had been there for the past year in advanced stages of colon cancer. His condition had taken a dive recently, and they urged her to hurry.

"About that—" Aaron moved in his seat toward her. "I'm sorry."

"Hmph."

Aaron shot her a look. "I'm serious."

Jolie glanced at him, then back to the road. "Why now? Aaron, if you're trying to get money—"

"I'm not, okay? It's not like that. Shit, give me a chance."

"When are you going to grow up, Aaron? Take responsibility for your life and do something."

Aaron rolled his eyes, as a black motorcycle sped past them.

"What did I do to make you hate me?" Jolie asked softly.

"I don't hate you—"

Jolie's grip tightened on the wheel. "You've always hated me. Like Liza."

The car settled into uncomfortable silence, and Aaron cleared his throat.

"I've always had a problem with how you abandoned me. How you *kept* doing it all these years. Even when I tried to have a relationship with you."

I abandoned him? I was the one abandoned. "I have never done that," Jolie retorted, frowning at him.

"When you left, you forgot about me. I looked up to you, Jolie." Aaron shifted his seat back, forcing his eyes on the road ahead. "You never came back. Then you changed your name, you went to school, you met all these people. I didn't matter in your life anymore. When you cut Mama off, you cut me off."

Jolie swallowed thickly. "You could have said something."

"What could I say at eleven? Mama let me do whatever I wanted, and I loved it. Stay out late. Drink. Smoke. She didn't care. After a while, I wanted someone to care. You were the one that cared for me in that house."

Jolie never thought about how her leaving would have consequences for Aaron. Exiting Liza's home had been such a relief, she'd never looked back.

"Who else did I have? My dad? He let Mama run the house. I saw how my friends' parents were and I knew it wasn't right after a while. You were the only one I'd ever had that was like a parent to me." Aaron stared out the front window.

She felt guilty and selfish.

"It's not like I had a choice." Jolie's voice broke, and Aaron watched her with a grim expression.

Never over the years did I think about Aaron on that night. I never cared about his feelings. I only cared about getting away. I abandoned him. Like Mama did me. Like I did to Cassian.

Aaron sighed. "I shouldn't have gone along with Mama, but I was angry. It was the only way I could express it."

"I didn't mean to abandon you. When I left, I was finally free. It felt so good, I didn't want to come back." Jolie cast her eyes downward, then to Aaron.

The car fell back into silence.

Aaron questioned softly, "What are you going to say to your dad?"

What could she say to a man she thought had been dead since she was three years old? There was so much she wanted to know. Why did he commit that crime? Why didn't he ever reach out to her? What was his relationship with Liza like? *Why? Why? Why?*

"I don't have a clue."

Aaron mulled that over. "I'm sorry, Jay."

Jolie swallowed, staring at her brother before focusing on the road. The rest of the ride was silent, and by the time they made it to the facility, her hands felt clammy and shaky.

Taking a moment to gather herself, she exited the car and walked into the reception area. Aaron caught her arm.

"Do you want me to go back with you?"

Jolie shook her head. She needed to do this alone.

"I'm fine."

Aaron sat in a chair in the waiting area as Jolie walked up to the front desk. "I'm looking for Lamar Francis."

Would he recognize her?

The older woman typed on the computer, then a grim expression appeared on her face.

"I'm sorry. Mr. Francis passed away."

The woman in front of her began to swirl and morph into multiple versions of herself. Jolie gripped the counter.

"What? When?"

"An hour ago."

Jolie's knees were weak, and she leaned against the counter. "Why didn't anyone notify me? I left my number. I'm…I'm his daughter. Did he leave anything behind—"

She nodded and stood, motioning toward the back. "This way, ma'am."

Jolie followed the woman through long, maze-like hallways. The walls were a muted paint and undecorated. The place was so abnormally quiet Jolie's steps seemed to reverberate off the shiny tile flooring as the woman led her to room 209.

"His things are in this box."

The room was small and nondescript. Bars on the only window. A small twin-size hospital bed with the sheets stripped. A small TV mounted on the wall. How long had he been in here? How had he done it for so long, alone?

Jolie walked slowly toward the brown box. She picked it up and started to leave, but paused. She pressed her hand onto the bed.

She thought she could still feel warmth there.

Outside, Aaron stood with a confused look on his face as she approached with the box.

"Wha—"

"I missed him by an hour."

Her body felt icy, and the need to scream and beg hit her like a tidal wave. It looked as if Aaron wanted to hug her, but Jolie brushed past him. Hurrying to the car, she tossed the box in the trunk, biting her lip and steeling herself against the tears.

An hour later, they sat in some hole-in-the-wall diner off the I-57 South in the backwoods of Kentucky.

She'd kept it together so far.

They stopped at the first diner they saw. Nothing like the gorgeous restaurants she had visited in San Francisco with Cassian. The thought of him sent another pain through her heart. What relationship was there without trust? She was worthy of a partner who recognized she was someone who was worth trusting, and she could not be with him if he didn't believe that. No matter what he professed in his text messages.

She sat outside on the curb, leaving Aaron to finish his food. The box sat in her lap, and she stared at it like it would grow legs and run off into the dense trees. The noise and rush from the interstate became muffled as Jolie shuffled through the random knickknacks before she picked up the stack of letters, opening the first one.

Jolie's mouth dropped at her mother's own scrawling handwriting.

Lamar,

I don't know how to start this letter. I've started dozens only to end up tossing them into the trash. I am livid with you. You are no good. My mama was right about you, and I regret the day we met. Do you even care how your actions have affected our family? I don't know how to tell the daughter YOU wanted that her father is in jail for murder. You told me when we ran away you'd take care of me.

My worst fear has come true. I'm alone. I have come to a final decision to let you go. I can't have you pulling me down even more.

Liza

It was dated April 1996, two months after he was sentenced. Jolie's vision blurred as she picked up another letter.

> *Lamar,*
>
> *Everyone whispers when I walk into the room. You've cursed me—especially this child you wanted. I hate you with every fiber of my being. How could you do this? You're not worthy of being a man I respect. You're nothing but a filthy criminal. I have to shake my feet of the dust of you. Don't contact us anymore. What good would come if Sparkle knew who you are? You can't provide for her. Protect her. Just nothing. You spread your sperm and left like a deadbeat. Stay out of my life —stay out of this child's life. It's for her own good if she thought you dead than the murdering bum you are.*
>
> *Liza*

Her hands shook. There were dozens of letters from her mother to her father. Her mother's letters increased in anger and insults. Through it all she demanded Lamar never contact Jolie. Eventually, Lamar's letters to Liza were returned. But those letters weren't addressed to her mother, they were addressed to *her*. It was a letter written on her wedding day.

> *Dear Jolie,*
>
> *I hope you find it in your heart to forgive me for never being in your life. I found you in the newspaper*

and saw you went by your middle name now. I'm so amazed by what you accomplished. The young man you're marrying, make sure he treats you well. Your mother thought it would be better that way and eventually I did too. I'm no good, and knowing me wouldn't have done no good. Most of my family cut me off but Marion. It's what I deserve in this life. I failed you as a father but I was lucky—you were young. You never stopped looking at me with stars in your eyes back then.

That's what I see each day I close my eyes in this cell. Your smile—though now you're a grown woman. I should have reached out sooner but I was scared. I'm sorry and now with this cancer... Sorry doesn't cut it, but to have your forgiveness would let my soul rest a little easier.

Your father,
Lamar

Her tears fell onto the letter, blurring the ink slightly. He wrote to her.

In the box was a photo of a younger Lamar. He looked...*alive.* A bright smile played across his face. He stared directly into the camera in a leather jacket and a bucket hat. *It would have been amazing to hear his story.*

"That's him?" Aaron appeared next to her, sitting down on the curb.

She tilted the photo of young Lamar toward Aaron.

"Wow." Aaron exhaled a shaky breath.

Jolie nodded, a sad smile creasing her face. "That's him."

This is him. He's part of me, as I'm part of him. That's all I have now.

He observed the picture closely. "That's a dope-ass outfit."

Jolie burst out laughing, and it broke the sadness within.

Aaron studied her.

"You have his smile."

"Do I?" Her finger traced his face. "I wish I could have heard his voice."

Aaron placed a hand on her shoulder. She stiffened before relaxing, leaning into his embrace.

"At least you have this picture now. The letters. You know what type of man he was."

"Someone who made a mistake, unfortunately. It cost him his life."

"I've been a shit brother for years. It won't make up for what I've done, but maybe we can try again?"

She gave him a look of surprise.

"I'm proud to have a sister like you."

Jolie smiled softly, holding the image of Lamar in front of them. "I'm sorry too. I shouldn't have been so mean."

"Bougie too?"

Jolie glared at him. "I don't apologize often. Don't ruin this."

Aaron grinned.

"I should have tried to stay in touch with you. Sorry doesn't cut it, but if you want a relationship, I'm willing."

Several seconds of silence passed before he asked, "What are you going to do now?"

Leaning her head on Aaron's shoulder, she inspected her father's photograph.

"Find his family."

thirty-one

. . .

"Should I beat your ass now or later?" Rock burst into Cassian's office. He'd been holed up in there for the past few days, engulfing himself in work to avoid contemplating his idiotic decisions regarding his wife.

"What'd I do now?"

"Why are you here instead of fixing your marriage?" Rock took the seat across from Cassian's desk. "You're hiding like a little bitch."

Cassian's suit was wrinkled, and dark circles had formed under his eyes. He leaned back in his seat, brows arched at Rock's harsh words. "My dad gave me this speech. I don't need another one."

"Obviously you need another one. You know your sister called me? Said that you've been a mean bastard and ignoring them. You've already lost your wife, now you're going to push away the family you supposedly care about?"

Cassian narrowed his eyes at Rock. "Watch it."

"You know it was Mayor Charles behind this. She's a conniving bitch. She tipped off that reporter at Jolie's job on a bogus tip."

"I—"

"That's disgusting, Cassian. To doubt Jolie," Rock snapped, a vein protruding from the side of his neck. "I've seen you be a cold-hearted bastard in the courtroom, but to hold a grudge against *your wife*—it's unhinged, man. Do the right thing."

Cassian stood abruptly, his chair banging against the window behind him. "I would fucking kill to be with my wife! I'll grovel till the ends of the damn earth and obey her every command if she ever responded to me! I don't exist to her now."

"That's what you deserve. Acting like an asshole because she has a family member that isn't the best."

Cassian exhaled, running a hand through his tight curls.

"I found out who was sending her threats." Rock reached into his bag, slamming an envelope on the desk. "Look at it."

Cassian's heart thundered as he approached the desk, picking up the envelope. He held a mugshot of a young man with spiky black hair. "Who is this?"

"Vince McMillian. An intern for Mayor Charles. Made the stupid mistake of using a friend's computer. His friend snitched. He was ordered to threaten Jolie."

Fucking Mayor Charles. I should have taken her down from the very beginning.

He should have listened to Jolie when she brought him her story. Rock glared at him. "Are you going to draw up the divorce papers too and hand them to her?"

"We're not divorced... Yet." He stared out the window toward downtown, the people moving briskly down the street.

If he wanted her back, he had to prove it. He couldn't give her an option to ignore him. He had to make her remember their love—*feel* their love once more.

"Do you want it to be done?" Rock asked. "Your relationship may have started out fake, but the two of you... When you're together, it's real."

Rock stood and tossed some files onto the desk.

"This is all the evidence you need to take down Kinsella and run off happily into the sunset. You can expose him. I can arrest him. It'll get the media off your back, and you might win this election. But at what cost?"

A jolt struck through Cassian's body, and he flipped through the file. Rock was right. Gerald had dug up phone records, payments, and letters detailing Kinsella and his camp hiding another car crash. The victim was waiting to record her story. This was what he'd always wanted, right here. Yet, he hesitated. Could he expose Kinsella and still feel glad, even after how he'd treated Jolie?

I failed her.

Rock headed toward the door as there was a knock. Paul stepped inside, and Rock gave him a dap before he disappeared, closing the door gently behind him.

"I have some news for you." a light sheen of sweat coated Paul's forehead. He set a folder on Cassian's desk.

"What are you doing here?"

Paul swallowed. "I was wrong."

That was another hit to the gut, and Cassian let the file drop, dread filling him.

"I went to her mother, and she confirmed Jolie didn't know. I can also attest to how horrible that woman is, and her hate for her daughter is deplorable."

"She wasn't lying. We fucked up," Cassian said, falling into his seat.

"I'm not usually one to say I'm wrong, but this time I am. I'm sorry about that, and—I was harsh. I need to apologize to Jolie. You need to get your wife back. And I miss having someone to argue with."

Cassian knew what he needed to do. Get on his knees, beg for his wife's forgiveness, tell her he couldn't live another day without her, but he was tired of trying.

"YOU'RE BACK! Are you feeling better?" Helena asked Jolie as she stepped off of the elevators at Channel 12.

Jolie was on a mission. No more crying. No regrets.

"You didn't call me after Memphis, just texted, and I—"

She gave Helena a sad smile. "I'm fine. Wish I got there in time."

Jolie only told Helena about Lamar's death two days after she returned home. She put his photo in a frame, setting it on her coffee table.

"I'm sorry, Jolie."

Months ago, she hadn't expected a story about a rent increase could lead to property laundering and scheming at the highest levels of city hall. Mrs. Lopez, Albert, and all those other people were counting on her. Fear swirled in her belly, but she stood strong. Regardless of what Cassian or anyone believed, this was *her story*. If she didn't speak up for them, nobody would. Mayor Charles and Martin Gomez would get away with it.

"It's fine."

Helena was on Jolie's heels as they entered the newsroom. Coworkers stared at Jolie, breaking out into furious whispers, but she held her head high.

"It's not! You found out the father you thought was dead was alive, and now he's really dead."

Jolie gave Helena a sharp look.

"That sounded bad."

"You think?"

Sitting down in her cubicle, Jolie fired up her computer to check her social media, which had exploded as she'd expected. *Dev should know now.*

"Cassian's debate with Governor Radcliffe is tonight at

Navy Pier." Helena rolled her chair over to Jolie's cubicle.

Pain shot through her heart at the mention of his name. Whenever she saw his face on the news, she had to change the channel.

"Good for him."

Helena pursed her lips but did not comment on Jolie's feign disinterest. "I don't like that look in your eye."

A throat cleared loudly, and they turned to find Travis standing with a smirk on his face. "Mrs. Anders has graced us with her return to the office. Isn't that wonderful?"

"What are you doing here, Travis?" Helena's voice dripped with distaste.

Jolie sat back in her seat, crossing her legs, and smiled at him. *Travis, Travis, Travis.*

"A little birdie of mine said things aren't looking too good for you or your husband. He's in deep shit again. Must suck." Travis glared at Jolie's smile.

Helena bared her teeth at him. "Shut up. Go do the job you barely do now."

Travis laughed; eyes focused on Jolie. "You blew your chances of the promotion. I hope you like reporting to me."

"It'll be a chilly day in hell before she answers to you." Helena hopped from her seat, ready to pounce.

"Calm down, Lena," Jolie urged, regarding Travis with a bored look.

"What does it feel like to blow the opportunity of a life-time?" Travis asked.

"Coldwell!"

Travis and Helena jumped, turning around to find Dev stalking toward them. Jolie sighed, relaxing in her chair as other coworkers paused their chatter, staring at Dev in shock.

Travis smiled evilly. "Bye-bye, Jolie."

Jolie stood, smoothing a hand down the front of her suit jacket. "Travis, suck a dick."

Travis gasped as if she'd slapped him. She turned to Dev.

"Dev—"

"Come with me. Now." Dev didn't stop as he breezed by her cubicle.

Shooting Helena a quick smile, Jolie left a sputtering Travis by her cubicle.

Dev was flushed red and his hair was in disarray as he paced behind his desk before ripping the chair back from it and planting himself in his seat. Jolie closed his office door, pausing for a moment facing the door. She forced herself to remain calm and turned.

"Now Dev—"

"Why, Jolie? Why go above my head and do this? The execs are freaking the fuck out. They want your head on a platter!"

The night before, Jolie had bribed an IT guy to post her investigation piece on Urban Properties and Mayor Charles to Channel 12's website on the front page. She attached every shred of evidence and the threats the mayor sent, and if people wanted to hear from Blue, Albert, and Mrs. Lopez, they could finish reading the piece on her new website.

No longer would this station continue to get her hard work, ignore her, and demean her. It was time for her to leave and find a place that could see the vibrancy and honesty in her world. In less than twelve hours, the article was gaining traction and a twitter hashtag #CrookedCharles had over fifty thousand tweets.

"People needed to know this *now*, Dev." Jolie's heart galloped in her chest.

"You went behind my back! The channel's back. You broke so many rules, we can't even list them all."

Jolie swallowed thickly, but remained firm. "I understand—"

Dev's black eyes impaled her. "You don't understand the severity of what you've done! An article like yours has to go through steps of approval. Especially with your history."

"My history? Are you referencing the countless hard-hitting stories I've produced? Or the spotlight attention I've brought us because of my exposé on Congressman Mills? The exclusives from my husband—" *Ouch, that hurt.* "My history has served you and the executives, and I took the hits, I was your *scapegoat* for everything that went wrong in this office and for every scandal because this channel wanted to look good to the right people." Jolie stood in front of Dev's desk with her arms crossed.

Dev scrubbed his face with his hand. "You're a fantastic reporter, but you don't know how to listen. You piss all over the social rules!"

"I don't care about social etiquette when people's homes are at stake! Urban Properties is a scam. Mayor Charles is at the center of it. There's nothing to discuss or try to figure out how to soften when I have evidence of those crimes."

Dev's frown deepened.

"You know what I did was right," Jolie declared.

"What you did was reckless. A blatant dismissal of company protocols. I'm going to have to let you go. You directly disobeyed the chain of command, and with your history of insubordination—the channel can't handle this pressure. Not now."

Jolie swallowed.

"You've left me no other choice, Jolie." Dev's voice cracked.

She stood. Her face was full of strength, shining with a steadfast determination.

"This station used to stand for something. *You* used to stand for something."

Dev's brows dipped, his voice losing its steely edge. "I admire you, Jolie, but my hands are tied, *by you.*"

"You and this channel used me, but believe whatever to sleep at night." Jolie turned and snatched open the office door.

"Jolie—"

She slammed it closed.

She forced herself not to look at the eyes on her as she packed the small things in her cubicle. Throughout it all, not a tear fell nor did her shoulders droop.

"Jolie! What's going on? What is—" Helena babbled.

There was a commotion coming from the hall. Three delivery men carrying giant vases of red roses entered the newsroom. The entire office went into a buzz as the men began stacking the vases in her former cubicle.

Helena reached for the first card.

"'I probably don't deserve it...'" Helena read the first card to Jolie, then found the second card. "'I want to ask for...'" She picked up the last card and sighed loudly. "'...*your forgiveness anyway. Cassian.*'"

Jolie felt a suffocating sensation tighten her throat. He would send her flowers the moment she was being fired.

"It's great to see you."

She turned so fast she almost snapped the heel of her pump. Cassian was *here*.

The gasps from her coworkers were a background buzz as she set eyes on him in what felt like the first time in forever. Anguish infused every pore in her body as the memory from the car hit her. Cassian's expression was tentative. She noticed the bags under his eyes and the weariness in his gaze. He looked hot as hell, but his pain was palpable.

Her façade broke, and she exhaled shakily. "What are you doing here?"

"I wanted to apologize to you—"

"Now?" she snapped.

Cassian's expression was like she'd slapped him. "I came here to publicly beg for your forgiveness. I'm sorry, Jolie. I was fucking stupid."

Jolie turned to her left to see almost every one of her coworkers standing in their cubicles watching.

Get out of here. Get the hell out of here, and away from Cassian.

She grabbed her things in one arm, and stormed past Travis and Dev, snatching Cassian by the wrist and dragging him out of the newsroom.

"Jolie!" Helena shouted.

The elevator ride to the garage was short and silent. As they exited into the empty parking lot, she whirled around and snapped.

"I can't believe you would show up at my job!"

Cassian's broad shoulders heaved. "You weren't answering my calls."

"It's because I didn't want to speak to you," she hissed.

She'd missed him so much. Her anger didn't stop her from longing to wrap her arms around him and bury herself in his embrace. She needed to get away from him before her heart won.

"I'm sorry. But I needed to speak to you." He took a step forward as if he wanted to touch her, but held back.

A cool breeze rushed through the garage, chilling the tears that escaped. She quickly wiped them away, frowning.

"You want to speak to me? It's too late for that."

"I don't deserve you giving me the time of day, but—"

"Roses? Is that supposed to make me forget how you humiliated me? Called me a liar and accused me of ruining your campaign? You're not that dumb."

Cassian's eyes darkened with pain. "I wouldn't dare think they could make up for what I've done, Jolie, but we aren't finished."

The man who broke my heart is here with fucking roses and plans for a public display of apology. I should tell him to kiss my ass. Why can't my feet move? Why can't I walk away from him for good?

Another damn tear fell. "If you mean the divorce, then no, we are not finished yet. Don't worry, I don't want a damn thing from you but my time wasted."

Cassian flinched. He acted as though her words were gutting him.

"I don't want a divorce."

Jolie closed her eyes briefly, her pulse racing. "There's no reason for us to stay married."

"I don't want us to end."

"What would that look like for your precious campaign, Cassian?" Jolie asked.

"I don't care about that."

"I don't believe you."

Jolie spun on her heel and hurried to her car. Cassian grabbed her elbow, spinning her around, caging her against the side of her car.

Gazing into his dark eyes, she watched him searching her expression. Something akin to hope swept across his features.

Let me go. I don't want to remember how it feels to be in your arms. I can't have more memories of how good it used to feel.

His arm circled her waist, and he pulled her flush against him.

"Let me go, Cas—"

Cupping her face, he claimed her lips.

Fire. It sizzled down her spine. Her stomach erupted into those familiar butterflies, and her blood coursed through her veins like a wild river.

Their mouths meshed, and she softened beneath him as he traced his tongue against her lips, begging for entry. Parting her lips, she succumbed to the still-flaming heat between them as her eyes closed.

Jolie moaned, leaning into him. She was weak as his fingers twisted in her hair, ruining her ponytail. Angling her head, he kissed her with fiercer pressure.

Don't do this to me, Cassian.

He showered kisses from her lips down the side of her neck, and she let out a mewl of pleasure that echoed in the garage. Cassian pressed her harder into the side of her Mini Cooper before reality hit her and she shoved him away.

"Don't. You don't get to just do that anymore," she gasped.

Cassian stumbled back, gathering himself. He wiped his bottom lip with his thumb.

"I know you didn't lie about your father. Your mother was truly the only one that knew."

"How did you know that?"

"Paul went to your mom."

Jolie's muscles quivered. "You went behind my back to my mother?"

Cassian licked his lips, trying to scramble together an excuse.

"Paul and I were wrong. Jolie, I'm begging you. Please, baby, however long it takes, I don't want us to divorce. I don't want to lose you. I let Kinsella and this election blind me to what was in front of me. You. I want to move on with *you*."

Jolie unlocked her car door. She paused, sparing him a sorrowful frown. "If it'll help you sleep at night, then I forgive you."

"No. Not like that."

"I'm not about to argue with you about this. You're forgiven. No hard feelings. Leave."

"I love you, Jolie."

Don't tell me that now. I don't want hope.

She gripped the car door. "Goodbye, Cassian."

"I can't." Cassian followed her, forcing the door open. "I'll do anything you want. Everything. Except leave you. I can't do that."

She shut her eyes to the naked need and genuineness in his tone. "Can't or won't?"

"Jolie…"

"How could you say you love me when you don't trust me?"

Jolie tugged the door to close it, but Cassian blocked it with his body, his eyes pleading with her.

"I trust you with my life and with my heart."

Cassian's anguished declaration threatened to shatter her last threads of control.

"It's better if we go our separate ways. You and Paul can spin whatever story you want. I'll take some more pictures once you're in office. We'll get this marriage annulled after."

"I can't." Cassian's grip tightened on the door. "I can't live without you."

"You betrayed me. You abandoned me when I needed you." Hurt, hope, and love screamed in her head and pulled her in opposite directions. "You screwed me over once. You won't get a second chance. Move."

"I love you, Jolie. Don't throw what we have away."

"Move, Cassian."

"I know you love me." His voice was muffled through the window. "Do you want to spend the rest of your life without me?"

"You can't love me." Jolie shook her head, a tear falling from her eyes as she tugged the door.

"I can't live without you," Cassian said. "Please."

In disbelief, she watched as he got down on his knee and withdrew a small box from his blazer. He opened it to reveal the ring she'd thrown back at him. "Be my wife again?"

A small sob tore through her, and she couldn't see him through the watery tears. More than anything she wanted his love, but maybe this was all an act for him to look good to gain voters back. Or only for him to realize getting revenge meant more than being her husband again. It all held her back.

"Goodbye, Cassian. Good luck with the debate tonight."

He backed away to avoid getting slammed by the door. The tires squealed as she left Cassian kneeling in her rearview mirror.

thirty-two

. . .

"**D**ammit, she's done it." Paul burst into Cassian's dressing room at Navy Pier.

Tonight was the night he'd been grinding for. The last debate in the race for the Illinois governor, the last chance to get voters on his side. He should be feeling motivated to win this debate and prove to the voters he was their best choice. Instead, he felt like a zombie, his body animated but his soul lost.

"I didn't do anything." Margarita frowned at Paul from the couch.

Paul rolled his eyes and turned the phone to Cassian. "*She* did it."

Cassian took it from Paul to see the headline:

MAYOR CHARLES AND MARTIN GOMEZ NAMED LEADS IN PROPERTY LAUNDERING SCAM

Jolie's article had gone viral. That made him feel more like shit. Cassian did a quick search of her name online.

All the stations in the city were talking about it, and it was getting national attention. There was a photo of a disgraced

305

Mayor Charles and Martin Gomez covering their faces as they fled city hall.

Charles's PR team had tried to attack Cassian as predicted, using the excuse that Jolie was trying to paint Gomez in a negative light to gain him favor with voters. It didn't work. Jolie had had years of bylines before she met Cassian, and the evidence against them was clear.

I should have listened to her from the beginning.

"Channel 8 did a poll on who's expected to win. You're favored against Radcliffe now."

Rock shot Cassian a smug look.

"The article helped." Paul's face filled with shame.

She was right all along.

"Gomez dropped out of the race, and Mayor Charles is fighting for her life in the press." Margarita took Paul's phone from him. "This is good. You won't be in the headlines anymore."

Margarita, Rock, and Paul shared a look as Cassian closed his eyes. He still had to perform. Get on stage and behave like a man who hadn't just lost the best thing in his life.

"Come on, smile, Cassian. This is what you wanted." Margarita stood, clapping a hand on each shoulder.

"You know why he can't smile," Rock said, pinning Cassian with a disapproving stare.

"You need to focus." Margarita shook Cassian slightly, forcing him to stare into her determined eyes. "This is everything you've wanted, and it's down the hallway. Pull it together."

Everything he wanted eluded him. He wanted Jolie. He wanted to come home to her. He wanted his marriage to be as long and as joyful as his parents'.

"Margarita is right. It's your last chance to convince people to choose you. Remind them why they support you." Paul's face was grim as he stood next to Margarita.

There was a knock at the door, and an assistant ducked their head in.

"It's time, Mr. Anders."

Straightening his tie in the mirror, Cassian sighed deeply. Paul was right. Setting his shoulders back, Cassian followed the assistant out of the room, his team following behind. This was days. Months. Years of work.

It all culminated to this moment.

The televised debate was not open to the public, but by private invitation only. The Aon Grand Ballroom glowed with red and blue lights, the eight-foot domed ceiling washed in thousands of dimmable lights that flickered, mimicking the night sky. The stage sat at the far wall commanding attention with *Anders vs. Radcliffe* projected in bold font.

A small audience sat before the stage intermingled with the cameras pointed toward the two podiums. The news anchor leading the debate was none other than Walter Cabot from Channel 12, and seeing the familiar staff and equipment made his heart skip.

"Speak from the heart. You won't go wrong." Margarita smiled encouragingly.

Margarita stood at the edge of the stage and squeezed his arm one last time. Then she hurried to her seat in the crowd.

"You...you've made me proud, Cassian. It's been an honor to work on this campaign." Paul's voice was apologetic. Cassian extended a hand, and to his surprise, Paul pulled him into a hug. Patting Cassian's back firmly, Paul followed Margarita.

Rock lingered. "She'll be watching."

She should be in the front row.

"You think so?" Hope crept into Cassian's voice.

"Feelings don't fade immediately. True love never dies."

Cassian smiled, dapping him up. "You're a poet now?"

"You learn some things watchin' chick flicks." Rock laughed. "You know what to do."

A producer led Cassian to the podium. After a quick lighting check, they attached his microphone and tested it. His head rose at the slight commotion he heard to his right.

Governor Radcliffe was approaching. The men made eye contact, a brooding expression on the governor's face.

Cassian held Radcliffe's stare until he was at the opposing podium.

"All right, let's start in three, two—" The producer made a motion, and the lights dimmed.

"Good evening to you, and welcome to the debate in the race for Illinois governor," Walter spoke to the camera. "I would like to announce that Martin Gomez has officially dropped out of the race for governor. Our two candidates today are Cassian Anders and Governor William Radcliffe."

The cameraman then panned to Cassian and Radcliffe, and they nodded.

"The candidates will each have one minute to answer questions, and the candidate who answers first will get thirty seconds for a rebuttal. Each candidate will also ask a question of their opponent, and they will then have another opportunity for a counterargument."

Cassian glanced into the crowd behind the cameras, and he spotted his mother, father, and sister. They all smiled and waved at him. His gaze was pinned to the empty seat next to his father.

"The order of the first question was determined by a random draw, and it is for Governor William Radcliffe." Walter turned from the camera to pick up his glasses and read the card in his hand. "Governor, a recently released article by a Channel 12 reporter alleges that you not only aided in the gentrification of several neighborhoods, you delayed in the reporting of thousands of dollars in income granted to several new tech companies in the city. It's incited claims that may lead to a criminal investigation against you. What do you say to that?"

The camera panned over to Radcliffe, and clearing his throat, he plastered on a snake-oil salesman smile.

"My administration was not notified of Mayor Charles's heinous actions—"

Cassian forced his face to remain neutral at the lie rolling out of the governor's mouth.

"For my last two terms as governor, I have acted with earnest integrity for the people of Illinois, and I will continue to do so."

"Mr. Anders, the allegations against the governor were produced by your wife. What do you say to critics that slam the article as a negative campaign tactic to get you into office after your scornful comments against Martin Gomez?"

Cassian spread his hands on the podium. "If we look at the record of my campaign, I have not responded to Governor Radcliffe's nor Martin Gomez's consistent attacks against me, though they have made many. My wife is a brilliant reporter. She has no personal stake in a negative ad campaign against Radcliffe, and quite frankly all it shows is that he's afraid of my legitimacy as a stronger candidate for office."

Paul and Margarita beamed, and his parents shot Radcliffe a dirty look before giving him a big thumbs-up.

Walter turned to Radcliffe. "Governor, your chance for a rebuttal."

Radcliffe turned to Cassian, controlled anger on his face.

"Shame on you for denying your negative attack toward me. There are several papers out there quoting you, denouncing my role as governor all over. I think the people of this state need to look more closely at your background, especially with the news of your wife's father. The governor is supposed to protect and honor our law force. Why should we have you in office when you're clearly related to someone willing to end the lives of our brave heroes?"

Cassian wanted to reply, but Walter called for attention.

"Next question."

You know what to do. Rock's words rang in his ear. *This can't wait till closing statements.*

"I would like to revisit that topic—"

"Next question, Mr. Anders."

He was breaking the decorum of the debate but a gut feeling told him continue. Even at the risk of them cutting him from it.

She needs to hear it. Your family needs it.

Cassian turned to the governor and spoke anyway. "It's shameful you choose to attack my family, when there have hardly been any claims against Dr. Radcliffe—"

"Mr. Anders, there are rules here."

Speak from your heart.

"I want to talk to the people. Not voters, *but people*, hardworking people in this city with family and friends and with a deep love of this place. Over the last few months, my intentions in my desire to run for governor have become skewed."

The crowd watched with wide eyes, and he made eye contact with his family, Margarita, and Paul. Rock gave a nod of affirmation.

"I was angry. Angry that twenty years ago my family and I were the victims of a drunk driver while coming home from an anniversary dinner." Cassian cut his eyes toward Governor Radcliffe, and the guilty expression on his face was damning. "That drunk driver was Attorney General Timothy Kinsella. My parents suffered injuries that still affect them today, and discovering this information put me on a path. I wanted justice. Isn't that what this country preaches? Liberty and justice for all? Instead, the act was covered up by numerous people, including Governor Radcliffe."

Margarita and Paul stood, rushing toward the producers as they pointed and whisper-yelled at Cassian to stop talking. He kept going.

"Justice slowly morphed into obsession. I needed this justice to move on with my life. It clouded my judgment and stole from me the reason why I began running. Helping and serving the boys at my outreach center. My clients. The people of this state. My obsession hit a low when it affected my personal relationship."

Cassian's eyes fell to his father. Edward gave him a firm nod.

"I lost my wife in my obsession. I wanted her to hide her story about Mayor Charles and Gomez so that I didn't lose my chance to get into office and finally seek justice against Kinsella. I was selfish. I knew how much her career meant to her, but I wanted her to ignore it to aid in my quest. I lost focus of myself and my mission for running. I now know what I need to do to earn back the trust of not only my wife and my family, but the public as well."

Cassian's heart thundered as his gaze passed over the faces of the crowd.

"I forgive Attorney General Kinsella, Governor Radcliffe, and those that aided in the cover-up. The people of this state, the boys of my outreach center, my clients, my family deserve the best of me, and I must let go of the past. My wife, Jolie—" Cassian looked directly into the camera as if she was there. "I've grown to admire her strength, tenacity, and dedication not only professionally but personally. She never compromised who she was faced with harsh challenges and revelations about a father she had never known."

Sweat beaded and ran down his forehead. He imagined Jolie sitting in the crowd, her smile bright, eyes mischievous, her expression egging him on.

"I did the worst thing a husband could do. On top of my selfishness, I turned my back on her in the foulest moment I could, and it's unforgivable. I wish I could take it back, Jolie. Please forgive me."

Everyone in the room stopped breathing as he stared directly into the camera.

"This isn't sticking to the script, and is grossly against the image I've portrayed, but I have to be honest. I want to love you and honor you all the days of our lives. I want to give myself to you without reservation in our marriage. Baby, I want those wedding rings we exchanged to remind you that you will always have my enduring love. I want to create a family with you. I want contentment, affection, and devotion with you. I want you. *I trust you.*"

"Yes!" Luna yelled, clapping her hands excitedly, and his mom's eyes were misty with tears as she smiled brightly.

"I'll be waiting for you, however long it takes. I vow to assist all the tenants of Urban Properties who have suffered or need legal services. All pro bono."

Cassian's eyes met his father's. Edward nodded, a bright smile on his face. *You've always been right, Dad.*

Margarita, Paul, and Rock clapped. The crowd looked mystified for a moment before slowly clapping along.

Governor Radcliffe shook his head. "Mr. Anders's claims of my involvement are defamatory and libelous! This is a completely inappropriate use of air time. We are discussing issues critical to our state. It's gross disrespect to use this time to confess love to your wife."

Walter cleared his throat, eying the camera with trepidation. "Let's continue with the debate."

JOLIE KNOCKED on the door of Mrs. Lopez's apartment, and it swung open.

"Jolie! What a joy it is to see you!" The older woman brought her in for a hug. For a frail-looking woman, Mrs. Lopez had a ton of strength in her body, and Jolie gasped for breath when she finally let her go.

"Hi, Mrs. Lopez."

The woman ushered her into the apartment. The smell of something good wafted up her nose.

"How are you today? Are you hungry?"

Jolie shook her head. "I'm fine."

"I'll make you a plate." Mrs. Lopez hurried to the kitchen as Jolie sat on the small couch.

Jolie closed her eyes briefly. Helena had furiously texted her to watch Cassian's debate with Governor Radcliffe, and she had caught his confession. He had gazed into the camera like he saw her through it.

He pleaded for me on live television.

She sobbed harder than she did rejecting him in the parking lot. *He's fighting for you.*

Jolie needed her heart to heal. She had been researching her father's family to discover this mysterious Marion. She discovered she was his sister in Lamar's small hometown outside of Memphis. She made the final decision to go full no-contact with her mother.

That relationship was irrevocably damaged.

Jolie focused on the happy photos lining the walls of Mrs. Lopez's apartment. That's when she noticed there were boxes and boxes filled with medical supplies.

"Uh, Mrs. Lopez?"

"Yes?" she called from the kitchen.

"You have a lot of boxes. Did you order something?"

Jolie advanced toward the box, and on top of it was a card.

Only a call away,
C.A.

She dropped the card, inhaling sharply. *No, he didn't...* The older woman came out of the kitchen with a plate of warm soup and bread. Mrs. Lopez set the plate in Jolie's hands.

"Come, sit and eat."

Jolie's gaze was pinned on the card. She sat on the worn couch, heart thundering.

"Mrs. Lopez? The boxes?"

"Oh yes, they came today." Mrs. Lopez smiled.

"Really?"

"Yes, from Mr. Cassian himself."

Her heart flooded with adrenaline and hope.

"It's a nine-month supply of Miguel's medicine. A lawyer named Meg…Meg Lincoln, I believe. She said she'll help me seek compensation." Mrs. Lopez beamed brightly, warming Jolie from the inside out. "Miss Arnell from the outreach center called me too. They found a new place for Miguel and me to stay with affordable rent. I've gotten people offering to help me with Miguel either at no or low charge. It's a blessing."

Mrs. Lopez's eyes watered. She looked lighter and happier than Jolie had ever seen her.

"You deserve it all." Jolie's voice was thick with emotion.

I miss Luna, Tisha, and Edward. Rock and Evelyn. Margarita. Paul's uptight ass.

"Isn't that wonderful of your husband?"

"Yes… Yes…"

I miss Cassian. I miss him most of all.

Jolie focused on scooping up some soup, ignoring the voice in her head telling her she needed to speak with him.

"I came to see how you're handling the news."

Mrs. Lopez wiped her eyes.

"I feel good. *Thrilled.* I finally have this burden off my shoulders. I don't see how the mayor could do those things. To people who voted for her."

Jolie set the bowl on the coffee table and spoke. "Some people think the end justifies the means. She wanted to fix the economic and job issues, but went about it horribly."

"I hope she prays for forgiveness."

Forgiveness was the word of the hour.

"It won't happen again. My hus—Cassian's running mate told me the prosecutor's office is pressing criminal charges. She's not getting away with this." Jolie's eyes shone with tears of happiness. "I told you I would help."

"You did, bless you, you did." The older woman launched herself at Jolie, pulling her into a hug. "Thank you for reading my email and listening."

"No, thank you. For entrusting me to tell your story. It means mo—" Jolie's voice broke. Her throat felt thick. "It means more than you'll ever know."

This is why I'm a reporter.

The women laughed in relief.

"You were the brave one."

Jolie shook her head. "No. It's you, Mrs. Lopez. Albert. All the others who were brave to tell their story. I only gave it a platform."

thirty-three

. . .

Election Day

"Are you really here right now?" Helena burst into Jolie's apartment.

Jolie sat on the couch watching the news report the polling numbers. Her eyes were riveted to Cassian's face on the screen as the votes for him continued to rise into the thousands.

He has to win. After everything, he has to.

"Why wouldn't I be?" Jolie frowned at Helena blocking the television.

"It's election day. You should be with your husband."

Jolie wanted to be there. Declare she loved him back and let him sweep her away, but that damn fear kept her pinned to the couch.

"Fake husband. Soon-to-be fake *ex-husband*."

The hurt ebbed and flowed each day, and some days she felt as if she couldn't breathe.

"I never wanted to beat your ass more than in this moment."

"Whose ass are we beating?" Her front door slammed, and Aaron entered the living room. He beamed at her, looking brighter and younger, now three weeks sober.

"Your sister's if she doesn't get her ass off this couch and go to her husband."

Aaron sucked his teeth, plopping on the couch next to Jolie. "Lena's right. You're miserable."

"Lena?" Jolie echoed, looking between her brother and best friend. "Since when are you two cool?"

Aaron sent Helena a look. Her friend sat in the accent chair angled to the right of the couch.

"We exchanged words. I told Aaron I'll have Nate, my butcher, and the rest of Nate's cohosts on *The Morning Crew* on his ass if he dared to step out of line with you again."

A deep, heartfelt laugh came from the pit of Jolie's belly. "What? Clark, the butcher you tried to set me up with at Magnifica?" *The night everything changed with Cassian.*

Helena shrugged. "You made a lasting impression on the man."

The three watched the screen. Radcliffe's face appeared opposite of Cassian's. His votes were rising.

"You miss that man, girl, and today is the most important day of his life. Be there," Helena implored.

"I still think he's a square-ass dude, but from what Lena told me about y'all, it's clear y'all love each other. Stop this dramatic shit and go be with him." Aaron put his legs up on Jolie's coffee table.

Jolie slapped Aaron's thigh and motioned for him to put his feet down. "It's better this way."

"For you or him? How many more ways do you need this man to show you he's sorry? That he loves you above everything?" Helena looked like she wanted to slap Jolie. "He used a televised debate to grovel to you."

Jolie sent her a dark look.

"Fine. Be stubborn. You need to get up anyway. We have to go vote. Nate's waiting outside. He'll drive us." Helena stood.

Aaron patted Jolie on the back, standing. "Let's go vote for my lame-ass brother-in-law."

Thirty minutes later, they were in line at the polling station. No one paid attention to the potential first lady waiting to vote. Instead, voters moved in orderly chaos as poll workers directed them to a booth.

Jolie observed the steady stream of voters entering and exiting the booths. She couldn't help but ponder who each person was voting for. Had Cassian done enough? Was his plea at the debate convincing? In the end, had her marriage to Cassian swayed them? Or did her article indeed hurt him?

"Don't look nervous," Helena told her.

Nate held Helena. "Yeah, ya man got this."

Aaron ruffled Jolie's hair, and she scoffed, swatting him away. The new brotherly affection was…unusual.

"Smile, Jay. It's gonna be all right."

Jolie exhaled shakily as they moved forward in line. "I'll try."

I wonder how Cassian feels right now. Jolie would bet a million dollars that he was pacing, worrying about the polls, then focusing on his family.

Tisha and Edward would be nearby, trying to calm him. Luna would tease Cassian to distract him. Margarita would probably light a cigarette, bragging to Paul about how her plan worked better than his. Paul would be stiff, eyes focused on the screen, as he used a handkerchief to wipe his forehead. Rock would crack open a bottle of champagne.

Who am I kidding? Helena was right. She missed Cassian. And his family and friends, who had become her family and friends. They'd become such an integral part of her existence, that life now felt weird and barren without them. Yes, her career mattered more than anything, but she had been uncompromising at times.

"Ma'am? Step up, please." A poll worker snapped her out of her thoughts.

Jolie stepped to the voting booth.

There were barriers on the front and sides, and she peered down at the voting sheet. *Cassian Anders*. He was the first name on the list. Flashbacks to those four days in Napa. Wine tasting, dinner, and dancing… The sex. Lots and lots of sex, but it hadn't been that or the luxury items that had made her love him.

It was just *him*.

His stubbornness and honesty. His compassion and devotion not only to his family and colleagues, to his outreach center and others. The way he listened to her rant about a story that excited her. The way his eyes lit up when he looked at her, making her feel like the most beautiful woman in the world. The way he catered to her emotionally and physically. The comfort and protection he offered lying in his arms after a long day.

Could she finally drop the heavy weight of isolated independence and let him in for good? Even if that meant he could still abandon her again?

Jolie picked up the pencil and made a mark by his name.

Whether or not he won, that didn't change his character. He would always be the best man she had ever known.

She exited the booth. Aaron, Helena, and Nate joined her, and they headed to a local restaurant. For the next few hours, they watched the election on the television.

Helena shook her head at Jolie. "Please, Jolie, don't be stubborn. You love the man. Admit that."

"I'm scared, Lena, and you know how much I hate to say that, but he turned once and didn't trust me. There is no relationship without trust. How do I know it won't happen again?" Jolie swallowed.

A glance at the news channel revealed footage of Cassian's campaign team. Paul, Margarita, Rock and Evelyn, his parents were all in attendance at his outreach center. Everyone except her.

"Jolie, think about your dad's letter. He loved you all these years and wanted you to have a family of your own." Helena reached for her hand across the table. "If you want to honor him, you do that by living. *Loving.* You can't get back the one that got away."

Damn, Helena was good.

"Speaking of jobs…" Jolie said.

Since being fired from Channel 12, she'd received a personal letter from the executives themselves begging her to return. Her article in fact was good for them, and now she was in their favor again. Dev called, offering her the promotion and an apology. *You deserve this, Jolie. We were wrong.*

"ABC News offered me the position of their lead editor and reporter for the political and crime section. I'll be investigating *and* be on air. It's national news, Lena. And I'll still be based here, and I won't have to move—"

"You're fucking kidding!" Helena screamed. Nate and Aaron looked at Helena like she was insane.

Jolie's website had crashed several times from the traffic, and apparently very important people had found her. There had been several job offers, but the hiring manager at ABC News offered Jolie what she needed. A step up. Something Channel 12 had denied her. Channel 12 would never respect her or stop othering her.

"Oh my God! I'm happy for you."

"Say the word, and I'll bring you over, Lena," Jolie said. Her friend was a fantastic reporter and deserved to be in a work environment that would respect her.

"Uh, duh! Don't turn into another Travis on me."

Jolie scoffed.

"Let's not distract from Cassian, though. You can't control life, and you can't be scared. Just like you're brave to take this new job, be brave in love with Cassian. Regardless of what could happen."

"It's difficult to throw away the instinct to protect myself."

Jolie glanced at the news again. Cassian was smiling and shaking the hands of some children in attendance. Everyone clamored around him, vying for his attention.

"Is he worth the risk?"

Jolie remembered the way he smiled against her mouth. She remembered how he held her. How they stood side by side making breakfast. Most importantly, it was the way he loved her. She wanted to feel it again. She needed to now more than anything.

I love him.

Her phone buzzed with an incoming email. The subject line read, *Family.*

Jolie,

I received your message, and it's great to hear from you. It's been so long since we last seen you. You had to be a baby back then and with Lamar's passing, we'd given up hope of seeing you again. Most of the family is still down here in Memphis and Kentucky, and some in Florida. Call me. I've attached a picture you may like.

Aunt Marion

She had more family. Jolie had gotten a lead that her aunt married a man with the last name Johnson and moved to St. Louis. She had contacted hundreds of Marion Johnsons in the hopes of finding her. She clicked on the photo, and the phone almost fell from her hand. Cupping a hand over her mouth, she exhaled shakily.

She'd never seen this photo before.

Lamar looked younger, no older than eighteen, with the same bright smile, holding an infant Jolie swaddled in a blanket.

A warm and solid feeling fell onto her shoulders, and Helena looked at her phone.

"Is that you and your dad?"

Aaron leaned over to glance at the photo. He grinned at her. "That's amazing, Jay."

She could only nod, staring at the picture for several

moments. Jolie looked up at the television screen, and Cassian was there.

"I have to go."

Helena beamed. "I'm glad you finally have some sense. Go get your man."

Jolie called for a ride and urged the driver to break several speed limits along the way.

She pondered what to say to him on the ride over. As she arrived in front of the outreach center, the words faded away.

Jolie pushed herself forward on shaky legs and followed the sounds of loud chatter and cheers. Her shoes squeaked against the linoleum floor as she opened the doors of the gym.

There were banners, streamers, and balloons hanging from the ceiling over several tables with blue and red tablecloths. People milled about laughing and talking, as the tally coverage continued on a projector screen.

No one noticed her at first. Cassian stood chatting with Miss Arnell, Paul, and Margarita, Evelyn and Rock flanking his sides. At a table close by, Tisha, Luna, and Edward sat taking pictures.

Suddenly the crowd parted for her. Cassian turned and glanced away before doubling back, shock etched across his features.

Jolie paused in the center of the room. Cassian stalked forward, ignoring whatever Paul was saying, eyes pinned on her. It felt like years since she last saw his face, and his cologne wafted up to her nose as he stood in front of her. She spoke first.

"Was it true?"

Cassian exhaled, his eyes not leaving hers. "I meant every word."

"Positive?"

He took a step toward her, pulling her into his embrace. Jolie could hear Tisha shriek across the room. Cassian and

Jolie turned to regard his mother with a humorous look before returning their focus to the other.

"I'm taking a chance with you again. Don't disappoint me, Cassian." Jolie's voice shook.

"You should know when I say something, I mean it."

She ducked her head as a short laugh escaped her. "Mr. Anders, should I call your bluff? I doubt I need to do that, right?"

"You shouldn't. Everything I said at the debate, that I'm saying now, is because I love you."

She felt an explosion of euphoria at his confession, and then there were no more shadows on her heart.

"I love you. I do."

Cassian cupped her cheeks with his hands, pulling her close. His breath ghosted over her lips.

"I love you, Mrs. Anders."

Cassian kissed her, and she wrapped her arms around his neck and gave herself over to him, leaving no space between their bodies. A chorus of gasps and cheers filled the air.

"Yes, God!" They broke apart to see Tisha clapping manically, with Luna and Edward watching with tender expressions. Rock winked at her, and Margarita waved. Lastly, her eyes fell on Paul, and he gave her an apologetic smile and nod.

Cassian leaned back, reaching inside the jacket of his suit to reveal a small box.

"Cassian…"

He opened it, revealing her wedding and engagement ring. "Will you wear it again? Forever this time?"

Tears filled her eyes, and she could only nod as she let him slide the ring back onto her finger. Back in its rightful place. She pressed her lips to his again, both of them reconfirming their vows to another with the kiss.

"Are you nervous?" Jolie murmured as she released his lips.

"Not with you here."

"Sweet-talker."

Jolie and Cassian laughed when someone shouted, pointing to the monitor on the screen. The last count was in. Everyone waited as Cassian's and Radcliffe's faces filled the screen. Then there was the declaration.

"Holy crap!"

"OH MY GOD!"

"Fuck, I knew it!" This last remark from Rock as he lifted Evelyn from her feet with a screech.

Cassian Anders was the new governor of Illinois.

The crowd went wild. The sound temporarily deafened Jolie as everyone rushed him. He held on to her. She pulled him down for another searing kiss.

"Hello, Mr. Governor."

"Hello, First Lady."

epilogue

. . .

You can read Jolie and Cassian's happily ever after at:
https://rb.gy/2fwxt3

sign up for my newsletter!

Would you like to see deleted scenes, epilogues, character interviews, new releases, and exclusive character art? Sign up for my newsletter:
https://rb.gy/bbemfx

connect with me!

You can connect with me on:
My Website: https://tiniamontford.com/
Facebook I Instagram I Pinterest I TikTok:
@tiniawritesbooks

Interested in listening to Jolie & Cassian's entire playlist?
https://rb.gy/txup0g

also by tinia montford

It Started with a List

A Loner. A Jock. A bucket list. What could go wrong?

It Started with a Dance

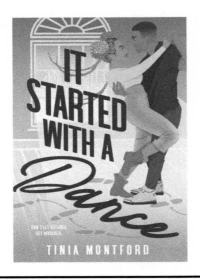

Can they pull off the perfect performance?

about tinia

Tinia (TUH-NIA) Montford is a Pisces who's a sap for romance, especially when there's (tons of) kissing. Loves eighties sitcoms and will consume anything with chocolate. She graduated from the University of San Francisco with a degree in English and Graphic Design.

If you can't catch her writing, you can bet she's overindulging on poke bowls, listening to the same four songs, or chilling with her adorbs doggie. She is currently pursuing her MFA in Fiction.

Ingram Content Group UK Ltd.
Milton Keynes UK
UKHW041535170323
418745UK00004B/289